DEADTOWN

NANCY HOLZNER

ACE BOOKS, NEW YORK

THE BERKLEY PUBLISHING GROUP
Published by the Penguin Group
Penguin Group (USA) Inc.
375 Hudson Street, New York, New York 10014, USA
Penguin Group (Canada), 90 Eglinton Avenue East, Suite 700, Toronto, Ontario M4P 2Y3, Canada
(a division of Pearson Penguin Canada Inc.)
Penguin Books Ltd., 80 Strand, London WC2R 0RL, England
Penguin Group Ireland, 25 St. Stephen's Green, Dublin 2, Ireland (a division of Penguin Books Ltd.)
Penguin Group (Australia), 250 Camberwell Road, Camberwell, Victoria 3124, Australia
(a division of Pearson Australia Group Pty. Ltd.)
Penguin Books India Pvt. Ltd., 11 Community Centre, Panchsheel Park, New Delhi—110 017, India
Penguin Group (NZ), 67 Apollo Drive, Rosedale, North Shore 0632, New Zealand
(a division of Pearson New Zealand Ltd.)
Penguin Books (South Africa) (Pty.) Ltd., 24 Sturdee Avenue, Rosebank, Johannesburg 2196,
South Africa

Penguin Books Ltd., Registered Offices: 80 Strand, London WC2R 0RL, England

DEADTOWN

An Ace Book / published by arrangement with the author

PRINTING HISTORY
Ace mass-market edition / January 2010

Copyright © 2010 by Nancy Holzner.
Cover art by Don Sipley.

ISBN: 978-0-441-01813-0

ACE
Ace Books are published by The Berkley Publishing Group,
a division of Penguin Group (USA) Inc.,
375 Hudson Street, New York, New York 10014.
ACE and the "A" design are trademarks of Penguin Group (USA) Inc.

PRINTED IN THE UNITED STATES OF AMERICA

10   9   8   7   6   5   4   3   2   1

To Steve, for more reasons than I can count

AND THEN THERE WERE ZOMBIES . . .

I was there when it hit. I was on my way to a drugstore near Downtown Crossing to buy lightbulbs before a lunch date with Kane. Funny how you remember little details like lightbulbs. One minute, I was in the middle of a crowd of lunchtime shoppers; the next, I was standing alone on the sidewalk, surrounded by fallen bodies. It was as if, on cue, everyone around me had agreed to play dead—except they weren't playing. I bent to the woman lying facedown at my feet. She'd hurried past me ten seconds ago; I'd admired her leather jacket. Now, her neck was warm, but my searching fingers could find no trace of a pulse. I turned her over. Her eyes were open, their whites bright red, and thin trails of blood trickled from her nose and mouth. She wasn't breathing. I checked another body, then another. They were all the same—whole and warm, with red eyes and dribbles of blood. And very, very dead.

I screamed and ran, not knowing where I was going; all I knew was that I had to get away before the same thing happened to me. But there was no "away." Every corner I turned, every block I ran down, was the same. Dead bodies. Everywhere. Dead bodies strewn all over the ground like trash at a landfill. Some wild part of my brain believed I was the only living thing left in the entire world.

Then, three days after the plague, the zombies began to rise. And Boston has never been the same.

Ace Books by Nancy Holzner

DEADTOWN
HELLFORGED

ACKNOWLEDGMENTS

I owe my biggest thanks to the amazing Cam Dufty, who plucked my manuscript from the slush pile and then edited it with equal measures of insight and enthusiasm—not an easy thing to pull off! And thank you, Cam, for your assistance and patience throughout the editorial and production cycles.

Gina Panettieri is an active, engaged, and tremendously helpful agent, and I'm grateful for her advocacy.

Don Sipley created the awesome cover art, and I wish he could have seen my jaw drop the first time I saw it. Thanks also go to art director Judy Murello and to Edwin Tse for cover type design.

Production editor Michelle Kasper and assistant production editor Andromeda Macri kept the production phase running smoothly. Thanks to copy editor Jessica McDonnell for her sharp eye and astute comments—and for saving me from a couple of real bloopers! I also appreciate the excellent work of proofreader Rob Farren and text designer Tiffany Estreicher. And thanks to my publicist, Rosanne Romanello, for her help in getting the word out.

My daughter (and newly converted urban fantasy fan) Tamsen Conner has always been supportive of my writing. Thanks, sweetie!

Finally, undying gratitude and love to my husband, Steven Holzner, who's published more than 120 books and understands what goes into writing one. He never minded when I'd disappear for hours into my fantasy world. And he bought me endless cups of coffee as I wrote, night after night after night, in coffee shops around town. His love and patience, his support and encouragement, are truly what made this book possible.

1

TWO RULES I LIVE BY: NEVER ADMIT TO BEING A SHAPE-shifter on a first, second, or third date with a human. And never, *ever* bring along a zombie apprentice wannabe on a demon kill.

Lately, given my lack of a social life and my kinda-sorta relationship with a workaholic werewolf lawyer, Rule Number One hadn't presented much of a problem. At the moment, it was Rule Number Two that was giving me trouble. Of course, I'd only formulated Rule Number Two about thirty seconds ago, but I intended to uphold it for the rest of my life—assuming that I'd make it out of here and have a rest of my life to live.

Rule Number Two was thanks to Tina, who—against my orders—had followed me into my client's dream. I was here to exterminate a pod of dream-demons, and the last thing I needed was a teenage zombie in a pink miniskirt.

"Hi, Vicky. I thought you might need this." Tina waved my flamethrower, then looked around. "Whoa. It's *weird* in here."

Weird didn't half describe it. We stood in the middle of a huge circus tent, the top stretching up and up until it disappeared somewhere in the stratosphere. Eerie music from an out-of-tune calliope swirled through the air. All around us loomed dozens of crate-sized boxes painted crayon-bright red, blue, and yellow. Suddenly, a box to my right flipped open. With an earsplitting screech, an evil-faced clown sprang out, jack-in-the-box-style. I raised my pistol, aimed, and squeezed the trigger. The bronze bullet nailed the demon-clown right between its eyes. It shrieked, bobbing around on its spring, then dissolved into a puff of sulfurous mist.

"Cool!" Tina brandished the flamethrower. "Let me do the next one."

"Uh-uh. You're getting out of here. Now. Before the client wakes up." I went over and nudged her toward the dream portal, but she shook me off and walked away.

"Don't worry. Georgie-poo's sleeping like a newborn baby."

"Mr. Funderburk to you."

"Whatever. Anyway, how can he wake up? That was, like, an industrial-strength sleeping pill you gave him. I want to look around. I've never been inside somebody's dreams before." Her mascaraed eyelashes fluttered against her spongy, gray-green skin. "Well, once, when I was alive, Joey Tomasino told me he had this dream and I was in it." She sighed. "But I didn't *know* I was in it, you know?"

I made a snatch for the flamethrower, but Tina spun around and danced out of reach. As she did, the ground rolled under our feet, sending up puffs of sawdust and making Tina stagger.

"What was that?" she asked.

"A bad sign." The ground shook again, ominous, like the shudder that runs up your spine before something really, *really* awful happens. "You're trespassing in Mr. Funderburk's dreamscape. You've gotta go."

She laughed. "I bet the earth moved more than that in Joey Tomasino's dream."

I grabbed her arm and tried to drag her toward the dream portal, but she dug in her heels. I'm stronger than a human, but zombies have incredible strength—something happened to their muscles between death and reanimation. I couldn't budge her.

The ground was rippling in steady waves now, making it hard to stay upright. "This is bad," I said, shaking Tina's arm. "If the client wakes up, we'll both fade into dream limbo. You want to be stuck in here forever?"

Tina yanked herself away and strolled across the bucking

ground, her arms out like those of a tightrope walker. She stopped beside a box and knocked on its lid. "Yoo-hoo. Any demons in there?"

The box flew open and a figure emerged. Tina stumbled backward and hoisted the flamethrower.

"Don't!" I shouted.

Too late. A blast of fire roared from the weapon, incinerating the figure and shooting past it to burn a hole in the wall of the circus tent. Tina fell, landing on her butt and dropping the flamethrower. The jet of fire whipped back and forth like an angry snake, igniting more jack-in-the-box boxes, the calliope, the Eiffel Tower—who knows how *that* got in here, but it was blazing now. I ran over and picked up the weapon, snapping the safety on before the whole damn place went up in flames.

Tina stared at the ashes of the box she'd blasted. "That wasn't a clown."

"No, it wasn't even a Drude." Drudes are dream-demons, the kind I'd been hired to exterminate. "You just torched Mr. Funderburk's mother." No question about it; I'd seen her photo on George's nightstand.

"Oops."

A howling began in the distance, from somewhere outside the dream. The noise got louder and louder, and the dreamscape bounced around like an earthquake redefining the Richter scale. The howling shaped itself into a word: "Mama! *Mamaaaa!*" Outside, George was moaning and shaking his head—signs he was waking up. If that happened, Tina and I would be trapped forever inside this freak-show circus or, worse, locked in the basement that stored the symbols and themes of George Funderburk's subconscious. I'd seen enough topside to know that was *not* a place I wanted to be.

"Mama!" George's heartbeat thundered through the dreamscape. Sleeping pill or no sleeping pill, he was working himself into a state that would catapult him out of his dream—the way it happens when you wake up suddenly, your heart pounding and a scream dying on your lips. We had ten, maybe fifteen seconds left. I shoved Tina, hard.

"Get through the portal! No more screwing around!"

This time, Tina listened. She scrambled, half-crawling, to the dream portal, a doorway of shimmering, multicolored light, then jumped into the beam. Immediately she bounced backward, like she'd tried to hurl herself through a trampoline.

All around us, the circus tent was going up in flames, roaring and popping, throwing lights and shadows across Tina's terrified face. George was screaming now; in here, it sounded like a million fingernails screeching down a million blackboards. Tina put her hands over her ears and again tried to shoulder her way into the portal.

"Vicky! I can't get through!"

I caught up with her. "There's an exit password. Keeps the Drudes in." I mouthed the secret word and shoved Tina into the portal. Her body shimmered for a second, dissolving into a Tina-shaped outline of sparkling colors. Then she disappeared, sucked back into the real world.

Damn, how I wanted to follow her. But I couldn't. Not until I'd finished the job.

With Tina gone, the place was shaking a little less, so maybe George was settling back down and I could—

An explosion ripped through the air, knocking me to the ground in a shower of sparks and hot ash. I scrambled for cover, then checked out the situation from behind an abandoned clown car. Fire raged through the big top as, one by one, the boxes blew up. That would get rid of some Drudes— and God knew what other dream figures were hiding in there—but I couldn't let the flames destroy George's whole dreamscape. If that happened, he'd never dream again, and that meant a one-way ticket to insanity. Not to mention the fact that I'd burn to cinders along with everything else.

Think, Vicky, think. Dreams don't follow the same rules as reality. I had to use dream logic to put out the fire, then try to repair the dreamscape—if the chaos in here didn't jolt George into waking up first. It was a plan, or the closest I could come to one at the moment.

I tried wishing the fire away. Sometimes that works in

dreams. Closing my eyes, I pictured a bright, happy circus scene: a bright, happy tent (flame-retardant) filled with bright, happy people. "Make it real," I whispered. "When I open my eyes, this is what I'll see." Taking a deep breath, I opened my eyes.

The ringmaster ran past me, screaming, his top hat on fire. To my right, a snack cart exploded, showering flaming cotton candy over the stands as spectators trampled each other while trying to find an exit. So much for bright and happy.

Time for dream logic, take two. I tried free association. Fire. Out. Water. Lots of water. As soon as I thought water, I thought of elephants—don't ask me why. It made perfect sense at the time. A line of elephants pedaled into the ring, each on its own tricycle, trumpeting sirenlike wails. It sounded a little bit like a brigade of off-key fire engines, and I crossed my fingers. The elephants triked over to the pool at the foot of the high-dive platform, then stopped. Each elephant rolled off its tricycle, did a ballerina-style pirouette, then began using its trunk to siphon up water and spray it on the flames. Sizzling sounds hissed through the air. Within seconds, the fire was out.

"Thanks, guys," I called, waving as the elephants floated skyward, then disappeared. Their trikes turned around and pedaled themselves out of the ring. Everything was back to normal, or as normal as it gets in a dream.

Except that all around me, everywhere I looked, George Funderburk's dreamscape lay in ruins. Steam rose from piles of wet, stinking ashes. The circus tent was three quarters gone; here and there, a few singed ribbons drooped. Beyond them, a charred, dreary landscape stretched out in all directions, the kind of dreamscape that brought depression and despair to waking life. Gray, gray, and more gray—the fire had burned out all the colors. Don't let anyone tell you that people dream in black and white; that's a severely damaged dreamscape. Dreams are supposed to be in hi-def, razor-sharp color. No way could I leave the place like this—the poor guy would be worse off than before he hired me.

Years ago during my training I learned a technique for rebooting a person's dreamscape, but I'd never actually tried it in the field. Today would be my chance—if I could remember what to do. It was the only hope I had of putting things right.

First things first, though. I couldn't attempt a reboot until I'd flushed out all the demons. Otherwise, they'd reinfest the place and we'd be back to square one. So before I did anything else, I'd finish the job I'd been hired to do. I pulled out the InDetect I wear on a cord around my neck and turned it on. It hummed to life, then was silent. Turning in a slow circle, I held it at arm's length and listened. After a quarter turn it clicked, softly at first, but as I took a few steps, sweeping the InDetect back and forth, the volume and the speed of the clicking picked up. Drude, dead ahead.

Following the clicking, I pulled out my pistol. I'd gone forward about a dozen feet when a demon leaped in front of me, gnashing its teeth and snarling. No more evil clowns. This one was in typical demon guise: long, pointed tongue and cloven hooves, bristling with sharp things—horns, fangs, claws—and spewing bad breath. It howled—whoa, make that *really* bad breath—then charged. I shot. One bronze bullet from my pistol, and the thing dissolved into a murky cloud and a whiff of rotten eggs.

I scoped out the rest of the dreamscape and blasted three more Drudes back into the ether. When the InDetect didn't pick up any more, I holstered my pistol, put my hands on my hips, and tried to remember the reboot technique. If I did it right, George would wake up demon free, with a vague memory of pleasant dreams. Tina's trespassing, Mama's live cremation, the trashing of his dreamscape—all of that would be gone. Overwritten. Not even a trace lingering downstairs in his subconscious.

If I did it right.

This much I remembered: to reboot somebody's dreams, you had to use the dream portal as a conduit to import, from the real world outside, the raw materials to rebuild the ruined dreamscape. Essences, not actual objects. I didn't want to pull in the bedroom dresser or, God forbid, Tina. Instead,

I needed colors, emotions, thoughts, memories—the ingredients we all use in an infinite variety of recipes to cook up our dreams.

There was a spell to pull in those essences. A word, a phrase maybe, that summoned the raw materials of dreams. What was it? Aunt Mab made me memorize it when she taught me how to use the dream portal, but damned if I could remember it now. I tried *essence* in English, then in Welsh. The dream portal sat there, empty, doing nothing but sparkling in shades of white and gray in this colorless world. Raw materials—I was sure the spell had something to do with that, so I tried all the synonyms I could think of: *ingredients, core, infrastructure, primary elements, source.* I also tried the Welsh equivalent when I knew it. I thought I'd had it when I tried *dream-stuff*, but nothing happened. Nothing worked.

Beneath my feet, the ground trembled and shifted. A sigh blew through the dreamscape like a gust of wind. George was stirring. I checked my watch, then shook it. The damn thing said it was 4:37 on Wednesday, February 1, 1792. The guy who'd sold it to me said it would work in here, and, like an idiot, I'd believed him. Time has no meaning in dreams, even though it keeps ticking away relentlessly in the real world. I must've been in here for hours by now; George's sleeping pill would wear off soon.

"Work, damn you!" I shouted at the portal, kicking it and causing a shower of sparks. My voice echoed, and the trembling intensified.

What was the magic phrase? I needed Aunt Mab's help. I'd have to try calling her on the dream phone. The Cerddorion, the race of Welsh shapeshifters to which I belong, have a psychic link to others of their kind that they can use while sleeping. All you have to do is concentrate on the person you want to connect with, and you open the connection. In your dream, the air begins to swirl and shimmer with that person's colors—all souls have their own colors—and, if they're willing to talk to you, you can have a conversation. Sometimes it worked when you called from inside another person's dreams. And Mab was powerful enough to answer even if she was awake.

I pictured her, a straight-backed, iron-haired woman sitting in the library of her house in North Wales. Like an out-of-focus black-and-white photo, the scene was blurred and Mab's usually sharp features were indistinct. I concentrated harder, envisioning her baggy cardigan, her long black dress, her sensible lace-up shoes. Her face was set in its familiar, you-can-do-better scowl. I watched for her colors, blue and silver, to emerge. Nothing. Just flat, blurry gray. And then I realized—I was in a place where there were no colors.

Now what? If Mab's colors couldn't get through, was I cut off from Mab? I had no clue. It had never been an issue before.

Mostly because I couldn't think of a plan B, I kept picturing my aunt. I took concentration to a whole new level, squeezing my eyes shut and scrunching up my forehead. I tried adding other senses: her sharp voice that contrasted so strangely with the softness of her accent, her scent of lavender water and mothballs. Gradually the image sharpened, like a figure emerging from the fog. Mab sat in her favorite wing chair by the fireplace, a book open on her lap.

"Mab, thank God you're there! I need to reboot this dreamscape, now."

Her mouth moved, but there was no sound. Damn. Bad connection. No wonder, since I was calling from someone else's damaged dreamscape. But I didn't have time to try again. Next time, the connection might be even worse.

She seemed to be able to hear me, so I asked, "What's the magic word?" She smiled, closed her book, and turned it so I could read the cover. *The Tempest*, by William Shakespeare. Something literary. It figured.

"For heaven's sake, Mab, I don't have time for English class! Just tell me. Write it on a piece of paper."

Mab tapped the side of her head, the gesture that meant, "Think, child." Her image began to fade. The book-lined walls of the room where she sat wavered and thinned. In a moment, all that remained was the damned book, floating in the air.

I remembered when Mab had made me read that play. I hated it—the language was old and hard to understand, and the story didn't make sense. A bunch of weird spirits and castaways running around on some island—it figured a book like that would hold the key to re-creating a dreamscape. There was something important in that play, something I needed to remember.

The ground convulsed, knocking me to my hands and knees, and a snort ricocheted around me. I was doomed. George was waking up, and Mab wanted me to read Shakespeare. Another snort, louder, knocked the book from the air. It whacked me hard on the back of the head, bounced, and landed on the ground in front of me. I sat back on my knees, rubbing my head. Jeez, if Mab could send a book through the dream phone, why couldn't she just send herself and get me out of this mess? But that wasn't how my aunt operated—never had been.

The book was open to a scene near the end, where the magician Prospero speaks to Ferdinand and Miranda. I scanned the words. *"Our revels now are ended. These our actors,"* blah blah blah. *"The cloud-capp'd towers, the gorgeous palaces,"* yadda yadda yadda. I'd never find it. I kept reading, faster, skimming over the words. Suddenly, my eyes hit the brakes. A phrase glowed and lifted itself off the page. *"We are such stuff as dreams are made on."* That was it. That was the spell. No wonder I'd felt close with *dream-stuff*.

"Such stuff as dreams are made on!" I shouted.

Immediately the portal expanded and a rainbow of colors poured in. Multihued streams of light shot around the dreamscape, touching things, washing them with color, bringing them to life. The portal widened further, and a strong wind entered, pushing me backward. Squinting through watering eyes, I peered into it. Dozens, hundreds of shadowy figures flew in, whirling through the dreamscape, breaking off into tornadoes that spun and leaped as far as I could see. Here and there, figures would jump out and strike a pose or sink down into the ground to wait their turn down cellar, in George's subconscious.

The lights and colors intensified, growing so bright I had to close my eyes. Next, sounds blasted their way in: voices, clanging, music, drumbeats, screeches, whistles, wails, chirping, sobbing—you name it. When every sound you might ever hear in a dream lets loose all at once, the din is unbelievable. I pressed my hands over my ears and crouched beside the portal. Blinded, deafened, pinned down by gale-force winds, I was helpless until the reboot was complete. *Don't wake up now, George,* I thought. *Please don't wake up now.* This dreamscape wasn't even such a great place to visit—I definitely did not want to live here.

The vortex of sounds, lights, and colors swirled and roared. Then, gradually, the chaos subsided, until a single sound emerged: *thumpa thumpa thumpa.* Fear tickled my spine. Was that George's about-to-wake-up heartbeat? No, it was too even for that. More like some kind of drumbeat. A rhythm track. Cautiously, I lifted my hands from my ears. Music—it was music. Not the calliope melody of before, this was dance music—loud, insistent, pulsing with a heavy bass line. I opened my eyes, then blinked. Spots flashed by in random patterns. It took me a minute to realize that they came from a mirror ball rotating overhead. The circus tent was gone. I now stood on the dance floor of the tackiest seventies-style disco you could imagine—raised dance floor, mirrored walls, a light show to make you seasick.

Over at the bar, George's mother waved to me. She raised her drink—something creamy and pink with skewers of fruit and a little umbrella stuck in the top—and smiled. She tossed the drink back in one gulp and wiped her mouth on her sleeve. Then she got up, tied on a frilly blue-and-white apron, and left.

Disco music is not my thing. I've got all the dance moves of a three-legged camel. But as soon as Mama was out the door, I felt an overwhelming compulsion to dance, to boogie, to get down and shake my groove thing. *Thumpa thumpa*

thumpa. The beat was hypnotic; the bass line throbbed through my bones. I tossed back my long black hair—which was odd because my hair is short and strawberry blonde. But I forgot about that as the music swept over me in waves of sound and moved my hips for me in a sexy, swaying motion. *Thumpa thumpa thumpa.* I looked down in surprise, wondering where I'd learned to move like that.

Oh, God. My clothes were dissolving. My T-shirt, which for some reason was soaking wet, was already half transparent, and my bra was missing. Okay, pretty obvious what kind of dream *this* was shaping up to be. No wonder George's mom had left. The dreamscape was rebooted and working just fine. A little too fine. And I was getting the hell out of here.

I ran for the portal, shouting the password, and dove into the beam.

2

GEORGE FUNDERBURK WAS AWAKE.

His open eyes were the first thing I saw as the bedroom materialized around me. Maybe my abrupt exit had woken him up, but I'd made it out of his dream with maybe half a second to spare.

His lips curling in a sleepy smile, George stared at me and murmured, "Wow, you're real. I thought I was dreaming." His comb-over had fallen across one eye; he pushed the hair back in place with stubby fingers.

"You *were* dreaming." Realizing what he was staring at, I crossed my arms over my chest. My shirt was still wet, and the bedroom was cold. "Tina, can you hand me my jacket, please?" I glanced in the mirror over the dresser to make sure everything else was back to normal. Strawberry blonde hair that I kept short because no matter what style I tried, it reverted back to this one after a shift. Heart-shaped face, amber eyes. Yep. That was me. Victory Vaughn, scourge of demons.

Tina, stationed in a chair by the window, tossed me the jacket and I put it on. The wet T-shirt remained clammy against my skin, but at least there was a nice, thick layer of leather between my nipples and George's leer.

"How are you feeling?" I asked him.

"Fine." He sat up in bed and stretched. Then he put his hands behind his head and regarded me. "I'm just sorry to wake up. I was having a great dream—first good one I've had in weeks." He waggled his eyebrows.

The best way to deal with this guy was to ignore the innuendo. Be professional. I opened my duffel bag and started packing my equipment. I unplugged the dream-portal generator (it shuts off automatically when a client wakes up) and wound the cord around its base. That went into the bag, followed by my InDetect, my utility belt, my pistol, and my extra bronze ammo. As I packed, I talked.

"Only sweet dreams for you from now on, George. You had about two dozen Drudes in there, but I got rid of them all."

"Hey, I helped." Tina sat up straight in her chair. Next to her loomed a small mountain of empty food containers: frozen pizza boxes, candy wrappers, an empty cellophane Oreo package, a squashed-flat potato chip bag. While I'd been putting out fires, she'd been cleaning out my client's kitchen. George glanced at her, then his eyes widened. Confusion etched lines across his forehead.

"Weren't you . . . ? I mean, didn't you . . . ?" He shook his head as if to clear his thoughts.

Holding up a warning hand to keep Tina quiet, I watched George as he struggled with the wisp of a memory of Tina invading his dreamscape. "What is it, George?"

He shook his head again. "Nothing. I thought I dreamed about a zombie, but I can't remember. It must be I saw her here, before I fell asleep, huh?"

"Must be." I needed to make sure the reboot had taken hold. "Do you remember anything else about your dreams tonight?"

His eyes returned to my chest, like he had X-ray vision through leather, and he smiled again. "You were there. In a disco."

"Anyone else?"

"Oh, um. My, uh, my mother." Poor George's cheeks couldn't have been redder if I'd given him the slap he deserved.

I shot Tina a look. She was scraping the bottom of a carton of butter pecan ice cream. She had no clue what a huge problem she'd caused. She dropped the empty carton on the floor, then ripped open a box of Twinkies. She'd popped two into her mouth before I caught her eye. She shrugged, then unwrapped another Twinkie.

I was feeling confident that George's dreamscape was whole and functioning, so I walked him through the usual post-extermination procedure. I read down the list of fears he'd provided at our first meeting: clowns, heights, elevators, falling, big dogs. With each item, he shook his head.

"Nope," he said. "None of that stuff bothers me now. Amazing. I've been scared of clowns since I was two years old." He scooched down in bed, closed his eyes, and started humming in a nasal falsetto. "Stayin' Alive"—the song from his dream-disco. Well, if he was picturing himself as a young John Travolta, he was *still* dreaming.

I sat on the edge of the bed and held out a list of instructions, rattling the paper in his face. He blinked and sat up again.

"Follow these post-extermination instructions. You've already arranged to stay home from work tomorrow, right?" He nodded. "Because you need a full day's rest. For the next week, no alcohol, no spicy food, no caffeine. And don't eat sugar or sugary foods after nine P.M., either." That last part shouldn't be hard, since Tina had scarfed down every speck of sugar in the place.

George nodded again, still humming. He shimmied his shoulders and made little pointing gestures that were almost in time with the song.

"George, knock it off for a minute and listen to me."

He blinked, slapped his own hand, and said, "Naughty Georgie."

Tina's bark of laughter sprayed Twinkie crumbs across the room.

I sighed and went on in my most businesslike tone. "It's important for you to understand that Drude extermination is a temporary measure. I can offer some relief, but only you can slay your personal demons once and for all. That's why I've included a list of local therapists who specialize in conquering phobias. Drudes feed on fear; unless you overcome your fears, the demons will return."

Like most clients, George didn't seem worried about that

now. The demons were gone, and that was all they cared about. For the first time in weeks, months—even years, for some clients—they'd be able to get a good night's sleep. And George was looking ready to snuggle back in for another round. His eyelids drooped and he leaned sideways on the pillow. His humming slowed to the tempo of a ballad, then faded out mid note.

"Hang on, George. We've got some paperwork to take care of."

I made Tina clean up the debris from her pig-out while George signed the standard forms and—my favorite part—wrote out a check. As he handed it to me, a shadow darkened the room, like a huge, fast, pitch-black cloud flying across the face of the sun. The temperature plummeted about twenty degrees; the sudden chill prickled the back of my neck and raised goose bumps all over. I was glancing at the window to see if Tina had opened it to the October night air, when pain shot through my head and gut like a million-volt shock, doubling me over. My right hand clenched into a fist so tight I thought my fingers were breaking. I couldn't breathe, couldn't even begin to remember how.

And then it was gone.

When I could speak, I said, "Holy— Did you feel that?"

"You know"—George scooted closer—"I've been feeling *something* ever since I woke up and saw you here. What do you say you and I have dinner tomorrow night?"

From the doorway, Tina made a sound halfway between a snort and a squeal.

I felt too shaken to glare at either of them. "Sorry. I don't date clients." The trembling in my voice surprised me. Physically, I felt fine. Now. A slight tingle in my right forearm was the only trace of whatever the hell had blown through that room.

"Too bad." George yawned. "Well, then, if you don't mind, I'm feeling kinda tired."

"We'll let ourselves out. You get some rest. Come on, Tina." I hoisted my duffel bag to my shoulder and walked to the doorway. Another chill hit me, and I looked back at George. He was already asleep, his mouth hanging slack like a child's.

"DID YOU NOTICE ANYTHING STRANGE BACK THERE?" I tried to keep the apprehension out of my voice as we cruised through predawn suburban streets toward Boston. My right arm still tingled from whatever I'd sensed—if it was anything more than my imagination. Sometimes a strong dreamscape can make the outside world feel surreal for a while.

Tina laughed. "Strange? Are you kidding? This has been the strangest night *ever*." She held her arms straight out in front of her, pretending she was turning a steering wheel. "Even sitting on this side of the car is kinda weird."

We rode in my baby, a 1964 E-type Jaguar in classic racing green. My father had shipped it across the Atlantic when he moved here from Wales in 1975. Because of its right-hand drive, I sometimes got puzzled looks from other drivers. But Dad had taught me to drive in this car, and I loved it.

"I don't mean ordinary strange," I said. "I mean, did you feel anything creepy right before we left?"

"I can't think of anything creepier than Georgie-poo asking you out on a date. He had snot in his moustache—did you see? Eww."

If Tina had felt the force that swept through that bedroom, she wouldn't be thinking about George Funderburk's snotty moustache. Whatever it was had felt—there was only one word for it—*evil*.

But Tina hadn't noticed. George hadn't seemed to, either. I relaxed a little, feeling like I'd been holding my breath since Concord. I rubbed the tingling spot on my arm. The sensation was fading. It must've been the aftereffect of spending all that time in George's dreamscape; I'd never been inside someone's dreams for so long.

"So anyway," Tina asked, "what happened in the big top after I got out of Weirdoland? I mean, you came through the portal looking like the third runner-up in a wet T-shirt contest."

I ignored the third-runner-up crack. So what if Tina, zombified at fifteen, had a couple cup sizes on me? Slender but strong—that was how I liked to think of myself. Besides, it was time to tell her off for the trouble she'd caused.

"I had to extinguish the fire you started, remember?"

"Yeah, right. Uh-huh." Tina's smirk was just visible in the light from the dashboard. "You sure lit Georgie's fire. Burn, baby, burn." She launched into "Disco Inferno" in an ear-splitting soprano.

Was I going to have to spend the entire night listening to *Disco's Greatest Hits for the Tone-Deaf*? I clicked on the radio, set to my favorite classic rock station, and turned it up loud. "Born to Run" blared from the speakers. No way Tina could compete with The Boss at full volume. After a minute of trying, she shut up. I reached over and turned the volume back to a level that didn't threaten hearing damage.

"So when's our next job?" Tina asked.

"*Our* next job? Let me see. That'd be when hell freezes over or snow falls in July. Take your pick."

"What's that supposed to mean?"

"It means there is no 'next job.' I'm not taking you with me again."

"But—"

"But nothing. You ignored everything I said and acted like Mr. Funderburk's dreamscape was your personal playground. That man hired me to kill his demons, not to cause permanent psychological damage—which you almost did. You blasted his mother with a flamethrower, for God's sake."

Tina didn't answer. She folded her arms and slouched in her seat. As much as a zombie can slouch.

"I said you could come with me tonight as research for your school project." Zombies had only recently gotten a school of their own. Tina had been in tenth grade when she died. Three years later, she was finally getting the chance to go back to high school. "I never said we were going into business together."

"But . . . you told me you had more work than you could handle."

It was true; I had said that. I was the only professional demon exterminator in Boston, and in the past year there'd been a spike in personal demon attacks. Not that I was complaining. The money was good, and I loved my work, being on the side of the forces of good and all that. It was just that sometimes I wouldn't mind a little help.

But not from Tina. She'd ignored my instructions by jumping into George's dream in the first place; once there, she made the proverbial bull in a china shop seem like some prim old lady at a tea party.

"Sorry, Tina. I'm not cut out for a partner. I work best alone."

She started arguing, and I turned up the radio again to tune her out.

Up ahead on the right was a 24/7 Donuts. At the moment, coffee seemed like a wonderful idea. I pulled into the lot. Tina sat up, then pumped her fist in the air and shouted "Yes!"

"Nothing like a little snack to lift your mood, huh?"

"Hey, zombies eat. It's what we do."

"Yeah, but all that sugar?" I chose a space and shifted into Park. "You ate enough back at Mr. Funderburk's to give an entire kindergarten class a week-long sugar rush."

"I could eat every donut in that shop and I wouldn't gain an ounce," she said, getting out of the car. "It's the only thing that doesn't suck about being reanimated."

The donut shop was typical of the kind you find in Boston—bright pinks and purples splashed across the walls and tabletops, long rows of donuts climbing the wall behind the counter. A fiftyish woman stood behind the cash register, her scowl clashing with her perky pink uniform. She held out her hand like a traffic cop.

"You got a permit for that thing?"

It took me a second to realize she was talking about Tina. Legally, restaurants couldn't refuse to serve a zombie unless the zombie had left Deadtown—the nickname for Designated Area 1, the part of Boston where all of us monsters had to live—without a permit. In that case, most humans would call the Removal Squad. And when that crew removed a zombie, the zombie never came back.

I slapped the permit on the counter. "My friend's name," I said, "is Tina. Not *That Thing*. Tina. Got it? And if you refuse to serve her, I'll have this place shut down so fast it'll make the cockroaches' heads spin." I could do it, too. That's what workaholic werewolf lawyer kinda-sorta boyfriends were for.

Gloria—that's what the woman's name tag said—gave me a look that I hoped she didn't use on the coffee. It'd be way too bitter. "What can I get you?" she growled.

"How about a new attitude?"

"Look, you wanna order something or are you just gonna stand there? We don't allow loitering, you know." She jerked her thumb over her shoulder at a sign that hung behind her. Sure enough, its big red letters proclaimed NO LOITERING.

I was half ready to turn around and walk out, but that would've made Gloria's day. So instead I smiled sweetly. "Ask Tina."

"Huh?"

"She's your customer. Ask her what she wants."

Clearly, Gloria did not want to ask Tina. She didn't even want to look at her. Suddenly, the woman seemed fascinated by the way her own fingers drummed the countertop. I hated that kind of attitude. Tina could have been Gloria's granddaughter. It was just chance—being in the very wrong place at the very wrong time—that had killed and reanimated the kid. Not to mention a couple thousand other Bostonians just like her.

"Are you refusing to serve my friend?"

Gloria mumbled something.

Tina stepped forward. "Did you say something, ma'am? I couldn't hear you."

"Whaddaya want?"

Tina looked up, down, and around, whistling. Then she turned to me. "I don't know who she's talking to, do you?"

"Yeah, you know, it's pretty confusing." There was nobody besides the three of us in the place. "I guess Gloria ought to use the name of the person she's talking to."

Gloria looked like she was ready to explode. "Goddamn it," she muttered under her breath. Then she looked Tina in the eye and said, "Whaddaya want, *Tina*?"

Tina bounced up and down on the balls of her feet. "Gee, Gloria, I thought you'd never ask. I'll take a dozen donuts. For starters."

Gloria whipped a box into shape, then Tina put her through a whole aerobics routine, bending and stretching and running back and forth as she hurried to retrieve the donuts Tina called out in rapid-fire succession: "A Boston creme, and a chocolate, and a cruller, and a buttermilk, ooh, and one of those pink-frosted ones with the sprinkles. No, make that two of those . . ."

After Tina had purchased a good part of their inventory, I ordered coffee and a pistachio muffin. "This is to go, right?" Gloria grumbled as she rang up the total.

"No, we're eating here," Tina said, wiping pink frosting off her face. Three boxes of donuts were tucked under her arm.

"It's to go," I said. "We need to get you home before sunrise."

I paid. Tina waggled her fingers at our server. "Ta-ta, Gloria. See you soon." She blew a kiss, then spun on her heel and flounced through the door.

In the parking lot, Tina dumped all three boxes into a trash can. Wordlessly, she got into the Jag.

"You okay?" I asked, buckling up.

"Fine. Just not hungry."

I backed out of the parking space, then glanced at her. Zombies can't cry. But if they could, Tina's face would've been wet with tears.

"I wish I could shapeshift like you," she said. "I'd have turned into a lion and torn that bitch's head off!"

"She's just a norm, Tina." *Norm* was a paranormal nickname for human—especially the clueless ones like Gloria.

But I understood how Tina felt. When I was her age, there'd been times when I'd wanted to do the same thing. Different norms, different insults, but I knew that feeling. I'd had to learn to push it down before the anger took hold and I really did shift into a lion or something equally dangerous. For Tina, it was just a fantasy.

Tina pressed fists against her eyes, blotting tears that couldn't fall. "Do you know that tonight's the first time I've been outside Deadtown in over two months? Every time I ask my parents if I can visit, they've got some stupid excuse. They wish I was dead, really dead. I know it." Her voice dropped to a whisper. "Everyone's forgetting me."

I wished I could say she was wrong, but I couldn't—the same thing was happening to all the zombies. Three years ago, after the terror and confusion of the plague, the rising of the zombies had been cause for citywide celebration. Everyone treated the newly reanimated victims like heroes: loved ones snatched back from death's craw. But the zombies were too different. Their skin was a funny shade of greenish gray, their movements stiff. They avoided sunlight and spent nights wide-awake. Their superhuman strength and insatiable hunger made them as terrifying as the zombies in any horror flick. And then there was the little problem of blood—the smell of fresh-spilt human blood sent them into a frenzy of hunger. You could calm them down with any kind of food, but the bloodlust did make things awkward sometimes.

Slowly, people like Tina's parents began to realize that they hadn't gotten their daughter back; instead, there was this creature, this monster, a mocking reminder of what they'd lost. Zombies couldn't cry, but they could still hurt. It was easier for the norms not to see that.

"I don't know why I even bother going to school," Tina said. "I'll never have a career. I'll end up doing manual labor like everyone else. That's all a zombie's good for."

"What about your teacher? She's a zombie with a career."

"That makes one."

Her voice sounded so utterly without hope that I found myself saying words I knew I would regret. But I said them anyway. "You really want to learn how to exterminate demons?"

She stared at her hands, folded in her lap. Then she nodded.

"Okay, I can teach you, but—"

"Great!" She bounced in her seat like one of George Funderburk's jack-in-the-boxes. "When's our next job?"

I shook my head. "Uh-uh. I said no, and I meant it. You can start learning the way I did: by studying."

She huffed and muttered *studying* in a tone more suited to a word like *maggots* or *entrails*. "Okay," she finally said, flipping her hair back over her shoulder. "How do I start?"

"I'll give you some textbooks. Once you've convinced me you know everything in them—and I mean *everything*— we'll go over the different pieces of equipment. Then we'll start practicing how to use each one. It's a long apprenticeship, Tina. It'll be years before you're ready to face a real demon." Suddenly, I felt like Aunt Mab. I'd just described the exact training program she'd used with me.

Tina chattered happily as we drove the last few miles back into town, but I tuned her out. I was busy wondering whether I was making the biggest mistake of my life. Probably. Well, so far, anyway—after all, I was still young.

3

WE WERE ABOUT THE TENTH CAR IN LINE AT THE TREMONT
Street checkpoint, waiting to enter Deadtown, the roughly
rectangular, several-block-long area that was home, by law,
to all of Boston's paranormals.

They'd opened the express lane for vampires, so it had to
be nearly sunrise. As we sat there, customers stumbled out of
the bars in the no-man's-land between Deadtown and human-
controlled Boston, a stretch everyone called the New Combat
Zone. The buildings here had stood vacant for a couple of
years; when bars began to open in the dusty storefronts, the
owners made no attempt to spruce things up. The more derelict and dangerous a place looked, the bigger the thrill for the
norms who ventured here to mingle with the monsters.

Tina nudged my arm. "Isn't that your roommate?"

I followed her gaze to a short, curvy woman with long
hair so black it had blue highlights. She stood in the doorway
of our usual hangout, a bar called Creature Comforts, nuz-
zling a man I'd never seen before. "Yeah, that's Juliet."

"Call her over. She can get us through the express lane."

Juliet wrapped one leg behind the guy's knees as he threw
back his head. "Does she look like she wants to be interrupted? Anyway, the Jag only has two seats."

"She can share with me. We'll fit."

"I don't think so. Watch. And don't blink."

Juliet released the human from her embrace. He staggered
backward, leaning against the wall, one hand pressed to his
throat. Juliet herself simply disappeared. One second she was
there, surveying her conquest with heavy-lidded eyes. The
next second, she was gone.

"Hey," said Tina. "Where'd she go?"

"Home. She's there by now."

"Really? How?"

"Vampire trick. Juliet doesn't like waiting in line, not even the express lane." You'd think a six-hundred-fifty-year-old vampire would've developed patience, but not Juliet.

"Can't she get in trouble for skipping the line?"

"Trouble?" I laughed. "Juliet's been poisoned, burned at the stake, thrown off cliffs, and dumped in the ocean to drown. Trouble doesn't faze her."

"God, I wish I were a vampire. They're, like, *so* much cooler than zombies—I mean, if you've gotta be undead. Check out that hot guy she was with."

On the sidewalk, Juliet's bedtime snack opened his eyes and blinked. He looked up the street, then down, then toward the Deadtown checkpoint. His shoulders slumped as he realized Juliet was gone. He pulled a scarf from his coat pocket, wrapped it twice around his neck, and walked toward the human checkpoint back into Boston. I couldn't tell for sure because the Jag's windows were rolled up, but he looked like he was whistling. Nothing like a vampire hickey to put a guy in a good mood.

"They should let zombies use the express lane," Tina complained as we moved up one car length. "The sun's not good for us, either."

"Yeah, but zombies don't go up in a puff of smoke."

"We don't heal, though. If I get sunburn, my skin will be all cratered and orange-splotched for life."

She sighed, and I knew we were thinking the same thing: whatever "for life" means to a zombie.

THREE YEARS AGO, THE ONLY PEOPLE IN BOSTON WHO believed in zombies were teenagers who'd watched *Night of the Living Dead* a few too many times. That was before the plague hit.

At the time, some of the city's monsters had begun venturing out of the closet, out of the coffin, out from under the bed. This was a change from when I was growing up, when someone like me had to keep my true nature hidden. I knew about my own kind, of course, but back then I had no clue that vampires and werewolves were more than scary bedtime stories. Then, about five years ago, in Boston and a few other cities around the country—Chicago, San Francisco, Dallas, Miami—paranormals began organizing for legal recognition and social acceptance. They were led by Alexander Kane, werewolf and lawyer. Oh, and my sometime companion for dinner, movies, and the occasional overnight romp. Kane's legal practice gave him a toehold of respectability among the humans, and his goal was full legal equity at the federal level for humans and monsters. (Except, if you're talking to Kane, don't say *monster*. Say *Paranormal American*, or PA for short.) He'd recruited a good-sized group to further the cause: werewolves, vampires, even a few humans. But no zombies. Because there *were* no zombies until the plague.

I was there when it hit. I was on my way to a drugstore near Downtown Crossing to buy lightbulbs before a lunch date with Kane. Funny how you remember little details like lightbulbs. One minute, I was in the middle of a crowd of lunchtime shoppers; the next, I was standing alone on the sidewalk, surrounded by fallen bodies. It was as if, on cue, everyone around me had agreed to play dead—except they weren't playing. I bent to the woman lying facedown at my feet. She'd hurried past me ten seconds ago; I'd admired her leather jacket. Now, her neck was warm, but my searching fingers could find no trace of a pulse. I turned her over. Her eyes were open, their whites bright red, and thin trails of blood trickled from her nose and mouth. She wasn't breathing. I checked another body, then another. They were all the same—whole and warm, with red eyes and dribbles of blood. And very, very dead.

I screamed and ran, not knowing where I was going; all I knew was that I had to get away before the same thing happened to me. But there was no "away." Every corner I turned, every block I ran down, was the same. Dead bodies. Everywhere. Dead bodies strewn all over the ground like trash at a landfill. Some wild part of my brain believed I was the only living thing left in the entire world.

Then I saw movement to my left. I quit running. A woman I knew from Kane's activist group, a werewolf, stood in the middle of the street, turning in slow circles. She stopped when she saw me. We stared. I was afraid that if I blinked, she'd disappear. The next thing I knew, we were holding each other like shipwreck survivors clinging to a raft in a shark-infested sea.

As scientists learned later, the virus was a one-in-a-billion mutation that happened to hit downtown Boston, the only place in the world to be so lucky. Only humans were vulnerable to it. The rest of us—werewolves, vampires, and yours truly, Boston's only active shapeshifter—were immune. The plague was the best thing that could've happened to human-PA relations in Massachusetts. Suddenly, the humans needed us.

We agreed to enforce a quarantine zone and gather up the dead. Every PA in Boston came forward to help. We strung up yellow DO NOT CROSS tape and spray-painted DED, for "Disease Enclosure District," on every available surface around the perimeter. (More than one norm noticed how *DED* could be pronounced as *dead*, and so Deadtown got its name. Well, from that and the fact that there were a couple thousand corpses within its borders.) We kept away the morbid thrill-seekers; nobody knew then that the virus had already mutated again, into something no worse than a bad cold. We gathered the dead and stored them in makeshift morgues. We went through belongings, making lists of the names and addresses of nearly two thousand humans who, in minutes, had been cut down. We even patrolled against possible invasion, since there were rumors of biological attack—a theory that's never been proved.

Then, three days after the plague, the zombies began to rise. And Boston has never been the same.

I LEFT TINA AT THE GROUP HOME SHE SHARED WITH FIVE other teenage zombies, promising to drop off some demonology textbooks before school the next night. Then I parked the Jag in the climate-controlled, secure garage I rented two blocks from my building. It was expensive, but I lived in a neighborhood where the residents possessed both super-human strength and nasty tempers. Besides, nothing was too good for my baby.

It was six thirty on a Wednesday morning, and Deadtown was quiet. The sun was high enough that all the vampires were tucked safely into their coffins or relaxing behind black-out window shades. Deadtown, the area where the plague had hit, looked pretty much like any other part of Boston. Shops, offices, apartment buildings. There was a lot of construction going on; restricting all of Boston's PAs—two thousand zombies and several hundred assorted other monsters—into such a compact area had created a demand for high-density housing. Offices got converted to studios, and high-rise apart-ment buildings sprouted all over. Everything was silent now, of course. All the work happened at night.

A figure passed on the other side of the street, wearing a wide-brimmed hat, sunglasses, and a scarf wrapped around its neck and the lower half of its face, looking more like a scarecrow than the zombie I knew it was. Zombie skin disin-tegrates when touched by direct sunlight—the "zombie sun-burn" Tina had mentioned—so the few zombies who venture outside in daylight look like walking piles of laundry. I turned the corner to my block, thinking about how good it would feel to crawl between the covers and sink into my mattress. Work was so busy I hadn't had a decent day's sleep all week.

And then there was a sight that made me stop in my tracks and forget about sleep—but not about crawling into bed.

On the sidewalk in front of my apartment building, a fig-ure paced, talking on a cell phone and gesturing. At the mo-ment, his back was to me, but I knew that back, broad and well muscled beneath the expensive wool coat. Kane. Plea-sure shivered through me as I paused to admire the powerful grace of his movements, the way his hair gleamed in the early morning light. Kane's hair was silver—not gray but really and truly silver. It gave him authority without making him look older than his thirty-one years.

He turned and saw me, then waved. He held up a finger in a "wait a minute" gesture, then bent his head and spoke into the phone. I waited, enjoying the chance to watch him. It was no accident that Kane spearheaded the campaign for PA rights. Besides his passion for the cause, he had the good looks and charm to be its perfect poster boy. The All-American Werewolf. When he appeared at a rally, leaping onto the stage with the animal grace that powered his every move, women cheered and swooned. I couldn't blame them. Watching him pace back and forth, I felt a little weak in the knees, myself.

After another minute, he shut his phone and clipped it onto his belt, beaming at me. God, that smile. Kane had the most dazzling, gorgeous, feel-it-all-the-way-down-to-your-toes smile. It made his gray eyes sparkle from within, like they had a light of their own. I smiled back. He picked up his briefcase, then came over and kissed me on the cheek. I inhaled the woodsy, musky scent of his aftershave.

"Hi," I said. "What are you doing out so early?" Most Deadtown residents were night creatures, but Kane, whose office was near Government Center, kept human hours.

"Early day at the office. But on my way out the door I realized it's been, what, over a week since I'd seen you." Actually, it had been two weeks, three days, and fifteen hours, but who was counting? "I hoped maybe you'd be putting on a pot of coffee." He nuzzled my neck. With his slightly rough lips exploring my skin, not only did I stop counting—I stopped seeing, stopped thinking, almost stopped breathing.

"What do you say?" he whispered. "Can I come up?"

For some reason, when I opened my mouth no sound emerged except heavy breathing. So I nodded, then grabbed Kane's arm and pulled him into the lobby. We stumbled inside, intertwined, trying to move forward and grope each other at the same time.

A harrumphing noise pushed its way through the lust-filled haze. "Good morning, Miss Vaughn. Mr. Kane." Clyde, the zombie doorman for my building, poured about a hundred gallons of prim disapproval into his voice.

"Oh, um, hi, Clyde." I put some distance between Kane and myself, feeling like a cheerleader who'd been caught making out under the bleachers. Kane, who never got frazzled, merely nodded at Clyde, then winked at me.

Clyde harrumphed again. His face remained blank enough for a poker tournament, but he managed to glare his reproach from behind his sunglasses. Clyde had been a minister while alive—Presbyterian, I think, or maybe Lutheran—and he frowned on public displays of affection. At the moment, he was frowning on us big-time.

I pressed the button for the elevator, and Kane and I waited side by side, not speaking and not quite touching. After a second, I forgot about Clyde's gaze burning holes in my back. Kane stood to my left; my body was so aware of his closeness that sparks of electricity skittered up and down my side.

The elevator door had barely closed when we pounced on each other, coming together in a full-body embrace, our lips hungry for each other's flesh. My hands sought the warmth inside his coat, inside his suit jacket, the smooth compactness of hard muscle under the Egyptian cotton shirt. By the time the elevator pinged at the fifth floor, I was half out of my leather jacket and Kane's necktie was on the floor.

As the doors opened, we came up for air. "I hope your roommate's asleep," Kane's voice, at once husky and breathy, sent tingles to places I didn't even know could tingle.

"Juliet hardly ever stays up past six."

"But I hear voices in there—don't you?"

"She probably left the TV on again." I don't think he understood what I said. It's hard to talk, nibble someone's ear, and turn the key in a lock all at the same time.

Finally, I got the door open. Inside, Juliet's huge television blared PNN, the Paranormal News Network. Kane's eyes locked onto the screen, his hands dropped away from my shoulders, and he stepped around me to get a better view. Damn. So much for the heart-racing promise of our ride up in the elevator. I walked to the coffee table and picked up the remote. Watching Kane's intent gaze, I was tempted to click the damn thing off; instead I lowered the volume to something slightly below "wake the dead"—which is pretty damn loud if you happen to live in my neighborhood. Juliet was nowhere to be seen.

Kane glanced at me. "Sorry, Vicky. I'll turn it off in a minute. I just want to see what's happening with this story." The reporter was talking about the zombies' application for a group permit to march in Boston's Halloween parade. Mayor Milliken had denied it. "This is why I'm going in early today," Kane said. "I'm filing an appeal as soon as City Hall opens. I was up half the night working on it." He flashed a half-apologetic smile and turned back to the screen.

So. There I stood, all revved up like an idling sports car with no one to slide into my driver's seat. For a moment I contemplated yanking Juliet's TV from the wall and hurling it out the window. The fantasy gave me a rush of pleasure— the only pleasure I was likely to get this morning, now—and my fingers itched to do it.

But I know a lost cause when I see one. I abandoned Kane to the news and went into the kitchen, where I measured coffee beans into the grinder. It was satisfying to hear the blades pulverize them into powder. I'd like to do the same thing to that giant, sixty-three-inch plasma monstrosity that dominated the living room like a yeti at a pixie convention. Juliet was fascinated by television and had insisted on buying the biggest, flattest, highest-definition set she could find. Even though she loved her TV, like most vampires, she couldn't maintain much of an interest in what was on it. After a few hundred years, the current pop culture trend or "crime of the century" news story just doesn't have the same impact, I guess. So Juliet was always turning on the TV and then wandering off to do something else. It was an annoying habit. Today, I'd promote it to super-annoying.

Not to mention Kane's ability to go from red-hot lover to news junkie in about one-point-three seconds. I sighed, then focused on inhaling that delicious coffee aroma. Nothing like

freshly ground, freshly brewed coffee to lift a girl's spirits.
Besides, I couldn't really complain about Kane's devotion to
his job. It was my fault as much as his that we hadn't seen
each other in two weeks (three days and fifteen hours). We
were both workaholics; it was one of the reasons we got
along.

By the time I carried two steaming mugs into the living
room, I was feeling better. Kane, sitting on the sofa, clicked
off the TV and turned to me. I handed him a mug. He put it
down on the coffee table and pulled me to him.

Mmm, I thought, snuggling in. This was more like it.

It wasn't the two sips of coffee making my heart race as
Kane's lips moved from my collarbone and up my neck, then
to·my ear. His breath warmed my skin and made me shiver—
both at the same time.

"Vicky," he whispered.

Instead of answering, I kissed him. Joined at the lips, our
bodies pressed their full lengths against each other. This was
definitely more like it. After a minute, he drew back—just a
little—and again I felt his warm breath at my ear.

"You know . . ." His murmur brushed me like a caress.
"Saturday's the full moon. Are you coming with me?"

Ever have a nice, steamy shower suddenly go ice-cold?
That's the effect his words had on me. I sat up, pushing him
away.

"Not this month. I'm busy."

Kane wanted me to go with him on his monthly werewolf
retreat. As a condition of getting limited legal rights in Massachusetts, werewolves were required to spend three days
each month—the time of the full moon—at a secure werewolf preserve: in Princeton, in Athol, or out in the Berkshires
in Savoy. For those three days, werewolves were free to un-
leash their inner beasts, as long as they stayed inside the
twelve-foot-high electrified fences topped with silver-coated
razor wire. The surveillance towers, staffed by sharpshooters,
made the local townsfolk feel secure enough that they didn't
show up with torches and pitchforks.

You'd think that Kane—campaigner for PA civil rights—

would object to what amounted to a three-day imprisonment of all werewolves every month. But that wasn't how he talked about it now.

"You have no idea how beautiful it is. The moon shining over the hills, almost as bright as day. Not a human anywhere. You can run and run, feeling all the raw power and strength that you've held back all month, let go of everything you've kept coiled inside." He moved back in, so close his lips brushed my ear as he spoke. "And making love is amazing. We can be who we really are."

He reached for me, but I pushed him away again. "Who *you* really are. I'm not a werewolf." I slid over to the far end of the sofa.

"But you can change into a wolf. You'd be just like one of us."

"Just like," I repeated darkly, reaching for my coffee. Just like nothing, I thought. Sure, I could change into a wolf. But I could never be one of them. I was a shapeshifter; my instincts were different. I didn't *want* to be a sham werewolf.

Why was it so hard to explain that?

Kane sighed, then picked up his coffee mug. We both sipped in silence for a minute.

"Besides," I said. "I already shifted once this month when I was doing a job over in the Back Bay. I've only got two left."

"So come on Saturday instead of Friday. Stay for two days."

"But then—" I tried to think of another excuse and came up dry.

"What are you afraid of, Vicky?" he asked, not looking at me.

"Nothing," I said, hoping the bright, professional voice I used on the phone would cover up the lie. "This month doesn't work for me, that's all."

His look—brows raised over skeptical eyes—said I didn't fool him for a second.

I opened my mouth, but he held up a hand. "Don't answer

me now—not if you're going to say no." He scooted next to me and lightly stroked my thigh. "We'll talk about it later, all right?"

"Later won't make any difference."

Another sigh. Then he sat up straight, checking his watch. "Damn, I've got to go." He was on his feet. "I'm giving a press conference in front of City Hall, and I need to get there early. There's a rumor that Baldwin might show up."

Seth Baldwin was running for governor on an anti-"Monsterchusetts" platform, vowing to take away the few rights PAs had won and drive us from the state. "You think he's going to crash your press conference?"

"I'd love to see him try. It'd be the perfect place to show the world what a bigoted ass he is, in front of all those rolling cameras."

Kane left so fast it was hard to believe he'd been panting for me a few minutes before. A quick peck on the cheek and he was gone.

IN BED, I BURROWED UNDER MY TWO LAYERS OF THICK down comforters. Juliet needed the apartment cold when she slept the sleep of the dead. In spite of the coffee, I was dead tired myself. Between Tina crashing George Funderburk's dream, me getting almost trapped inside his dreamscape, and now the feeling that I'd let Kane down—it had been a long night.

I tossed to one side, then turned to the other, sleep hovering just beyond the edges of my consciousness. Kane's disappointed face floated against my eyelids, even when I buried my head under the pillow. He was asking too much. I wasn't going to alter my nature, not even for him. I was a shapeshifter, not a werewolf. I was Cerddorion—part of a long line of Welsh shapeshifters stretching all the way back to the goddess Ceridwen—and I was proud of my heritage. Like others of my kind, I could change into any sentient creature, and I could do it just three times each moon cycle. So if I started hanging out with Kane and his lupine buddies every month, I'd be stuck in wolf mode. Each retreat was three nights— that'd be it for my three changes.

What are you afraid of? he'd asked. There was the answer. I was afraid he wanted me to become something I wasn't.

But I was also afraid that if I didn't, I'd lose him.

Sleep swallowed me suddenly and deeply, like I'd tumbled into a pitch-black well. No dreams. I'd had enough of dreams for one night.

Or so I thought. Like any self-respecting demon-fighter, I have lucid dreams—I know when I'm dreaming and I stay in control. But somewhere in the depths of my sleep I heard a hammering. Loud. Insistent. And I couldn't tell where it was coming from. No images, just blackness. I went deeper into sleep, searching for the cause of the sound. It got louder, but I wasn't getting any closer. The sound eluded me, always just around the corner. But there *were* no corners. Was something wrong with my dreamscape?

Wham! The crash of a redwood falling, an avalanche booming, a cannon firing—or something that loud—resounded through the apartment. I half-leaped out of bed, getting tangled in the sweaty sheet and falling onto my side. The room, darkened by blackout shades, was as inscrutable as my sleep. Was I still dreaming? Was I awake? How the hell could I not know?

My bedroom door burst open, and light stabbed into the room. Two shapes hulked in the doorway. Somehow, I didn't think they'd stopped by to wish me sweet dreams.

4

"FREEZE!" SHOUTED A MAN'S VOICE. "THIS IS THE HUMAN-Paranormal Joint Task Force!"

The Goon Squad? What the hell was the Goon Squad doing in my apartment? I squinted toward the doorway. Pointing two guns at my head, that was what.

"Whoa, whoa. Take it easy." I slowly raised both hands. "What's the problem?"

Somebody found the light switch. A blinding glare, and I could make out the features of my visitors: one human, one really big zombie. The human stepped forward, his gun steady. "You're the problem, you damn freak."

The zombie behind him, so tall he stooped in the doorway, growled. Not a pleasant sound.

"Shut up, Sykes," said the human, who seemed to be in charge. "And cuff her."

"Hey, wait a minute—" I began, but the zombie picked me up and flipped me over like he was a short-order cook making flapjacks. In two seconds he'd cuffed my hands behind my back. In another three, I was half-standing, half-hanging from Sykes's superhuman grip as he dragged me over to his partner. Thank God I'd put on sweatpants and a T-shirt. Often I didn't bother with pajamas.

The human cop holstered his gun. He was short, ugly, and mean-looking. He put himself right in my face, so close I could see the pores that pitted his oily skin. His breath smelled like onions and cheap cigars.

I was scared as hell. The Goon Squad meant business—police business. The Boston cops sent the Goons into Deadtown to do the dirty jobs. But I wasn't going to let this bozo see one drop of fear. Squaring my shoulders as much as I could, given Zombie Sykes's death grip on my arm, I glared at the human and said, "You'd better tell me what this is about. My attorney is Alexander Kane, and he'll—"

"Hah!" Sykes snorted again. "Hear that, Norden? Your favorite lawyer."

Hatred dimmed Norden's eyes. He leaned in even closer. "I don't care if he's the Attorney General of the United States. I don't have to tell you a goddamn thing."

It was true. Paranormals didn't have the same rights as humans. The cops could haul us in for no reason at all—which appeared to be happening to me at the moment.

I slumped, and Norden grinned. His smile didn't make him any prettier. "Goddamn monster," he said.

"Hey," said Sykes. "Cut the 'goddamn monster' crap, blood bag. All right?" Norden glared at *blood bag*—undead slang for *human*—then stomped out of the bedroom.

I looked up at Sykes, which took a bit of neck-craning. He wasn't bad-looking for a zombie. The flesh on his face was barely rotted, his color only slightly green. To tell the truth, he was better looking than his partner. I smiled in what I hoped was a buddy-buddy kind of way—we monsters gotta stick together and all.

"So what's this about?"

He opened his mouth, paused, then closed it again. After a glance over his shoulder into the living room, he said in a low voice, "Some out-of-town cops have a couple of questions they wanna ask you."

Norden rocketed back into the room like he'd been shot out of a cannon. "Shut up, Sykes." For a minute, I thought he was going to smack the big zombie. That'd be interesting. But instead he took a slow, deep breath and jerked his head toward the door. "Let's get her out of here." He strode out of the bedroom like he wanted to show us how it's done.

Sykes tugged my arm, but I dug in my heels. It wouldn't do much good except for maybe surprising him enough to buy me three seconds of time to think. My mind was reeling, so much that I still felt like I was dreaming. Out-of-town cops? I hardly ever left Boston. Other than last night's demon extermination in Concord, I hadn't been out of the city for a month. What could they possibly want to ask me?

"Come on, Ms. Vaughn," said Sykes, his voice almost gentle. "Don't make me carry you."

He could, of course. A zombie that size could juggle three of me with one hand. But he wasn't using his full strength yet. As he hesitated, a thought pushed its way through the confusion buzzing in my mind. I was not going to let anybody, not even the Goon Squad, drag me out of my home in handcuffs.

I closed my eyes and concentrated on slimness. I thought only of skinny things: drinking straws, uncooked spaghetti, beanpoles (not that I've ever seen an actual beanpole). My pulse sped up, and energy bubbled under my skin. I felt my limbs contract. Not too much—I didn't want to shift all the way into a snake or something—just enough to make myself a bit more slender. It's a neat trick when I want to fit into a skintight little black dress. Or get out of a pair of handcuffs.

The cuffs dropped to the floor with a clatter.

"What the hell are you doing in there, Sykes?" Norden reappeared in the doorway, and I gave him a friendly wave. His eyes bugged out when he realized my hands were free.

In a second, he'd pulled his gun and was pointing it at my chest. But now that I knew the cops needed answers to some questions—and thought I could provide them—I was ready to call his bluff.

I folded my arms and put on my best stubborn look. (It's a good one, if I do say so myself.) "I'll go with you. I'll answer your questions. But I won't be treated like a criminal. Put the gun away, and forget about any handcuffs."

Norden's mouth was a grim line. "I'm not messing around, freak. This thing's loaded with silver bullets."

I laughed. "What, Norden, you skip the chapter on shapeshifters in the monster manual? I'm not a werewolf. Silver isn't lethal to me."

At least, it wasn't any more lethal than any other kind of bullet. Put a big enough hole in me, and whether you made that hole with silver, lead, steel—whatever—I'd bleed, then die. I didn't have a werewolf's miraculous healing powers or the undead advantage of a vampire or zombie.

Sykes picked up the handcuffs from the floor and dangled them from one massive finger. "I used the silver-plated cuffs," he remarked.

"See? If I had a problem with silver, I couldn't have gotten out of them."

The gun didn't move, but Norden's face was all red and puffed up; he looked like a volcano ready to explode. I could see I'd gained maybe a millimeter of an advantage, so I pressed it. "You liked that trick? Put the gun away, and I'll go with you. But if you keep threatening me, I'll shift into a wisp of smoke. Try putting handcuffs on that."

It was another bluff, of course. I couldn't turn into smoke. Shapeshifters can only change into animate creatures. But it was clear that Norden didn't know squat about my kind. Besides, whether I turned into a mosquito or an elephant, I didn't much like my chances against Sykes's strength and Norden's gun.

I closed my eyes and tried to look like someone about to vanish in a wisp of smoke.

"Goddamn it!" Norden stomped his foot. But he holstered the pistol.

"Okay, boys," I said. "Let's go."

I led the way through my living room. Sykes held my left arm in a near-crushing grip. Norden followed so close behind us I could feel his onion-and-cigar breath on my neck. I was in the clutches of the Goon Squad, but I was walking out of here on my own.

IN THE LOBBY, CLYDE SHOOK HIS HEAD LIKE HE'D EXPECTED to see something like this. He probably thought they were hauling me in for public indecency. But his face creased into a frown when his gaze shifted to Norden, who stuck as close as he could without actually touching me. Nobody in Dead-town liked the Goons, and most felt that norm cops had no business inside our borders. "Is everything all right, Miss Vaughn?" he asked, still staring at the cop.

"Just peachy, Clyde. Would you mind giving Kane a call? Tell him to meet me at Goon Squad headquarters ASAP."

"Very good, Miss Vaughn." He reached for the phone.

"Goddamn monster with a goddamn lawyer," Norden grumbled. "And the lawyer's a monster, too. What next?"

The big zombie growled, and the human half turned in his direction. "Shut up, Sykes."

Sykes gave his partner a look that would reduce most norms to a quaking puddle of fear. The two stared at each other, tense, fists clenched on both sides. Then Sykes pulled up his hood, put on his sunglasses, and shambled out the door, sorting his fingers into gloves.

Norden watched him go, his lip curled in pure hatred. Odd. Most norm cops joined the Goon Squad because they thought hanging out with the monsters made them tough. This one seemed to be here because he hated us. Wasn't I lucky the lucky one, drawing him as my dance partner.

Poor Norden, though. It just wasn't his day. I wasn't playing nice, his partner was snarling at him, and he couldn't even have the fun of dragging me into headquarters in handcuffs. The guy was mad, and he was looking for someone to take it out on. He picked me, shoving me hard toward the door.

"Mr. Kane is out of the office, Miss Vaughn," Clyde said, putting the phone down. Damn, I'd forgotten about the press conference. "But I left an urgent message."

"Thanks, Clyde. And could you send someone up to fix my front door? The Goons kicked it in. The lock's busted, and Juliet's asleep in her coffin."

Clyde picked up the phone again as Norden hustled me out the door. Good old Clyde. He'd have the door fixed before Juliet woke up. Good thing, too, I thought, looking at Norden. In this neighborhood, you couldn't be too careful.

5

THE GOON SQUAD WAS HEADQUARTERED IN THE BASE-
ment of a rundown building in the New Combat Zone, down
one flight of rickety stairs. Sykes gripped my arm as we
marched down a featureless hallway with gray metal doors
lining each side. The sound of our footsteps ricocheted off
the anonymous walls, and I tried not to wonder what lurked
behind the doors. Offices, probably, but the place had an
eerie sense of despair, as though people were trapped and
forgotten behind those blank doors. We stopped in front of
one, seemingly at random. Norden rapped once, then turned
the knob and went inside. Sykes propelled me in behind him.

"Here's your freak," Norden said. He spun around, shot
me one of his piggy-eyed frowns, then pushed past me and
out the door. "C'mon, Sykes," he said from the hallway.

Sykes regarded me over the top of his sunglasses, looking
like he wanted to say something. Instead of tender farewells,
though, he settled for a nod. Then he shambled into the hallway, closing the door behind him.

The room was small, with scuffed, white, windowless
walls. Two people sat at a banged-up metal table—a woman
directly across from me, and a man to my left. There was no
third chair, no place for me to sit down.

I glared at the woman, who cringed, then I turned my evil
eye on the man. At least, I tried to. It's hard to glare into a
pair of astonishingly blue eyes with a hint of a smile crin-
kling the edges. I blinked and took in the rest of the view: a
headful of curly blond hair—half an inch too long for a
cop—high cheekbones, and a strong jaw. He wore a suit, not
a uniform, so I must have been looking at a detective. I didn't

know they made detectives that good-looking. The guy should've been modeling Armani suits instead of having me hauled in by the Goon Squad. I looked him over again. Nah, he wasn't pretty enough to be a model. More like the kind of actor who makes a gazillion bucks playing tough-but-sensitive action heroes. Whatever. He still looked damn good.

He stood and picked up his chair, carrying it around to my side of the table. "Here, why don't you sit down?" he asked. "I'll find us another seat."

I sat, and he actually held the chair for me as I did. Wow. A gentleman. Under other circumstances, I'd enjoy meeting this guy. Circumstances that didn't involve my being pulled out of my bed and dragged here in my pj's by the Goon Squad.

Suddenly I realized I hadn't even had time to comb my hair. I must look like a total mess. Thank God the interrogation room, or whatever it was, didn't have one of those one-way mirrors. I didn't want to see.

The detective disappeared through the door, which shut with a bang but no click. Was it unlocked? Norden hadn't used a key to get in. I thought of reaching over to try the knob and glanced at the female detective. She sat across from me, silent, blinking like a startled owl. She was on the far side of forty, with frizzy hair, scanty eyebrows, and saucer-sized dark circles under her eyes. Her jacket, green plaid with linebacker shoulder pads, could've been an exhibit in a 1980s museum. She swallowed, looking terrified. I thought about how easy it would be to walk out of there—stand up, open the unlocked door, waltz down that hallway and up the rickety stairs. She'd be too paralyzed to stop me.

But they'd just send the Goon Squad again to haul me right back.

The door opened, and the good-looking detective wrestled a metal folding chair into the room. He hefted it over my head to place it at the end of the table, then sat and gave me a dazzling smile.

Suddenly, everything about him annoyed me: the good manners, the even better looks, the two-hundred-watt smile.

Who the hell was he to look so attractive and friendly and . . . attractive? This was the guy who'd sicced the Goons on me.

He opened his mouth to say something, but I beat him to it.

"I have no clue why you dragged me out of bed and brought me here against my will. But you'd better know right now that I'm not saying a word until my lawyer arrives."

The two detectives exchanged a look, increasing my annoyance factor. "My attorney, by the way, is Alexander Kane. Ever heard of him?"

"I—" the good-looking detective began.

"Kane will be *most* interested in the civil rights aspect of my treatment today. I'm a demi-human, you know." You'd think that would give me half the rights of a human, but it didn't work that way. Shapeshifters were either active, like me, or inactive, like my sister, Gwen, a suburban wife and mom. Inactive demi-humans had the same rights as humans; we active ones had no rights at all. Kane had several civil rights cases grinding their way through the courts, trying to get such issues in front of the Supreme Court. He wouldn't rest until all the monsters had rights.

"But—" the detective tried again.

"But nothing. That's what you'll get from me without my attorney present—nothing. Do you understand that? Not a word." I sat back in the chair and folded my arms across my chest. Hah. That told them.

The female detective looked suitably bludgeoned by my words. I glanced at her partner. He was biting his lip, trying to suppress a smile.

"Something amusing you, Detective?" His smile broadened to a grin. "What the hell is so damn funny?"

"It's just that, well, for someone determined not to say anything, you haven't let me get a word in edgewise."

Heat rose in my cheeks as I realized he was right. He gave me a look that might have included a wink—it was too fast to know for sure—then angled his chair toward me.

"Listen," he said, leaning forward, "I promise we won't ask you any questions until you feel comfortable answering them. We'll certainly wait for your attorney. In the meantime, do you mind if my colleague and I introduce ourselves?"

I sat there staring at the scuffed tabletop, feeling—and probably looking—like a sulking child.

He laughed and held up both hands in a gesture of surrender. "Sorry, sorry. That was a question." He shrugged and sat back.

"Go ahead," I said, trying to sound like I was doing them some huge favor. "Introduce away."

"Great. I'm Daniel Costello, Boston PD," he said. "And this is Detective Stephanie Hagopian. She works in Concord." He nodded toward the frizzy-haired woman, who blinked again.

"I thought you both were from out of town," I said.

Costello shook his head. "Concord requested our assistance."

"Why?"

"Because they believe the case has paranormal elements."

"You're on the Goon Squad?" He sure didn't look like one of the goons. And why hadn't he come to pick me up? I almost wouldn't have minded waking up to find *him* in my bedroom. Almost.

He shook his head. "I'm in Homicide."

Homicide? Now we were getting down to it. I leaned forward to hear what this was all about.

But Costello chose that moment to stop talking. He sat back, gazed somewhere over Hagopian's head, and drummed his fingers on the table.

My mind started putting the pieces together. Costello was a Homicide detective. Hagopian was from Concord. I'd been in Concord last night. My God. As soon as the thought struck me, I blurted it out. "Is it George? George Funderburk— you're not saying he's dead?"

He shrugged. "I'm not saying anything yet, Ms. Vaughn. I think we'd better wait for Mr. Kane before we proceed," he said. He checked his watch. "Would you like to call and see what's delaying him?" He unclipped a cell phone from his belt and slid it toward me.

I stared at the phone, not really seeing it while my mind whirred at two hundred miles a minute. It couldn't be true. George had been fine when I left. But Concord, homicide—it had to be. Oh, God. What if Tina had caused more damage to his dreamscape than I'd realized? But that was ridiculous— no one ever died from a damaged dreamscape. Or did they? Just because I'd never heard of it didn't mean it was impossible.

But then maybe it wasn't George. I'd left the guy snoozing happily just a few hours ago. Everything had been normal, routine. Everything except— A chill swept over me as I remembered. Everything except that weird feeling, that sense of evil, that had passed through the room. God, I wished Kane was here—maybe he could help me make sense of this. Fingers trembling, I reached for Costello's phone.

At that moment, the door opened and Kane strode in. "Vicky," he said, breathless, "I got here as soon as I could."

Seeing him, his silver hair gleaming, his expression both worried and determined, was like seeing the sun break through the clouds. In his immaculate gray suit and steel-blue tie, he looked like the ultimate power broker. Definitely not someone to mess with. And he was on my side. I wanted to jump up and throw my arms around his neck, but I merely nodded.

Introductions were made. Kane's nostrils flared as he shook hands with Costello, his werewolf senses working overtime to sniff out an opinion of the guy. They seemed to have a couple of acquaintances in common—not unusual for a police detective and a lawyer. Hagopian still didn't say anything. Kane glanced at her, and I could see him decide that Costello was the one to deal with. He leaned on the table with both hands and gave Costello a smile that straddled the line between camaraderie and aggression: be a pal or get your throat torn out—your call.

"I may need a private conference with my client before she can answer any questions, Detective. But it would be helpful to have some idea of what this is all about." He stood and spread his hands, reprising that chummy, sharp-toothed smile.

"Certainly. As Ms. Vaughn already suspects, we're investigating the death of one of her clients. George Funderburk."

I slumped in my chair, chilled all the way through by fear and guilt. I shouldn't have left him alone. I should have cleared out that horrible presence, whatever the hell it was. But the truth was I'd been afraid, even then. I'd been in a hurry to go. "He was fine when I left," I said, my voice barely a whimper.

"Are you bringing charges against her?" Kane asked.

Costello shook his head, but he was looking at me, not at Kane. His blue eyes regarded me with something I could've sworn was concern.

"We're not questioning you as a suspect, Ms. Vaughn," Costello said. "We're consulting you as an expert."

"Then why the hell did you have her dragged in here like some kind of criminal?"

"I'm sorry about that." Costello never shifted his gaze from me. He looked like he meant it about being sorry, a shadow deepening the blue of his eyes. "I haven't had a lot of experience with . . . with Paranormal Americans. I was following standard procedure." I started to look away, but something in those eyes held me, that and a note of urgency in his voice. "I'll know better next time."

Kane stepped between us. "Let's make sure there won't be any next time, Detective." He crouched beside my chair, his hand brushing my thigh. "Are you willing to talk to them, Vicky?"

"What do you want to know?"

Costello let out his breath as though he'd been holding it for an hour. "Thank you," he said, once more seeking and holding my gaze. Then he glanced at Detective Hagopian. To be honest, with all the testosterone floating around, I'd forgotten she was in the room. "Stephanie?"

Hagopian jumped. Then she nodded and opened a notebook. She cleared her throat twice. "The death was . . . well, it wasn't normal," she said. "We know from documents found at the scene that you were there last night in your, ah, professional capacity. We'd like your opinion on whether Funderburk died as the result of a demon attack."

I shook my head. "I exterminated the whole pod. Besides, demons don't kill. They torment. That's how they feed. If the victim dies, the party's over."

"What do you mean?"

"Demons are conjured entities. They don't exist until someone invokes them. That someone can be a sorcerer out to hurt someone—that's where Harpies come from—or it can be the victim himself." Hagopian flinched, and I added, "Or herself."

"People conjure demons against themselves?" She raised a plucked-half-to-death eyebrow.

"Not on purpose. But strong feelings of guilt or shame or fear can bring demons swarming to a victim like honeybees to a rose garden. Eidolons are personal demons that feed on guilt. Drudes feed on fear. They're pretty similar, except Eidolons attack while you're lying awake at night and Drudes invade your dreams."

Hagopian shuddered, and I got the feeling she'd had a personal encounter with a demon or two. Too bad that now wasn't the time to make my sales pitch. Not that she'd be buying, seeing as how my last client turned up dead. I remembered his happy, off-key humming after the extermination. Poor old George.

"Harpies," I continued, "are revenge demons. Eidolons and Drudes can take many forms, but Harpies always look the same: They've got vulture bodies and Medusa heads, with snakes for hair and a beak for a mouth. They smell like garbage that's baked in the sun for a week. Their screeching"—I tried to find a way to describe the brain-shredding noise Harpies made, but there were no words for it—"well, their screeching alone can drive a person insane."

Both detectives were watching me openmouthed, like kids listening to a scary campfire story they didn't want to hear.

Too bad. They'd dragged me here; they deserved all the juicy details. "Harpies attack from the outside. You're lying in bed, and suddenly you can't move. These hideous things—worse than any nightmare—fly through the wall and land on you, tearing into you with their talons. Then they begin to feed. It feels like they're ripping out your vital organs. The agony lasts all night. The next morning, there's no physical damage. But you can count on them returning night after night after night."

"What about the other kinds, the"—Hagopian consulted her notebook—"the Eidolons and the Drudes?" Her voice had diminished to a croak. Costello shot her a questioning look, but her eyes were fixed on me.

"Eidolons attack from the inside," I answered, "like you've got some huge, venomous parasite gnawing on your bones. Guilt brought to life. Some victims can see their Eidolons; others just feel unbearable agony. Drudes are unpredictable, like dreams, and they're the source of most nightmares. If you're plagued by horrible dreams, swarming with everything you fear, you've got a Drude infestation." I glanced at Detective Hagopian, who'd closed her eyes and was breathing shallowly through her mouth. Yep. Drude victim for sure. I turned back to Costello. "Demon attacks are terrifying and painful. Hell on earth. But they're not fatal. When a victim dies, that person's demons cease to exist. That's why demons don't kill."

They chewed on that for a moment, and I had a thought. "It's not uncommon for demon victims to commit suicide. Could George have—?" Even as I asked the question, I wondered why Funderburk would kill himself. He'd been in such a terrific, disco-dancing mood.

Costello shook his head. "He was . . ." He shuddered. "*Cooked*. From the inside out. The body looked perfectly normal, even felt cold to the touch like you'd expect in a corpse. But when the paramedics lifted the victim onto the gurney, his mouth fell open. A jet of steam shot out and scalded one of the EMTs. The EMT ended up in the burn unit." *Oh God,* I was thinking. *This can't be.* Costello didn't see the expression on my face, because he kept on talking. "Ice-cold skin but, well, boiling inside."

The roaring in my ears drowned out his voice, and my vision shrank to a pinprick. Something squeezed all the air out of me, and I couldn't catch a breath. I closed my eyes and pushed everything away: the detectives, George Funderburk, this whole goddamn conversation. *No,* I thought. *No. Not here. Not that.*

A hand rubbed my back, and something pressed against my lips. A voice drifted down from the ceiling. "Vicky? Are you all right? Do you want to stop?"

I opened my eyes to see Kane's face hovering inches from my own. He was trying to get me to take a sip of water. "Drink this."

He was too close. They all were. I couldn't breathe. Damn it, I wanted them all *away* from me. My arm tingled. It was a warning. I tried to push down the feeling, but I couldn't. I couldn't. The tingle intensified to a burn, the heat racing through my veins. And then it hit me like a tsunami—the rage. Pure, white-hot rage. I wanted to crush the cup Kane held to my lips. I wanted to tear apart the goddamn room and everything in it. I wanted to pound and kick those detectives, both of them, and even Kane, over and over, until they were nothing but a bloody pulp on the floor. Smash everything— just *smash* it. My fists clenched so hard that my nails cut into my palms, drawing blood.

The sharpness of the pain brought me back a little. I remembered who I was—me, Vicky. I remembered that the others in this room weren't enemies, weren't ants to be crushed and flicked away. No. Kane—I knew Kane. Those cops—just humans trying to understand a death. *No more deaths,* I chanted mentally, *no more deaths*. And I fought down the urge to destroy; it was like trying to tame a gale-force wind into a gentle breeze. How easy, how *satisfying* it would be to slaughter them all. No. I had to fight it. Inch by inch, I did. Inch by inch. The burning subsided; drew back gradually until my arm was my own again.

"I'm okay." I pushed the cup away, gently, then thought better of it. Putting both my hands around Kane's to keep the cup from shaking, I took a deep swallow. The water soothed me, and I drank it all.

When I spoke again, my voice was clear and steady. That surprised me, because I was still quaking inside. "I was wrong, Detective Costello. From what you describe, a demon did murder George Funderburk."

"But you said demons don't kill."

"Most don't. But we're not talking about an ordinary demon." I hesitated, not wanting to say the words, as if saying them would make it real. But it was real already. Whatever I might wish for, it was real. "George died of a Hellion attack."

Hellion. As I said the word, a tingle teased my arm. I ignored it.

"Oh, Vicky," Kane murmured, still rubbing my back. "I'm so sorry."

The detectives glanced at each other. Hagopian, her face drained of color, looked bewildered and scared. "What's a Hellion?"

"It's a demon, but nothing like the kind I was telling you about." I wished I had another cup of water. "Those are personal demons. If you want to get technical, they're of the genus *Inimicus*. Hellions are a different class altogether, genus *Eversio*. They exist to destroy. Usually, they don't bother with individuals—they're a lot more interested in wreaking havoc in society. Whenever something really nasty happens, you can bet Hellions are there."

"Like what?"

"Earthquakes, wars, genocide. Anything that causes massive suffering and destruction."

"Like the plague." This came from Hagopian.

"Yes. Events like that attract Hellions by the legion."

Kane cut in. "Right after the plague, when we realized Hellions were massing, the witches of Boston put up a shield to keep them out."

"So how did a Hellion get to Funderburk?"

"The shield protects Boston itself. It forms a circle that

reaches as far as Somerville, Cambridge, Brookline, Dorchester, and the harbor," Kane said, drawing a circle in the air. "The larger the area, the weaker the shield. Besides, the plague was localized in town."

"In a legion, Hellions are a terrifying destructive force. Individually, though, they're usually not tormenters," I said. "Instead, they find somebody with a crack in their moral armor, somebody who can be tempted by evil. They incite. They whisper, insinuate, nudge."

Costello looked confused. "So you're saying that a demon, a Hellion, talked somebody into killing Funderburk? But—the way he died . . ."

"No. I wasn't quite finished. Even though they're inciters, Hellions are also violent themselves. Brutally so. Sometimes a sorcerer will try to bind a Hellion into service."

"Bind it?"

"It's a dangerous thing to do. A powerful sorcerer can force a Hellion to do his bidding. But the Hellion doesn't like it one bit. A bound Hellion is surly, rebellious, and difficult to control. It'll kill its master if it gets the chance. But if you can keep it under your thumb, a Hellion in bondage is a powerful weapon."

"Let me get this straight. Somebody, some sorcerer, called up a Hellion and used it to kill Funderburk."

I nodded.

"Why?"

"I don't know."

"I think I do." Kane patted my back and moved to the front of the room. "It's the election."

We all turned to him. Detective Hagopian spoke. "The victim wasn't involved in politics. He sold used cars."

"That's the point," Kane looked angry. "Just a normal citizen. An ordinary, law-abiding citizen killed by the monsters."

"Not monsters," I said, surprised to hear Kane use that word, "a Hellion."

He shrugged. "What's the difference?"

"PAs have independent existence. Demons are conjured entities—"

"You know that. I know that. Even the good detectives here know that now. But the average voter has no clue. To them, anything that isn't human is a monster. They're not going to waste time on fine distinctions. When this hits the news . . ." Kane turned to Detective Costello. "Who called the police?"

Hagopian answered. "His neighbors, reporting loud noises from his house. They described the sound as"—she flipped back a few pages in her notebook—"'repeated banging, like hammering.' Officers arrived at oh-seven-twenty. The front door was open, so they went in. They found the victim in his bedroom. There was no sign of a struggle. The body was tangled in the sheets, nothing more."

"I locked it," I said. Everyone looked at me. "The front door. I always double-check that all doors are locked when I leave." I could see myself watching Tina skip to the Jag, then testing the lock. I held the picture in my mind. Partly to be sure I was right, but mostly to hold back the memory of the last time I'd seen a Hellion victim.

"Did the neighbors talk to the press?" Kane asked.

"How would I know that?" Hagopian asked. "No reporters have called for a statement. That I know of, anyway."

"What about the victim's family? Are they likely to run screaming to the press?"

Hagopian shrugged. "They think he had a heart attack. The autopsy won't contradict that for several days, anyway."

Kane paced in the small space near the door. "Somebody will leak it. It's just a question of timing—how close to election day. All they have to do is whip up a little panic, and Baldwin wins."

"Aren't you overlooking something?" Kane stopped pacing and looked at me. "That Hellion didn't attack at random. It went after my client, right after I exterminated those Drudes. What if it's here for me?" My voice betrayed more panic than I wanted to show.

"Vicky, I don't think—"

"Hang on a minute, Mr. Kane." Costello squinted at me with intense interest, his blue eyes glinting. "Why do you think a Hellion would be after you?"

The roaring started in my ears again, but I swallowed hard and pushed it down. "Why, Detective Costello . . . ?" God, it hurt even to think it. I didn't know if I could force the words out. Another hard swallow. "Ten years ago, a Hellion murdered my father. Because of me."

6

MY FATHER NAMED ME. ONE YEAR BEFORE I WAS BORN—TO the day—he was visited in a dream by Saint Michael, sworn enemy of demons, and Saint David, patron saint of Wales. Saint Michael brandished his flaming sword and declared, "A girl child shall be born unto you, and her name shall be Victory." Saint David nodded and made a gesture of blessing, then the two ascended—into heaven, I guess, or wherever saints go after they've delivered a prophecy. Dad thought they were growing taller, until he realized they were rising into the air. He could see the toenails of their sandaled feet at eye level for a moment, and then they were gone.

Funny, Dad said, he'd never thought about archangels, or even saints, having toenails. But that was my favorite part of the story when I was a girl. Clean, pinkish toenails peeking out of golden sandals.

Mom wanted to call me Rhiannon. But she was loopy on painkillers when my father filled out the birth certificate, so Victory I became.

My childhood was normal enough, I suppose, for a demi-human whose birth had been foretold by a prophecy. We lived on the top floor of a Somerville triple-decker. Dad juggled three or four part-time teaching jobs at local colleges, and Mom stayed home with us two girls. When money got tight, she'd sell magazine subscriptions by phone from the kitchen. My parents were both Cerddorion—a race more common in their native Wales than in their adopted home of Boston—and I grew up trying to master the trick of being proud of my heritage while keeping it an absolute secret from the norms around me.

I got by in school, played softball in Foss Park, and alternately fought with and confided in my older sister, Gwen. And then puberty hit—as if that weren't tough enough—bringing with it the sudden, hard-to-control "gift" of shape-shifting. As I tried to learn how *not* to become a rampaging gorilla when I was angry or dissolve into a hyena when laughing, I also began my long education in demon slaying.

No more softball. During the summer I was shipped off to my aunt's manor house in North Wales to fulfill my destiny as a demon slayer. It was like school, only harder. I struggled to memorize entire books of information—the taxonomy of demons, their habits and habitats, the history of my family's conflict with them—and Aunt Mab drilled me endlessly, peering disapprovingly over her glasses, her lips scrunched up like she'd tasted something awful. Outside, the green hills of Snowdonia, the woods and brooks and neighboring farms, called to me to explore. On the days when I got everything right, I could go run around outside. When I made a mistake, I had to stay in and study. I spent a lot of time indoors.

But I loved Mab. Dad said she could fight with a flaming sword. Although I found that hard to picture, with her frizzy steel-wool hair and her high-necked, long-skirted, old-fashioned dresses, I didn't doubt it for a minute. There was something formidable about my aunt, something that said *don't mess with me*. I could believe she was the scourge of demonkind. Fashion sense aside, I wanted to be just like her. On the days when I pleased her, her brisk "well done, child," accompanied by a fleeting smile, was a real reward for my hard work.

And year by year, drill by drill, I was learning. When I was fifteen, Aunt Mab declared that the book-learning portion of my education was finished. "I believe you've been through every book in my library," she declared, as we sat by the fire on a cool June evening.

"I think you're right," I said. "All but that one."

"Which?"

"The one Dad says is bound in human skin." I laughed,

too old now for Dad's scary stories, expecting her to laugh with me.

But she didn't laugh. Her face shut, quickly and completely, like someone yanking down a window shade. "That is not something to speak of," she said. "Never mention it again."

I gulped. "Okay." Involuntarily, I glanced at the shelf that held the book. There it was, its spine a pale ivory shade, unlike the calf-bound books around it.

Mab grasped my arm. Her hand was gnarled and spotted with age, but her grip was iron-strong and her eyes burned like coals. "Do not touch it, do not speak of it. Do not even think of it. Never, Victory. Do you understand?"

Mute, I nodded. And for that summer and the years that followed, I tried my best to comply with her warning. It wasn't hard. Mab was teaching me weaponry: fencing, archery, marksmanship, knife fighting. Now that was more like it. I loved the jeweled, bronze-bladed dagger she gave me for my sixteenth birthday. Who cared about books, even *that* book, when I was learning the best ways to fillet a demon?

The only part that bothered me was that I'd never yet seen an actual demon. And I was getting impatient to try out my new fighting skills on real, live nasties instead of paper targets and straw-stuffed bags. What I really wanted was to use a broadsword like Mab's, the one she called the sword of Saint Michael, the kind that bursts into flame in the presence of a demon. But instead of a heavy sword with a gleaming bronze blade, Mab started me off with two pieces of wood nailed into a cross shape. Feeling like a kid playing pirates, I protested.

Mab *tsk*ed at me in her no-nonsense way, and I knew it was hopeless. It was always the same with Mab: first, technique, then practice—she was big on practice. Next summer, maybe, we'd hunt some demons together. "Small ones," she said, her voice stern but her accent lilting. "'Tis always wise to start small, child." And so I practiced with a Peter Pan sword.

The next summer, I was eighteen years old, a high school

graduate, and feeling more than ready to graduate from Mab's training program, as well. I was all grown up now, and this would be the summer I finally got to kick some demon ass. When my father decided to spend a couple of weeks in Wales with me, I was eager to show him how impressive my skills had become, to make him and Aunt Mab both proud.

But the day after we arrived, right after breakfast, Mab tossed me the goofy wooden sword. I caught it, surprised, wincing as a splinter slid into my palm. "Broadsword practice in ten minutes," she announced. "Undoubtedly you've forgotten everything I taught you."

Mab always began the summer with a comment like that, but in front of Dad, it stung. And it was almost like a curse. At practice that day, and the next several days, I was slow, I was clumsy, and I felt like I *should* be using a stupid wooden sword. Dad standing there watching, saying *relax, don't try so hard*, just made it worse. From the look in Mab's eyes, I just knew that she wouldn't be taking me demon hunting this summer. Not even for the small ones.

Well, why should I wait for her? I'd trained for six years. I was tired of endless drills and exercises. I wanted to kill a demon. And I thought I knew where to find one.

On the night of July 8—a date burned into my memory—I snuck into Mab's library and got down the book, the one bound in human skin. My fingers tingled when I touched the spine, and I had a clear vision of a corpse lying on a table and a vat of something bubbling nearby, as a hooded, black-robed figure approached with a curved knife. As the knife made its first cut, the corpse moaned and bright red blood welled from the wound. It wasn't a corpse at all; someone had been skinned alive to make this book.

I gasped and shoved the book back on the shelf. The vision faded. My pulse hammered through my veins; pain seared the fingers that had touched the book. This was crazy. I wasn't going to mess with some book that gave you waking nightmares just from touching it. I headed toward the door.

But something made me turn around.

Hundreds of times since that night, I've relived that moment, trying to figure out why the hell I couldn't just walk out of that library and go to bed. Did a spirit call to me? Did some entity possess my body long enough to turn me back toward that book? Or was it just my own stubbornness? I'll never know.

But turn around I did. I strode back to the bookcase like a woman on a mission and yanked the book from its shelf. This time, there were no visions, no odd sensations. I laughed. It was just a book. I carried the volume over to the window where the moonlight streamed in so that I could read without turning on a light. Flipping through the pages, I glanced at the illustrations until I found the one I was looking for. A demon. A real one.

The thing was hideous. Its skin was deep blue, and flames shot from its eyes. Its mouth bristled with teeth too long and sharp for lips to hide. It hunched over like an ape, its hands on the ground; its fingers and toes ended in nails that looked like daggers. I stared at the picture, fascinated by my own repulsion. *This* was the kind of thing I wanted to fight.

The words under the picture belonged to a language I didn't know. Not Welsh—too many vowels. Definitely not English or French. Latin, maybe. Dad would know, but I didn't dare ask him, because then he'd know I'd been looking at the forbidden book.

Almost idly, I sounded out the words. I don't think I pronounced them anywhere near correctly. As I spoke, I visualized myself fighting this demon, wielding my flaming sword like Saint Michael himself. The blade whirled and flashed, rending the air with blinding speed. I visualized—I can admit it now, although I couldn't for years—my father there, cheering me on, as I sliced the demon into little bits of barbecued ghoul.

One thing I'm sure of: I stopped speaking the words before I got to the last one. The book still scared me enough that I wasn't going to read an entire spell from it out loud. Even though I'd gone to the library determined to conjure a demon so I could kick its ass, the power of that book had shown me I was still out of my league. I'd rebelled against my aunt by taking down the book. That was enough.

I put the book back in its place, making sure its spine was exactly even with the others. A cloud covered the moon, and the room felt dark and cold. I shivered, eager to get back to bed. I tried to hurry across the Persian rug, but my body wouldn't cooperate. I moved slowly, like I was wading through a river of molasses. My heart pounded with the effort, but I couldn't make any forward progress. The room felt even colder, and I wondered if I was coming down with something.

Too tired to take another step, I sat down in the middle of the floor. *I'll just close my eyes for a minute,* I thought. But I was shivering too violently to sleep. Goose bumps rose on my limbs, on the back of my neck. My teeth chattered so hard they made my head hurt. What was wrong with me?

I heard a bang, like a door slamming, somewhere deep in the house. *Great,* I thought, *Aunt Mab. I'll really catch it now.*

Another bang, closer, then another. The banging grew rhythmic, a steady hammering. What *was* that? Why would Aunt Mab call in carpenters in the middle of the night? But the next noise wasn't from a carpenter—it was a horrible, skull-splitting screech, somewhere between a howl and a scream, a sound of pain and rage and something else. The screech came again, and I knew what the something else was—pure, unremitting evil. Fear shot through me like a hundred arrows. I tried to get up, but my legs buckled, unable hold my weight. I stayed there in a heap on the floor, as whatever was making that noise screamed again. Right outside the library door.

I was crying, but I didn't even have strength to wipe the tears from my face. "Please, God," I said. "Please, please . . ." I couldn't think of anything else to say. Every prayer I'd ever learned had evaporated from my mind. All I could do was beg.

The door exploded, leaping from its hinges and shattering into splinters. A hot wind roared through the room, stinking of sulfur and rotted meat. The wind toppled the leather chairs, cycloned papers off Aunt Mab's desk, hurled the desk itself into the far wall. It didn't budge me, though. I squinted into the doorway and could distinguish, barely, a massive blue shape.

This demon made the one in the book look like a cartoon. It must have been twelve feet tall, because its head brushed the library ceiling. Jets of blue and yellow flames shot from its eyes. It snarled and snapped, showing hundreds of sharp, daggerlike teeth. It moved its head blindly back and forth, then locked on me, sitting there helpless on the floor. It screeched again, striking at the air with its ten-inch claws, and started toward me.

I screamed. The demon laughed and came closer.

Another step and the flames touched my arm. The pain was indescribable. Heat scorched me from the inside. Flames leaped across my skin, not singeing a hair. But inside my flesh was on fire, my blood literally boiling. I closed my eyes, the world nothing but an inferno of heat and pain and fear and screaming.

And then it stopped.

I looked up. My father stood in the doorway, brandishing Aunt Mab's sword. The demon had turned to him. As soon as its eyes were off me, the burning stopped. But when it looked at my father, the sword burst into flame.

My father said some words I didn't understand. Then he said, in English, "Difethwr, I banish thee back to the Hell whence thou came."

The demon paused. It even staggered—I'm sure it staggered back a little. My father's power weakened it. I wanted to laugh with triumph. My father would kill this hideous demon, and then he'd teach me how to use the sword. Together we'd become the invincible scourge of the demonic world.

The demon roared, and its eyes shot flames at my father. Dad raised the sword in a defensive posture, using both hands to hold it horizontal, deflecting the jets of flame. He stepped forward with great effort, as though he were pushing back a brick wall. I closed my eyes to utter a prayer of thanksgiving.

And then I heard the sound that has haunted my dreams for ten years. A quiet sound, not like the demon's din. Half-gasp, half-moan, it came from my father. I opened my eyes to see him on his knees. The sword, its flame extinguished, slanted loosely in his hand, its tip resting on the floor. He was engulfed in a sphere of fire. Although the flame didn't appear to hurt him—his hair didn't burn, his skin didn't blacken—I knew what it was doing to him on the inside.

He groaned and fell forward. The flames followed him, flattening and lengthening to encase his prone body. I screamed and crawled forward to help him, but I was afraid of those flames. I couldn't force myself to go near them.

My father writhed, and now his screams mingled with my own. The demon was killing him, and I was too paralyzed with fear to do anything.

The flames that consumed my father's body began to subside, until all that was left was a greenish flickering over his skin. He lay still. Desperate, I searched for some sign that he was okay—a twitching finger or a fluttering eyelid, the slightest rise or fall of his chest—but there was nothing. Nothing at all.

"Dad?" I stretched my hand toward him. "Daddy . . . ?" The burn on my arm hit me with fresh pain, worse than before. I screamed and crumpled in agony. Demonic laughter rumbled through the room. From my curled-up position, I watched twin jets of flame sweep across the carpet. Toward me. I closed my eyes and waited for their excruciating touch.

I wondered what it would feel like to die.

But the flames didn't reach me. The deep, floor-shaking laugh faltered, then slid up, up, up in pitch into a scream.

I raised my head and looked.

The demon was on its knees, writhing in its own flames. Aunt Mab stood over it like an avenging angel. She carried a sword I'd never seen before; it was as long as Mab was tall, but she wielded it with ease and skill. The sword gleamed like pure sunlight and gave off a dazzling rainbow of flames. These held the cringing demon in a cage of light. Mab's lips moved, but I couldn't make out what she was saying over the thing's screams.

Aunt Mab took a step forward, and the demon shrank into a tighter ball. Slowly, she took another step, still reciting the unknown words. The fiery sphere around the demon grew smaller, then smaller still. I couldn't believe it. That huge, monstrous demon was shrinking. Still Mab advanced. Now the thing was the size of a doll. One more step and it vanished. Only a scorched spot on the carpet remained.

"Mab! You killed it!"

My aunt glanced at me with a single, decisive shake of her head. She bent over my father, laid a hand on his forehead, like a mother checking on a sick child. "Oh, Evan," she breathed. She closed her eyes, for a moment looking very old and very tired. Then she crossed herself and straightened.

"No!" I shouted. I tried to stand, but still my legs wouldn't hold my weight. I crawled over to my father and put my cheek against his. His skin was already cold. "No," I sobbed. It was the only word in the universe. *No, no, no.*

IN MY NARROW BEDROOM UNDER THE EAVES, I SAT ON THE bed and stared at the floor with its wide wooden boards. Aunt Mab had sent me there, saying to stay out of the way, that she'd handle everything. From my high window overlooking the courtyard, I'd watched a single police car arrive—no lights, no siren—followed by an ambulance. A few minutes later, a small black car disgorged a priest, who carried a heavy-looking bag. He paused on the doorstep and crossed himself before entering our house.

I tried to convince myself that the ambulance meant there was hope. But I knew it wasn't true, and I wasn't surprised when the ambulance men wheeled out the gurney with a sheet draped over Dad's body.

I sat on the bed, numb. The world was divided into Before and After, as neatly and completely as if someone had split it with a butcher's cleaver. Before, I'd woken up in this bed, and

Dad had been alive. Before, I'd gone down to breakfast, and Dad had been alive. Before, I'd run up here to change out of the sweats I wore for sword practice, and Dad had been alive. The clothes still draped the chair where I'd tossed them.

I told myself I should put them away, but I couldn't bear to touch them, as if moving them would make it real.

A glass of water sat on my nightstand. Thirsty, I reached for it. Before, I thought, when I'd filled up that glass . . . My hand dropped to my lap.

I was trapped in a world of After. Even if nothing in this room ever changed, even if I sat forever on the thin mattress, the eternal caretaker of Before, I could never get back there. This long night couldn't last forever. The moon would move across the sky. The sun would come up. And so would begin the first day of After, the first day of a world without my father in it.

I knew that. Even so, I sat absolutely still, some part of me believing that if I didn't move, didn't speak, didn't cry, I could somehow keep time from snapping the thin thread that connected me to this day. To my living father.

Soon, I heard Mab's tread on the stairs. She rapped once on the closed door. When I didn't answer, she rapped again and opened it.

I kept my gaze on the floor. I didn't want to have this conversation, didn't want it to carry me further into the After.

Mab didn't speak. She sat next to me on the bed and patted my knee. Minutes went by. Mab sighed. She patted me again. "Your father : . ." she began.

At the sound of her voice, the last remnants of Before shattered like a funhouse mirror and crashed at my feet. Dead. My father was dead. There was no going back.

I howled with the pain of it and sobbed into my aunt's shoulder. Mab didn't respond, just carefully put her arms around me. There was nothing comforting in her stiff embrace.

"Victory—"

"Don't call me that! Don't call me that ever again. I killed my father, Mab—it was all my fault. I killed him!"

She pushed me back and held me at arm's length, giving my shoulders a little shake. "You most certainly did not. He was killed by a demon of Hell. By Difethwr, the Destroyer."

"You don't understand! I summoned the demon. I got down your book—" I didn't want to continue, but I forced myself to say the words. "And I spoke the spell." Mab's grip tightened on my arms. "I didn't say all of it. I swear I didn't. But the demon came anyway."

"Tell me exactly what happened."

I did. She interrupted only once, to ask me what I was thinking as I sounded out the words of the spell. When I told her, she shut her eyes and bit her lip, then nodded. I finished my story, and she nodded again, then looked at me. Her eyes were clear, and when she spoke, her voice was calm.

"Evan was fated to die at a demon's hands. He knew that. He's known it since he was your age, even younger. When he confronted the Destroyer, he knew exactly what was coming."

"But I should have helped him! And I didn't. I was too afraid of that fire. I couldn't reach into it to get the sword because I couldn't stand the thought of getting burned again."

Mab looked at me sharply. "The Destroyer's flames touched you?"

I nodded.

"Where?"

I held out my right forearm. It looked completely normal. It felt normal, too, except for an itchy tingling. "You can't see it now. The demon was burning my arm with its eyes when Dad came in." Mab pursed her lips as she ran her fingers over my arm. She shook her head and muttered something I couldn't make out. My heart sank. She didn't believe me. She probably thought I was lying to make up a reason for not helping Dad. Tears welled in my eyes.

My stupid arm didn't even hurt anymore. Maybe I *was* making it up. Maybe I was so scared of the demon that I'd only imagined the pain. The tears spilled over.

Mab reached into her pocket, and I thought she'd hand me a tissue. Instead, she gripped my right arm and slashed a blade across the forearm. I saw the blood before I felt the cut.

I stared at my aunt, openmouthed. In her right hand she held a jeweled dagger, its blade shiny with my blood.

Then the pain hit. Not the pain of the knife slash, although that stung, but a roaring, hot, fiery pain, like she'd stuffed burning coals under my skin. I screamed and twisted, but she wouldn't let me pull away. Blood streamed from the wound, and from it rose puffs of yellowish steam that smelled like sulfur and rotting meat. The steam—billows of it—filled the small room, choking off my screams into coughs. The blood ran down my arm and made a sticky pool on the floorboards. Gradually it slowed. Mab's grip remained iron until it stopped. Then she got up and opened the window, her figure vague through the yellow steam though she was only three steps away.

She muttered something, and the steam swirled into a coil. At a sharp gesture from Mab, it shot out the window. The air was instantly clear. I could breathe again. Mab stood by the window, looking out toward the courtyard.

I gaped at her, unable to speak. Was she punishing me? Making me suffer because I'd caused my father's death? Even with the pain that seared my arm, it wasn't enough. Nothing could ever be enough.

"I had to let the fire out," she said, still looking outside, "or it would have continued to burn." She spoke matter-of-factly, as if telling me we were having lamb chops for dinner. It was that matter-of-fact tone that made me lose it.

"You *cut* me!" I shouted. "You stupid bitch!" I clutched my arm against my stomach, bloodying my shirt. "You act like you're some mysterious, powerful force, but you couldn't stop that thing from killing my father! You didn't care about him. You have no feelings. You're not human!"

"No," she said softly. "I'm not human. And neither are you, Victory."

"I told you—don't call me that."

She sat next to me again, took my chin in her fingers, and turned my face to hers. "Victory—Vicky. Listen to me. There's something you must understand about what happened tonight. When those flames touched your arm, that demon marked you."

"I wish it had killed me."

A slap stung my face. "Your father died to save you. How *dare* you dishonor his sacrifice."

She was right, of course. I hung my head.

When she spoke again, her voice had softened. "Evan saved your life. But you bear the mark of the Destroyer."

Fear gripped my gut. "What does that mean?"

"What it means, young Vicky, is that you'll have to be strong. You've been poisoned by the essence of that demon."

The essence of the Destroyer—the flames, that fetid yellow steam. I felt sick to my stomach. "But you got it out, right? That's why you cut my arm."

She nodded. "If I hadn't opened the skin, the essence would have spread. Let's hope the mark remains small." She wasn't talking about the scar from the knife wound. "Bearing the Destroyer's mark will change you. You might find feelings like anger harder to control. You may sometimes feel a powerful urge to smash things. Or this arm could strike out when you wish no harm."

I was beginning to understand. "You mean that . . . that *thing* is inside me? For good?" My stomach clenched, then heaved. I managed to run across the hall to the bathroom before I threw up. Kneeling on the cold tile floor, I retched and retched until I was weak and shaking, until it felt like there was nothing left inside me.

Nothing except the essence of a Hellion.

Mab came in and knelt next to me. She stroked my hair, then lifted my arm and inspected it. "The essence of the Destroyer is inside all of us. Some more than others. The Hellion's gaze has called forth the part of you that destroys. Brought it to the surface, at least in this spot." She ran her finger along the cut, smearing the blood. "But you can learn to control it."

7

"AND YOU THINK IT'S THE SAME DEMON?" DETECTIVE Costello asked.

I nodded. "I'm sure of it. Different Hellions kill in different ways, according to their nature. Some flay their victims alive, stripping off an inch of skin at a time. Others are big on strangling victims with their own entrails. What happened to George, that internal burning, that's the Destroyer's signature."

"The Destroyer? That's its name?" He grinned, like he was trying to lighten things up. "Doesn't sound big enough or bad enough for a Hellion."

"Exactly. That's why it's the safest name to use," I said and watched the grin fade. Well, this was serious stuff. "The Destroyer has hundreds of names, Detective. This one"—I snatched Hagopian's notebook and wrote *Difethwr* on the page—"is its name among the Cerddorion. Our conflict with the Destroyer goes back thousands of years."

He looked at the page. "How do you pronounce that?"

"You don't. Saying that name out loud is like issuing an invitation. Just call it the Destroyer."

He nodded and passed the notebook back to Hagopian. She glanced at the name, then crossed it out. Superstitious, but smart. The woman had seen enough of personal demons to know not to mess with a big one.

"Are we done here?" Kane asked, checking his watch. "I've got to get back to the office. Any more questions, Detective?" He looked at Costello, who glanced at Hagopian, then shook his head. "Thank you for your time, both of you," Costello said.

Kane gave me a peck on the cheek and asked me to drop by Creature Comforts after midnight. I replied with a firm maybe—I had a lead on a client, which could mean a job tonight. Story of our lives, I thought, watching him hurry out the door. All work and no romps in the hay.

After Kane had gone, I turned to Hagopian. "Has there been an autopsy yet?"

She shook her head. "Next week, maybe."

"Uh-uh. Make it today. The sooner the better. And have someone there to perform an exorcism."

"Exorcism? You mean, like, a priest?"

"Sure, a priest will do." Like the priest Aunt Mab had called to banish Difethwr's filth from my father's corpse. She'd told me about it, later. "So would a sorcerer or a witch, even. Somebody who knows how to undo a demonic possession."

"What's the point?" Costello asked. "The victim's dead."

"His body's dead. But his soul is burning." Even dead, poor George was in agony while we sat around talking. "You need to have someone exorcise the Hellion when the medical examiner cuts open the body. I'm not joking about this. If you don't, George's soul will keep burning and burning until it's completely destroyed."

Hagopian nodded, doing her scared-owl blink again.

"Before sundown today," I added. "You don't have long. *George* doesn't have long."

Unexpectedly, Costello caught my hand, pressing it in both of his and regarding me with urgent sincerity. God, those eyes were gorgeous. "We'll take care of it. I promise."

"Make sure you do. The utter destruction of a human soul is an unspeakable thing."

He nodded, his gaze holding mine.

"Also," he said, "I just want to let you know that I'm sorry—personally sorry—for authorizing the Goons to bring you here. Next time . . ." He paused, and I wondered if he meant the pause to be meaningful. "Next time, I'll call."

"I'm in the book," I said, wondering why my face suddenly felt hot.

* * *

IT WAS TWELVE THIRTY BY THE TIME I GOT BACK TO MY apartment. Juliet was awake. A vampire her age needs only a few hours of sleep each day. She reclined on the living room sofa with blackout shades down to block all sunlight, and was filing her nails. *Sharpening* would be a better word. Each finger looked like a lethal weapon.

"You had two phone calls." She put down the file and held out a slip of paper.

"Thanks," I said, taking it.

She waved dismissively, her scarlet nails streaking the air. "If I'm going to play secretary, I'm going to start demanding a living wage." She laughed, tilting her head back and showing her fangs. "That's funny, isn't it? A vampire getting a living wage. I should've said an *undead* wage."

I smacked my forehead. In all my life, I'd never met a vampire who could tell a joke. "If you don't want to take my calls, let voice mail pick up."

Juliet went back to filing her nails. "Where were you, anyway?"

I told her about the morning's events. She was outraged. Not on my behalf, of course—vampires are the most self-centered creatures in the universe—but because the Goon Squad had busted down our door.

"They broke in while I was asleep!" she fumed. To be fair, it was a serious issue. When vampires sleep, they're dead to the world, or, as Juliet puts it, they "resume the shroud." So a sleeping vampire is helpless. "That's intolerable! Absolutely intolerable. I'm taking this to Hadrian."

Hadrian represented the vampire contingent on the Council of Three, which governed Deadtown. Besides Hadrian, the Council consisted of one werewolf and one zombie, but everyone knew that Hadrian pulled all the strings. When it comes to being manipulative, you can't beat vampires—even if they'd never make it in stand-up comedy.

I had my doubts, though, that even Hadrian could do much. The Goons worked for Boston PD. And the Council of Three had zero power beyond the narrow boundaries of Deadtown. The only reason the humans gave the Council any authority at all was in the hope that somebody else would keep the monsters under control. If the Goon Squad wanted to break down a vampire's door in broad daylight, the Goon Squad would do it. The Council could protest all night and all day, but no norm would care. Besides, Hadrian was smart enough to choose his battles.

While Juliet stormed off to call Hadrian, I looked at my messages. Both calls were from potential clients. Good. I could use some money because the Jag needed a checkup. She'd been making this whiny noise I didn't like.

The first message had dollar signs written all over it. It was a reminder about my appointment with Frank Lucado that afternoon. Lucado was well known in Boston; he was a real estate developer with a shady reputation who'd been indicted a couple of times but never convicted of anything. Guys like that—lots of money, lots of enemies—were frequent targets of Harpy attacks. Some tough-guy wannabe trying to horn in on their action would pay a sorcerer big bucks to conjure up a few Harpies for nightly visits. I checked my watch. I had forty-five minutes before the one thirty appointment. Just enough time to return the other call.

The other caller's name—Sheila Gravett—also sounded familiar, but I couldn't place it. I had a feeling I'd seen the name Gravett in the paper recently, but for what I didn't know.

Down the hall, Juliet swore and slammed a door, so I figured the phone was free. I dialed Gravett's number.

She answered on the third ring. "Dr. Gravett." Doctor, huh? Good—she could afford me. I never did pro bono work. A girl had to make a living, after all.

"Hello, Doctor. This is Victory Vaughn returning your call."

A gasp came over the line. "Oh, hello. Oh, I'm *so* glad you called." Her voice rose in pitch, breathless, like she was the winning caller on a radio show.

"Why don't you start off by telling me a little about your problem? Once I know what kind of infestation you're dealing with, we can work out a strategy for getting rid of them."

"Getting rid of what?"

"Your demons." Silence. "You called about demon extermination, right?"

"Demon—? Oh, no." She laughed, a trill that started high
and tripped down the scale. "No, Ms. Vaughn, that's not why
I called. Although I do want to hire you."

"Sorry, I don't understand."

"Let me explain. I'm a research scientist." She stopped
there, as though that actually explained something.

"That's great, but I still don't see—"

"I'm the principal researcher at Gravett Biotech. We specialize in paranormal biology. And we're very interested in
mapping the shapeshifter genome. In fact, you may have
heard of our work with werewolf DNA."

"I'm not a werewolf, Dr. Gravett. I'm Cerddorion. It's not
the same at all." I sighed. I got so tired of giving this lecture.
"Werewolves become wolves—they can't change into any other
animal—and when the moon is full, they have no choice.
They have to change. Cerddorion can shift up to three times
per lunar cycle, whatever the moon phase, and we can shift
into any kind of sentient being. We can choose to shift, or
sometimes very strong emotion can force a shift. So, if you're
studying werewolves, you don't want me."

"Yes, yes, I know all that." Her voice sharpened, its tone
suggesting that Dr. Gravett was *not* one to suffer fools gladly.
"Werewolf biology is becoming better understood each year.
But shapeshifter biology—that field's wide open. You're the
only active shapeshifter in the state. If Gravett Biotech can
unlock the secrets of your DNA . . ." Her voice trailed off, as
though the possibility were too wonderful to describe.

I finished her sentence for her. "You'd get damn rich. Off
me."

Now I remembered where I'd heard of Gravett Biotech.
They'd tried to clone a werewolf. The story had been re-
ported very differently, depending on whether you followed
the human press or the PA press. Norms tended to view the

research as key to understanding—read *controlling*—the monsters. PAs saw the experiments (which had been conducted in New Hampshire, a state where PAs had no legal rights) as abuse, plain and simple. Whichever way you spun the story, though, it was clear that Gravett Biotech had created an abomination—a weak, incompletely shifted, hairless thing that was about the size of a Chihuahua and stayed stuck between canine and human forms. The poor creature had survived less than a week. No way I'd let that lab get hold of one speck of my genetic material.

She was still talking, going on about science and the pursuit of knowledge and the greater good and all kinds of other crap. Her voice rose with enthusiasm. "This is such a wonderful opportunity for me—well, I mean for science, you know. If we can understand what you are—"

"*I* understand what I am just fine. I don't need a bunch of sadists in white coats to tell me that."

She drew in a sharp breath and, for the first time in our conversation, didn't seem to know what to say. I smiled into the phone.

"Was that all, Dr. Gravett? Because I'm not interested."

"Wait!" Her voice sounded panicked. "You haven't heard me out yet. We're prepared to offer comfortable lodgings and substantial compensation if you'll agree to change shape under controlled circumstances in our lab."

"Where's the lab?"

"Not far. About an hour north of Boston."

"Oh, you mean in New Hampshire? No, thanks."

"All right, yes, it is in New Hampshire, but we'll guarantee—"

"I told you, no, thanks."

"Sixty thousand dollars, Ms. Vaughn. For one month of observation. And one half of one percent of any profits on patents that stem directly from this research. You can't earn that kind of money as a freelance demon exterminator."

That was true. Sixty thousand dollars in one month worked out to a nice two thousand bucks a day. But I earned my money on my terms. The thought of a bunch of scientists poking and prodding me, coming at me with all kinds of electrodes and needles—I shuddered. I hate needles. I wouldn't do it.

"Sorry, Dr. Gravett. I'm not playing lab rat for you or for anyone else."

"But—" I didn't hear the rest of her argument, because I'd already hung up the phone.

8

A NAP WOULD'VE FELT LIKE HEAVEN SINCE, THANKS TO THE Goons, I was running on less than three hours' sleep. But there was no time. I was meeting Frank Lucado at a construction site on Milk Street in twenty minutes. It wasn't far, a ten-minute walk. So no nap, but I could just about beat the world record for fastest shower. I hopped in, hopped out, and toweled my hair dry. Then I pulled on a fresh pair of black leather jeans and a red turtleneck. Add a new pair of pointy-toed, stiletto-heeled black patent leather boots, and I was the poster girl for kick-ass demon killers. Lucado would hire me in a second.

Or so I hoped, anyway. I grabbed my black leather jacket and raced out the door.

A few minutes later, I was there—and right on time. I stood in front of a half-built office building, a couple of blocks past the point where the New Combat Zone gives way to human-controlled Boston. A plywood wall surrounded the site, repeating the name LUCADO CONSTRUCTION, INC. every ten feet or so, interspersed among warnings that you were about to enter a hard-hat site and counts of how many days the site had been accident-free. Ninety-four so far. Not bad. I stepped inside the gate and looked around. I didn't see anyone, but saws buzzed and hammers banged somewhere inside.

"Hey!" said a voice right behind me, so close it made me jump. "This is a construction site. Filene's is that way."

I turned to see a big-bellied guy in a dirty T-shirt and a yellow hard hat, pointing west. I didn't bother to let him know that Filene's had been bought by Macy's a few years back. Or that the old Filene's building was now in the middle of Deadtown.

The guy dropped his arm and looked me up and down with the kind of leer only a construction worker can give. If they have a leering class in construction-worker school, this guy had aced it, for sure. He licked his lips and said, "Hey, if you wanna come back later, I get off at five."

"As tempting as that offer is"—I smiled sweetly—"I'd rather eat nails." That got a surprised laugh out of him. I went on before he could tell me I was "feisty." "I have an appointment with Mr. Lucado."

"You're here to see Frank? Jeez, why didn't you say so? Hang on a minute and I'll take you to him."

He turned and walked into the trailer that served as the site office, treating me to a view of the gap between his T-shirt and his too-low jeans, which were dragged down by his tool belt. The gap stopped short of his butt crack. Thank heaven for small mercies.

When he returned, he was carrying a hard hat. A fluorescent orange one. "Here." He held it out to me. "Can't let you on the site without one."

"Thanks, um . . ."

"Everyone calls me Buddy."

"Thanks, Buddy." I put the hideous orange hat on, and it promptly tipped forward over my eyes.

"Hey," said Buddy. "You're all set for Halloween. Orange and black. You look just like the Great Pumpkin."

"It's too big. Don't you have something smaller?"

"Nah, it'll do. You're just gonna talk to Frank, right?"

Yeah, I thought. Looking like the Great Pumpkin. So much for the demon-killer poster girl.

Buddy led the way to an elevator. As we went deeper into the building, the construction sounds intensified. Country music blared from a radio somewhere, and voices occasionally shouted over the din. Scraps of wood and other debris littered the floor. The air smelled like sawdust and oil.

We got out on the tenth floor and walked into a huge open space partitioned here and there by hanging plastic sheets.

The noises were louder up here. Buddy pointed toward a group of men about forty feet away. "That's Frank," he said, "in the brown suit. I gotta go back downstairs." He pressed the button for the elevator.

I started toward the man he'd pointed out, but Buddy grabbed my arm. "You ever meet Frank before?"

"No. We've spoken on the phone."

The elevator door opened, and Buddy stepped inside. "Don't let him scare you," he said and winked. The door closed.

I laughed. Big, gallant Buddy, worried I'd be afraid of some businessman. Me, who dated a werewolf, shared an apartment with a vampire, and went demon hunting six nights a week. Like I couldn't handle a human real estate developer. Even one with a reputation for a shady deal or two.

I started across the open space to where the men stood. The one in the brown suit, Lucado, had his back to me. He was medium height, a slight stoop to his shoulders. Four other men huddled around him, all wearing hard hats (not a fluorescent orange one among them, I noticed) and reading blueprints. Lucado gestured and pointed, then shook his head.

The damn hard hat kept sliding down over my eyes. Trying to watch Lucado and adjust the hat at the same time, I tripped over some tool left lying on the floor. I sprawled forward, landing on my stomach with an *oof!* and getting the wind knocked out of me. The hat flew off and rolled away. I lay there motionless, trying to get some air back into my lungs.

A pair of shiny brown wingtips appeared in my field of vision, followed by a hand. I batted the hand aside—I was not going to begin this interview being helped to my feet by a potential client—and pushed myself up onto my hands and knees. My breath came back in a whoosh, and for a minute I just stayed there, gulping in air, head hanging down, grateful I'd remembered how to breathe. The brown wingtips never moved.

I made it to my feet, squared my shoulders, and looked into the most terrifying face I'd ever seen—on a human, anyway. Victory, meet Frank Lucado.

He had the face of a man who'd stared down violence and ended in a draw. It was the scar. A meaty red streak slashed his face in two, running from his right eyebrow across a milky, sightless eye to the corner of his thin-lipped mouth. Some men would've worn an eye patch to hide the bad eye. Not this guy. He was looking at me with a smug amusement that showed he thought he'd already won—whatever our battle would turn out to be—before we even exchanged names. I could tell that he used his scar as a weapon, to keep opponents off balance.

"Mr. Lucado?" I extended my hand. "I'm Victory Vaughn."

"You? You're—?" He threw back his head and laughed. He picked up the orange hard hat and put it on my head, patting the top twice like I was a cute little kindergartner. The damn thing promptly tilted over my forehead. "You're the demon killer? You gotta be kidding me. Honey, my demons would eat you alive." He started walking back to the group of men.

Jerk. I pushed the hat as far back as I could without having it fall off my head. "I made the time to come out here," I said. "The least you could do is shake my hand."

He stopped and looked back at me over his shoulder. "You wanna shake hands?" He shrugged. Then he turned around, strode back, and grasped my right hand. He squeezed it hard; he was trying to make it hurt. But I squeezed harder.

This asshole was *not* going to dismiss me as a clumsy little girl. I poured all my shapeshifter strength into my grip. Lucado's eyes widened, then bulged. He tried to pull his hand away, but I wouldn't let go. My fingers tightened around the delicate bones of his hand. Just a little more pressure and I'd crush them. My arm started to tingle, then burn, and I thrilled in my power over this norm. The urge grew to crush, to snap, to pulverize his hand into a mess of smashed flesh and bone. I could do it. I could destroy his hand, and then I could kill him. The thought made me laugh. My forearm felt like it was on fire, blazing with strength. Lucado squeaked out a strangled whimper, and I glanced at the group of men. They still studied the blueprints. *Yes, I could do it,* I thought. *I could kill this jerk.* He was mean and weak and pathetic. Who needed him?

A rumble of laughter rolled through my thoughts. I knew that sound—the laugh of the Destroyer. I flashed on a vision of its hideous blue face, triumph in its eyes.

My God, I was letting the mark take over. No, I thought, that's not me. I willed the vision away, blocked my ears to Difethwr's laughter, forced down the urge to destroy. My arm flared with pain, but I pushed past the feeling. Fighting the demon essence, I held myself on just this side of crushing the man's hand, until the impulse to annihilate began to subside. Then I made myself relax each finger, one by one. Lucado snatched his hand away.

"Jesus," he whispered. "What are you?"

I felt a little queasy from that surge of destructive power, but I cleared my throat and made an effort to speak coherently. "I'm the demon killer."

Lucado pointed his scar at me and blinked his sightless eye. I'd scared him; now he was trying to scare me back.

"You don't want to hire me?" I shrugged. "Fine. Go ahead and lie awake in bed each night, having your liver ripped out by disgusting, stinking bird-women." It was a guess, but Lucado's demon problem had to be Harpies. Hard to believe, but even a guy this sweet and charming might have an enemy or two out for revenge.

He stared at me, his jaw hanging, the hand I'd nearly crushed cradled against his belly. It was my turn to start walking away.

"No, wait!" Desperation rang in his voice. I kept going, the click of my heels ringing through the construction noise like gunshots.

"Please!" Ah, the magic word. I stopped and turned around, eyebrows raised.

Lucado practically ran over to me. He glanced over his shoulder at the other men. "I've told nobody about that. Nobody. How did you know?"

"I know my demons, Mr. Lucado. So, are you ready to talk business?"

He smiled, stretching the scar. The smile touched his good eye, almost making it twinkle. "A businesswoman. Now *that* I can understand. Demons and shit"—he shuddered, then shook his head—"that stuff's too spooky for me. All I know is I've gotta get rid of those things."

"I can do that for you."

He smiled again, shaking his head. "I believe you. I wouldn't have thought it to look at you, but man . . ." He rubbed his sore hand.

We discussed terms. I was still a little pissed at the guy, so I added twenty percent to my usual fee. He didn't bat an eyelash, just wrote a check for the first half, the other half payable after the job was done. I wanted to schedule the extermination for the next night—I was still down on sleep—but Lucado wouldn't wait that long. Now, he insisted, tonight. He wouldn't budge on that, but I'd expected it. By the time clients get around to calling me, they're usually pretty desperate, even a tough guy like Lucado. *Especially* a tough guy like Lucado. Guys like him think they can handle it themselves—until the Harpies have tormented them to the brink of insanity.

After we'd agreed on terms, I needed some information. I pulled out my notebook to take it down. First I got his address and phone number. He lived in a two-story condo at the top of a brand-new building on Commodore Wharf, in the North End. Nice location. He'd developed the building.

"What time do you usually go to bed?"

"Around eleven. Why?"

"I need to know when the Harpies are likely to show up."

"Oh. I guess that makes sense."

"Bedroom on the top floor?"

"Yeah. In the front."

"Which direction does it face?"

He had to think about that for a minute. "East, I guess. Yeah, east. The bedroom overlooks the harbor. It's got a balcony and a big picture window."

"Is that where the Harpies enter?"

He closed his eyes, his face pale. The scar stood out in a

scarlet slash. "Yeah. When I moved in, I loved that window. Loved the balcony even more. Great view. Now I can't stand to look at it. I've thought about bricking it up."

"That wouldn't stop the demons."

"Yeah, I figured that out. Every night they smash through the glass. But in the morning it ain't broken."

For a moment, the scar made him appear pathetic—defeated—instead of brutal. He looked so exhausted and afraid that I felt a little sorry for him. Well, almost.

I handed him a copy of my standard instruction sheet for Harpy exterminations. "Tonight, you need to do exactly what this sheet says."

He nodded and looked it over. "Wait a minute. It says I gotta take a sleeping pill. I don't do pills."

"Tonight you do." It was one of my hard-and-fast rules. "This one," I added, holding out a bottle with a single pill rattling around inside. I had a special license that allowed me to dispense them to my clients.

He didn't take it. "But I want to see you kill those bastards."

"Clients often do. I don't blame you, but it's a bad idea. You'd get in my way, for one thing. But the battle can be traumatizing. You could get hurt."

"I can handle it."

"Maybe you can. But we play by my rules, or I don't take the job." I rattled the pill at him.

Lucado's dead eye stared at me like a marble statue. He ran a finger along the scar, from just under his eye to the corner of his mouth. Up and down, up and down. When I didn't blink, he shrugged.

"Okay," he said, taking the bottle. "You win. But I want to see the carcasses when you come back in the morning. I want to see those damn things dead."

"I can do that." I headed for the elevator. But then I stopped and turned around. "I always win, Mr. Lucado. Whether it's demons or clients, I always win."

He laughed and nodded. "I bet you do."

9

I HEADED HOME THROUGH THE NEW COMBAT ZONE, which was deserted in the afternoon. Things never got hopping here until well after midnight. I walked past storefronts with cracked, dusty windows. A sheet of newspaper somersaulted down the street, then wrapped itself around a lamppost. Now and then I had to step around the prone form of a vampire junkie sprawled across the sidewalk. Vampire saliva is both narcotic and mildly hallucinogenic to humans. Combine that with a vampire who gets carried away and sucks out more than the legally allowed pint of blood, or with a junkie who goes around offering dinner to several vampires all in the same night, and you've got zonked-out humans sleeping it off wherever they happen to fall. When closing time rolls around, bartenders in the Zone simply drag 'em out by the feet and dump 'em on the sidewalk. And when the bars open again after dark, the junkies are back on their bar stools, hitting on the vampires for another fix.

Nobody bothered about the junkies because nobody patrolled the New Combat Zone—nobody besides the Goon Squad, and they didn't care. I stepped over a junkie who lay on his back, snoring. At least the guy had a smile on his face.

As I walked, I clenched and unclenched my fist, trying to diminish the tingling in my arm. The demon mark wouldn't leave me alone; it itched and burned. Okay, so Difethwr was in Massachusetts. The Hellion's proximity would probably make the mark flare up. But at least I was safe in Boston, safe inside the shield.

But it wasn't *my* safety I was worried about. Since the

Destroyer had reappeared in my life, I'd nearly lost control twice. Over nothing. In the Goon Squad interview room, one minute I'd felt upset and crowded; the next minute those feelings had ballooned into a murderous rage. And all Lucado had wanted was a pissing contest. So the jerk thought he could squeeze the little girl's hand until she said "Ouchie." That was no reason to kill him—and I'd come way too close.

I seriously needed to work on my anger management, at least until the Destroyer found some other place to play. The mark amplified rage; it brought the anger too close to the surface. What if, losing control, I shifted? This close to the full moon, I couldn't count on my human personality to keep an enraged predator—a tiger or grizzly or something like that—under control.

I'd have to be careful. Whatever happened, I was not going to let the Destroyer make me into its instrument of destruction.

AT HOME, JULIET WAS STILL IN HER ROOM WITH THE DOOR closed. I went into my bedroom and stood in front of the bookcase that held my demonology library. It was puny compared to Aunt Mab's, and it certainly held no mystical books bound in human skin. But these were the books that had built my foundation in demon slaying, and I liked having them around. I ran a finger along the spines, feeling the smooth leather of the bindings, until I found the book I was looking for: Russom's Demonology. Or, more precisely, *Russom's Demoniacal Taxonomy*. I pulled it from its place, inhaling its pleasantly musty, old-book smell.

This book had been the starting point for my training. It was a classic; my copy had been published in 1924, and that was the twelfth edition. *Russom's* classified all known demons and described their characteristics. It was comprehensive, but dry as old toast. At first, I could usually get through about half a page before I fell asleep. But thanks to Aunt Mab's relentless quizzes—at lesson times, at meals, even when we passed in the hallway—I learned its contents. I could still hear her crisp, accented tones: "To what phylum do Drudes belong?" "Name three demons of the order *Terrificus*." I thought I'd never get it. But once I finally did learn the stuff, I never forgot it.

Now I'd be putting Tina through the same drill. I still had misgivings about teaching her, especially with the Destroyer around, but I had a feeling her lessons wouldn't last long. Tina, I suspected, was a lot more interested in the latest celebrity gossip than in memorizing the nocturnal habits of wraith demons.

Shaking my head, I tucked *Russom's* in my bag and headed out. I nodded to Clyde as I passed through the lobby and thanked him for getting my front door fixed so fast. He touched his cap, looking pleased. Or at least the death grimace that stretched his lips tight across his pitted, greenish face sort of resembled a smile. At any rate, I was glad I'd acknowledged his effort. People didn't say "thank you" to zombies very often.

I dropped off *Russom's* at the group home where Tina lived. She wasn't up yet, so I left it with the house mother, along with a note to read the first twenty-five pages. I checked my watch; it was a little after three. Lucado and I had agreed I'd get to his place around ten to set up. I wanted to get there early, to make sure the guy would actually take the sleeping pill I'd given him. I'd learned the hard way that it was a bad idea to have a client awake and watching while I did my job. I still visited that client in the psych ward every year around Christmas.

So I had seven hours, give or take a few minutes. Plenty of time to zip out to the suburbs to visit my sister, Gwen, as long as I took a tub of coffee along for the ride. Gwen had made Halloween costumes for her kids and wanted to show them to me before, as she put it, "the little brutes trash them." A quick phone call, and she said now would be perfect.

I didn't want to drive the Jag, not with that whiny noise. Going by commuter rail out to Needham and back, I could return to Boston by nine, pick up my supplies, and get over to Frank's condo in the North End before ten. I was overdue for a visit to my sister's. So I'd chat with Gwen, *ooh* and *ahh* over the kids, and let her talk me into staying for supper. Gwen was a terrific cook. My own efforts in the kitchen tended toward the frozen-dinner-and-microwave approach.

I caught the train at South Station, right on time, and dozed a bit on the ride. After a quick forty minutes, I was waving to Gwen as I got off at Needham Heights.

Most people are surprised to learn that Gwen and I are sisters. It's not that there's no family resemblance—you can see that if you look for it, in our amber eyes and heart-shaped faces. It's more that our lifestyles make us look like we come from different planets. I favor wash-n-wear hair and leather jeans. Gwen looks exactly like the role she's chosen: a stay-at-home mom in a pricey Boston suburb. Her chinos and polo shirts are designer brands, and she wears her chin-length auburn hair in one of those elegantly casual styles that requires twice-a-week maintenance at a salon. She probably spends as much on her hair each month as I spend on rent—and even with a roommate, my apartment isn't cheap. And although Gwen isn't exactly overweight, she plumped up some with the birth of each child: Maria, a ten-year-old tree-climber; Zachary, a frighteningly energetic five-year-old; and Justin, still the baby at two. Great kids. Gwen, of course, believed they were the most adorable children on Earth. As their aunt, I tended to agree.

"Where are the kids?" I asked as I strapped myself into the minivan. It was rare to see Gwen without a munchkin or three in tow.

"They're at the neighbors', putting on their costumes. I think they plan to scare you when you arrive."

"Thanks for the warning. For your kids, I'll go all the way to terrified."

Gwen smiled and navigated the minivan through the maze of suburban streets. I could always find my way around a city, but put me in suburbia, among all those green lawns and picket fences, and I got hopelessly lost.

Gwen lived in a Cape Cod–style house in the Birds Hill neighborhood. The area was developed after World War II, filled with compact ranches and Capes where returning veterans and their sweethearts raised their families. The next generation, though, seemed to demand more from its homes. Every time I came out here, another ranch house had been razed to make room for a mini mansion. Scaled-down faux French châteaux and English manor houses loomed over the more modest homes that had given Birds Hill its family feel. If you asked me, the huge houses looked silly on their quarter-acre lots. Somehow, though, I didn't think the owners of those million-dollar homes were falling over each other to get my opinion.

Gwen's block, at least, still had that cozy neighborhood feel. It was the kind of place where everybody knew their neighbors and went to monthly potluck dinners. We pulled into the driveway, and a costumed figure burst from behind the garage, where he'd obviously been watching for us.

"Arrrrh!" yelled Zachary. "Ahoy, mateys!" He was the cutest—I mean *fiercest*—pint-sized pirate I'd ever seen. He wore a black tricornered hat, an eye patch, and a blue coat with silver buttons. A drawn-on moustache curled unsteadily over his mouth. The stuffed parrot perched on his shoulder wobbled as he waved his cutlass.

"Zack, be careful with that," warned his mother.

I cowered in my seat. "You're not going to make us walk the plank, are you?"

Zack giggled with delight and nodded vigorously. He jumped up and down, chanting, "Walk the plank! Walk the plank!"

Gwen got out and went around the front of the van. She put a hand on Zack's parrot-free shoulder and held it there until he stopped jumping. "If you keep telling Aunt Vicky you're going to make her walk the plank, she won't get out of the car."

"Oh." Zack considered this. "Okay, Aunt Vicky, I won't make you walk the plank." His eyes sparkled with mischief. "This time."

"Thanks, Captain." I climbed down from my seat. "That's a terrific costume you've got there."

"Mommy made it." A movement in the next yard caught Zack's eye, and he took off, yelling "Ahoy! Ahoy!"

"Zack!" yelled Gwen. "If you ruin your costume, you can't go trick-or-treating!"

"Okaaaaay, Mommm . . ." His voice faded in the distance.

Gwen stood with her hands on her hips, smiling in the direction he'd disappeared. "Now where are those other two?"

"Come *on*, Justin." Maria's voice came around the corner of the garage. A second later, she appeared, leading her baby brother by the hand. Justin, dressed as a teddy bear, toddled along unsteadily, his eyes round. When he saw me, he smiled that heart-melting baby smile, held out his arms, and said, "Twick or tweat, Aunt Vicky!"

Maria giggled. "Not yet, silly. Trick-or-treating's not 'til Friday." Maria had her long sandy hair pulled back in a ponytail; she wore a black turtleneck sweater and black jeans.

"What are you, Maria?" I asked.

She glanced at her mom, a little nervously. Gwen said, "Why aren't you wearing your costume?"

"It took *forever* to get Justin ready, Mom."

"Well, go put yours on now." Gwen picked up Justin, perching him on her hip, while Maria zoomed off around the corner of the house.

"Wait'll you see her costume," Gwen said. "It took me a week to make it. She's a fairy princess bride. It was really hard getting the wings right."

Justin stared at me with wide eyes. "Twick or tweat?" he tried again.

I patted my pockets. "Sorry, Justin, I'm fresh out of candy." I really should try to remember to pack a few lollipops or something when I go to see Gwen's kids.

Maria peeked around the corner of the garage, then stepped out. She didn't look like any fairy princess bride I'd ever seen, but then I didn't have a lot of experience with such things. She was still dressed all in black, but she'd added a double holster with two toy guns and a plastic dagger stuck in the belt, and there was something on the back of her head.

Gwen stared at her daughter as Maria walked shyly toward us. When she got to the edge of the driveway, she turned around, showing the plastic lion mask she wore on the back of her head.

"Maria, what on earth—?" Gwen began.

The girl turned back to face us, beaming. "I made it myself, Mom. Don't you get it? I'm Aunt Vicky."

Uh-oh.

The enthusiasm in Maria's voice picked up as she explained. "See, on this side, I'm a demon fighter." She drew a gun, made shooting motions, then holstered it. She turned again to reveal the lion mask. "And on this side, I'm a shapeshifter. Pretty cool, huh? I found the mask at the church thrift store, and that gave me the idea."

"What about your bride costume?" Gwen's voice sounded strangled.

"Oh, I gave it to Brittany." Brittany was Maria's best friend. "She likes that girly stuff."

"Young lady, you are *not* going to—" Gwen glanced sideways at me. "We'll talk about this later. Now go change Justin back into his play clothes."

Maria's face crumpled, and a tear leaked from the corner of her eye. She blinked rapidly, then turned to me. The elastic from her mask made a line across her forehead. "You like my costume, don't you, Aunt Vicky?"

Oh, boy. How was I gonna answer this one? My options seemed to be upset Maria or make Gwen mad.

"It's a great compliment, Maria. I'm really flattered."

Maria beamed at me, then flashed her mom a look that was half triumphant and half an acknowledgment that she was in big trouble. She lifted Justin out of Gwen's arms and led him around the garage toward the back door. Justin gazed back at me, looking like he was still trying to figure out why the magic words had failed to produce any candy.

Gwen watched them go, arms folded, her mouth a tight line. Then she turned and marched up the front steps.

Wonderful. I'd been here five minutes and had already caused an argument. Ah, the joys of family.

I SAT IN MY SISTER'S LIVING ROOM—COLONIAL-STYLE, a Wedgwood blue sofa, two beige wing chairs by the fireplace—while Gwen banged things around in the kitchen. She said she was making coffee, but mostly she seemed to be taking her feelings out on her appliances. A cupboard door slammed hard, and the floor vibrated under my feet.

I knew why Gwen was angry about Maria's self-made costume, and I couldn't blame her. Well, I *could* blame her, but I could also understand. Ever since Gwen's firstborn had turned out to be a girl, she'd been terrified that the child would grow up to become a shapeshifter. Just like Aunt Vicky.

Among the Cerddorion, only females have the ability to shift. And that ability manifests with the onset of puberty. With each year that went by, Gwen grew a little more afraid that Maria was going to turn out to be one of the monsters.

Well, not a monster, not really. A demi-human. That was the official classification for Gwen and me both. The only difference was that I was classified as demi-human (active) and Gwen as demi-human (inactive). That meant she no longer had the ability to shift; she just had some funky stuff going on with her DNA that could create more demi-humans down the line. So Gwen had all the rights of any norm—she could vote, travel freely, live outside Deadtown—and I had all the restrictions of a PA.

Gwen hadn't always been ashamed of what we are. She's four years older than me, and she'd started shifting before I could. And she loved it. In fact, hardly a month went by when she didn't use up all three shifts. PAs weren't out at that time, so she had to be discreet, but Dad encouraged her to experiment. Even Mom, always the worrier, remembered the early thrill of shifting and loosened the tight leash she normally kept on us girls.

Gwen's favorite shift was a seagull; she adored soaring over open water. But she also tried out life as a cat, a squirrel, a deer in the woods. She even shifted into a baby elephant to do an undercover exposé for the school newspaper on animal cruelty at the circus—her English teacher couldn't stop praising her for how vividly she'd imagined the life of a circus animal. Everything was great until Gwen landed the lead in her senior class play.

They were doing *Our Town*; her role was Emily. For weeks, all she could talk about was acting, the theater, how she was going to major in drama and become a Broadway star. She lost interest in shifting—which I thought was grossly unfair, because I'd just started. For stagestruck Gwen, though, nothing compared to the thrill of the theater, and she spent all her time at rehearsals and hanging out with her acting-crazed friends. I missed her. I volunteered to help backstage, but for the first time ever Gwen treated me like the pesky little sister, tagging along.

On the play's opening night, disaster struck. My sister got stage fright. She walked confidently onto the stage, then froze up, her eyes wide and glassy. Her mouth opened, closed, opened, but all that came out was a piteous squeak. Then she shuddered and bent double, her limbs twisting, as though she were having a seizure.

I realized what was happening and ran to close the curtain, yelling at the other actors to get off the stage, to give my sister some room. Mom and Dad were with us in a flash, emerging from the audience to hold the teachers at bay.

Gwen writhed on the floor. Fur covered her face; her ears slid around to the top of her head. Her nose lengthened, and she sprouted whiskers. The shift's energy field blasted out, billowing the curtain and shredding her costume to ribbons. All the while, she shrunk smaller and smaller. Soon, all that could be seen of her was a rustling inside the remnants of Emily's dress. Gwen had changed into a mouse.

I scooped up my sister and carefully slipped her into my pocket as Mom gathered the scraps of costume. Dad spoke to the teacher who had directed the play and convinced her we'd already carried Gwen out to the car. The director made an announcement that Gwen had become ill and the scene started over, with the understudy thrilled to step in. No big deal. The audience thought Gwen had fainted. Back in those days, most norms had an enormous capacity to ignore what they'd seen in favor of what they'd prefer to believe.

But Gwen was inconsolable. Her life, she insisted, was over. She refused to go to school for a week. And when she finally returned, it was to be shunned by her former friends. They blamed her for ruining the play, and someone—we never found out who—had seen something of Gwen's shift. Rumors flew around the school, most of them even crazier than the truth. Gwen was called a freak, an alien, a mutant. Maybe if the monsters had been public then, kids would have thought she was cool. Maybe if Aunt Mab had taken on Gwen as her apprentice demon-fighter instead of me, my sister would have felt like there was some point to shifting. As it was, she felt like everything she'd ever wanted—her friends, popularity, a career as an actress—had been ripped away from her. Because she was Cerddorion. And she'd die, she insisted, if anyone ever found out.

Gwen never shifted again. She gave up her college plans and dropped out of high school. My parents objected. They pleaded. They even tried a threat or two. Gwen wouldn't budge—stubbornness is a family trait. She found her own tiny studio in Medford and took a job at a pizza place near Tufts. And her mission in life became finding the right guy to get her pregnant. When a Cerddorion female gives birth, she becomes inactive, losing the ability to shift. Once being "normal" became Gwen's driving force, she set out to catch a norm, with the intensity of a hunter stalking big game. Within three years, she'd married Nick Santini and gotten pregnant—not in that order. Nick was exactly the catch she was looking for. A Tufts grad who worked in finance, on campus for his five-year class reunion, he fell in love at first sight with the pretty waitress at the his old student hangout. Gwen was twenty-two years old the spring Maria was born. And with the birth of her child, she dedicated herself to out-humaning all the human moms in her picket-fence suburban neighborhood.

Dad and I saw Gwen's embracing of normhood as a rejection of everything that we were. Mom had a different view—after all, she'd made the same decision once. "Don't judge your sister too harshly, Vicky," she'd told me. "Maybe she's not pushing her heritage away so much as she's reaching toward something else." I had no clue what Mom was talking about. All I could see was that Gwen wanted to be a norm.

Now, as if to prove that she was indeed the epitome of norm homemaking, she appeared in the doorway carrying a tray loaded with coffee and various pastries. All home-baked, I was sure. Gwen would rather die than have a store-bought cookie in her house. She smiled as brightly as any TV mom, kind of like Carol Brady, Clair Huxtable, and June Cleaver all rolled into one.

She put the tray on the coffee table and poured me a mug. We both like our coffee the same way, strong and black, but Gwen had set out a creamer and a little bowl of sugar cubes, complete with tongs. In the Santini household, appearances counted big-time. I warmed my hands around the steaming mug, breathing in that wonderful fresh-coffee scent.

"Gwen, about Maria's costume—"

"Don't worry about it. I overreacted. It's just that I put a lot of time into the bride's costume." That wasn't it at all, and we both knew it. She sighed. "I'm glad that Maria looks up to you. It's just . . ."

"It's just that you don't want her to *be* me." I tried to keep the bitterness out of my voice, but it crept in anyway.

"I'm so scared that she'll turn out to be Cerddorion."

"What's so awful about that, Gwen? I'm not the only Cerddorion around, you know. You're Cerddorion, Mom's Cerddorion. If Maria's one of us, so what?"

"Each year, she grows up a little more. She's ten already. In a couple more years—"

"In a couple more years you'll know whether or not she needs some specialized guidance. If she's Cerddorion, I can help her."

"You know, I married Nick partly because he's pure Italian. I was hoping that that would . . . I don't know . . . *dilute* my DNA or something."

"Maria will be fine, Gwen. She's a great kid. That's what counts."

Gwen looked at me dubiously. She was about to say something else when the doorbell rang, and the expression on her face changed to a strange combination of guilt and hope. Uh-oh. I'd seen that look before.

"Are you expecting someone?" I asked.

"I wasn't sure. A friend of Nick's said he might drop by." She checked her watch. "He must have gotten off work early."

"Gwen, you didn't." Even as I said it, I knew she had. No matter how many times I asked her not to, my sister was always—*always*—trying to set me up with a human boyfriend. She didn't approve of my dating a werewolf. Can't imagine why.

She got up and started toward the front hall, smiling sheepishly—but not quite sheepishly enough to hide her delight. "This guy's great. His name's Andy. He just joined Nick's investment firm. He's really cute—and he went to Harvard. As soon as you said you were coming, I called Nick and told him to invite Andy for dinner."

"I'm not—" But she was gone. Damn. I did *not* want to sit there and play nice on some blind date I didn't even know I was having. So I did what any self-respecting, happily single woman would do. I ran and hid in the bathroom.

I closed the door, locked it, and leaned my forehead against the cool tile wall. How was I going to convince Gwen to stop doing this? The last time she'd fixed me up with one of Nick's friends, I'd agreed, reluctantly, to meet the guy for dinner. When I got to the restaurant, he was waiting for me in the bar, sipping a Scotch on the rocks. I don't think it was his first one, either—he weaved a little as we followed the maître d' to our table. The way he stared made me feel like some kind of zoo animal. Before our appetizers arrived, he got down to business: "So you're a shapeshifter, huh?" I nodded, and with shining eyes he took a rolled-up magazine from his jacket pocket. "Can you change into this?" The centerfold dropped open, and there was Miss July in all her silicone glory.

My last image of that date was Scotch dripping off his nose and chin.

Through the bathroom window, I could see Gwen's kids running around in the backyard. They were playing tag, from the look of things. Maria ran very, very slowly, arms and legs pumping exaggeratedly, so little Justin could catch up and tag her. Gwen didn't have a thing to worry about with that girl.

Muffled voices penetrated the door. Even by pressing my ear against the wood, though, I couldn't make out what they were saying or who was speaking. I gazed longingly toward the window. Maybe I could climb out and join the kids in their game of tag. I'd even volunteer to be It.

I actually had my hand on the window latch before I could admit how silly I was being. I regularly confronted the nastiest demons in Boston, but I was afraid to be introduced to a norm in my sister's living room? Okay, okay. I could do this. I unlocked the door, sighing. At least I got to be fully armed when I went to meet the demons. I didn't have so much as a slingshot to keep Andy at bay.

As I opened the door, Gwen was talking, for some reason, about the heights and weights of her kids at their births. Andy must have been riveted. I almost felt a stab of pity for him. I walked down the short hallway and peered around the corner into the living room. Gwen sat on the sofa, her back to me. Facing her in one of the wing chairs was an elegant, fortyish woman in a taupe business suit. She wore her blonde hair up in a twist. Half-glasses perched on her nose as she wrote in a notebook, nodding.

No Andy. I was safe. I strode into the living room. When the woman saw me, her face lit up like a kid who'd just watched Santa Claus emerge from the fireplace. "Hi," I said. "I'm Vicky, Gwen's sister."

The woman stood and extended her hand. "Yes, I know," she said. "I'm so pleased to meet you." Her hand was cold and a little damp. She shook hands vigorously and seemed reluctant to let go. I tugged my hand away, and we both sat down.

"Vicky, this is Sheila Gravett. She's a doctor. She's offering free health screenings to selected children from Maria's school."

Gravett—I knew that name. The woman watched me with intense interest, and a chill swept over me as I realized who she was. Gravett Biotech. The werewolf cloner. And she was here to ask Gwen about her *kids*? I narrowed my eyes at her.

"Why don't you tell my sister the truth, Dr. Gravett?"

Gwen gaped at me. Gravett smoothed a hand over her already smooth hair and smiled, like she was glad I'd seen through her lie. She started to say something, but I cut her off. "The good doctor isn't a pediatrician. She's a research scientist—and president of Gravett Biotech. She's trying to decode the Cerddorion genome so that her company can make a fortune off it. Isn't that right, Doctor?"

"What I'm doing is in the interest of science. As I explained to you on the phone—"

Gwen blinked rapidly, like she was trying to process what was going on. "You lied to me? You wanted to"—she searched for the right word—"to *study* my children under the pretense of a medical exam?"

"I'm sorry, Mrs. Santini. In fact, I'm relieved your sister has revealed the truth. I don't like to fabricate lies." She shot me a cool glance. "But Vicky has been uncooperative, and I wanted a chance to meet you in person, to explain that this research can unlock the hidden mysteries of shapeshifting, for the good of your children, your family—for the good of this great nation."

Oh, please. All we needed was a waving flag and the "Star-Spangled Banner" swelling in the background. "Okay, Dr. Gravett," I said, "you've made your case. As you can see, Gwen isn't interested. The front door's that way."

Gravett didn't move. She leaned forward in her chair, watching Gwen, who twisted her hands in her lap.

I stood up and stepped toward the researcher. "Out," I

said. "I'll pick you up and throw you out myself if you don't get moving. I'm not kidding."

Gravett looked at me, a challenge in her eyes. Her expression suggested she'd like nothing better than a chance to witness my paranormal strength. After another glance at Gwen, she sighed and got to her feet.

That's when Gwen looked up. "Wait. If you decode this genome, does that mean—" Her eyes shone. "Does that mean you could find a cure?"

"A cure?" I couldn't believe I'd heard her right. "For God's sake, Gwen, it's not a disease. It's what we are."

My sister turned to me, her face cold. "It's what *you* are. I'm not. And I don't want my daughter to be, either."

Gravett pushed past me to sit down next to Gwen. "Once we understand how the shapeshifter gene works, we may be able to deactivate it, yes."

The wheels were spinning behind Gwen's eyes. You could almost see her calculating how much time the research might take versus how much time Maria had left until puberty. I wanted to shake her, to tell her to let her daughter be what she was—Cerddorion or human.

The grandfather clock in the corner chimed five. Gwen blinked, looking like she'd just come out of a dream. She stood. "I have to start supper," she said. "I'll think about it, Dr. Gravett. I have your card. I'll call you."

Gravett stood too, smiling that damned smug smile, and Gwen walked her to the front door.

"Gwen—" I began when she came back.

"Don't start, Vicky. Just don't. I'm not going to discuss it with you now." She pushed past me and went into the kitchen. This time, no banging sounds emerged. The silence was scarier.

I didn't stay for dinner. Besides the fact that I still didn't want to be introduced to Andy, the bad feelings between Gwen and me meant that this was not a good night to be sharing lasagna around the Santini family table. So I took a taxi to Needham Heights Station and caught an early train back to Boston. After the conductor punched my ticket, I sat and stared out the window. The light faded as we sped past graffiti-covered walls, gradually showing nothing but my own scowling face reflected in the glass. I was glad the light was gone, plunging Boston into the world of vampires, zombies, and other night creatures. The meeting with Gravett the mad scientist had put me in a bad mood. I was ready to kill some demons.

10

BOSTON'S NORTH END IS A WARREN OF NARROW, TWIST-ing streets lined with brownstones, mom-and-pop grocery stores, wholesalers, and some of the best Italian restaurants you'll find outside of Tuscany. I drove down North Street and turned right on Lewis—the Jag whined in protest as I turned the wheel, then coughed a couple of times. Damn, I really needed to get that checked. I made a left on Commercial, which brought me to Atlantic and the waterfront. There it was, Commodore Wharf. I had to hand it to Lucado—he'd put up a good-looking building. Tasteful, even. Mostly brick, it rose ten stories and sported balconies, arched windows, and lots of glass. Modern, luxurious, but not out of place in Boston's oldest neighborhood.

I parked in a visitor's space and breezed past the door-man, who waved me through when I told him who I was there to see. The lobby was as classy as the building's exterior: marble floors, dark wood paneling, leather chairs clustered here and there in conversation groups. Nice.

When I rang Lucado's doorbell, it was a few minutes before ten. The door was opened by a massive chest with pumped-up pecs. At least, that's what it looked like until I craned my head back to see the guy's face. He was well over six feet tall, and he had the face of a prizefighter who'd won himself more poundings than prizes: beady eyes and a zig-zagging nose that'd been broken in at least three places. Be-sides a too-tight T-shirt, he wore jeans and black boots. Strange uniform for a butler, so I was guessing this must be Lucado's bodyguard.

"You the demon killer?" His basso profundo voice sounded skeptical.

"That's me."

"Lemme see some ID."

I handed him my state-issued PA identification card. Its photo was better than the mug shot on my driver's license, not that I cared what Lucado's pet ape thought. He squinted at it for a long time. I was about to offer help sounding out the words, when he handed it back to me. Then he stood there, filling up the doorway, the Man-Mountain of Massachusetts.

"I need to talk to Mr. Lucado before I set up." I went to push past him. He didn't budge. I shoved a bit harder. I might as well have tried to move the wall. Then I realized the game he was playing. He must have heard about how I'd half-crushed Lucado's hand; now he wanted to test my strength against his. Despite his size, I could pick this guy up and toss him over my shoulder if I felt like it, but I liked to conserve my strength when I was on the job. Worse, tapping into my full strength could cause the demon essence to stir—not a good way to start a new acquaintance, especially when the guy was already annoying me. So I'd let the ape think he'd won. This time. I stepped back and waited.

After a second, he moved aside. I think I saw the shadow of a smile way up there in the stratosphere.

"Leave your bags here," he said. I didn't like to be separated from my weapons at work, but I could understand a bodyguard's reluctance to let them in the house. Some clients are funny that way. The second bag was more or less empty; it was for packing up the Harpy carcasses after the job. I let both bags drop where I stood.

"Frank's in the living room." He jerked his head back, then sat down in the chair beside the front door and opened a comic book. I'm not sure, but I think he was reading Casper the Friendly Ghost.

Lucado must have paid his interior decorator a fortune. Everything about the place said "old money," even though

rumor had it that most of Frank's money was of the freshly
laundered variety. Oil paintings in gilt frames adorned the
walls, antique furniture was placed in artful arrangements,
and the Persian carpet under my feet looked way too pricey
to be walking on.

In the living room, Frank sat in a leather club chair, holding a brandy snifter. He looked up as I approached. The scar
nearly made me flinch. I'd forgotten how impressive it was.
If shock value could be measured in dollars, that scar would
be worth a couple million, at least.

"You shouldn't be drinking, Frank. You've got a sleeping
pill to take, remember?"

"A little nightcap won't hurt." He swirled the liquid
around in his glass, then took a swig. "Besides, I told you—I
don't take pills."

"You're taking one tonight, or I'm leaving."

We stared at each other, tension in the air between us.
Neither of us blinked. Finally, Frank banged down his glass,
brandy sloshing up the side.

"They don't work," he said.

"What do you mean?"

"Sleeping pills. They don't work worth crap." A shadow
of desperation crossed his face, making the scar stand out
like lightning at midnight. "Like I said, I don't do pills. But
these attacks—it's been so damn horrible, I've already tried
sleeping pills. I thought if I knocked myself out, I'd sleep
through it." His hand, resting on the arm of the chair, clenched
into a fist. "Didn't happen. They woke me up somehow, and
it was the same as every other goddamn night."

"Tonight will be different. I'll kill the Harpies before they
can get to you. You'll sleep like a baby, and tomorrow will be
a fresh new day."

"A fresh new day. La-di-dah. You sound like a song from
a musical." He glowered at me. "I hate musicals."

But he picked up the sleeping pill from a tray on the table
beside him. He held the tablet between his thumb and fore-
finger, pointed to it with his other hand, and then made a big

show of putting it in his mouth. He swallowed it, then washed it down with the rest of his brandy.

"Good boy," I said. "Now it's time for bed. That pill works fast. You've got about three minutes to haul your butt between the sheets."

"Listen to her," he remarked. Already his words were slurring. "Haul my butt. Nobody talks to Frankie like that."

He got halfway to his feet, then collapsed back into the chair. Jeez, how many brandies had he had? I went over to check his pulse. He didn't blink when I put my fingers on his neck. The pulse was a little slow, but strong and steady. He'd be okay.

In the front hall, I said to the bodyguard, "Your boss needs some help getting upstairs. Be sure you tuck him in nice and tight."

I picked up my bag and got ready to work.

IT TOOK SOME CONVINCING BEFORE THE BODYGUARD would let me into Frank's bedroom with my duffel bag full of weapons. He had real trouble with the idea that I was there to help his boss, not attack him. A two-pronged argument finally penetrated that thick skull: (a) if Frank had hired me to do a job, and the bodyguard didn't let me do it, Frank would be pissed off; and (b) if I harmed Frank in some way, I'd still have to get past the bodyguard. I promised to let him check on Frank before I left, scout's honor. He really made me say that, too—"scout's honor." No matter that I'd dropped out of Girl Scouts after Brownies. It seemed to satisfy him, so what the heck.

Once he was gone, I set to work. Demon slaying is part science, part art, part ritual. First, know your battlefield. Frank's bedroom was large, about sixteen by twenty. It was more spartan than the antique-filled living room—the only furniture was a king-sized bed, a nightstand, a dresser, and two slipper chairs. That was good. It meant there'd be less stuff in the way if the battle got complicated.

The carpet and walls were white; the furniture was black. Cushions and a couple of paintings added primary colors to the mix. The bed where Frank lay snoring was against the north wall; two closed doors occupied the west wall. I went over and opened each of them: bathroom and walk-in closet, both clear. The south wall displayed a huge painting, scribbles and drips of color on a white canvas. If anyone had been taking bets, I'd have put my money on Jackson Pollock. The slipper chairs were set side by side, facing by the east wall, which was almost entirely glass and overlooked the harbor. Must be an awesome place to watch the sun rise. There was a glass door on the right side of the window-wall, which opened onto a balcony. Frank had said that the Harpies, three of them, entered through the window, so this area would be my focus. The trick would be to nail all three Harpies without shattering all that nice glass.

I picked up one chair and moved it out of the way, over near the closet. I pulled the other chair to the side so I could wait in it and aim parallel to the windows, not straight at them. Surprise would give me an advantage of a second, maybe two. With any luck, it'd be three quick shots, three dead Harpies.

Time to prepare the equipment. I carried my weapons bag over to the dresser, whose top held a tray with a comb, pocket change, cuff links, and a wristwatch. I carried the tray into the bathroom and left it on the vanity. Back in the bedroom, I unzipped the bag, took out my rolled-up altar cloth, and spread it across the top of the dresser. A deep red cloth embroidered in gold, its symbols included swords (for Saint Michael) and harps (for Saint David).

I reached back into the bag, got out my automatic pistol, and checked the clip. All loaded up with bronze ammo. Bronze is lethal to demons, so all my tools—arrows, daggers, swords— were bronze at the business end. I got the silencer and screwed it in place. I wasn't worried about waking Frank; with the magically charged sleeping pill I'd given him, I could tap-dance on his pillow and he'd just keep snoring. But I definitely didn't want the bodyguard charging into the bedroom in the middle of a Harpy fight.

I placed the gun on the cloth and took out my dagger, the one Aunt Mab had given me at sixteen. It was a wickedly beautiful piece of work. Shaped like a cross, its handle was set with rubies and sapphires; its bronze blade shone dully in the light. Next was my backup dagger. This one was smaller and plainer, its curved blade etched with mystical symbols. I laid out the weapons in a row on the altar cloth.

As I reached into the bag for the vial of sacramental wine, my fingers brushed the pommel of my sword. Should I prepare that, too? It seemed like overkill. Swords were for bigger game than Harpies; I didn't even know why I'd brought it. Knowing Difethwr was around had made me uneasy. But that was silly; I wasn't out in Concord tonight. I was still in Boston, protected by the shield. I left the sword in the bag.

I closed my eyes and took three deep breaths, grounding myself. Then I murmured a prayer invoking Saint Michael, killer of demons, and Saint David, protector of Wales. I asked for their aid and assistance in dispatching these Harpies back into the ether. Amen. I unscrewed the top from the vial of the wine, which had been blessed by three sages of three different faiths, and touched a single drop to each weapon. The drop glowed; the glow spread, and for a moment each weapon shone like pure gold. When the glow faded, I was ready. I stuck the jeweled dagger in my belt and snugged the curved dagger into a sheath strapped to my ankle. I clicked the safety off the pistol and sat by the window to wait.

Lucado kept snoring, a weird combination of buzzes and snorts. The glowing green numbers on his nightstand alarm clock said 10:57. Soon, the Harpies would attack.

I dabbed some menthol cream into each nostril. I braced myself, then opened my senses to the demonic plane. Most people can't perceive any demons besides their own. As one of the Cerddorion, I had the ability to step into the dimension where demons reign—and believe me, the demon-haunted world is not a nice place. The moment I tuned in, I was hit by a cacophony of shrieks and screaming, gibbering and cruel laughter. Colors dimmed, overlaid by a gray film of smoke and shadows. And the stench—a nauseating combination of raw sewage, rotting meat, sulfur, and sweat. The smell could knock you backward when it hit. That's what the menthol was for.

I focused, sifting through the racket of thousands of demons tormenting hundreds of Bostonians. Through all that din, I was listening for one particular sound, the sound of frenzied Harpies approaching their prey, like a million out-of-tune violins shrieking out the music from the shower scene in *Psycho*. After about two minutes I heard it, and it was getting louder as the demons made a beeline for Frank's bedroom. Showtime.

Keeping an ear tuned to the Harpies' approach, I jumped up and turned the chair around. I knelt on the seat and braced my arms on the chair's back. The shrieks grew louder, louder—waves of earsplitting screeching pounded my skull. My finger tightened on the trigger.

Crash! The Harpies slammed through the window. In the demonic plane, it shattered, shards flying everywhere. Pieces stung my face, my arms, but I didn't flinch. I squeezed the trigger. *Pop, pop, pop.* One, two, three, the Harpies dropped from the air and thudded to the floor. The demons hadn't made it more than two feet inside. Not even a hole in the wall; bronze bullets don't pass through demon bodies. Clean, fast, complete. Nice work, if I did say so myself.

I stood, clicking on the safety and holstering the gun. In the bed, Frank moaned and turned onto his side. Some part of him sensed there were Harpies in the room, even dead ones. "No," he murmured, then went quiet. At least he'd stopped snoring.

I fetched the second duffel bag and went over to collect the Harpy corpses. Even after ten years of exterminating these demons, I was still jolted by their vileness. Harpies have the body of a vulture—with extra-long, extra-sharp steel talons—and the head of a Gorgon, a creature that looked something like a woman, but with snakes for hair and a cruel, hooked beak. That Gorgon head was said to turn humans into stone, and that's what it did—paralyzed them with fear and horror so that the victim had no defense against the creature as it tore into his guts.

The duffel bag was lined with aromatic herbs and pine branches to help counter the stink of dead Harpies. I opened it, then picked up the first Harpy by its feet and stuffed it into the bag. The second soon joined it. As I reached for the third, Frank moaned again. I turned to check that he was okay, and a deafening screech split the air as a slash of pain ripped across my arm. I spun around—the third Harpy no longer lay still and silent on the floor. It had taken to the air, hovering near the ceiling, its snake hair writhing in a spitting, hissing cloud around its head, its beak snapping open and shut. I barely had time to register its position before it dived.

Hurtling toward me, feet first, its steel talons targeted my eyes. I dropped and rolled, yanking the dagger from my belt. Shrieking with rage, the Harpy hit the ground hard, skidding across the floor and gouging twin tracks out of the carpet. I lunged for the thing and missed, and it made like a road-runner for Frank's bed.

"No, you don't!" I shouted, throwing myself at it, but grasping only a few tail feathers. They yanked out, and the demon spun around, howling in fury. It paused, torn between going after me or its victim.

"Come on, you damn demon." I crouched, gripping the dagger, ready. The Harpy flapped its wings, lifting heavily into the air, but not getting higher than head level. Three feet away, its snakes strained toward me, trying to strike. I could see now that I'd only grazed it with the gun, under the left wing. I couldn't use the pistol here, though; not this close to Frank's bed. What if I missed? As the demon turned its head back and forth between me and Frank, I advanced. It moved away, trying to gain some height, and I pressed forward, herding it toward the back wall, away from the bed.

When it realized what I was doing, it struggled upward another couple of feet, then dived again. This time, I was ready. I stood my ground as the shrieking, hissing thing plummeted toward me, and at the last second I raised the dagger. It screamed as it impaled itself on the blade.

I kept my arm braced, took the impact and the weight. Then I lowered the dagger, and the Harpy slid to the floor.

The beak still gaped open, but the beady eyes had lost their fire, and the snakes lay limp and unmoving. Steam curled from the place where bronze had pierced its flesh. I poked the demon with the toe of my boot. No response, just dead-weight. Within a minute the Harpy had joined its sisters in the duffel bag.

In the bed, Frank had resumed snoring. I surveyed the room. On the demonic plane, it was a mess—shattered window, expensive white carpet torn and stained. I went into the bathroom to wash the gooey, smelly, green-black Harpy blood off my dagger. In the mirror, I was a mess, too—my face flicked with a dozen cuts, my arm gashed by a Harpy bite. Gazing at my reflection, I closed my senses to the world of the demons. As if by magic, the cuts closed up, faded, then disappeared. When I returned to the bedroom, normal reality showed the room in its previous condition, except for a whiff of sulfur in the air. If that wasn't gone by morning, Frank's carpet would need a good steam cleaning.

CARRYING MY TWO DUFFEL BAGS, I TROTTED DOWN THE stairs. By the front door, the bodyguard sat with his chair tilted back against the wall. He leaned there, mouth open, snoring like he was trying to beat the boss in a snoring com-petition.

The smell of sulfur still clung to me. I needed fresh air. I remembered there was a balcony on this floor, too, off the living room. I'd take a minute to step outside, get my head clear. Walking through the darkened living room, I dropped my bag by the chair where Frank had sipped brandy earlier. Then I opened the balcony door and slipped outside.

The night was chilly, with a hint of frost, but sparkling clear. Perfect. I stood with my hands on the cold railing, fac-ing the harbor, and inhaled the crystalline air, cleansing my lungs of the foulness of demons. It was about eleven forty, and it was quiet. Blessedly quiet. I could perceive a faint echo of the screams and groans in the demonic plane, but as I stood and focused on my breathing, those subsided, then faded out entirely. Revitalized, I went back inside.

In the front hall, I stopped and regarded the big norm sleeping in his chair. Some bodyguard. Hmm, I wondered, how should I awaken Sleeping Beauty? A gentle shake of the shoulder—or a good swift kick to send the chair flying out from under him? Decisions, decisions.

Before I could make up my mind, a funny feeling prickled along my arms, goose-bumping my flesh. I looked around. Nothing. The feeling returned, stronger, like an electric current. It raced up my arms and past my shoulders to make the hair on the back of my neck stand at attention. What *was* that?

I stepped forward, and the feeling intensified. I stopped and listened, straining to hear past the bodyguard's snores. Somewhere in the distance, but inside the building, I heard a bang, like a door slamming. The sound sent shivers through my bones.

Get a grip, Vicky. This is a condo development. People slam doors.

Something banged again. Louder.

I ran across the hall, grabbed the bodyguard's shirt, and shook him. The T-shirt tore like tissue. He sputtered and grabbed for his gun, but I held his arms fast. His eyes widened when he realized it was me, or maybe when he realized that I could force him to hold still. "What the—?" he began.

"You've gotta tell me something." My voice sounded wild. "Do people slam doors in this building?"

"Slam—?" He looked bewildered. His eyes had lost that heavy-lidded, sleepy look, but there was drool on his chin. "Hey, let me go. What the hell are you talking about, slamming doors?"

Another bang.

"Like that."

A frown creased his forehead. "Nah. I never heard that before. Frankie built this place real good. It's got sound-proofing." He flexed his biceps, then strained both arms outward, but he couldn't break my hold. "Come on," he said, "lemme go." I released his arms, and he wiped his chin with the back of his hand.

That's when the screeching started.

This time, the bodyguard grabbed my arm. "What the hell was that?"

I yanked away. "Which way's the kitchen?"

He looked at me funny, like maybe he was thinking this was no time for a coffee break, but he pointed to the right. "Through those doors."

I took off running before the words were out of his mouth and slammed through the swinging doors. The kitchen was modern, all granite and chrome, and every surface was empty. No salt shaker on the table or the stove. I began opening cabinets, one after another, but I couldn't find what I was looking for.

Another horrible screech sounded, and the bodyguard stood in the doorway. "What do you think you're doing? And what's making that noise?"

"Salt!" I yelled, and he looked at me like I was insane. "Where does Frank keep the salt?" He gaped at me, not answering. "Don't just stand there, damn it! We've got to stop that demon!"

That got him moving. He was surprisingly fast for someone the size of a battleship. He opened a cupboard next to the stove and took out a round blue container.

"Iodized?" he asked.

"Doesn't matter. Get back out there. Sprinkle a line of salt across the doorway. If the thing comes in anyway, throw a handful at it. Aim for the eyes."

The screeching was in the outer hallway now. The bodyguard stared at me with bug eyes. "You want me to throw salt at it."

"Aim for the eyes," I repeated, pushing him out the door. In the hallway, I quit pushing and split off toward the living room. The bodyguard stopped in his tracks and stared at me over his shoulder. He looked scared. "I'll be there in a minute," I said. "I've got to prepare."

But there was no time. The front door burst open, and Difethwr loomed on the threshold, hideous, making Lucado's bodyguard look like a midget. The Hellion was even more terrifying than I remembered it. Its warty blue skin glistened with slime that dripped from its body in long, mucouslike strings. It stretched its mouth into a horrible grin, revealing row upon row of razor-sharp teeth—hundreds of them. Flames shot from its eyes, its mouth. The bodyguard stopped, craned his neck to get a look at the thing, and then keeled over in a dead faint. Shit.

I ran to him, grabbed the salt from his hand, and poured it around his prone body in a lopsided circle, silently chanting words of protection, charging the salt with their power. Difethwr advanced, filling the room with screeches so painful you wanted to cut off your ears. I looked up and saw the yellow eye-flames sweep toward me. And I froze. It was the worst night of my life all over again. I was back in Aunt Mab's library, helplessly watching this creature destroy my father, Dad's body twisting in agony.

No, no, no.

The Hellion laughed, exactly as it had laughed that night, and I snapped back to the here and now. This demon was not going to make a victim of me twice.

I poured salt into my hand, the grains spilling over the edges of my palm and skittering across the hardwood floor. I charged the salt with my intention—*Stopiwch! Arhosa!*—commands to halt, to immobilize. Salt wouldn't destroy a Hellion, but it would make the thing hurt and slow it down. As I finished the spell, I clenched my hand into a fist. The charged salt vibrated with power, and I felt a twinge in my arm. Difethwr had stopped by the fallen bodyguard and was streaming fire at him.

The flames bounced and sparked off the bubble of protection that shielded the man. Inside the circle, he lay unharmed, looking like he was asleep. The Hellion roared with fury, then raised its eyes to me.

I drew back my arm and took aim. The tingling in my arm intensified. It felt like a swarm of spiders crawling under my skin. The salt in my fist grew hot—blisteringly, unbearably hot. I couldn't hold it. My fingers opened; the salt fell to the floor. And the pain—my whole arm blazed with a fiery ache that tormented like the touch of Difethwr's flames. Weak and useless, the arm dropped to my side. I couldn't make it move. The demon mark glowed a fiery red.

Difethwr laughed again, and I understood. The arm that bore the Hellion's mark would not act against the demon.

Well, the rest of me could still fight. Hastily, I knelt and scooped up a pile of salt with my left hand. Still on my knees, I hurled the salt as hard as I could left-handed.

My aim was off, and most of the salt sailed past its right shoulder. But some hit the target. The demon clawed at its eyes, its shrieks rising to a whole new level. "Difethwr," I shouted over the din, "I banish thee back to the Hell whence thou came."

The last words my father ever spoke.

The Hellion staggered back, and I ran for the living room. I opened the duffel bag and reached in with my left hand— my right arm still hung limp—and fumbled around until I found the sword. I grasped the hilt and pulled it out. Heavy footsteps approached from the hall. Moving as fast as I could, I got the sanctified wine out, but I couldn't get the top off with just one hand. Flames danced over the edge of the Persian rug. I looked up. Difethwr stood in the doorway. My sword's blade remained cold and dull.

I looked wildly around the room. Too much to hope for that Lucado would have a little sanctified wine lying around, but then I saw the brandy decanter. It was worth a try. As Difethwr advanced, I grabbed the decanter with my left hand, yanked out the glass stopper with my teeth, spit it out, and poured brandy along the blade. As I did, I whispered the ancient spell. A faint glow played along the edge of the blade— or was it the reflection of Hellion fire?

Come on, I whispered, *come on.*

Difethwr laughed, and the back of my neck tensed, anticipating a blast of Hellion fire. But I kept my focus on the sword.

The blade glowed. A flicker ran along one edge. And then the blade burst into flame. I straightened, and turned to face the Destroyer.

The sword felt awkward and heavy in my left hand as I raised it. Not six feet away, the demon stopped. It pulled back its flames until all I could see of them was a smolder behind its eyes. We faced each other.

Difethwr chuckled, a deep, gravelly rumble. And then it spoke my name. Its voice sounded like a dozen demons speaking together, not quite in unison, in a huge, echoing chamber. "Victory Vaughn," it said, "thy true name is Vanquished." Another rumbling laugh. "Prepare to join thy sire."

"Don't you dare talk about my father, Hellion."

"True. 'Tis senseless to speak of things that are no more." The thing regarded me, running its pointed black tongue over all those teeth. I tightened my grip on the sword. God, I wished I could use my right arm. "No trace remains of thy father. We destroyed his soul."

"That's a lie!" I hoisted the heavy sword, my left arm trembling, and charged.

Difethwr leaped to my right, and I missed it entirely. I spun as fire erupted from its eyes. I tried to block with the sword, but it was too unwieldy, my left arm too slow. The twin flames sped toward my face. This was it. I was going to die in excruciating agony, just like my father.

Then, so close that they singed my eyebrows, the flames stopped. I stepped back. Difethwr groaned and muttered something. I heard it say, "No, Master. The shapeshifter is here." Then it growled. Slowly, as if the effort caused it pain, the Hellion reeled the flames back into its eye sockets, inch by inch. Again, the eyes glowed dully.

The Hellion raised its slime-dripping arm and pointed at me. A flame danced at the end of its clawed finger. "It is not yet thy time, daughter of Ceridwen. But soon. Soon we will destroy thee and reduce this city to ashes and rubble. And thou wilt have no power to stop us."

As if to confirm the demon's taunt, the flame along the blade of my sword dimmed. Difethwr laughed, throwing back its head. Huge, slime-covered blue warts covered its neck and jaw. I spoke the spell frantically, whispering the words too fast, slurring them. It did no good. The sword's flames faltered, then went out.

Difethwr's laughter cut off abruptly, and the demon cocked its head, as if listening. Rage twisted its face. "Yes, Master. We obey," it said, each syllable yanked out like a tooth being pulled. The Hellion wavered, fading, becoming transparent.

"Who bound you, Difethwr? Whose call do you answer?"

It regarded me with scorn. "One far stronger than thou, foolish daughter of Ceridwen." It was almost gone now, like night fog touched by dawn.

"Too strong for you, though, huh? So the Big Bad Destroyer can be forced to bow to a human master. Who'd have thought it?"

The demon's howl of rage was muted, its body a dim blue haze. "Thy time is coming soon." Its voice was all that remained now, like the stink of cold ashes after a fire. And even that was fading. "Soon."

11

I NEEDED A DRINK—AND I'M NOT MUCH OF A DRINKER. BUT part of me felt like downing a lot of shots of . . . well, *something*, and in rapid succession. What I really needed was to sit down, get my nerves steady, and figure out what the hell was going on.

So I headed for Creature Comforts. I'd told Kane I'd try to meet him there, anyway. Maybe he could help me make sense of what had just happened. Somehow, a Hellion had breached the shield and invaded normal reality.

I drove home like a maniac, parked the Jag, and left my duffel bags locked inside. Then I ran toward Creature Comforts as fast as my stilettos would carry me. *Calm down, Vicky. You'll figure this out. The Hellion isn't coming back tonight.* I slowed my pace. In a few minutes, I was there.

Creature Comforts, like most bars in the New Combat Zone, didn't look like much on the outside. But once you pushed open the heavy oak door—well, it didn't look like much on the inside, either. It was dim, like you'd expect a monster bar to be, with sticky linoleum floors and dark wood paneling on the walls. To the left of the door stretched the longest bar in the Zone, with stools spaced haphazardly along its length. Square tables took up the main floor area, and four-seater booths lined the right and back walls. Above each booth hung a single light fixture with a black shade and a forty-watt bulb; the seats sported ancient red vinyl cushions zigzagged with cracks, some patched with duct tape. The air smelled of beer, cigarettes (no one tried to enforce any smoking bans here), and, underneath it all, the vaguest whiff of human blood.

There was a rumor that Axel, the owner and bartender, pumped in a special blood-scented air freshener to attract the vampires—just enough to get them feeling kind of edgy but not go all blood-crazed predator on the norms. I didn't believe it. Most of the vamps seemed to show up with blood already on their breath. Whatever. Creature Comforts was definitely the place to be for vampires, their junkies, the occasional werewolf, and a few human thrill-seekers.

I liked it because it felt like home. And that's why I'd come here now.

A quick glance around the room failed to find Kane. It was already half past midnight, but because of our crazy schedules, we were each used to the other one showing up late.

Axel loomed behind the bar. Nobody knew for sure exactly what Axel was. Few would even hazard a guess—mostly because, if you guessed wrong and offended the guy, Axel looked like he'd eat you for an hors d'oeuvre. The guy was huge—too big to be human—and regulars said the more you drank, the bigger he looked. Not a bad quality in a bartender who doubled as bouncer. Axel had a sort of caveman vibe going on: shaggy beard, big nose, long arms so hairy there were whispers he was part bear. Since his lair—er, *apartment*—was in the cellar below Creature Comforts, the whisperers might not be too far off.

I spotted Juliet at the bar, where she sat with her back to me. The guy next to her leaned in so close he half fell off his stool. He looked like a college kid—baseball hat, baggy jeans, a hooded sweatshirt that read HUSKIES.

"No way," Husky Boy exclaimed as I approached. "No friggin' way!"

"It's true. I swear on my own grave," Juliet said, stirring her Bloody Mary. She ordered that cocktail not because she liked it, but because it freaked out the norms—they assumed it was made with real blood. Most norms think that vampires can't eat food, but that's not true. They can eat whatever they want, but only human blood gives them nourishment. Juliet's complexion glowed like she was in a cosmetics ad, which meant she'd already fed tonight. But it couldn't have been much more than an appetizer, or she wouldn't be bothering with a drunken frat boy.

Unless, of course, he happened to be taking a Shakespeare class. Juliet was a sucker (pun intended) for an English major.

I sat next to Juliet, on the side opposite Husky Boy and his buddy, and waved to get Axel's attention. When Juliet saw me, she smiled, showing fangs stained slightly red—whether with tomato juice or something else, I didn't know. "Ah, here's my roommate," Juliet said. "She'll tell you."

The kid leaned over so far he was almost lying on the bar. "She's shittin' me, right? She's not the real Juliet. You know, like in *Romeo and*—?"

Axel lumbered over. I ordered a tequila, straight up. He raised his eyebrows but moved silently down the bar. Then I turned to the kid and shrugged. "Her name is Giulietta Capulet. And she's been a vampire for six hundred fifty years. Sounds about right to me."

"Yeah, but how—"

"Think about it," Juliet said. "I died. I was buried in the family tomb. And then I came back to life."

"Yeah, 'cause that monk guy gave you a potion."

"Friar Lawrence? And what kind of potion was that?" The kid looked at her blankly. "Your culture has 'modern medicine.' Seriously, do you know of any drug that causes temporary death? No pulse, no breath, rigor mortis setting in?"

"The plague did."

Juliet tossed back her black hair, then ran a hand down her ivory neck and across her bosom. The kid's tongue hung out—kind of like a real husky's—as he watched. "Do I look like a zombie?" she asked.

Husky Boy shook his head, staring.

"Lawrence was no potion-maker; he was a vampire. He turned me. I was dead—truly dead—then I woke up undead." She smiled again. "Happens every day."

Husky Boy's forehead furrowed in confusion. His friend leaned over and whispered to him, making him perk up. "Yeah!" he said. He turned back toward Juliet. "If you're really Juliet, say, 'Romeo, Romeo, wherefore art thou Romeo?' Say the whole thing."

Juliet snorted, sounding like she'd gotten Bloody Mary up her nose. "The balcony scene? Oh, please. Shakespeare was a hack. He got the story all wrong. For one thing, I was twenty-two, not fourteen. For another, Tybalt—you know, Shakespeare calls him 'fiery Tybalt'? Well, Tybalt was a wuss who ran away crying when Romeo challenged him."

"So, what about Romeo? Dying for love of you and all that. Is that part wrong?"

Juliet's eyes glittered in the dim light. "Only partly. He did come to look for me in the tomb. He arrived just before I awakened."

"And he killed himself because he thought you were dead."

"No."

"You mean he didn't die?"

"Oh, yes, he died, all right." She smiled. "When I woke up, I was famished."

"LIME?"

Axel deposited my tequila in front of me. I shook my head, picked up the shot glass, and downed the drink in one gulp, leaving Juliet to mess with the mind of Husky Boy. The liquor burned my throat, but I managed not to cough. I slammed the glass down on the bar. "Another," I said, my voice hoarse from the fire in my throat.

Up went the eyebrows again, but he nodded and moved to fetch the bottle. In case you haven't noticed, Axel doesn't talk much.

This time, after he poured the tequila, he stood and waited, bottle in hand. I threw the second shot back. This one burned less, and a pleasant warmth rose through my body. Tension seeped out of my shoulders, my neck, my back. Axel looked as sympathetic as a seven-foot-tall Cro-Magnon could, and I motioned to him for another refill.

By now, Juliet had turned on her stool to look at me.

"Axel, how many shots is that for Vicky?"

He held up three salami-sized fingers.

Juliet's eyes widened. She scrutinized me, looking almost shocked. For a second, I felt proud of myself. It takes a lot to shock a vampire.

"Three shots? What's up with you?" She paused. "You look terrible."

"Thanks," I said. The warm, rosy feeling drained away, replaced by something cold and hard as I considered how to answer Juliet's question. I fingered my shot glass, but thinking about Difethwr made me feel queasy enough. "There's a Hellion loose in Boston."

Juliet's eyes got wider, then she laughed. "Some kind of Halloween joke, right?"

"No joke. I saw it. Over in the North End."

"But that can't be. Boston's shielded against those things."

"That's what I thought, too." I told her what had happened at Lucado's condo. When I got to the part where Difethwr spoke my name and told me it wasn't yet my time, I picked up the glass, threw back my head, and sent the third shot down the hatch to join the first two.

"A Hellion running around Boston," Juliet said, then shrugged. "Bummer for the humans." She looked at my empty tequila glass. "Oh, and for you, too. I mean, I know you've got a history with this thing. You really think it came here looking for you?"

"It called me by name. It mentioned my father." I closed my eyes, but that made the room tilt, so I opened them again. "What are we going to do?"

"About what?" said a man's voice behind me. "Or am I interrupting a private conversation?"

"Yeah, you are, so just—" I turned around to tell whoever it was to take a hike. I found myself staring into cornflower-blue eyes beneath blond curls. My heart picked up its pace. "Detective Costello," I said. "I, um, I didn't recognize you without the suit."

He looked good. In fact, he took looking good to a whole new level. He was wearing a *very* well-fitting pair of black jeans and with a soft-looking crewneck sweater the same blue as his eyes. He smiled, making his eyes go a shade deeper. "Do you always start talking before you know who you're talking to?"

"Yes," Juliet said, "she does."

Costello's smile broadened, and Juliet gave me a look that said, *Better eat this one while he's hot.*

"Why don't you go play with your English major?" I said.

Juliet laughed and licked her fangs. Costello's gaze went back and forth between us, looking confused and more than a little worried.

"I take it you don't come here much," I said.

He let out a breath and shook his head. "First time. I heard you tell Attorney Kane you'd try to meet him here tonight. I wanted to talk to you."

"More questions about George?"

He grinned. "That, too."

COSTELLO ORDERED BEER, A KILLIAN'S. AS FOR ME, I'D HAD more than enough alcohol for one night, so I had Axel pour me a club soda. We moved to a booth, where I repeated the story of seeing the Destroyer.

"I'm not up on all this paranormal stuff," Costello said. "Life used to be a lot simpler."

"It only seemed simple, you know. We've been here all along. Don't you think it's better to have the monsters out in the open instead of lurking in dark alleys?"

He didn't answer. For a moment, the look on his face made me think I didn't really want to hear his reply. Then he blinked and shook himself. "What can you tell me about this shield?" he asked. "The one that's supposed to keep these Hellions out of the city."

"It was created after the plague by a consortium of white witches, representatives from all the local covens: Beacon Hill, the Back Bay, Southie, Cambridge, Somerville, all over. Something had to be done fast, because Hellions were already creating havoc. You remember what it was like then, don't you? Riots, looting, arson. That kind of havoc attracts even more Hellions—it spirals. So an emergency magical response team was put together. Sorcerers drove out the Hellions that were already here. Then the witches erected the shield keep them out."

"Doesn't seem to have worked."

"It did, though. I've never seen a Hellion in Boston." Until tonight. "The shield must have been breached somehow."

"So we have to tell the witches to fix it."

I shook my head. "It's not that easy. The Destroyer was inside the city tonight. If it's still around, repairing the shield would trap it inside."

"And then?"

"It would never rest until it had destroyed the city and everyone in it." As it was already threatening to do.

We looked at each other. Daniel picked up his beer and took a swig. I felt kind of sorry for him. Boston was his city, and as a cop it was his job to protect it. But he had no clue what he was up against here.

"There's another thing about the shield," I said. "I think someone cut a hole in it on purpose. If that's the case, the breach will be hidden. Even with the best witches, it could take a while to find the hole and repair the damage."

"Why on earth would anyone purposely put a hole in the shield that protects the city?"

"Somebody summoned the Destroyer. Whoever did that has plans for it—and is way ahead of us."

Daniel was silent for a few minutes, staring at the table, taking it all in. Then he looked up. "So what do you suggest?"

"Talk to the witches who created the shield. The Department of Magic has their names. They can start searching for the hole. And they might have some idea of who made it."

"But what about the demon?"

"Demons are my department." Costello gave me a long, searching look, then opened his mouth like he was going to try to talk me out of it. "It's mine, Detective. That Hellion murdered my father. I'm going to kill the damn thing."

A FEW MINUTES LATER, THE DOOR BANGED OPEN AND Kane stood in the doorway, surveying the bar. His silver hair gleamed like a warrior's helmet, and he still wore the gray suit, looking as sharp as it had this morning. He did a double take when he saw me sitting with Costello, then nodded at us. He came inside, followed by two zombies. And then a guy with a TV camera. And then a whole troupe of other people I didn't know who were carrying lights and bags and clipboards.

There was a stir when the zombies came in. Humans turned in their seats to get a better look. We were only a couple of blocks outside of Deadtown, but you just didn't see zombies at Creature Comforts very often. Even the New Combat Zone was off-limits to zombies without a permit.

After a word with Axel, Kane strode right over to our booth, his gray eyes lit up with a strange glow. "Detective Costello," he said, extending his hand. "I have to admit I never expected to see you here."

"I needed to ask Vicky a couple of questions."

When Costello used my first name, Kane raised an eyebrow, then frowned in my direction. For a moment I could've sworn he was jealous. "You shouldn't talk to the police unless I'm present," he said. Of course. His disapproval of my sitting here with a handsome detective was purely professional. Silly me.

"Daniel's not on duty, so I figured it was okay." It was the first time I'd said Costello's first name out loud. I kind of liked the way it sounded, especially because this time Kane really did look jealous. "Don't worry, Kane. I didn't give away any classified PA information. The secret handshake is safe."

Kane shot me a look that promised we'd continue this discussion later. Then he turned to look at the door, where the zombies stood awkwardly. There were two of them, a male and a female. They both looked like they'd died young—late twenties, maybe. They were good-looking for zombies. No holes in their faces, no missing limbs, just a couple of fingers gone from the guy's left hand. He wore a Red Sox sweatshirt and jeans; the female zombie was in an orange dress that didn't flatter the greenish tone of her skin. She clutched her handbag to her chest, as if she were drowning and it was a life vest.

"What are those two doing here?" I asked. "And what's with the camera crew?"

Kane had been trying to wave them over to join us, but they stood where they were. "They're here to make a point," he said. He went to the door, took both zombies by the hand, and led them over to us.

"Well, Detective, aren't you going to arrest them? Aren't these citizens committing a crime by leaving Designated Area One without a permit?"

Costello leaned back in the booth and squinted at the zombies. "I don't make a habit of pestering people for IDs when I'm off duty, Counselor. As far as I can tell, these are a couple of college kids in their Halloween costumes."

I realized what Kane was doing. "Don't drag Daniel into this," I said. "Make your propaganda without him."

"It's not propaganda; you know that." He turned to Costello. "We're taping a paid political advertisement to rebut Baldwin's claims that Paranormal Americans are a threat to humans. Will you say on camera that you can't tell these previously deceased humans from college students?" He gestured to the cameraman.

"Sorry. Can't do something like that without running it past the chief first. We're not allowed to take sides publicly in politics." He slid along the booth's vinyl seat and stood up.

Kane stepped close in front of him. Tense, they measured each other up. Fists clenched. Chests puffed. You could almost smell the testosterone. Axel came halfway around the bar, watching. The cop and the werewolf stared at each other, eye to eye, almost exactly the same height. I would've enjoyed the view if I hadn't been worried that in half a second they'd start tearing each other apart.

Then Daniel relaxed just a hair, but enough to signal to Kane's werewolf senses, loud and clear, that he wasn't interested in fighting. A lot of werewolves would take that as a sign of submission, but Kane didn't press it. He stepped back, relaxing as well, his hands unclenching.

They nodded to each other. Daniel turned and walked toward the door. I couldn't pick up any fear in the way he carried himself. Pretty brave for a human, turning his back on a werewolf.

Over at the bar, Axel picked up his towel and started wiping glasses.

Kane watched Daniel until the oak door closed behind him. I thought I heard a low growl, but maybe it was just the buzz of conversation around us. He went back to his frightened-looking zombies and started herding them around.

"One more thing."

I looked up, again into those blue eyes. Why did Daniel Costello's eyes always draw my gaze like a magnet?

"I thought you left," I said.

"I did. But I came back to tell you something."

"Yes, Detective?"

The eyes went all crinkly with his smile. "Call me Daniel. I like the way it sounds when you say it."

I didn't answer. Anything I said would've come out as a squeak.

"Here," he said, handing me a card. "I wanted to give you this." It was his business card, listing his precinct address and phone number. He touched my hand—I hoped he couldn't feel how that made my pulse race—and twisted slightly to flip the card over. There was another phone number written in pencil on the back.

"That's my home number. Please don't hesitate to call me, at either one."

"You mean about the Hellion?"

Just the slightest increase in pressure on my hand. You couldn't call it a squeeze, but it was—something. "About anything." He smiled and exited Creature Comforts for the second time that evening.

12

KANE SHOOED AWAY THE COLLEGE BOYS WHO'D BEEN SIT-
ting next to Juliet. They grumbled, and Husky Boy shook his
fist in Kane's face, clueless that this was a stupid thing to do
to a werewolf. Lucky for him, Kane was in public-relations
mode tonight. Juliet leaned over and whispered something to
the angry kid, and he moved off to one side, although he
clearly wasn't happy about it.

Next, Kane arranged the zombies at the bar, getting the
male a beer and the female a glass of white wine. He kept
telling them to relax, but they were both stiff. What else could
you expect from zombies?

Someone from the camera crew set up lights around the
zombies, and a woman in black leggings and a silvery tunic
started patting powder all over their faces. Makeup on zombies! It seemed, well, overkill. Zombies had spongy, green-
gray flesh. Everyone knew that. If Kane wanted people to
accept the zombies as they were, trying to make these two
look more human could easily backfire. The makeup girl
fluttered her powder puff across Juliet's face. So she'd be on
camera, too. Nothing like a sexy vampire to give the zombies
some credibility, I guess. Of course, as Tina had pointed out,
there's undead, and then there's *undead*. All you had to do
was glance at these three to see that.

Kane came over and put his hand on my arm. "Do you
want to be in the shoot?"

"No, thanks. I have no ambition whatsoever to be on TV."

"You sure? Might be good for business."

"You're not making a commercial for my business, Kane.

You want me there because I look human. I can sit next to the big bad zombies and not look scared."

"And what's wrong with that?" He smiled one of those smiles that melted you all the way down to your toes. How come he was always looked so damn good when he was trying to talk me into something?

"Nothing, I guess." I shrugged; I wasn't in the mood to melt. "I just don't want to be on TV." I nodded at Husky Boy, now skulking at a table. He wore his baseball cap sideways, making him look like he hadn't yet perfected his dressing-himself skills. "Why not use a real human?"

"Those kids are drunk. They'd just make goofy faces at the camera." But he seemed to like the idea. He scanned the crowd, then went over to talk to a woman who was sitting at a table with three others. She had that Midwestern tourist vibe going on. She shook her head and batted Kane away, but she was laughing. Kane whispered something to her and treated her to one of his trademark smiles. I've yet to see a woman who could resist the Kane charm when he had it going full blast. A minute later, she was seated at the bar getting powdered.

The lights guy had finished setting up, and the guy with the clipboard—who must be the director—said, "Listen up, people! Everybody in position, now. Let's get started."

Kane stepped in front of the group at the bar, adjusting his tie and closing his eyes as he got the powder-puff treatment. The director moved everyone around a little, so that Juliet and the male zombie could be seen behind Kane to his left; the female zombie and the tourist sat to his right. He squeezed them in close to fit everyone in the shot.

"Hey! Zombie boy!" yelled Husky Boy. "Hands off my lady!" His friend laughed and punched him on the shoulder.

"Quiet on the set!" The director glared around the room until everyone settled down. He addressed the group at the bar. "Relax. You're out having a good time. Look like you're having fun. That's all you have to do while Mr. Kane says his lines. Got it?" Juliet flicked back a strand of hair while the other three nodded in unison, looking various degrees of terrified.

The director pulled out a handkerchief and mopped his forehead. "Take one." He nodded to Kane.

Kane flashed his smile at the camera. "Hello. I'm Attorney Alexander Kane. After a hard day at work, Bostonians like to unwind. And we have many options for unwinding: a home-cooked meal, a quiet evening in front of the television, a visit to a neighborhood tavern. Previously deceased Bostonians, innocent victims of a now-dormant virus, also work hard. They also like to unwind, just like you and me."

The female zombie was stuffing her face with peanuts. Handful after handful, she crammed them into her mouth. If there's food around, zombies will eat it; and besides that, she was nervous. It was distracting to watch her, so much so that I forgot to listen to Kane.

"Cut!" yelled the director. "Cut, cut, cut! Somebody take those peanuts away from that zombie."

"Previously deceased hu—" Kane started to correct him, when some of those peanuts went down the wrong way. The female zombie clutched at her throat and started coughing, spraying chewed-up peanut crumbs all over the norm woman sitting next to her. The woman squealed and jumped off her stool, brushing at her clothes like they were on fire, while Axel leaned over the bar to pound the coughing zombie on the back.

She shuddered and gasped and eventually stopped coughing. She drained her glass of wine, then looked around unhappily. "Sorry," she said, and hiccupped.

Axel refilled the zombie's wineglass. She picked it up and promptly spilled it down the front of her orange dress.

The college boys howled with laughter and high-fived each other. Kane looked ready to toss them out of the bar—he could've done it without wrinkling his suit—but he must have decided they weren't worth bothering with, because he merely smoothed his jacket and waited while the makeup girl dealt with the flustered zombie, blotting her dress and applying more powder.

"Let's get it right this time, people. You guys at the bar—
no eating, no drinking. Just sit there and smile while Mr.
Kane speaks. All right? Okay, go. Take two."

The camera began rolling again, and Kane repeated his
speech. He made it past the first cut, and continued: "The
previously deceased *are* Bostonians. They are our spouses, our
family members, our friends." His brow clouded, just enough
to make him smokily handsome. "But Seth Baldwin calls them
monsters. If Baldwin becomes governor, he'll take away their
limited rights and force them from their homes. Haven't the
previously deceased suffered en—"

Husky Boy leaped to his feet, pumping his fist in the air
and yelling, "Baldwin for Governor! Woo-hoo! Yeah!" His
friend, laughing, added a couple of rebel yells. The two of
them made so much noise I could barely hear the director's
"Cut!" over their racket.

Kane glared at them. Juliet rolled her eyes. The tourist
slid off her bar stool and returned to her table. The zombies
looked lost. When Kane started toward the college boys wearing his scary face—an expression that was way more werewolf than public-relations exec—I followed. This looked like
a situation where a little backup couldn't hurt.

By the time I got there, the less drunk kid was holding the
other one back. Husky Boy was red-faced, shouting at Kane.
"It's a free goddamn country, and I'll say whatever I goddamn please." Drops of spittle, lit up by the TV lights, sprayed
from his mouth. "Humans got freedom of speech, ya know!"

"I think it's time you boys went back to the dorm." Kane
took an arm in each hand. The students tried to shake him
off, but he was too strong, which only made Husky Boy yell
louder and add more obscenities to his words. Kane ignored
him, propelling them both toward the door.

"Lemme go!" Husky Boy struggled, jerking his arm
around and dragging his feet. Kane kept moving toward the
door; the kid had no choice but to go with him.

I opened the door for the trio. Kane pitched both norms
onto the sidewalk, just hard enough to make his point. Husky
Boy, who'd lost his baseball cap, lay on his back and shouted,

"You let goddamn freakin' zombies in there an' throw out real Americans!" As I closed the door, his friend was saying, "C'mon, man, let's just go."

Kane was halfway across the room when the door burst open and the angry kid came after him, waving a broken beer bottle. Kane turned, swinging his arm out, and Husky Boy ran smack into it, nose to elbow. He went down like someone had kicked his legs out from under him. His nose spouted a fountain of blood, and he'd cut his own arm on the broken bottle.

The moment the smell of blood hit the air—real blood, and lots of it—everything went still. For a long moment, nobody uttered a sound, nobody flicked an eyelid.

Then Juliet licked her lips.

Vampires rose to their feet. Both zombies sniffed the air and looked at Husky Boy, who'd rolled on his side and was trying to get up. As if hypnotized, they got down from their stools and staggered toward him.

I grabbed a handful of napkins and handed them to the kid. "Here," I said, "you'd better stop that bleeding." I raised him to his feet, but his knees kept buckling. So I picked him up like a child and turned to carry him out the door. Six vampires, their eyes glowing, blocked our way. Behind us, heavy zombie footsteps came closer.

"Kane!" I yelled, but even he was staring at the bleeding college student with a gleam in his eye. Even the most assimilated PAs can get stirred up by the smell of fresh blood.

To make things worse, the kid I was holding started flailing around. He still clutched the broken bottle, and I had to drop him to avoid being cut. He lashed out as he went down, slashing the leg of a norm tourist sitting next to us. Great—more blood. A woman screamed. A man jumped up, yelling, "Back off, you damn monsters!"

One of the zombies—the male, I think—bumped me from behind. A greenish arm reached around me, grasping, trying to get at one of the bleeders. I shoved backward so he crashed into the other zombie. I heard twin grunts as they hit the floor. From the front, a female vampire levitated, then flew straight at Husky Boy, fangs bared. I picked him up and threw him over my shoulder in a fireman's carry, then grabbed the bleeding tourist with my other hand. "Follow me," I shouted.

A dozen humans stampeded for the door. Kane had gotten himself under control and was growling at the vampires, hackles raised, in an effort to convince them that eating these norms would be a bad idea. I glanced behind us to see where the zombies were; both of them had crawled to the spot where the student went down and were licking his blood from the floor.

"Axel!" I yelled on my way out. "Toss the zombies some pretzels." Once their hunger gets stirred up, zombies have to eat—they have no choice.

Outside, Husky Boy's friend had snagged a taxi. I put both bleeders in the back and ordered the driver to take them to Mass General. I didn't think either one was really hurt, but better safe than sorry. And better still to get them out of here as fast as possible. The taxi took off with a screech as the bar door flew open and three vampires leaped outside. Someone else came out behind them, but I couldn't see who it was. I had three hungry vampires to calm down.

"Stop right there, all of you. There's no food here," I said.

The humans who'd run out with me had all disappeared. Either they'd taken off in their cars or had run for the human-controlled part of Boston, where the worst thing they'd face was a mugger with a gun. They might get robbed and killed, but at least they wouldn't get eaten.

The vampires sniffed the air. Suddenly one was right in my face, thanks to that superfast now-you-don't-see-'em, now-you-do movement they do. I knew this guy; he was one of Juliet's friends.

"They're gone, Gregor."

"You smell like blood." His eyes glowed like a cat's.

I looked down at my clothes. Husky Boy had bled all over me, down my front and probably down the back, too. Blood streaked my sweater and was beginning to stiffen the leather of my jeans. I was covered in the stuff.

"It's not mine, Gregor. I'm not human; I'm a shapeshifter, remember? Juliet's roommate?"

He blinked, as if my face had just come into focus. The light in his eyes faded. Vampires won't drink shifter or were-wolf blood. They don't like how it affects them. Those old legends that tell of vampires becoming bats and wolves? They're not legends. That's what happens when a vampire drinks the wrong kind of blood.

Gregor didn't apologize—I'd never met a vampire who apologized for anything. He just turned and walked back toward the bar. The other two followed him. They stopped briefly to sniff at the other person who'd come out. It was the cameraman, still filming. I hadn't realized it before, but the cameraman must've been a werewolf, because after a couple of sniffs the vampires left him and went back inside. He followed, camera on his shoulder.

Great. Footage like that would really boost Kane's pro-monster PR campaign.

When the door opened, frantic yelling erupted from inside. I heard Kane's voice: "Stop, damn it! Get off him!" Apparently, the fun wasn't over yet. I ran back inside.

In the middle of the room stood the director, screaming. He had a vampire hanging off his neck; the female zombie chewed on his ankle. Kane held the zombie by her feet and was trying to pull her away. Her green toes wiggled in his hands. One of her shoes had fallen off and lay on its side. Zombie Cinderella, dragged kicking and screaming from the ball.

Looked like the vampire was my job. With vampires, the trick is to get them to pull off voluntarily, so their fangs don't make hamburger out of the victim's flesh. The way the director was thrashing around, he was in danger of having some serious damage done to his neck.

Axel stood behind the vampire, holding a silver stake. A silver stake would immobilize a vampire but not kill him, unless it went directly through his heart. But it'd certainly hurt like hell. Other vampires stood in a semicircle, watching with keen eyes. None of the vamps would mess with Axel.

He liked to think it was because he was so tough, but the real reason was that they didn't want to get banned from Creature Comforts.

"Don't stake him, Axel," I called. "Not yet." My words made the vampire open his eyes and regard me over the director's neck. His throat pulsed as he swallowed. "Hold still," I said to the director, "or you're gonna lose a big chunk of your neck." He stopped struggling. Either my advice scared him or he was losing strength.

The vampire watched me, his eyes glowing yellow, as I came up to him, real close. I didn't know this vamp—some out-of-towner. The New Combat Zone attracted PA tourists as well as human ones. I placed my finger and thumb behind his ears and squeezed. It was almost like picking up a kitten by the scruff of its neck. If you're strong enough, sometimes this move can make a vampire retract his fangs. But this vamp was enjoying his feed too much for that.

"Okay," I whispered. "Here's plan A: You let go of this norm's neck willingly. If that doesn't happen, we move on to plan B. You wouldn't like plan B. It involves a silver stake and a very pissed-off bartender."

I squeezed a little harder. The vampire gasped—a good sign; he'd broken suction. But his fangs still pierced the director's flesh.

"Axel?" I said. "You ready?"

"Ready." Axel lifted the stake.

"Mmph, mmph! All right!" The vampire retracted his fangs and pulled back from the director, who collapsed on the floor. I checked his neck wound. Two small punctures, but no tearing. He'd have one hell of a hickey in the morning, but he'd be okay. The zombie, finally pulled off by Kane, hadn't done much more than fray the hem of the director's jeans. All told, he was in damn good shape for someone who'd survived a double-monster attack. The cameraman, finally putting down his camera, bent over his boss.

"Bar's closed," Axel said. "Everybody out. And you—" He looked at the out-of-town vampire, whose lips were crimson with the director's blood. "You'd better get out of here now, before the cops arrive. It'd be a really smart idea if you left town within, oh, the next five minutes or so."

It was the longest speech I'd ever heard Axel make. He must've been really angry.

Silently, the vampires dispersed. Juliet brushed my arm. "I'll see you at home," she said.

The director had regained consciousness. He sat up woozily, then leaned back against the cameraman. "Cut," he croaked. Then he smiled as the vampire-saliva high hit.

"Don't worry, I got the whole thing," the cameraman said. "Every minute."

"Hold on," said Kane. He'd settled the zombies back at the bar and given them a couple of cases of potato chips to munch on. They crunched away happily. "I demand that you give me the tape."

The drugged-out director squinted at him. "Huh?"

The werewolf cameraman stepped in between them. "No way. I'm selling that tape to the highest bidder. You want to make an offer, fine. You can bid against all the news outlets— and Baldwin's campaign."

Kane grabbed the camera, but the cameraman had already removed the tape. He patted his jacket. "Want to fight me for it?" he snarled.

Kane's hackles rose, and for a minute I thought he'd go for it. Then Axel spoke up. "No werewolf brawls in here tonight. Take it outside if you're gonna settle things that way."

"Don't worry, Axel." I stepped in front of Kane and smoothed his lapel. Trust me to get between two snarling werewolves. "We've got bigger things to worry about right now."

"Bigger things?" Kane said. "If Baldwin's camp gets its hands on that tape, it'll send PA rights back to the Stone Age." He turned to the director, who was back on his feet and looking blissful, like he could hear choirs of angels singing "Happy Birthday" to him. "I paid both of you to be here tonight," Kane said. "That tape is legally mine. In fact, I'm going to find a judge and slap an injunction on you so fast—"

"What?" said the werewolf. "My head will spin? Somehow, after what happened tonight, that doesn't worry me too much. Come on, Joe, let's get out of here." He put an arm around the director and helped him across the room.

When they reached the door, the cameraman turned back. "See you on TV." He sneered and was gone.

What a night. I'd been threatened by a Hellion, questioned by a cop (a hot cop, admittedly), and caught in the middle of a monster-human bar fight. And by tomorrow morning, my blood-smeared face would be all over TV.

13

IT WAS ALMOST THREE IN THE MORNING WHEN KANE AND I walked together along Washington Street in the New Combat Zone. The night was cold and clear. Stars shone overhead, and the waxing moon lit our way. He should've had his arm around me, or at least been holding my hand. Instead, we each held hands with a zombie.

Kane led the male, and I towed the female along behind me. Both zombies were exhausted, wiped out by the evening's excitement. Human blood had that effect on zombies: frenzied bloodlust, followed by extreme torpor. That's why you didn't find a whole lot of zombie orderlies in hospital emergency rooms. Left alone, our zombies would've sunk down in the street and stayed there until the sun started eating into their skin, so it was up to us to get them home. But guiding this zombie through the streets was about as easy as dragging a refrigerator. I tugged, she took a half-step, then fell forward against me.

"What were you thinking, anyway," I asked irritably, "putting zombies in a television commercial?"

Kane, trying to lift his zombie in a fireman's hold, scowled at me. "Don't call them zombies; it's insulting. They're previously deceased humans." He gave up trying to carry his "previously deceased human" and resumed half-dragging, half-leading the guy. "Previously deceased" was right. A corpse couldn't be any stiffer than a zonked-out zombie.

"Can the politically correct labels, Counselor," I said. "I'm not in the mood to have my language policed."

"They deserve our respect, just like anyone else," he said,

manhandling his zombie off the curb. "Which term do *you* prefer: Cerddorion or freak?"

For a moment, the Goon Squad's Norden flashed across my mind, the way he'd sneered, calling me just that: a freak. Okay, so it wasn't my favorite memory. Maybe Kane had a point. Not that I was going to admit it.

"You're avoiding my question, Kane. Why did you bring these . . . um . . . these two into Creature Comforts?"

"I wanted to show that PAs—not just the previously deceased, but *all* of us—can mix with humans without fear or threat of danger to either side." He shook his head, then sighed. "Didn't quite work out that way, did it?"

He dropped his head, his silver hair touched by the moonlight. He looked so despondent that I softened a little. I squeezed his shoulder with my free hand. "That human kid started it. Everything was going fine before he tried to jump you." And before the monsters gave the concept of bloodlust a whole new meaning. But I didn't say that part.

Kane's shoulder rose and fell under my hand in a shrug. "Yeah, but do you think the media's going to show that? Tomorrow morning, every news channel, every newspaper, every Web site and blog will feature one image: that director with a vampire sucking on his neck and a zombie chomping his ankle." The fact that Kane had used the word *zombie* showed how upset he was. "I knew I should've hired PAs only."

Well, that werewolf cameraman had been willing to fight Kane for the tape, and probably to the death, knowing werewolves. But I didn't say that, either. After all, when the opportunity to make a quick buck arises, PAs and norms come out even in the greed stakes.

Up ahead, on the other side of the street, two figures appeared at the corner. They were too far away for me to make out their features, but something about them made me think of my earlier visitors—the ones who'd broken down my door. "Goon Squad!" I hissed in a loud whisper, shoving my zombie sideways into the shadows of a recessed doorway.

The zombie tripped first, going over like a bowling pin. I

sprawled on top of her. Underneath us, something groaned and cursed, sounding more sleepy and annoyed than hurt. We'd stumbled over a vampire junkie sleeping it off.

A silhouette loomed over us, features indistinguishable with the moonlight behind. I braced myself, expecting to see Norden's gun shoved in my face. By now, he'd undoubtedly read up on shapeshifters enough to know that, yes, guns could hurt me. Bad.

"What are you doing?" Kane asked, his voice perfectly calm.

"Shh. Didn't you see? Goon Squad patrol." I rolled deeper into the doorway, motioning to Kane to follow. If the Goons hadn't seen us, we could still hide. "Don't step on the junkie."

He stayed where he was.

"Kane, are you crazy? If they catch these two out of Deadtown without a permit, they'll take them away."

He laughed, a deep, silvery chuckle that gradually rose in pitch and intensity. I peered out of my hiding place. Kane held his stomach and threw back his head, looking ready to howl at the moon. Except he was laughing. Usually I like Kane's laugh—and heaven knew he could use one right then— but it's hard to enjoy somebody's mirth when you have no idea what's so goddamn funny.

"I'm sorry," he said, wiping his eyes. "It's just that, well, you took off so fast, and then, *boom!*" He clutched his stomach again. Across the street, the figures stopped. And looked directly at us. They weren't Norden and Sykes, but they were definitely Goons. They stepped into the street and headed our way.

They got bigger and meaner-looking as they got closer. Showdown time. I stood and stepped out of the doorway. The zombies were out of it, and Kane had finally cracked under all the pressure or something. It was up to me to handle the situation.

The only problem was, I didn't have a clue how.

I tensed, ready for a fight. The human Goon I could take easily, but not his zombie partner. Not on my own. There was only one way. I'd have to shift. Into something big and dangerous and preferably armor plated. I didn't like to shift this close to the full moon—it made the animal consciousness stronger—but if I was going to protect Kane and these zombies, I had no choice.

I closed my eyes and focused. A rhinoceros. It was the only thing I could think of that might work. I'd seen one on a rampage on a nature show, trampling everything in its path. I brought that image to mind and tried to feel the rhino's anger. Threat . . . rage . . . protect my own. I felt a bubbling sensation under my skin as the shift began, a hardening at the tip of my nose, my limbs starting to thicken. God, I hoped I could hang on to enough of my personality to keep from goring the Goons to death. Then the bubbling intensified into a throb, and I didn't care anymore. Pain shot through my head as my skull began to lengthen and grow.

A hand on my arm startled me out of my concentration. How dare—? But the touch was gentle, and I opened my eyes to see somebody . . . No, wait, I knew this being. Kane. It was Kane, looking perfectly normal and in control. "Don't, Vicky," he said. "It's not necessary."

Not necessary. Not necessary. The meaning of those words got through, and I tried to slam on the brakes. Once a shift has started, it takes a huge amount of effort and will to cut it short. I staggered backward, thinking, *Stop, stop, stop.* I pictured my image in the mirror, my strawberry blonde hair, my heart-shaped face. I focused on what it feels like to be me—me, in my body. No armor plating, no horns. The pain in my confused body doubled me over, and I clutched my stomach as the throbbing subsided back to a bubbling, then gave way to nausea and a splitting headache. If Kane had waited five seconds longer to say "not necessary," it would've been too late.

"She all right?" a voice asked.

"Fine, fine," I heard Kane reply, sounding all hale and hearty and aren't-we-all-good-old-boys. "A little too much to drink, that's all."

Thanks, Kane. Here I was, ready to risk my life to protect him, and he's telling the cops I'm a drunk. I'd kick his ass for that. As soon as I could stand up straight again.

Kane and the Goons were discussing what a fine evening it was. As the world gradually came back into focus around me, I saw Kane hand some papers to the human Goon. He inspected them for a moment, then gave them back.

"Need help getting everyone home?" he asked, sounding downright friendly.

I stepped forward. More like a weave, really, but it was forward. "No, thanks." My voice came out as a bellow, sounding like, well, an angry rhino. I cleared my throat. "We're fine."

The human Goon shook his head and shot Kane a sympathetic look. Then he and his partner resumed their patrol, and I smacked Kane in the shoulder.

"I thought you didn't have permits for those zombies!"

He looked surprised. "Why would you think that?"

"At Creature Comforts. You told Daniel you'd taken them out of Deadtown without a permit."

"Stop saying 'zombie.' Anyway, I'm a lawyer. Do you seriously think I'd break the law *and* risk the lives of these two people? Of course I got permits."

He tugged on his half-asleep zombie, who shambled forward, and they moved along Washington Street. I was faced with the problem of getting my zombie back on her feet. She lay facedown in the doorway, one arm thrown across the vampire junkie. They looked almost cozy together—or would have, if either of them had looked a little less like death warmed over.

I yanked on her arm, which raised her off the ground a bit, but she was so stiff—nothing would bend the way it was supposed to—that I couldn't get her to her feet.

"Will you hurry up?" Kane called from down the street. "I've got at least two dozen phone calls I should be making right now."

I looked down at my zombie and her junkie companion, then stepped over the pair of them to get behind her. Crouching, I got both arms under her, one at the armpit and the other at midthigh. I called on the remnants of brute rhinoceros strength and heaved. As I straightened, I lifted her from the ground. I stepped over the junkie and out of the doorway. It was like carrying a plank, but I had her.

The zombie groaned and squirmed a bit, and I shushed her like a mother comforting a half-awake infant. As we passed under a streetlight, I could see clumps of powder sticking to her greenish-gray cheek. This female may have been human once, but she sure as hell wasn't now. She was a zombie—and she'd still be a zombie no matter what politically correct name Kane or anybody else called her. She uttered another small groan.

"C'mon, hon," I said, "Let's get you home." Still weaving a little, I hurried down the block after Kane.

WE PASSED THROUGH THE TREMONT STREET CHECKPOINT into Deadtown and almost immediately ran into Tina and one of her friends. They both wore low-slung jeans and tight belly shirts that showed off a couple of inches of zombie pelvis. The temperature was close to freezing, but the undead don't feel the cold.

"What's with the crashed-out zombies?" Tina asked.

"Don't call them zombies," Kane said. "It's demeaning to them and you both."

Tina rolled her bloodred eyes in the way only a teenage girl can, and then looked at me inquiringly.

"Kane was making a political commercial."

Tina's jaw dropped. "A commercial? Like for TV? Why didn't you ask me? I would've—"

"You had school," I reminded her. "In fact, is school even out for the night yet?"

Tina and her friend exchanged a look.

"Tina, you of all people should know better." Tina and a friend—this one, maybe—had gotten zombified because they'd skipped school to go shopping. If Tina hadn't cut class that day, she would've been miles away from the plague zone.

She shrugged. "So what? I mean, what's gonna happen to us now? We're already dead."

Good point. But still. "If you want to learn demon-fighting, you've got to be willing to study."

"I am! I'm reading that book you gave me. Jenna even saw me, didn't you, Jenna?" Tina's friend nodded and popped her gum. "Anyway," Tina said, "stop trying to change the subject." She planted herself directly in front of Kane, fists on her skinny hips. "How come you didn't ask me to be on TV? I'd be way better than those two corpses. Are you sure they're even reanimated?"

"I don't have time for this nonsense." Kane moved on, guiding his zombie around the two girls.

"Hey—"

"Tina, don't bug him now. He's had a bad night."

"Oh, yeah? Well, what about me? I—"

"You," I said, "should be studying. I'll come over and quiz you on the first twenty-five pages of Russom—"

"*Twenty-five?* But that's—"

"The first twenty-five pages, tomorrow night, before school. Six o'clock—be ready."

"Or what?"

"Or our deal's off. If you're not going to be serious, I'm not going to teach you."

Tina kicked at the curb. "Could you at least bring your flamethrower? That was cool."

It was my turn for an eye-roll. It was a pretty good one, I thought, for an old lady of twenty-eight.

BOTH ZOMBIES WERE SAFE IN THEIR BEDS, SLEEPING IT OFF. They'd snooze through the day and wake up around sunset, starving, but no longer craving human blood. Five or six pizzas each, and they'd be as good as new. Or as good as newly risen, anyway.

Kane put his arm around me and pulled me close as we walked. I snuggled in, enjoying his warmth, the solidity of his body. I sighed contentedly, happy to be in this moment.

Safe and warm. Then I ducked out from under his arm. The things I had to discuss with Kane weren't exactly cuddly.

He looked at me, surprised, when I pulled away.

"Kane," I said, "I know you're worried about that tape, but I wasn't exaggerating when I said we've got bigger things to worry about."

"Yes?"

I told him about what happened on Commodore Wharf: killing the Harpies, Difethwr's arrival, its message and sudden departure. Goose bumps prickled my arms as I talked, and when I mentioned the Destroyer the demon mark itched. Kane listened intently, nodding from time to time.

"This is what you were talking to Costello about?"

"Yeah." I watched for any flash of jealousy but came up empty. Kane was focused on our Hellion problem. Well, that was good. I guess. "He's going to talk to the Witches of the Shield, see if they have any idea who punched a hole in it."

"And whether they can find the hole and repair it?"

"They can't do that! Not while the Destroyer is running around Boston. They'd trap it inside the city. It'll tear the place apart."

"From what you say, that's its plan, anyway. They've got to fix the shield soon, Vicky, or more Hellions will come."

I was worried about that, too. A legion of Hellions would attack in one terrifying strike, destroying everything in its path. No building left standing, no survivors. It was possible that Difethwr, or the sorcerer who'd bound it, was calling to others of its kind. A sorcerer would have to be insane to try to raise a legion of Hellions—but any sorcerer who'd dare to bind Difethwr was already just plain crazy or else too arrogant to be on speaking terms with reality.

Kane half turned toward me. "Was the Hellion there for you or for your client?"

"Me. Definitely me. I didn't force it off, Kane. I didn't fight it at all, except for throwing some salt around. It delivered a message to me, then it left."

"Are you sure, though? It killed one of your clients already, and it didn't speak to you then. It didn't even show up while you were there."

I remembered that evil presence in George Funderburk's bedroom and shivered. True, the Hellion hadn't spoken to me then. But it had been close by. Very close by. My demon mark tingled at the memory. That night, perhaps the sorcerer had called the Destroyer but not yet bound it. And the Hellion, searching for the source of the call, had responded to its own essence. In me. The thought made me queasy.

Kane was still speaking. "You can't assume that the connection is you. It might be something else entirely."

"Like what?"

"Well, both men had been suffering from demon infestations."

"Drudes versus Harpies. Not the same at all."

"Okay, I'll take your word for that. So it's not the clients' demons. But my point still holds. There might be another connection, one we're not seeing."

I stopped in my tracks. "Are you even *listening* to me? The Hellion said my name. It went there to find me." My voice sounded shrill, even to my own ears.

"Maybe you're right." He took my hand. "Maybe I just don't want something that nasty to be coming after you." We walked for a while in silence. His hand felt strong, clasped around mine.

We stopped at Kane's building on Winter Street. He folded his arms around me and drew me close against him. I pressed my face into his muscled chest. He was warm, so warm, and even here in the middle of the city he smelled like a forest after a summer rain.

He stroked my hair. "Do you want to come in?"

Yes, I thought. More than anything, I wanted to go up to Kane's apartment and feel warm and protected in his king-sized bed. I was tired of standing alone against the demons. I wanted Kane to hold me and fill me with his strength and let me know that everything was all right. But I had things to do. I sighed, rubbing my cheek against his jacket. "I thought you had two dozen phone calls to make."

"I can make them later." He put a finger under my chin and gently lifted my face to his. His lips met mine, and the kiss melted through me like warm chocolate. I wanted to press myself closer to him, explore more deeply, feel those lips touch my skin all over. But I shook my head.

"I can't. I've got to get cleaned up, then go back to the North End to collect the rest of my fee from Lucado."

All that melting warmth evaporated as Kane went rigid. His arms dropped away from me as he stepped back. His eyes narrowed. "Did you say Lucado—*Frank* Lucado?"

"Yeah. The real estate developer. He was my client to-night."

"You did a job for Frank Lucado."

"I just said I did. So what?"

He made an exasperated noise. "Vicky, Lucado is one of the biggest contributors to Seth Baldwin's campaign."

"So?"

"So? *So?* How can you say 'so'? You helped a guy who wants to drive us out of the state."

"I didn't help him. I did a job for him. When I'm on the job, I don't care what my client's politics are."

"It's not a matter of his personal politics. Lucado has spent a couple million dollars to support a candidate who'd strip PAs of all legal rights and protections. *All* of them, Vicky. If Baldwin wins, any human could kill you or me and still be acting within the law."

"I know that."

"And you don't care, do you? Anything to make a buck. Even if it comes out of the pocket of a bigoted criminal."

"Lucado's never been convicted of anything. And just be-cause the guy's a jerk doesn't mean he deserves to suffer Harpy attacks night after night. I don't discriminate in my clients."

"No, not you. Only if they're poor. Then demons can tor-ment them forever, for all you care."

That was a low blow. In truth, most of my clients were wealthy because the wealthy had more demons. Take Har-pies. Rich people had rich enemies. Hiring a sorcerer to sic a flock of Harpies on somebody was illegal, and that meant it wasn't cheap. People with no money usually took a more direct route—like using their fists—to settle their differences. But I wasn't going to argue that point with Kane tonight.

I glared at him. "You have no right to tell me who I can or can't take on as a client."

"And you have no principles." That was Kane—he lived for peace, justice, and the American way. Oh, and turning into a huge, slavering, bloodthirsty wolf whenever the moon was full. He squared his shoulders, making a visible effort to control his anger. "Well, you've already done the job, so there's no point in arguing about it. Just stay away from him from now on, all right?"

"I don't know. I thought I'd invite him to go down to Baldwin's campaign headquarters and stuff envelopes with me."

"Not funny. Vicky—" He put his hand on my arm, and I jerked away. For a moment, I thought with longing about how close we'd been, how warm I was, just a few minutes ago. Oh, the hell with it. I wasn't going to take orders from a politically correct werewolf. Or anybody else, for that matter. I turned away.

"Wait—" For a second, I thought he was going to apologize, and a little warm spot opened up inside me. I looked at Kane, ready to be generous, ready to accept his admission that he was wrong. "I just thought of something," he said, his eyes thoughtful. The warm spot froze over. How could I forget—Kane was always right. In Kane's own mind, anyway.

"What?"

"That Hellion showed up at Lucado's condo, right?"

"Yes." Whatever Kane was thinking, it was so interesting to him that he didn't notice I was throwing icy monosyllables at him.

"What if the Destroyer *was* after Lucado? You took the job just yesterday, didn't you?"

"Right."

"So, what if the Hellion went there to claim another victim? Then it saw you there and got sidetracked."

"What if it did? I don't see where you're going with this."

"Maybe the sorcerer is on *our* side. If Lucado's dead, Baldwin loses a big source of revenue. The election is less than a week away. Both sides are pouring money into their campaigns. By taking out Lucado, someone's trying to slow Baldwin down."

He gestured as though he'd just finished his closing argument to a jury. Clearly, he thought he'd nailed it. I shook my head. Time for the rebuttal.

"If the sorcerer had wanted Lucado dead, he'd be dead." And so would I. "Whoever sent the Destroyer called it away after it had delivered the message. It was a warning, Kane, not politics."

He didn't look convinced. "Besides," I continued, "the Destroyer boasted that it's going to obliterate the whole city. If Boston's toast, it doesn't exactly matter who wins the election."

"Someone's got to be governor. Might as well be our guy." Kane's eyes shone. He was really taken with the idea that someone was trying to rub out Baldwin's biggest supporter. "Okay, you did the job. Fine. But now stay away from Lucado. It's not safe."

"I've got to collect the money he owes me."

"Sure, sure. But after that, you're done with the guy, right?"

The truth was, I didn't have any reason to hang around Lucado after he'd handed over the second half of his payment. But I didn't want Kane to think I was doing what he told me to do. "We'll see."

He sighed. "You're impossible, Vicky." He leaned over and gave me a peck on the cheek. "But I do kinda like you."

"Kinda, huh? Be still my heart." I said it lightly, but part of me was still mad at him. And another part—a very big part—was aching for another one of those long, deep kisses. Clearly, and in too many ways to count, tonight was not my lucky night.

After Kane went into his building, I headed home, thinking about what he'd said. For all his high-and-mighty principles, Kane would be thrilled if somebody offed Lucado. Just to undermine Baldwin's campaign. Kane would never attack Lucado himself, but I was pretty sure that he wouldn't lift a finger to save the guy, either. For me, ethics were a lot simpler. If you had a problem and you could afford my fee, I'd help you out. And if you were a demon and you came after me, I'd kill you. So I wouldn't win the Nobel Peace Prize any time soon. My system worked for me.

14

JULIET WASN'T THERE WHEN I GOT HOME. PROBABLY ALL that bloodlust at Creature Comforts had sent her out on the prowl. I peeled off my bloodstained clothes and checked the mirror. I'd cleaned up a little in the ladies' room at the bar, but I was in dire need of a shower. I took a quick one and then crawled into bed. I was due back at Lucado's at seven to show him the dead Harpies and finish our business. I set the alarm for six thirty—a mere three hours away—and was fast asleep two minutes later.

I dreamed of my father, or tried to.

I tried to call him on the dream phone. I pictured him the way he looked at my high school graduation—my proud, happy father, his temples touched with gray, standing up and cheering, putting two fingers in his mouth to whistle. The vision was so clear I could feel the hot June sun beating down, could smell the roses he'd given me when I collected my diploma. I reached out to touch his arm, but there was some kind of invisible barrier between us. So I just pictured him. I visualized and visualized, but his colors, purple and green, didn't appear. The connection remained closed.

I wasn't surprised that the call failed. I'd sometimes tried to contact my father in the years since his death—every night, at first—and never succeeded. But I was still disappointed. I didn't know whether the dead were simply beyond our reach, behind that invisible barrier, or whether Difethwr's taunt was true. What if the Hellion *had* obliterated my father's soul? It was a question whose answer I didn't dare pursue.

The vision of my father faded, and I fell into a deep, dreamless sleep. It felt like falling into despair.

* * *

THE JAG WOULDN'T START. WELL, I GUESS I KNEW WHERE the money from last night's job was going. My poor baby needed a checkup.

I jogged to the edge of Deadtown, the bag with the dead Harpies banging against my knees, and flagged down a cab. All the way to the North End, the driver kept sniffing, but he didn't ask what the smell was. He'd probably had worse-smelling things in his backseat.

I stepped onto Commodore Wharf just in time to see the sun rise over Boston Harbor. Streaks of red, purple, and gold stretched across the sky, reflected in the placid water. No wonder the norms associate this kind of glorious sky with new beginnings. The darkness is gone, the night creatures have fled back to their lairs, a new beauty tinges the earth. It was the perfect time to show Frank Lucado that his demons were a thing of the past.

But the Frank Lucado who answered the door did not look happy. He scowled violently, his scar bisecting his face, and jerked his head to indicate I should follow him inside. Since inside was where his checkbook was, I did. He closed the door behind me.

"What the hell did you do to Wendy?"

"Who?"

"My bodyguard. I woke up this morning, the guy was a puddle on the floor. He roused himself long enough to tell me he quit. Then he ran outa here like a kid making a break from the principal's office."

"Wait. Your bodyguard's name is Wendy?" I couldn't quite put that name together with the six-and-a-half-foot Man Mountain who'd welcomed me the night before.

"Wendy, yeah. Short for Wendell." Somehow Wendell didn't seem to fit either, but at least it didn't sound like Peter Pan's girlfriend. Wendy. Jeez. No wonder the guy had an attitude. "So what'd you do to him?" Lucado said. "I've never seen anyone so scared."

"Nothing." Nothing besides saving his life, but I wasn't

really eager to fill Lucado in on those details. I just wanted to get my money and get out. "Some people are just spooked by demons, I guess. How'd you sleep, by the way?"

He smiled, looking relaxed for the first time since I'd met him. "Like a newborn babe in his mother's arms," he said.

"Well, get used to it. Those three Harpies won't be bothering you anymore."

"You got all three?" he asked. I nodded. "Let's see 'em."

I opened the bag. Even though I'd packed the carcasses in lavender, mint, and pine boughs, the stench of dead Harpies blasted into the room. Nothing could cover up that smell. Lucado, who'd been leaning over the bag to look inside, covered his nose with both hands and took three steps backward.

"Jesus, those things stink," he said. "One night without them, and already I'd forgotten how bad."

"They're worse when they're dead. Here—" I pulled the menthol cream from my pocket. "Dab some of this under your nose. It'll help."

"Naw, that's okay." Pinching his nostrils shut, he looked into the open bag. Three dead Harpies stared back at him with open beaks, their snaky hair in limp tangles. "All right. Zip it up." As I did, he went to a desk and pulled out his checkbook. I gave him my boilerplate affidavit to sign, affirming that I'd performed the service for which he'd hired me, and he signed it with a flourish. It would've been nice to have Wendy there as a witness, but this would do.

"What do you do with those things?" Lucado asked, nodding at the body bag.

"Burn them."

He nodded his approval. "I thought of having one of the bastards stuffed, but I never want to see 'em again. Ever."

"Taxidermy wouldn't work, anyway. Nobody can see them except you and me."

"No kidding? Can they smell them?"

"Sort of. When somebody passes through a place where Harpies have been recently, they sometimes get a whiff of that smell. They might wrinkle their noses or check the bottom of their shoes, but usually they don't know what it is."

He made a face. "Smells like somebody puked on a pile of dead rats." Wow, the guy was a poet. But it was a pretty accurate description, actually.

Lucado opened a closet door and started putting on a wool coat and scarf. "You need a ride?" he asked. "My limo's waiting downstairs."

"Uh, yeah. Sure. Thanks." Usually I don't accept any favors from clients after the job is done and we're all square. But I'd never been in a limo. And I'd decided to warn Lucado about Difethwr. Kane wouldn't like that, but I owed the guy a warning. Neglecting to mention the Hellion's visit didn't seem like playing fair. See? I did have principles. They didn't always line up with Kane's, that's all.

The limo was one of those stretch jobs, black with little lights around the windows. Inside it was even roomier than I'd expected. It had a curved bench seat made of supersoft leather. I could've stretched out full length on it. Not that I tried. I didn't turn on the flat-screen TV, play with the electric windows, or rifle through the bar, either, even though I was tempted. There are occasions when a girl's gotta show some class.

"Where you headed?" Lucado asked.

"Back to Deadtown."

"Is my Milk Street site close enough?"

"Sure." Not only did the limo have a TV, it had a video game console, a sound system, and a computer. I wondered if the computer had online access. Also, a mini fridge. Hell, I could live in there—it had all the comforts of home.

But I needed to talk to Lucado about Difethwr. I didn't think he was in danger, but on the off chance Kane might be right, I didn't want to leave him unprepared. "Mr. Lucado, about your bodyguard—"

"Frank."

"I thought you said his name was Wendy—Wendell."

"No, me. Call me Frank. Mr. Lucado's my old man. Everybody calls me Frank or Frankie."

"Frank. Okay. Well, Frank, I want to talk to you about

what happened last night, while you were asleep. I know why Wendell quit."

"Good man, Wendy. He'll come back. He's been with me for fifteen years. Doesn't scare easy, but those damn demons must've scared the hell out of him. I don't blame—" He stopped, then frowned. "I thought you said nobody else could see 'em."

"That's right. But those Harpies weren't the only demons at your place last night." I told him about Difethwr's visit. I told him that I'd encountered the Hellion before. The only part I held back was about Dad. Some things are too painful to turn into stories.

As he listened, Lucado's face moved from attentiveness to a scowl, the scar puckering his eyebrow, his dead eye looking at nothing.

"I don't think it was coming for you," I said, finishing up. "As I said, I've got a history with this thing. But I thought I should warn you, anyway. What you need to do is find a competent witch and buy a good, strong demon-repelling charm. Tell the witch you need protection against Hellions."

I'd hired a witch to create a Hellion-repelling charm for Gwen's house, right after the plague, because Needham is outside Boston's shield. It was expensive, but the witch renewed it monthly, and it worked like, well, a charm.

"I can recommend a witch, if you'd like," I told Frank.

"Not good enough." He turned his head so that it looked like he was staring at me with his blind eye. The only part of his face I could see was violently slashed by his scar. It was unnerving. I don't think anyone who saw the scar ever asked Frank what had happened to the other guy. You just didn't want to know.

But if I could look a Gorgon-headed Harpy in the eye, I could do the same with Frank Lucado. I stared at him straight on. "What do you mean, not good enough? There's a Hellion loose in Boston. A charm can keep it away from you."

"That's not how I figure it." He rolled his eyes, but since I couldn't see his good eye, the blind one just seemed to ricochet around its socket. I shifted in my seat and leaned over so I could see both eyes.

"What do you mean?"

"Here's how it looks to me. I hire you to do a job—"

"Which I did."

"True. I'll give you that. But you did a hell of a lot more."

Uh-oh. Suddenly I had a feeling I knew where this was going.

Frank held up his hand and, as he spoke, ticked items off on his fingers. "You killed those Harpies, but from what you're telling me, you lured something worse into my home. What did you call it?"

"A Hellion," I muttered, slumping in the leather seat.

"Right. A Hellion. So this Hellion, a thing I never even heard of before, may or may not be out to get me. Now I've got to go out and buy an expensive charm just in case. Besides that, you scared off the best bodyguard I ever had, leaving me with no protection. That sound about right to you?"

I wasn't the one who had scared off Wendy, but it seemed like a moot point. I shrugged. Frank was going to stop payment on his check, I could just feel it. If I had to take him to court to make him pay up, even with the signed affidavit, it'd cost me more in time and court fees than the check was worth.

"So," Frank continued, "the way I figure it, you owe me some protection."

I glared at him. "I don't work for free."

He smiled. "I like you, Vaughn. You say what's on your mind." He looked out the window. We were only a block from Lucado's construction site on Milk Street. I was just beginning to think that maybe he'd let me off the hook after all when he turned to me again. "What's your beef with this Hellion?"

His question took me by surprise, but I still wasn't going to say what it had done to my father. "My family has been at war with demons for centuries."

"So that's it, huh? Some ancient blood feud?" He nodded. "I can understand that."

The limo glided to a halt. The driver started to get out, but Frank punched the intercom button. "Take it once around the block," he said.

"I've got things to do," I protested.

"Hear me out first."

I looked at him, then nodded. Frank rapped on the glass divider, and the limo pulled back into traffic as smoothly as a sailboat on a glassy lake.

"So talk," I said.

Frank looked me up and down, not like he was leering, but like he was sizing me up. The look held both assessment and respect. "We need to come to a new arrangement," he said. "I'm gonna put you on the payroll."

I shook my head. "Uh-uh. Sorry, Frank. I'm a free agent. I work for myself."

"I need protection. Thanks to you, I ain't got any right now, *and* I got some kinda demon from Hell on my tail. You wanna kill the demon. It's a match made in heaven."

Somehow, I couldn't think of Frank and myself in those terms. I started to say so, but he interrupted. We were coming up on the drop-off point again.

"Look at it this way: who's going to pay you to kill that Hellion if I don't? You can settle your blood feud—and get paid for it. I can go back to sleeping at night. It's what I call a mutually beneficial situation."

"Mutually beneficial, huh?" He had a point, now that I thought about it. But then I thought of an entirely different point. Kane would *not* be happy if I agreed to protect Lucado. Not one bit. I remembered how he'd looked in front of his building, pulling away from me and trying to order me to stay away from Lucado. The annoyance I'd felt then flared up again now. So he wouldn't like it. So what? Nobody, not even Kane in alpha mode, could tell me what to do.

"All right, Frank. I'll sign on as your protection until the Hellion is killed. You pay me five hundred a day, plus expenses."

"Three hundred flat."

"Three-fifty. And you provide meals on the job."

He stuck out his hand. "Welcome to the team."

I explained that Difethwr would attack only at night, and I needed to get some supplies before I started my first shift. We agreed that I'd meet him at his condo at seven and stand guard overnight. In the meantime, I'd grab some much-needed sleep. I climbed out of the limo, trying to look like I rode in a car like that every day, surreptitiously glancing around to see if anyone I knew was watching. No such luck.

Of course, now that I was on the team, I might catch a ride home this way every day. Me, on Frank Lucado's team. God, what would Kane say?

15

WHEN I GOT OFF THE ELEVATOR, I COULD ALREADY HEAR Juliet's TV blaring through the closed door of our apartment. I unlocked the door and walked inside—to see myself, in all my life-sized, blood-spattered glory, in a still photo behind an overdressed anchorwoman. The caption read "Boston shapeshifter saves human." Lovely.

Juliet hadn't gone to bed yet. She sat on the sofa, a bowl of popcorn in her lap.

"How bad is it?" I asked.

She glanced at me and smiled, showing her fangs. "We're famous," she said. "Top story on CNN; they're showing the tape almost continuously. I look good, but you're definitely the star. Look, it's coming on again." She nodded at the screen and tossed some popcorn in her mouth.

My God. The segment started with the humans stampeding out of Creature Comforts, then cut to me, blood all over my face, hands, and clothes, yelling "There's no food here" at the vampires. Then the picture jumped inside the bar, showing the director screaming while the out-of-town vampire and the female zombie gnawed on various body parts. Kane was shouting and trying to drag the zombie away. There was a close-up of Juliet, watching with an amused half-smile and stirring her Bloody Mary, then I charged in like the cavalry to grab the vampire and detach him from the director's neck. And that was it. That was America's view of what had happened in Creature Comforts last night.

From there, the network cut to a talking head in a studio: a female professor of paranormal zoology at Boston University. Her commentary didn't help much. She didn't support outlawing PAs, but even as she spoke in favor of keeping PAs legal, she managed to convey the impression that we monsters were a bunch of wild animals. She was more interested in studying PAs than in learning to live with us—like Sheila Gravett and her biotech lab.

While the so-called expert was prattling away, CNN replayed the part of the tape that showed Kane pulling on the zombie's ankles and me pinching the nape of the vampire's neck. The director's face contorted and his eyes squinched shut as he screamed. The images definitely didn't convey an impression of "let's all get along and live happily ever after." The BU professor never even bothered to point out that the guy's saviors—Kane and me—were every bit as paranormal as the creatures attacking him.

Watching the CNN coverage was like witnessing a car wreck. You didn't want to see it, but you couldn't look away. Kane was going to be livid.

The network cut to a story about some pop singer who'd been arrested for drunk driving, and Juliet hit the Mute button. "Has Kane called?" I asked.

Juliet selected a piece of popcorn from the bowl as she shook her head. "That cop did, though. The good-looking human one from the bar."

"Daniel?" I felt a flutter in my stomach, then remembered the only thing I'd put in it since last night had been three shots of tequila. That would explain the fluttery feeling. Sure it would. "What did he say?"

"He wants you to call him. Something about witches—he didn't say more than that. You know how cops are. Especially norm cops." She held up a piece of popcorn, then stuck out her tongue and placed the piece on the tip. She curled her tongue around the kernel and drew it into her mouth. "Mmm." Trust Juliet to turn eating popcorn into soft-core porn.

"Did you write down his message?"

Juliet waved vaguely in the direction of the phone. She crunched another piece of popcorn, then licked her fingers, one by one. "He likes you, you know."

"I'm helping him with an investigation."

"Hah, that's amusing. I'm sure he'd enjoy investigating you." She threw a piece of popcorn into the air and caught it between her teeth, then let it fall into her mouth.

"Don't be ridiculous. And look, this is how you're supposed to eat popcorn." I grabbed a handful and shoved it into my mouth. I could feel my cheeks bulge like a chipmunk's. When I swallowed, my stomach felt a little more normal. "Not everything has to be a sex act, you know."

"Who's acting?" Juliet's leer showed her fangs in their full glory. "Stop changing the subject. That delicious-looking cop wants to get to know you better. Are you going to do anything about it?"

"I'm a witness in one of his cases—cops can't fool around with their witnesses, you know. Plus, I'm already dating someone." Although I wondered whether that would still be true after Kane found out that I was on assignment for Lucado.

"Dating? When's the last time you and Kane had an actual date? You both work too hard. You see each other, what, maybe once every ten days? That's three whole times a month."

More like twice a month, unless he had to rescue me from the Goon Squad, but I wasn't going to admit that. "Our work is important to us. That's why we're good together. Neither of us makes demands on the other."

"You call that being *good* together?"

"Well, what do you call it?"

She shook her head. "When that oh-so-yummy cop looks at you, the whole room starts buzzing. You shouldn't let that kind of attraction go to waste."

"You're telling me I should cheat on Kane?"

"You're the one who insists that you two aren't 'going steady.'" Her voice took on a sarcastic tone as her bloodred nails wiggled quotation marks in the air.

"Yeah, but that's only because we're both too busy to date anyone else."

Juliet sighed. "You're impossible. If I had a good-looking norm panting over me like that . . ." She paused, licking her lips. "Well, I do, of course. Several of them. All I'm saying is that perhaps you should go for a little pleasure once in a while, instead of work and . . . and whatever it is you and Kane do."

The Creature Comforts story was coming on again. I watched myself staring down the hungry vampires outside the bar. How many times could they show the damn thing? Wanting to think about something—anything—else, I asked, "Were there any other phone calls?"

"Only about a million. You're in demand, Vicky. Every news station in town is begging for an interview. And that's just the beginning. Have you ever wanted to be on *Oprah*?"

"Is that supposed to be a joke?"

She shook her head. "The phone wouldn't stop ringing. I finally unplugged it and let voice mail take over. I changed the message, though." Juliet loved changing the message for our voice mail, just like she loved turning on the TV. She changed it about three times a week. Now, she licked her lips and lowered her voice to a deep, husky tone that would've been perfect for phone sex. "Hello. You've reached the voice mail of Vicky and Juliet. Our phone's been a little busy lately, but we will get back to you. Maybe. If you're a human calling to offer yourself to Juliet for her pleasure, please call her private number. If you don't have that number, worse luck for you. If you'd like to schedule an interview with Vicky, please contact the office of her lawyer, Alexander Kane. Otherwise, leave us a message at the beep."

"You told reporters to call Kane's office? Please tell me you didn't."

"Why not? He'd want to handle it."

"Yeah, but he'll expect me to actually talk to them. I'm not going to do that."

"Not even Oprah?"

I sighed. "Kane's going to be impossible about this."

"Speak of the devil." Juliet was staring at the TV.

I shifted my gaze back to the screen. It showed the same studio where the BU professor had blathered on, but the set now had two chairs, occupied by Kane and an older, well-dressed man. In his black suit and red tie, Kane looked spiffy but tired. He must've been up all night trying to run damage control. "Turn up the volume, will you?" I said.

Juliet pointed the remote and hit a button.

The announcer was finishing up the introductions. Besides Kane, the other guest was Seth Baldwin, the anti-PA candidate for governor. Baldwin must've been over fifty, but he was a young-looking fifty. Even in his tailored, pin-striped suit, the man boasted an athletic build. His hair was full and a rich brown, and his strong jaw made him look like he could've worn the white hat in an old Western. This was the candidate Kane would do almost anything to stop, and there they sat, side by side in the studio. This should be interesting. I sat down and grabbed a handful of popcorn.

The tape from inside the bar rolled yet again, zooming in as Kane yanked at the female zombie's ankles. Then the scene switched back to the studio, showing Kane and Baldwin, two handsome professionals who might've had lunch together on Beacon Hill—if they could make it through a lunch without killing each other. Then the screen showed Brenda Salamanca, the interviewer. A pert blonde in a sunny yellow suit, Brenda sat in the Washington bureau, interviewing them remotely. Better to keep your distance from those werewolves, I guess. And politicians could be scary, too.

Even though the tape had played about a zillion times in the ten minutes I'd been home, Brenda shook her head, artfully furrowing her brow, as though she'd never seen it before. "Shocking," she said, lip gloss glistening on her frowning mouth. Then she flipped her expression over to a bright smile and said, "Mr. Kane. As we saw on the tape, you were there last night. Why don't you tell us your view of what happened?"

The camera zoomed in on Kane's face. A label appeared at the bottom of the screen: *Alexander Kane: attorney and werewolf.* Kane looked straight into the camera. His expression was serious yet appealing. He resembled a therapist or a favorite professor, someone who knew how to listen and cared about what you had to say. He told me once he'd spent years perfecting that look for the courtroom.

"Thank you, Brenda. Yes, I will. Last night I took two previously deceased humans—"

"You mean zombies," Baldwin cut in. The camera pulled back to show them both.

"No, Mr. Baldwin, I mean what I said: previously deceased humans. They're as human as you are. The only difference is that you had the good fortune to be out of town when the plague struck."

"Woo-hoo! Score one for Kane!" Juliet licked her finger and made an imaginary mark in the air.

"One thing that I want to emphasize," Kane continued as the camera centered on his face again, "is that most of what happened last night does not appear on that tape. A number of events combined to create a complex situation." From there, he gave his account of what had happened. He was a master at giving his story just the right spin. Nothing he said was untrue, but the way he told it, the fight wasn't really anyone's fault. Instead of pointing out that a human had started the whole thing, he suggested that college hijinks had, unfortunately, gotten out of hand—many of us could remember what it was like to have a few too many at that age. Fights break out every day. It was just one of those things.

I thought he did a good job. He managed to put the incident into a context that most humans could understand, without placing any blame. As a PA, the last thing he wanted to do was make it look like he was blaming anyone. It made the norms nuts when the monsters tried to come across as victims of society. For some reason, most people didn't buy the idea that a "victim" could tear your throat out while bouncing bullets off its hide.

Back in the Washington bureau, Brenda also seemed impressed. "Thank you, Mr. Kane, for reminding us that there's often more to the news than meets the eye." She flicked on her high-beam smile again. "Our next guest is Seth Baldwin, who's challenging current Massachusetts governor Paul Sugden in next week's election. It's a tight race. Mr. Baldwin. You've made no secret of the fact that you'd like to make Paranormal Americans illegal in Massachusetts. How do last night's events in Boston's so-called New Combat Zone affect your position?"

Baldwin's face filled the screen. Close-up, his face looked craggier, more weathered, than it did from a distance. As he nodded, it was clear that he'd also practiced his serious-but-caring look.

"He's hot," Juliet said.

"You think everybody's hot."

She arched an eyebrow at me. "And your point is?"

I shushed her so I could hear what Baldwin had to say.

"I believe that there's a place for monsters in the world, but Massachusetts is not that place. Mr. Kane says the tape doesn't show us everything. But what it does show is clear, irrefutable evidence that humans and monsters cannot mix." I waited for Kane to jump in and correct Baldwin's *monsters* to *Paranormal Americans*, but he remained silent, listening. He wasn't going to let Baldwin blow off his terminology the way he'd blown off *zombies* earlier. Smart.

"Monsters"—Baldwin shot Kane a look—"whether we're talking about zombies, vampires, or, yes, even werewolves like Mr. Kane here, represent a danger to human beings. What the world saw on that tape was no ordinary bar fight." Obligingly, CNN played the tape again, Baldwin's voice intoning over it like the narrator in a movie. "Yes, humans do fight each other. I'm not saying that fighting is right, but it's part of human nature. Notice I said *human* nature. But I think I speak not only for myself, but for every human being who ever lived, when I say that never, ever have I seen a simple bar fight in which one human being attempted to eat another."

Juliet grinned at me. "The man has a point," she said. "I wouldn't mind having him for a snack. What do you think his blood type is? I'd bet anything he's an A neg. He looks juicy."

Baldwin shook a finger in the air to drive home his point. "Last night's attack was on a human being who was in that bar trying to help the monsters. Mr. Kane admits he hired the man to make a paid political advertisement against my campaign. And that attack merely shows that humans and monsters cannot live together. This country belongs to human beings. It was founded by human beings, on human values."

"Aaron Burr was a werewolf," Juliet remarked.

I stared at her. "Who?"

Juliet rolled her eyes. "Don't they teach you any history in school? In the early nineteenth century, he was in a duel with, um, what's-his-name."

"Are you talking about Alexander Hamilton?"

"Yeah, him. Hamilton had a regular bullet in his pistol, not silver. So Burr couldn't lose."

I wondered if Kane knew that the guy on ten-dollar bills had been outwitted in a duel to the death by one of his kind. Human values, indeed.

Baldwin was still speaking. "I don't say kill the monsters, but I *do* say let them start their own country. Somewhere far from human civilization. Antarctica, maybe. But I promise, if the people of Massachusetts elect me as their governor, we will never see a repeat of last night's tragedy. No more 'Monsterchusetts'—my administration will restore Massachusetts to the great commonwealth it was before these inhuman . . . *creatures* started demanding special privileges."

"Mr. Baldwin—" Kane began, but the picture went back to Washington. Brenda beamed at the camera, thanking them both for being there, then introduced the weather report. A giant weather map appeared, accompanied by another glossy female with sprayed-stiff hair and a fixed smile.

"Wow," Juliet said, squinting at the weather girl. "Look at all those teeth. She'd make a great vampire." She muted the TV again, and the silence sounded a whole lot better than all that yammering. "I wonder what Kane's doing now," she mused. "Do you think he's ripping out Baldwin's jugular?"

"I'm sure he wants to. But you know Kane, always trying to prove that the monsters are as good as the humans. Better, even. They're probably shaking hands and thumping each other on the back, saying they'll have their people get in touch." Even if that's precisely what they were doing, Kane was furious right now—no doubt about that. In any debate, he believed it was essential to have the last word. And Brenda had cut him off before he could rebut Baldwin.

"Who do you think won?" Juliet asked. "I gave them one point each."

"Baldwin turned the whole thing into a campaign speech. That guy's smart. He knows an opportunity when he sees it. I bet he gained himself some votes today." I glanced at Juliet, who covered her mouth as she yawned. "You don't seem too worried about what will happen to us if he wins."

"Another purge against the monsters?" She yawned again, as if the subject bored her. "What's to worry about? I'm one of those vampires who always lands on her feet, like a cat." She stretched, looking very much like a cat, and put the popcorn bowl on the coffee table. "That's it for me. I'm going to resume the shroud."

She paused in the doorway, silhouetted against the hall light. "Why didn't Oprah's people call me? I looked damn good sitting at the bar."

"Next time she does a show on vampire beauty tips, I'm sure you'll be first on the guest list."

After Juliet left to crawl into her coffin, I stretched out on the sofa, hugging the popcorn bowl for solace. I munched popcorn while CNN started the tape yet again. Then I picked up the remote and turned off the TV. I couldn't face seeing that disaster another time. Poor Kane. His political ad had turned into a public relations nightmare. Baldwin had milked the sensationalism for all it was worth, and he'd gotten in the last word. All things considered, Kane must be in a very bad mood.

So how was I going to tell him I was still on the job for Frank Lucado?

16

STEAM BILLOWED OFF THE WATER THAT POURED INTO THE tub as I measured out a capful of bubble bath. In the past ten hours, I'd stared down a Hellion, gotten involved in an interspecies bar brawl, argued with my sort-of boyfriend, taken on his archenemy as a client, and become the top story on CNN. And the day was just getting started. Right now, all I wanted was a nice, long, fragrant soak and an even longer nap. Then I'd be able to face things.

I'd called Daniel at the police station, but he wasn't in yet. I left a voice mail to let him know I'd returned his call. As I hung up, I'd flipped over Daniel's card and stared at his home number. "Please don't hesitate to call me," he'd said. My heart did a little tap dance. Then I stuck the card in the back pocket of my jeans. Forget it. I wasn't going to call the guy at home unless I had a good reason. Returning a call wasn't it.

I left my clothes in a pile on the floor and eased into the tub. The water embraced my limbs. It was a little too hot, reddening my skin as I lowered myself, inch by inch, into the water. Ahhh. Just the way I like it.

Submerged under a mountain range of bubbles, I laid my head back and closed my eyes. Warm scents of lavender and vanilla filled my nostrils, and I sighed blissfully. The bath was an oasis, a place where I could finally unwind. I needed this.

The door banged open, making me jump a mile and blowing wisps of bubbles across the tub. There stood Kane, scowling. He looked like he'd come straight from the studio; he still wore his black interview suit, although he'd loosened the tie. The look on his face made me wonder whether giving him a key to my apartment had been such a great idea. "Why don't you answer your damn phone?" he growled.

It doesn't matter how many times you've spent the night at someone's apartment (well, just two so far)—when you're about to have an argument with that someone, you definitely don't want to be lying bare-assed naked in a bubble-filled tub.

"Let me finish washing and put on my bathrobe. I'll be out in five minutes."

He checked his watch. "No time. If you'd picked up your phone instead of making me traipse all the way over here to talk to you—" He shook his head, too annoyed to finish the sentence. "Besides, this won't take five minutes. I just need to confirm the times for your interviews." He pulled out his BlackBerry and jabbed at the keys.

"I'm not doing any interviews."

He raised his eyes from the BlackBerry to look at me, then huffed an exasperated sigh. "This is no time to be camera-shy, Vicky. You're the hero of the day, the PA who stepped in to rescue humans. You're the one who can really swing public opinion to our side. We should've had you on already."

Have you ever had a fully dressed werewolf standing over you while you're wet and naked and you know that what you're about to say is going to make him really, really mad? I don't recommend it. I pushed around some bubbles to make sure I was decent, then took a deep breath.

"I am not going on television, Kane. Period. End of discussion."

He stared at me so hard I wondered whether werewolves had X-ray vision. Through bubbles, anyway. "I know you always say that you're not interested in politics. I don't understand that, but all right. It's your choice. But this isn't about you, Vicky. It isn't even about the PAs in Massachusetts. Every single state in the country is watching us right now. What happens next could put human-PA relations on an equal footing—or declare open season on PAs. Literally."

"You're being melodramatic. By tomorrow there'll be some

other big story and the media will run after it like blood-hounds." Kane frowned. Maybe the bloodhound analogy wasn't the best choice to use with a werewolf. "The point is, this will all blow over in a day or two. People forget old news as fast as they toss out yesterday's newspaper."

"You're wrong. This story has national implications. Inter-national, even." The United States was one of three countries in the world that had any form of PA rights, the other two being Great Britain and Italy. And Massachusetts was the most accepting state in America; or it had been, until Baldwin's campaign gained steam. "If we handle this correctly, PAs will be able to get passports, travel openly—even live openly—anywhere in the world."

"'If we handle this correctly.' By *we*, you mean *me*. And I'm not going to do it." Maybe I could get away with pure stubbornness as my excuse. Kane spent enough time com-plaining about that facet of my personality.

But he changed tack. "This could be great for your busi-ness, you know. Think of all the publicity. We can make sure that they introduce you as a professional demon extermina-tor. You'll have clients coming out of the woodwork."

"The demons are the things that come out of the wood-work." He didn't smile. "It's *because* of business that I won't do it."

He didn't say anything, just raised an eyebrow, so I con-tinued. "I'm on a long-term assignment. It's good money, and it requires some . . ." What was the word I wanted? Got it: "Some *discretion*. It would cause problems for my client if I started doing these interviews you want me to do."

"Why?"

The water was getting cold. Goose bumps rose along my skin, and I wanted more than ever to get out of the damn tub. I'd had enough of this argument. I wasn't going to play poli-tics for Kane, and I wasn't going to stay trapped in this cool-ing, dirty water. I also wasn't going to sugarcoat anything for him. So I just said it: "Because the client is Frank Lucado, okay?"

Kane closed his eyes and gave his head a shake, as though

he was the one with water in his ears. "But you finished your job for that blood bag. If you're worried he'll stop payment on his check—"

"I killed his Harpies, yeah, but I left the guy in a bad position. Thanks to me, he's got a Hellion stalking him and no bodyguard." My mind flashed on the image of Wendy, Lucado's big, scary bodyguard, passed out on the floor. "I agreed to be his nighttime bodyguard."

"You're going to be Frank Lucado's bodyguard." Kane repeated the words slowly, like he had to say them out loud to understand them. "Let me get this straight. I tell you I wouldn't mind seeing the guy dead, and the first thing you do is run over there and offer to protect him." He turned and slapped the wall, hard; the water in the bathtub rippled. "Of all the rich assholes in Boston, why pick him? Why not Baldwin himself?"

I tried to defuse the situation with a lame joke. "Lucado made me an offer I couldn't refuse?"

Kane didn't crack a smile. He didn't even bother to roll his eyes. Instead, he focused on me with a laser-beam gaze. Now it wasn't the bath water giving me goose bumps; his stare was frightening. "You did it to hurt me," he said. "There can't be any other reason. You know how important this election is to me, and you just don't give a damn. You don't give a damn about me, and you don't give a damn about Boston's PAs. You don't give a damn about anybody besides yourself." He slapped the wall again, then wheeled around and stormed out of the bathroom, slamming the door behind him.

Before I could reach for a towel, the door flew open and he stormed right back in. "No, I take that back. You don't give a damn about yourself, either. You're not one of them, Vicky; you're one of us. If PAs are outlawed in Massachusetts, that includes you." His eyes narrowed. "Unless you're planning to become a brood mare like your sister."

"A brood mare!" That was too much. "Don't you dare say that about Gwen. I don't agree with some of her choices, but that's no reason to insult her." I wished I had something to throw at him, but somehow a handful of bubbles wouldn't make the statement I was going for, so I shot him my fiercest glare instead. "Don't you tell me who I do or don't care about, Mr. Big-shot Werewolf Lawyer. You don't know why I took the job. You weren't there, and you won't shut up long enough to let me explain."

He folded his arms and squinted at me. "So explain."

"Hand me a towel first."

He growled, but he snatched a towel from the rack and flung it toward the tub. I barely managed to catch it before it hit the water. I spread the towel wide, making a curtain, then stood. I wrapped the towel around myself, tucking in the end, then took another from the rack and twisted it around my head in a turban. Kane drummed his fingers impatiently on the sink.

Wearing a towel was only marginally better than being in the tub, but at least I wasn't lying down. I turned to face Kane, eye to eye. "You may not care whether the Destroyer comes back and kills Lucado," I said, "but I do. I don't leave my clients in danger."

"You already said that. If that's the only—"

"No, it's not the only reason. I'm going to kill that Hellion, Kane. No matter what else happens, I'm going to obliterate that thing from the face of the earth. It knows Lucado; it's been to his condo. The Destroyer is not one to let a victim go. Once it fastens on someone, it won't rest until it destroys him." For a moment, I saw my father, writhing on the floor of Aunt Mab's library. I pushed the image away. "Last night, the Destroyer's master called it away. But it'll be back. Sticking close to Lucado is my best chance to find it."

"Bullshit. You've got this perverse streak in you that makes you want to go against what's right."

"Keeping my client alive is what's right. Killing the Destroyer is right." I took a deep breath to calm my suddenly pounding heart. "Avenging my father's murder is right."

"I'll tell you what's right." He opened his mouth, then closed it, shaking his head. "Why bother? You don't know or care about what's right, Vicky. You never have." He stalked out of the room. And this time, he didn't come back.

* * *

SLEEP WOULDN'T COME. HOW CAN IT BE THAT ONE MIN-ute you're so exhausted you can hardly see your way to bed, and then the next minute, as soon as you hit the sheets, you're wide awake? The more I thought "I need to sleep," the wider awake I became. Kane's angry stare. Kane slamming the door. I wished we hadn't argued. But he expected too much. He had no right—none—to tell me who I could work for or what my politics should be.

Sighing, I turned on my side. The room was cold, but I was sweating, comforters pushed aside, the sheet twisted around me in damp coils. I turned over my pillow to find a cool spot, punching it into shape. I punched it again, and then again, harder. Hitting felt good. My right forearm twitched; the demon mark was fiery red, feverish. Now I knew why I felt so hot, and why I wanted so badly to hit something. The urge was like a desperate itch that needed hard, vigorous scratching *right now*, and who cared if you scratched yourself bloody? Hitting wouldn't be enough. If I let myself, I'd tear the whole bedroom apart.

I flopped over onto my back again and stared at the ceiling, willing myself to lie still until the urge subsided. Gradually, it did. Gray light struggled through the blinds, making everything look flat and dull. A dusty, abandoned cobweb hung down where the ceiling met the wall, stirring with air currents I couldn't feel.

You don't know or care about what's right, Kane had said. He didn't understand. How could he? As a lone wolf, *un solitaire* in the tradition of his French-Canadian pack, he'd left his family group to strike out on his own. It had been his choice to leave behind his father and mother, his brothers and sisters, to pursue his work. It was different for me. I hadn't left my family; they'd left me. When Gwen married Nick, she was rejecting our Cerddorion heritage to become as human as she could. My father died—no leaving was more final than that. After his death, my mother took off for a retirement community in Florida. In her view, Florida was perfect because everyone there had left the past behind, along with the snow, the kids, the careers they'd retired from. Nobody cared about your past there, she said; everyone was living for the moment.

What the hell was so great about living for the moment? What about honoring the past? What about holding on to those things you could touch only in memories? I shifted my gaze to my dresser, to the dim outline of a rectangular frame that sat there. I didn't need light to see the photo it held. My father and I stood on a Welsh hillside, wind blowing our hair across our faces, our arms draped across each other's shoulders. I was smiling; my father's mouth was half open. "Hurry up, Mab!" he'd said. "Snap the picture before this wind blows us into the valley." The photo was taken the day before he died. Now, my father, like that moment, belonged to the past. I'd never feel his arm on my shoulders, never hear his voice. Only in memories—my memories. They were all that kept him alive.

Nothing would make me give him up. Nothing. Not even Kane, so devoted to his cause that he'd sacrifice anything for it. I wondered if that included me.

I'd told Kane, but he didn't get it. I was going to kill Difethwr to avenge my father's death. That was my cause.

17

AFTER A COUPLE OF HOURS OF TOSSING AND TURNING, I gave up and got out of bed. The wood floor felt chilly on my bare feet as I walked down the hall to the living room. The oversize Harvard T-shirt I wore wasn't exactly warm, so I stopped in the bathroom to grab my terry cloth robe. In the living room, I sat on the sofa, tucking my feet under me, and picked up the phone. I had to call the garage to come and tow the Jag, then fix whatever was wrong with it.

A stutter tone sounded on the line, indicating voice mail. Maybe Kane had called to apologize, I thought. After I'd called the garage, I punched in the access code, knowing as I did so that any message from Kane would not hold an apology.

"You have twenty-seven new messages," a computerized female voice chirped. Oh, goody. I picked up a pen and a pad of paper and started going through them. Twenty-four were reporters requesting interviews; I deleted all of those. Nothing from Kane. Only three were worth returning: one from Daniel, one from Gwen, and one from a possible new client. I wouldn't be able to take on any more clients while I was working for Lucado, but I'd call her back anyway. If her infestation wasn't too bad, I might be able to put her off for a week.

I called Gwen first, maybe because I'd been thinking about family instead of sleeping. Or maybe because I still wasn't sure what to do about the stomach flutter I'd felt when I heard Daniel's voice. Gwen answered on the second ring. I could hear one of the kids, probably little Justin, crying in the background.

"Bad time?" I asked.

"Give me a minute. Can you hang on or should I call you back?"

"I'll hang on."

She put down the phone, and I could hear her soothing the crying child. Gwen was a good mother. And being a mother was good for her. It wasn't the choice I'd have made, but then, her life wasn't about me. Maybe Mom had been right. Maybe my sister's longing for children had been less about rejecting what we were and more about giving herself something she needed.

I hadn't gotten very far with that line of thought when Gwen came back on the phone. "Sorry," she said. "I was making pumpkin cookies for the neighborhood Halloween party. The minute I turned my back to answer the phone, Justin managed to pull the mixing bowl off the counter and onto his head. What a mess."

"Is he okay?"

"He's fine. Just covered with cookie dough. He wants to say hi to you." A second later, Justin's voice said, "Hello?"

"Hi, kiddo. Do you know who this is?"

Silence. I pictured him shaking his head.

"This is your Aunt Vicky."

"Aunt Vicky?" More silence.

Pretty good phone skills for a two-year-old. "Can you put Mommy back on?" I could hear him breathing, with those thick breaths that follow a child's crying bout. "Give Mommy the phone now, Justin, okay?" No response. How did you make a toddler give up the phone? I had an idea. "Say bye-bye now, Justin."

"Bye-bye!" he shouted. I was right—he'd been waiting for his exit line. Hey, I wasn't so bad with kids myself. At a distance, of course.

Gwen got back on the line. "Ugh," she said. "The handset is all sticky with cookie dough. Not to mention my entire kitchen." She sighed. "I guess our homemade Halloween cookies will be the kind you get at the bakery."

"Speaking of Halloween, did you work things out with Maria? About her costume?"

Gwen sighed. "How on earth did you manage to get on television, Vic? Now that you're a celebrity, there's no way Maria's giving up that costume. She's told everyone in the neighborhood you're her aunt." The line hissed as she caught her breath. "Not that that's a bad thing. You know I don't mean that. It's just—"

"Don't worry, Gwen. I know what you mean." And part of what she meant, even though she'd never admit it to my face, was that she'd rather the neighbors didn't know her sister was a monster who jumped into interspecies bar fights. Oh, well. I loved her anyway. "Hopefully CNN will get sick of that story soon. Kane tried to sign me up for a truckload of interviews, but I'm not doing any. Once they get tired of playing that damn tape, I'll be off the air for good."

"Good. Uh, good for you, I mean. It must be awful to have reporters hounding you."

"It's a pain, yeah, but they'll give up sooner or later. It's a good thing most norms are too scared to venture into Deadtown. Otherwise I'd have reporters camped out on my doorstep. But who wants a campsite crawling with zombies, right?"

Gwen didn't respond. She held the typical norm beliefs about Deadtown and had never liked that I lived there. She'd never been to my apartment or met Juliet. I'd tried to explain that the PA zone was the only place where I felt normal, but she didn't get it. She preferred to think I lived here because state laws required it.

"So anyway," I said, "why'd you call earlier?"

"Oh, right. The kids and I are coming into Boston on Saturday, and I was hoping you could meet us for lunch."

"You coming in for the parade?" Over the past couple of years, Boston's Halloween parade had become one of the largest in the country. And why not, since we had the most monsters living openly here. The parade was a free-for-all with norms dressing up and reveling in the streets, like Mardi Gras with a spooky theme. And this year, the zombies wanted in on the fun, applying for a group permit to march. No way the mayor would allow that. But Kane— A twinge of guilt hit me as I realized I never asked him how his appeal had gone.

"The parade?" Gwen was saying. "Lord, no. I don't want to try to keep track of the kids in all that craziness. Plus Nick has a business dinner we have to attend, so I've got to be home by five to get dressed."

Good, I thought. I didn't want my sister's family in Boston after dark with a Hellion on the loose.

"So how about it, Vicky? Can you do lunch?"

"Sure. I'd love to." We decided to meet at noon at a pizza place in Quincy Market. The area would be crammed with tourists, but it would also be fun for the kids. Suddenly, Gwen let out a shriek.

"Oh, no! Zack let the dog in, and now she's getting into the pumpkin mess. Lady, no!" Barking and high-pitched kids' shouts resounded in the background. "Oh, God," Gwen said into the phone, "she's tracking it into the living room. Gotta go. Bye!" She hung up.

I held the phone, feeling uneasy. It seemed like a bad idea for Gwen and the kids to come to Boston with the Destroyer threatening to demolish the city. But I was worrying too much. Demons are restricted to the demonic plane during daylight, and the Santini clan would be out of the danger zone long before dark. Plus, I had the feeling that lunch was a peace offering from Gwen. She'd think I was snubbing her if I suggested we make it another time—like the day after I'd sent the Hellion back to Hell.

I hit the Talk button for a dial tone. Should I call Daniel next? The butterflies started dancing a ballet in my stomach, and I chickened out, calling the potential client instead. The phone rang several times. I was about to hang up when she answered.

"Hello?"

"Hi, is this Mrs. . . ." I squinted at my own lousy handwriting. "Mrs. Williams?"

"Who is this?" Her voice sounded suspicious, or maybe a little nervous.

"My name is Victory Vaughn. I'm returning your call."

"Oh! Oh, yes. Thank heavens you called. I can't tell you, dear, how *horrible* it's been." My heart sank at the eagerness in her voice. She sounded like a sweet old lady, and I was going to have to put her off.

"Mrs. Williams, I'm sorry, but I'm all booked up right now. If you can wait a week—"

"Booked up?"

"Every night, I'm afraid."

"But . . . but I can't . . ." She started to cry. Damn. I can't stand hearing sweet old ladies cry.

"Why don't you tell me a little bit about your situation, Mrs. Williams? Maybe I can help over the phone."

She let out a wail, making me feel like the kind of person who snatches lollipops away from small children. "That's impossible. It's not even here now. Every night, this horrible creature torments me—and you think you can help me over the *phone*?"

I tried to make my voice soothing. "What's the creature like? Can you tell me that?"

"It . . . it . . . it's like it rises through the bed and possesses my body. Terrible pains shoot through my limbs, agonizing, like it's eating me from the inside out. It's dreadful, I tell you. Dreadful!" Her voice dissolved in a torrent of tears.

It sounded like a classic Eidolon attack—a guilt demon. That was good news, for her and me both. Eidolons were conjured, unknowingly, by their victims. Although I could fight guilt demons in the normal way, they usually came back in a few weeks. Eidolons were like weeds; you had to go down deep to root them out, or they'd just keep springing up again. The only way to get rid of an Eidolon for good was to purge the guilt that summoned it. And I could do that in daylight, using hypnosis.

I explained all this to Mrs. Williams. Her crying turned into little fluttering sounds of excitement. "You can come today? In an hour—at noon?"

"Actually, I—"

"Oh, you must help me. You simply *must*. If I have to endure another night of that torment, I'll . . . I'll kill myself!"

Great. The suicide card. It was why I was always at a disadvantage when I tried to negotiate with my clients. I sighed.

"All right. Where are you?" She gave me an address in South Boston. "Got it. I'll see you in an hour. Between now and then, don't take any kind of stimulant, not even coffee or tea. If you can, play some calming music, sit down, and close your eyes. Take deep breaths. The more relaxed you are when we start the session, the better."

"Oh, thank you, thank you, dear girl!"

I hung up the phone, suddenly feeling like I could go back to bed and sleep until dusk. Oh, well. I'd just kissed any chance of sleep good-bye. Whether or not the Destroyer showed up at Lucado's, it was going to be a long night.

I WAS ALMOST READY TO LEAVE TO MEET MRS. WILLIAMS when I decided to call Daniel back. I fought down those dancing butterflies, telling myself I was being silly. Juliet's assessment of Daniel didn't mean a thing. This was business.

So how come my heart was pounding so hard as I listened to the phone ring?

"Costello."

Business, I reminded myself, and put on my professional voice. "This is Vicky Vaughn. I got a message saying that you wanted me to call."

"Vicky." There was a smile in his voice. "Thanks for calling back."

The warmth in his voice flowed through the phone and spread down to my toes. Could Juliet be right? And if she was, how did I feel about that? Thank goodness blushing doesn't show up over the phone. "My roommate said you called about the witches. Did you meet with them?"

"No, your timing is perfect. I've set up a meeting at three. I want you to be there with me."

Not just be there. Be there *with him*. Business, I reminded myself again. "A civilian at a police interview? Is that a good idea?"

He gave a soft laugh. "Officially, no. But you know more about demons than anyone in Boston. I'm worried that I won't ask the right questions if I go on my own." He paused, and I remembered how he'd paused last night and looked at me with those blue eyes. "Please say yes."

"Yes." The word flew out of my mouth. "I mean—"

"Great. Meet me at the station at quarter to three. I really appreciate this, Vicky. Really."

When I hung up the phone, butterflies were dancing all over the room.

FIFTY MINUTES AND TWO BUS TRANSFERS LATER, I STOOD on a deserted street scratching my head. Somehow, I'd gotten Mrs. Williams's address wrong. According to the address in my hand, the derelict warehouse in front of me should be Mrs. Williams's apartment. The building was clearly abandoned. Shattered windows gaped like eyeless sockets, and at one point the roof had caved in. At street level, signs proclaiming DANGER! and KEEP OUT! were plastered across the walls and doors as high as the workers had been able to reach. Across the street was a closed autobody shop, and next to that stood a triple-decker apartment building with boarded-up windows and graffiti scrawled all over.

Not a single little old lady in sight.

Now what? I didn't carry a cell phone—I'd lost too many—so I looked around for a pay phone. No luck, of course. Who used pay phones anymore, besides me? Over toward the waterfront, I could see a crane swinging slowly, a huge container dangling from its cable. There'd be people over there. Maybe somebody would let me borrow a cell phone or at least point me toward a pay phone. Poor Mrs. Williams. I pictured her sitting in a rocking chair, trying to relax but wringing her lace-trimmed handkerchief and looking anxiously out the window, waiting for a demon slayer who wasn't appearing.

So I'd head toward the pier, using the crane as my guide. I'd taken about three steps when I heard an engine rev, hard. Tires screamed. A black van shot around the corner and bumped up onto the sidewalk, screeching to a stop in front of me. The side panel jerked open, and two big men in ski masks jumped out. They charged right at me, but somehow I didn't think they'd stopped to ask directions. I braced for a fight.

The first one ran at me, opening his arms like he wanted to give me a bear hug. I slammed both hands into his wide-open chest and shoved. He flew backward and crashed into the side of the van, denting it. I heard a crack as his head hit. Then he slithered down the van and sat lopsided on the ground.

I spun to locate the second one. He jumped back as I turned. Behind the mask, his eyes were wide, like he couldn't believe I'd hit his buddy that hard. He jogged from side to side like a prizefighter, watching me, and when I swung at him he grabbed my arm and spun me around, twisting my arm behind my back. Pain shot down from my shoulder and lit up the demon mark like a bonfire. I screamed with anger— this one was going to be sorry he'd messed with me. But the way my arm was twisted, I couldn't wrench it free. He got his other arm around my neck and tried to drag me toward the van. No way was I getting in there. Using my free hand, I gripped the arm that held my neck, finding and squeezing the wrist. At the same time, I kicked backward. My heel met only air.

"Let go of me now," I said, my voice a choked half-whisper, "or I'll crush every bone in your wrist."

He tightened his hold on my neck, cutting off my air. Panic hit. I couldn't get a breath. I stopped squeezing his wrist and clawed at his arm. "Hey!" he yelled toward the van. "I need some help over here. Ken's knocked out, and I can't hold this wildcat and stick her at the same time."

The driver's door flew open and a third man got out. He also wore a mask. If I hadn't been choking to death, I'd have made some comment about how Halloween was still two days away. But blackness was closing in on my peripheral vision, and bright spots swirled before my eyes like sun sparkles on a lake. A lake that was drowning me.

The thug from the van advanced, holding something. A needle. I *hate* needles—even worse than I hate ski-mask-wearing thugs. I kicked backward again, hard, and this time my heel bashed my captor's knee. I felt the kneecap move and heard it go *pop* a split second before he let out the most god-awful, earsplitting yowl I'd ever heard come from a human. He let go, thrusting me away. Still on one leg, I lost my balance and collapsed sideways, gasping. The guy who'd been holding me hopped around, gripping his knee and howling. But the other guy, the one with the needle, was bearing down on me like a sprinter with his eye on the finish line. I didn't have the breath to get up and run. I watched the guy come, and I snarled.

The moment I made the sound, I could feel the shift begin.

It started in my fingers and toes, as my nails lengthened, hardened, honed themselves into sharp points. That sent ripples of energy charging up my arms and legs, like a flash fire across a wheat field. My limbs contracted, coiled, then reformed in a new shape. The muscles in my chest, my back, and my thighs bunched and thickened; black fur sprang up along my arms. For an agonizing moment, it felt like my head was being crushed in a vise, but then the skull gave and adjusted. I blinked. The colors around me had changed. Sounds, distant and impossibly high-pitched, pricked my ears.

And then the smells. The world reshaped itself into smells. Too many at first; too powerful. Confusing. Oil, burning, metal, ocean, sweat. One smell, sharp and salty with a metallic tang, rose up. Fear. Delicious. My limbs tensed with desire. I growled low in my throat.

There. The source of that mouthwatering fear smell. A human. Or some creature like a human. It had something over its face, but I could see its eyes. Wide, white with fear. A creature paralyzed by fear is such easy prey. I growled again.

Hungry. When you're hungry, nothing smells better than terror.

I licked my lips. Teeth sharp and strong under my tongue. I laid back my ears, tensed my limbs. Claws eager to pierce flesh. Ready to spring.

"Jesus God!" screamed the prey. And then it ran.

I leaped, claws out. I landed on its back, felt skin give way as claws sank in, gripped. The prey went down. Blood flowed, that metallic-sweet scent. I went for the throat. The prey's arm got in the way, and my teeth sank into a bicep, tore. More blood scent. I growled, lunged again, claws holding firm. My teeth grazed skin. I couldn't get at the throat.

A sound behind. I swiveled my ears back. Too late. Something slammed into my haunch. A blast of pain, like a tree had fallen on me. I snarled, jumped, spun. Another human. It stood two leaps away, holding a club. The club was in both hands, lifted above its head.

It shouted: "Get away, you damn monster!"

I growled, ears back. Tensed to spring.

Another sound, from the west. I swiveled an ear. Shrill, piercing. Getting louder. I sniffed, but I couldn't smell the source. Looked back at the human. Hungry. Smells of blood and fear so strong.

Still, though, that sound. It bothered me. Something told me: *Danger*. Louder still. The human glanced toward the sound. Yes, danger. It wasn't safe here. I had to run.

I leaped over the human that should've been my meat. It was on its back. As I jumped, the human shouted. A sting on my leg, like a wasp. But danger was coming. I ran, hard. As hard as I could. Away from these humans. Away from the danger sound.

I ran down the street, around a corner. Behind a building. Hard ground under my paws. High, I should get up high. But there were no trees.

Something was wrong. My legs felt heavy. My head felt heavy, too. Slow. I felt slow. Still no trees. I crawled between a big metal box and a wall, exhausted. Dark, narrow space. Like a den. It felt safe.

Good smells came from the metal box. I was still hungry. But tired, too tired to explore. I sank to the ground.

My back leg ached, throbbed. I turned to lick the spot. Something strange hung there, lying against the black fur. Gently, I took the thing in my teeth and pulled it out. Like a thorn. I tossed the thing away from me. I wanted to lick the sting, but my head felt heavy, so heavy. Too heavy to hold up. I lowered my head to the ground. Closed my eyes. Good smells close by. Food smells. Then darkness.

18

TWO BEADY, CLOSE-SET EYES PEERED AT ME THROUGH THE
gloom, an inch from my face. Something moved in my hair,
then brushed against my cheek. Whiskers—oh, God, it was
a rat.

I screamed and sat up, flailing my arms at the rodent. It
skittered away.

It was dark, and I was cold. My shoulder hurt; I'd scraped
it against something when I sat up. Where the hell was I? In a
narrow space between—I felt behind me—a brick wall and a
Dumpster. It had to be a Dumpster. The stomach-churning
stench of ripe garbage was unmistakable. And I was completely naked—as in completely, bare-ass, buck naked. Okay,
I'd shifted. That much was clear. But into what? What had
happened?

Reaching back in my memory, I groped for the last thing I
could remember. Phone calls—I remembered returning some
phone calls. Mrs. Williams, the little old lady I was going to
hypnotize. South Boston, the wrong address, the black van.
Thugs in ski masks rushing me.

From there the quality of the memories changed. They
became impressions, flashes, actions without words to shape
them into thoughts. I remembered smells—all kinds of smells—
and hunger, blood, danger, food. I remembered sleek black
fur, powerful limbs, claws hooking into flesh. I remembered
tearing, biting, running.

A panther. The anger and fear I'd felt during the attack
had shifted me into a panther.

I peeked out from my hiding place. The streets were

deserted—not that they'd been busy during the day. The moon was descending in the western sky. I had no way of knowing exactly how long I'd been out, except that it was night and I was back in human form. Shifts could last anywhere between two and twelve hours, so it was impossible to tell how long I'd been a panther. But whatever that thug had jabbed me with had really knocked me out, and I had no clue how long its effects might have lasted. For all I knew, I could have been sleeping naked behind this Dumpster for two days.

I felt around me, patting the ground gingerly. My fingertips touched gravel, cardboard, broken glass, but not what I was looking for. I could see a little in the dim light, but it would've been nice if I still had a panther's superior night vision. Leaning forward, I extended my reach and felt the cylindrical shape I'd been searching for: the hypodermic needle I'd pulled from my leg.

Crawling out from behind the Dumpster, I looked around again. Not a soul in sight. I held the needle up toward a streetlight so I could see it better. Light glinted off a clear liquid that almost filled the syringe. The guy who'd stuck it in me hadn't depressed the plunger, so I couldn't have gotten more than a few drops in me. Whatever it was, the stuff had hit me so hard that I never would've made it to the end of the block if I'd taken the full dose.

I remembered the needle; I'd seen it before I shifted. But the memories of what came next wouldn't jell; they swirled and changed like patterns in a kaleidoscope. I'd been hungry, I knew, and on the hunt. I held my hand up to the light. There was blood under my nails, staining my fingers. A man's screams echoed in my ears.

Sirens, I thought, suddenly. I remembered hearing a siren. That was the danger sound that sent me running. So what had happened when the cops arrived? I had a strong feeling, like a memory in my bones, that I'd mauled one of my attackers. Maybe killed him. Shit.

I'd never killed anything besides demons.

The law was strict, no loopholes, about PAs who killed

humans. The sentence was always death. Extenuating circumstances, self-defense, who started it—none of that stuff mattered. If that thug was dead, so was I.

Had I killed him? I couldn't remember.

I needed to know. But the first thing to do was figure out how to get out of here. Even if the cops were after me, I wasn't going to spend the night sitting behind a Dumpster, hanging out with Boston's rat population. But I wouldn't get very far stark naked.

I always carry a spare set of clothes. Always. Precisely in case something like this happens. But not today. My head was so full of worries about Kane and butterflies about Daniel that I'd just stuck twenty dollars, my keys, and my ID in the back pocket of my jeans when I left the apartment. Just a simple hypnosis of a sweet little old lady; I'd be back in two hours. No need to tote all my gear across town.

Brilliant, huh?

Okay, no use beating myself up about that. Right now, my problem was how to get home. It was tempting to shift again. I could turn into an ordinary house cat and run through the city unnoticed. The worst that would happen was I'd get chased by a dog or two. But three things made me hesitate. One, I was still hungry, and this alley was crawling with rats that would taste mighty good to a cat. I didn't want to burp up rat flavor after I'd shifted back to my normal form.

Two, it was always a good idea to let a day pass between shifts, to let my form readjust to its usual shape before twisting it again. Aunt Mab told me once about a Cerddorion relative— a second or third cousin, I think—who'd done too many consecutive shifts and had ended up with pointy ears and fur on his face. Permanently.

The third reason, though, was the biggie. This was my second shift this month—three weeks ago, I'd had to shift into an eagle to fight some particularly tough Harpies. The full moon, after which my powers would renew themselves, was still a couple of days away. And I was planning to kill Difethwr before that, if I could. I wanted to have at least one shift left for that battle. I needed that weapon in my arsenal—

for fighting a Hellion, I needed every morsel of help I could get.

So shifting was not an option. I'd have to figure out another way to slink unnoticed through the nighttime streets of Boston. I half-stood, peeking over the top of the Dumpster, and looked around. Nothing but deserted parking lots, boarded-up buildings, and looming warehouses. Not exactly the fashion district. There wasn't even a pedestrian whose coat I could borrow or steal. I slapped the Dumpster in frustration.

And bam! I had my solution.

I stood on tiptoe to reach into the Dumpster. The thing was full of crushed boxes, bottles, sheets of plastic—jeez, didn't people around here know about recycling?—all of it coated with slimy goo that I preferred not to contemplate. Something rustled near my hand, and I batted away another rat. It clambered to the Dumpster's rim and jumped, squealing, to the street. "Get your own Dumpster," I said. It sat up on its hind legs and stared at me, eyes gleaming.

In another minute, I'd found what I was looking for: a black plastic garbage bag. I hoisted it from the Dumpster. It was tied, and I worked at the knot. The cold was starting to get to me, making my fingers stiff. I picked and picked at the tight knot until it finally gave.

As soon as I opened the bag, the pungent odor of overripe garbage attacked my nose. My eyes watered, and I gagged. I had to turn my face away. Even as I did, my hunger flared for a second. I guess garbage smells like din-din to a panther. Gross. At my feet, the rat I'd chased away advanced, its whiskers quivering.

"It's all yours," I said. I turned the bag upside down, letting a shower of garbage rain over the rat and flow into the street. The rat practically did somersaults of joy.

The empty bag was equally slimy and disgusting inside and out. I didn't know if I could go through with what I was about to do. But I couldn't think of a plan B. Using my nails, I tore a hole in the bottom of the bag, then another in each side. Then I closed my eyes, pinched my nose, and slid the bag over my head. I pushed my head and my arms through the holes, trying not to think about the smell or about the slimy, unknown substances making contact with my skin. I tried, but I failed. I bent over and retched, but it had been so long since I'd eaten that nothing came up. That didn't stop my body from trying to puke up my empty stomach.

After a couple of minutes, I straightened. I grasped the plastic of the bag with two fingers and pulled it away from my torso. Voilà. Cinderella, ready to go to the ball. All I needed was a rotten pumpkin and another rat for a coachman.

Well, at least I was decent. A whole new definition of decent, I thought, trying to get used to the smell so I wouldn't have to hold my nose. I ventured out from behind the Dumpster and started walking. Barefoot, freezing, and completely disgusting, but covered.

I needed to get home, but first I wanted to see the scene where I'd shifted. If I was incredibly lucky, I'd find some piece of clothing that hadn't shredded when I'd changed. If I was incredibly *un*lucky, I'd come across a police crime scene, complete with a chalk outline of that thug's body.

But my luck was middle of the road tonight. When I got to the place where those three guys had jumped me, there was nothing—barely a sign they'd ever been there. Some skid marks, a bloodstain in the road (not too large, I noted), and a couple of tatters of leather. At least there was no chalk outline, no police tape. That was something, anyway. I picked up a strip of black leather and rubbed it against my cheek. Damn. Those had been my favorite jeans.

If the cops had been here, collecting evidence, they'd have picked up these scraps of leather, right? The thought made me feel a little better. Then another thought struck me like a blow to the head: They'd have picked up my paranormal ID, too. They'd know exactly who had attacked that norm. I scouted around but couldn't find the card anywhere. Maybe the energy-field blast of the shift had shredded it, along with my clothes. God, I hoped so.

There was nothing else left. The only thing I could do was go home—a two-and-a-half-mile hike. I jogged down the middle of deserted D Street, trying not to notice the feel of slimy plastic sliding and sticking against my skin. And the smell—God. If anything, it got worse. Demons stink, but I'd never smelled anything like the odor of garbage mingled with sweat that currently surrounded me like a cloud of flies.

As I approached a cross street, a car slowed and started to turn toward me. When the headlights swept across me, the car stopped, then turned and skidded away in the opposite direction. Apparently, the driver wasn't impressed by my fashion choices tonight.

But the encounter made me realize that I needed to be more careful. If someone was looking for me—the cops or maybe those thugs, back for a second round—I was making it way too easy for them. I ducked into the shadow of a building. As I made my way back to Deadtown, I chose backstreets and alleyways, staying close against buildings, darting across intersections only when the coast was clear. I ran from shadow to shadow, exactly like some kind of monster trying to stay out of sight of the humans.

BY THE TIME I KNOCKED ON MY FRONT DOOR, I WAS ready to call it a night. Without my ID, I'd had to sneak back into Deadtown—not impossible, but tricky. And then . . . It's not easy looking like a freak on a street full of zombies, but tonight I'd managed to accomplish just that. Zombies pointed, laughed, crossed the street to get out of sniffing range. Even Clyde couldn't keep a poker face as I stomped through the lobby. No "Good evening, Miss Vaughn"—it was more like "Oh, my lord, what on earth have you done now?" And I heard snickering, definite snickering, as I waited for the elevator. Clyde could just kiss his Halloween bonus good-bye.

I was in a foul mood, not least of which because I *couldn't* call it a night. I still had to go to Lucado's condo and watch for Difethwr. The way I was feeling right now, if that Hellion showed up tonight, it wouldn't stand a chance.

"What in the name of Hades is that horrible smell?" Juliet

said as she opened the door. When she saw me, her jaw dropped so far I could see past her fangs all the way to her tonsils. "Are you wearing a *garbage bag*?"

"I don't want to talk about it."

"How did you—?"

"I said I don't want to talk about it. All I want right now is to stand under an industrial-strength, boiling-hot shower until my fingertips wrinkle up like prunes. Then I've got to try to sort out the mess my life has become."

I flounced past her with all the dignity I could muster— which was slightly less than zero, given the circumstances. I went into the bathroom and closed the door. Then, remembering how Kane had barged in earlier, I clicked the lock. I turned on the hot tap full blast and peeled off that damn trash bag. Steam billowed in hot, delicious puffs from the shower stall as I crumpled up my never-again gown, lifted the lid to the trash can, and slam dunked the bag, letting the lid bang shut. I took a deep breath, then sniffed, and sniffed again. I could still smell it. Then I realized the smell was coming from me. The stench of garbage had sunk into my pores. I jumped into the shower and started soaping up. I lathered and scrubbed, lathered and scrubbed, lathered and scrubbed, until the bar of deodorant soap I'd started with dissolved into a tiny sliver.

It felt good to put on real clothes—a scoop-neck yellow cashmere sweater and black jeans—even if the leather of the jeans was kind of stiff. They were a new pair; it'd take a while to break them in. Zipping up my black ankle boots, I felt like a whole new person.

I grabbed a spare apartment key out of my dresser and stuck my driver's license in my pocket—that would get me through the checkpoints until I could replace my paranormal ID card. Then I went into the living room, where Juliet sat watching the local news. "Any good murders today?" I asked, trying to sound casual. To anyone else, it would have seemed an odd question. But like most vampires, Juliet enjoyed hearing the gory details of a murder. Preferably one with lots of blood.

She shook her head. "Nothing interesting."

Well, that was a relief. Unless some norm being mauled to death by a panther in the middle of South Boston didn't count as interesting to a vampire.

The sports anchor was listing high school football scores. Juliet tore her gaze away from the TV and regarded me.

"Going out?"

"To Commodore Wharf. I've got a job for the next few nights." I had to get over there fast. It was past eleven—I was already over four hours late. I had a feeling that, sooner or later, Difethwr would show up again. I said a silent prayer that it hadn't shown up already.

Juliet's eyes rounded. "You shifted tonight! That's why you—you know."

"Disappeared for twelve hours and came home without my clothes? Gee, when I say it like that, it sounds like I should've had a hell of a lot more fun than I did. Yeah, I shifted into a panther. Some guys jumped me, and I lost control while I was fighting them off."

"So that's why you asked about murder." She grinned and clapped her hands in delight. "You killed someone, didn't you?"

"I don't know."

"You don't? Wow. Must've been some shift."

"I mauled one of the thugs. If I didn't kill him, the only reason was because I heard sirens coming." My fingers twitched involuntarily, remembering how it felt to sink my claws into his skin. I'd wanted *so much* to lap up his blood, to tear chunks of meat from his bones and swallow them whole. And it wasn't morals or compassion or any of that good, reasoning human stuff that had stopped me. It was fear. The sound of a siren had alerted the panther's instinct for danger. If I hadn't heard it, I'd have eaten that thug.

What the hell was wrong with me? I'd never lost control like that before. Was it because the shift was so close to the full moon? Or, with the Destroyer in town, was the Hellion's essence taking over?

No. It couldn't be that. I wouldn't let it.

But what if I couldn't stop it?

I shuddered and blinked. Juliet looked at me expectantly. "Sorry," I said. "Did you say something?"

"I was wondering about the men who attacked you. They were norms?"

I nodded. "I'm pretty sure."

"How many?"

"Three. With ski masks and a black van."

"But why? Who would want to kidnap you?"

I frowned. I'd been thinking about that, too. And the only answer I could come up with was the worst possible one, the one I didn't want to be true. I couldn't even state my theory; I had to make it a question. "Do you . . . uh . . . do you think Kane could do something like that?" I tried to swallow the basketball-sized lump that materialized in my throat. "To me?"

Juliet tilted her head, thinking, which meant she didn't consider it a stupid question. I kind of wished she did. "Kane would do just about anything to advance his cause. But I don't think he'd hurt you." She didn't *think* he would. Well, it was something. "Besides, how would kidnapping you help him politically?"

"By keeping me away from my new client. Frank Lucado. Kane was furious when I told him I'm Lucado's new bodyguard. He'd like to see the guy dead."

Juliet nodded. "A lot of vampires would, too. Hadrian especially. But I don't think Kane would hurt you. The moon's not full yet."

"The kidnappers weren't supposed to hurt me. They were supposed to knock me out with a sedative and bundle me off who knows where." To keep me out of the way until the election was over. Or until Difethwr murdered the man I'd promised to protect, like it had murdered my father.

Which was why I had to go to Lucado's condo now. I was going to do my job. But more important, I was going to track down that Hellion and kill it before the Destroyer destroyed anything else. To hell with it—literally. And to hell with anyone who tried to stop me. Even Kane.

"I'M TELLING YOU, SWEETHEART, THERE'S NO WAY YOU'RE going up to Mr. Lucado's condo. Nobody gets in tonight. I got my orders from Frankie hisself."

I glared at the norm who stood blocking my way. He looked as much like a doorman as I looked like Snoopy. Instead of a uniform, he wore black on black on black: a shiny black suit, black shirt, black tie. This bodyguard wasn't as tall as Wendy, but he was still big and powerfully built. He had a bull neck and biceps that threatened to pop the seams of his jacket. He had squinty eyes and a chipped front tooth that gave him a slight lisp. But you could bet he pounded the hell out of anyone who teased him about it.

"First of all, I'm not your sweetheart. Got it?" His response was an ugly leer. I sighed and pressed on. "I work for Frank. I was supposed to be here earlier but I was, uh, unavoidably delayed. Now that I'm here, I'm sure he'd want you to let me in."

"Nobody gets in."

"If you'd just check the list. The name's Vaughn."

"You check it." He went over to the desk, picked up a three-ring binder, and shoved it in my face. I had to blink and push it back a couple of inches to bring the words into focus. "See?" he said, his thick finger stabbing at a line. "Right there. You was on the list, but you got crossed off. Mr. Lucado called down around nine. He said nobody gets in—'specially not you."

He was right. On the second line, I could make out my name under a scribble of black ink.

"Look, Frank only said that because he was mad I was late. Tonight was supposed to be my first night on the job. I understand he's annoyed with me, but if I can explain to him what happened, I'm sure we can set this straight."

I started toward the elevators, but in a flash he was in front of me again. The leer got uglier as he looked me up and down. "First night on the job, huh? And what kind of job would a sexy lady like you be doing upstairs at midnight? Might as well accept it, sweetheart. No fun and games tonight. Frankie got tired of waiting and went to sleep. Old guys do that. Now, if you're interested in a man with some staying power, there's a storeroom we can use."

I ignored that remark as I considered my options: sweet-talk my way past this bozo or pound his face in and waltz upstairs. Since we both worked for Lucado, violence probably wasn't the best option. Pity. "If you'd just call upstairs and ask him—"

He laughed. "Sweetheart, I sure as hell ain't waking up the boss to tell him the hooker finally got here."

My hand flashed out and grabbed his tie. He made a strangled noise as I pulled him down to eye level. "I told you, I am *not* your sweetheart. I am not a prostitute, either. Frank hired me as a bodyguard."

Even half-strangled, the guy managed to laugh in my face. "A broad for a bodyguard? That's a good one."

I twisted his tie around my hand, cutting off a little more air, and pulled him closer. I forced his head to one side so I could whisper in his cauliflower ear. "If you'd like a demonstration of my skills, I'd be happy to throw you through that window."

"Frankie wouldn't like that," he choked out. "Anyway, I'd shoot you first." Something poked my ribs. I thrust the doorman back an inch, enough to see the pistol in his hand. "Let go," he said, "or I'll shoot you right now."

Not a good situation. If I released my grip, he might shoot me anyway. "Okay, okay," I said, "let's both cool off a little. I don't think either of us wants to hurt anybody, right?"

His hate-filled glare suggested otherwise, but he said, "Right."

"So you put the gun down on the desk, and then I'll let go. Agreed?"

I could almost see his mind working overtime, chugging away at a speed of, oh, about ten miles an hour, trying to

figure out how he could come out ahead. And to him, I suspected that coming out ahead included finding a way to hurt
me—bad.

"Okay," he croaked. "But then you'll leave. Pronto."

"All right." I walked him over to the desk, and he laid the
gun on its surface. "Now," I said, "we're going to move over
there, near the door." I pushed him backward until I was sure
I could get out before he could reach the gun. Then I let go.

He took in a huge gulp of air, one hand going to his throat.
The other hand produced a second, smaller pistol. But I was
gone through the glass doors, disappearing into the dark night,
before he could aim.

Outside, I looked up at Lucado's darkened condo on the
top two floors. Good way to strain my neck, but it wasn't
going to get me inside. And I wasn't about to try scaling the
wall with my bare hands—besides the fact that I'd fallen off
the climbing wall at the Y (twice), I needed my duffel bag
with my weapons. If Difethwr was coming, I couldn't face
the Hellion empty-handed. Facing it one-handed would be
bad enough.

There had to be another way in. No metal fire escape zigzagged down the outside—this building was too new and
classy for that. Around the back of the building was a blank
metal door, no knob or handle—probably an emergency exit.
And I'd bet a week's pay that it was hooked up to an alarm. I
couldn't risk it. The last thing I needed right now was to set
off an alarm and bring the cops screaming in.

I stood in the visitors' parking lot. A ramp led down under
the building to a parking garage for residents. Instead of a
door, it had a gate, an arm that swung up to let you through
when you waved a card at a reader. I didn't want to park;
I just wanted to get inside. I walked around the gate and
went in.

I kept toward the outer wall, crouching so I was no taller
than the cars, as I searched for the interior door. That gate
seemed pretty low security; I wouldn't have been surprised if
Frank had posted a bodyguard on duty in there, too. But I
didn't see anyone.

The building entrance was about halfway through the garage. There was a security camera pointed right at it. Did the doorman watch security cameras from behind the desk, or was that someone else's job? Maybe the cameras just recorded, without anyone watching. The way my luck was running, I wouldn't count on it. But I didn't have a choice. I had to get inside, and this was the only way.

I walked over to the door and pulled. It didn't open. I tugged harder, but I knew it wouldn't give. There was a card reader next to the door, like the one that raised the gate to drive into the garage. And I didn't have a keycard.

This would be a great time for someone to come home late, so I could be rooting through my bag, pretending to look for my keycard, and then gratefully let them open the door for me. But in the wee hours of a Friday morning, the chances of that happening were slim. Pizza delivery? No, it was too late for that, too. Anyway, the delivery guy would go through the lobby.

My next thought was to smash the glass door. That didn't seem like such a hot idea, either. First of all, it could be wired to set off an alarm. And second, it was likely to make Frank even more pissed off than he already was. I looked around. There was a phone by the door. Maybe I could reason with Frank after all. Worth a try. I picked it up and dialed Lucado's phone number.

He picked up on the second ring. "What is it?" His voice was thick with sleep and disoriented. I had a feeling that Frank handled a lot of problem calls in the middle of the night.

"Is everything okay?" I asked.

"What the hell? Who is this?"

"Victory Vaughn. I know I'm late, but—"

"You're way past late. You're fired. Don't call me again."

He hung up.

I stared at the phone in my hand. Well, Frank was still alive; that much was clear. But with more than five hours to go before sunrise, Difethwr still had plenty of time to show up. I wasn't going to leave Frank to be a sitting duck. And I wasn't going to miss out on my best chance to confront the Hellion.

I'd been in front of the security camera for a couple of minutes now, and the bodyguard hadn't come running and waving his guns around. That was something. I inspected the glass of the door. There were no wires that I could see. That was something, too.

Okay, Frank, I thought, *you've left me no choice.* Whether he wanted my protection or not, he was stuck with it. I went outside and selected a couple of good-sized rocks from an ornamental border around some bushes. Then I walked back through the garage to the residents' door. I stepped back, just under the security camera, and hoisted my arm.

Roger Clemens never sent a ball flying across the plate more perfectly than I threw that rock. It smashed a fist-sized hole right through the center of the door. Bull's-eye. I held my breath, listening. No alarms, no running footsteps. That lunkhead of a bodyguard was probably snoozing at the desk. Or maybe he was off in the storeroom, playing all by himself.

I went to the door and used my arm, encased in my nice, thick leather jacket, to widen the hole. Safety glass rained onto the floor. When the hole was big enough, I tossed my duffel bag through it, then stepped inside.

Better not chance the elevator. I took the stairs, climbing the nine flights to Lucado's condo. Ten, since I'd started in the basement. So I was a little winded by the time I stood in front of unit 901. I listened with my ear to the door. Quiet. I opened my senses to the demonic plane and listened again. All around was the usual din, but none of it came from Lucado's place.

I sat down on the thick carpet, my back against Lucado's door. From my duffel bag, I removed my broadsword and the vial of sacramental wine. I whispered the prayer and anointed the sword, held it flat across my knees, hilt in my left hand, and then settled in to wait. I had a feeling it was going to be a long night.

19

AT SOME POINT BETWEEN FOUR AND FIVE IN THE MORN-
ing, the elevator dinged. I gripped the sword and stood, even
as my rational mind told me that demons don't use elevators.

The man who stepped out had white hair and glasses. He
was reaching into the *Boston Globe* bag at his side when
he noticed me. He stopped short, his eyes wide behind his
glasses, and stared. Can't imagine why. Didn't he regularly
encounter leather-clad women carrying broadswords on his
paper route?

"Thanks," I said, reaching for the paper.

He let me take it, then turned back to the elevator and
stabbed at the button. Then he must've had second thoughts
about standing with his back to me, because he yanked open
the stairwell door and disappeared inside.

I resumed my post by Frank's door, unfolded the paper,
and scanned the headlines.

I was relieved to see that the Creature Comforts brawl had
moved off the front page. Today, the top story was about a
teenage boy who'd shot his girlfriend's parents to death because they wouldn't let her go to a motel with him.

And they say the monsters are heartless killers.

The Opinion section featured competing columns by
Governor Sugden and Seth Baldwin, commenting on the Creature Comforts fight and laying out their positions on Paranormal Americans. Baldwin repeated the rant I'd seen on TV,
vowing to drive out the monsters if he was elected. Sugden
took a milder approach. Kane liked Sugden, as a politician
and a person. Sugden's daughter had been zombified in the
plague, so he had a personal stake in making sure the zom-

bies were treated right. More than that, though, the governor saw PA rights as a civil rights issue, just like Kane did, believing that the monsters were intelligent beings who could contribute to society. I'd vote for the guy—except, of course, as a PA I couldn't vote.

Leafing through the paper, I saw nothing about a bloodthirsty panther on the loose. Nothing about a man having been mysteriously killed in South Boston. Good. I was starting to believe that maybe I really *hadn't* killed that thug. Not that he deserved to get away, but still. I'd prefer not to add "murderer" to my résumé this week.

It bothered me that my usual self—my personality, the part of me I thought of as *me*—had lost control of my animal self. Could I, Vicky, really disappear that completely? I flipped through the pages of the newspaper, reading financial news, the advice column, sports scores, even the classifieds, not wanting to face the question that pushed at me from the edges of my mind: Was Difethwr's closeness boosting the demon essence inside me, infecting me like a virus—not with a disease, but with the urge to kill?

It was, damn it. As soon as I let myself ask the question, I knew the answer. I could hold back—barely—if the mark flared up when I was just me. When I'd shifted, though, there'd been no such restraint. None at all. Maybe keeping a shift in reserve for when I fought Difethwr wasn't such a great idea after all. I could no longer trust myself in a different form.

What the hell was I doing reading the lost and found ads? I folded the newspaper and tossed it to one side. I had to practice. Now. I had to be so ready to fight that Hellion that its mark on me wouldn't matter. And I had to be ready to fight the thing as me, as Victory Vaughn, Cerddorion demon slayer and avenger of my father.

Hefting my broadsword in my left hand, I went through the first routine Aunt Mab had taught me. Cut, parry, thrust; cut, parry, thrust. The sword felt heavy, and my movements were awkward. I let my right arm dangle by my side; I couldn't even trust it to help me with balance. The thick carpet absorbed any noise I made as I danced up and down the hallway. Within twenty minutes, my arm ached. Within half an hour, my muscles trembled uncontrollably. But I kept going. When I felt I'd made progress with the first routine, I moved on to the second, then the third. I didn't quit until the window at the end of the hall lightened enough to chase all the demons back into the shadows.

I put my sword away and sat on the floor again, leaning back against Lucado's door to wait. Frank and I still had a thing or two to discuss.

ABOUT TEN MINUTES LATER, I HEARD THE LOCK CLICK BEhind me. I sat where I was, lifting Frank's paper above my head like the Statue of Liberty raising her torch.

The door opened. I heard a stifled curse. Then the paper disappeared from my hand.

"You're still fired." He shut the door.

I got up and rang the bell. No response. I rang it again. And again. And again. And—

The door flew open. Lucado stood there in a blue and burgundy silk bathrobe, looking like he hadn't had his coffee yet. *"What?!"*

"You can't fire me, Frank. I'm not your employee. I work for myself, remember?"

He snorted. "Whatever. The bottom line is you're gone. And I ain't paying you for last night, neither."

He started to close the door again, but this time I pushed back. After a second of tension, he gave way. The door opened wide.

"Hell," he said. He turned and went into the kitchen. Smelling coffee, I followed him. Lucado stood with his back to me, pouring the steaming brew into a mug.

"So, Frank," I said, leaning against the granite counter, "anything nasty show up last night?"

He turned, glared at me, and sat down at the kitchen table. "Just you. How'd you get in, anyway?"

I shrugged.

He stared at me, running his finger along his scar. Then he

jumped up and ran over to a phone on the wall. He punched in a few numbers, listened for a second, then hung up without speaking.

"Rosie's still at the desk. Jesus, for a minute I thought you'd scared him off, too."

"Rosie? Do all your bodyguards have girls' names?"

"Yeah. All of 'em except you. And, as we both already agreed, you don't work for me. So why the hell are you in my kitchen?"

I strolled over to the coffeemaker and opened cupboards until I found a mug. I filled the mug with coffee, inhaling deeply. Took a sip. Mmm. Frank bought the good stuff.

I turned to him. "I'm trying to track down the demon that was here the other night. Not the Harpies I killed; the big one. The Hellion. I think it'll be back."

Lucado swigged his coffee and waved dismissively. "Yeah, yeah. The big bad demon. The one I ain't never seen. You know what I figure? I figure you and Wendy cooked up that story between the two of you to extort money out of me. After I've paid you a bundle, you'll give me another damn sleeping pill. Next morning, you'll say, 'Good for me, Frankie. I killed the demon. Thanks for the dough.' Only you won't have killed anything, 'cause there wasn't no Hellcat in the first place."

"Hellion."

"Huh?"

"The demon is a Hellion, not a Hellcat."

"What's it matter what I call it? It doesn't exist."

"Interesting theory." I sipped at my coffee. Lucado looked gratified, like I'd admitted he was right. "Only one problem with it."

"Yeah, what's that?"

"You're paying me by the day. If I was going to rip you off by protecting you from an imaginary demon, I'd show up the first night, wouldn't I? And a whole lot more nights after that." I slammed the mug down on the counter. Lucado jumped. Coffee splashed on my hand. "Did it ever occur to you that it's *costing* me money to protect you? You know how much I get for a Harpy extermination—you paid me for one." I'd overcharged him, but he didn't know that. "While I'm working for you, I'm losing clients."

Lucado didn't answer. I could see him thinking it over. Money was something he understood.

I decided to take advantage of his silence. "Besides, you never asked why I was late last night. Maybe I had a good excuse."

He lifted his chin, and his thoughtful expression switched to skepticism. "Yeah? Like what?"

I told him all about yesterday's kidnapping attempt. Well, okay, not *all* about it—I skipped the parts where I almost ate a guy and slunk home in a garbage bag. Lucado listened, stone-faced. When I'd finished, he shook his head.

"You expect me to believe a word of that crap?" He checked his watch. "I gotta get dressed. I want you out of here before I leave for work."

"I know it sounds far-fetched—"

"Far-fetched? Honey, you must've gone to Jupiter and back to fetch that story." He stood. "Out. Now."

Shit. Difethwr hadn't attacked last night, but I knew it would return soon. It was locked on to Lucado; I could feel it. Lucado would be dead, and I'd be responsible for another Hellion victim. I couldn't let that happen.

"You deaf or something? I said get out." He pointed. "Door's that way."

"Wait—don't you see? Somebody wants me out of the way so he can kill you." It wasn't exactly Kane's plan—Kane only wanted to keep me out of the way until someone *else* knocked Lucado off—but it was close enough. And it got Lucado's attention.

"You've got enemies, right?" He didn't answer, but at least he didn't argue. "I mean, it's obvious. Someone conjured those Harpies to attack you." He was listening now, stroking his scar. "I killed the Harpies, and I chased the Hellion away." Okay, so that part wasn't strictly true, either. But I needed Lucado to believe I could protect him. "I'm the only one who can look out for you, Frank, and that Hellion knows it. If you want to be free of demons, really free, I'm your only chance."

"So you're saying this Hellcat—Hellion, whatever—didn't show up last night because the grab went south. With you still running around, they didn't want to take a chance on sending the demon." He paused, thinking. I could practically see those wheels turning behind his eyes. His good eye, anyway. "Okay, Vaughn. I'll give you another try. You don't show up, though, don't bother pushing your way into my kitchen tomorrow morning."

He put his coffee mug in the sink, then turned to me, puzzled. "How *did* you get in?"

"I, um, might have broken that glass door to the garage. A little bit."

He scowled. "That's coming out of your pay." The phone rang, and he crossed the kitchen. "And I still ain't paying you for last night." He picked up the phone. "What?"

His demeanor changed, became almost deferential. "Oh, hi. Yes . . . Yes, I know. But I'm having a discussion with my new bodyguard . . . Yeah, the one I told you about." He looked up, scowled at me, and waved his hand to shoo me out of the room.

I left, letting the door swing shut behind me. No sense in annoying my client, now that he was my client again. I sat by the door, in Wendy's chair, and waited. A few minutes later, Lucado came out of the kitchen and went upstairs. A few minutes after that, he came downstairs dressed in a dark olive suit with a beige shirt and a green-and-brown-striped tie.

"Come on," he said. "Limo's waiting."

I COULD GET USED TO THIS, I THOUGHT, SINKING INTO THE leather seat. "You can drop me off at Milk Street again," I said.

"Uh-uh. You still owe me a couple hours' work, seeing as you were so late last night."

"You said you weren't paying me for last night."

"If you can manage to keep from annoying me for the next hour—which I doubt—I'll forget I said that. I'll forget about the door you smashed, too."

One hour for all that? I'd be on my best behavior.

"So where are we going?" I asked, settling back in my seat.

"Out for breakfast. Ain't you hungry?"

"I had coffee back at your place. That's plenty of breakfast for me."

"Humor me." Lucado looked out the window, making it clear that the discussion was over.

It was early, about seven fifteen, but there was a lot of traffic. The limo sat behind a double-parked delivery truck while the truck driver stacked boxes on a dolly and rolled them around the corner into an alley. We were on a one-way street, cars parked on both sides, so there wasn't enough room to ease past the truck.

Frank leaned forward, knocked on the partition between us and the driver, and then saw that there wasn't a damn thing the driver could do. "Never mind," he growled, then sat back hard, huffing. He looked out the window, drumming his fingers on his knee.

When the truck driver reappeared, wheeling an empty dolly and with his clipboard tucked under his arm, Lucado pressed a button and his window glided open.

"Hey, asshole! Think you own the street or sumthin'?"

The deliveryman gave him the finger, then climbed into his truck, whistling.

"How do you like that?" Lucado said. "Guy's mother never taught him any damn manners."

Once the truck started moving, we inched forward, although pedestrians were easily passing us. When we'd moved up half the block, I could see why the parking was so tight here. News vans lined the street; one was parked on the sidewalk. We turned the corner and stopped in front of the Liberty Diner. Even from the limo, I could see that the reporters from all those vans were packed inside.

"This is the place," Frank said.

I stared at him. "In there? With all those reporters?" I shook my head. "Uh-uh. Not me."

He scowled, turning his head so the scar dominated his face. The guy had a hell of a scowl. "Don't be ridiculous. There's someone in there wants to talk to you."

"Yeah, I can see that—about a dozen reporters. I'm not being interviewed. I wouldn't do it for Kane, and I sure as hell won't do it for you."

I sounded angry, but inside I was panicking. What if Lucado tried to drag me out of the limo? He wouldn't win, but we'd make a lot of noise, and reporters would come running. Wouldn't Kane love seeing that on today's news? Lucado trying to haul me ass-first out of a limo? I braced myself.

But instead of arguing, Lucado started to laugh. "What makes you think those reporters want to talk to you?"

I must have looked flabbergasted, because he laughed harder. He laughed until he had to wipe his eyes with his handkerchief.

"Didn't you see me on CNN yesterday?"

"What, that freak show in the Zone? Honey, that's yesterday's news." He wiped his eyes again, then stuffed the handkerchief back in his pocket. "The reporters ain't here for you; they're here for the guy inside, the guy who wants to talk to you."

"Who's that?"

"Aw, now you wanna ruin my surprise. Okay, okay. It's Seth Baldwin, our next governor."

Baldwin? Oh, my God. I'd rather have a nice little chat with Difethwr. The only thing Kane would hate more than seeing me getting out of a limo with Lucado would be seeing me cozy up to his idea of the Antichrist over a plate of scrambled eggs and sausage.

"What does Baldwin want to talk to me for?"

"That's what we're going inside to find out."

I shook my head. "There is no way in hell I'm going in that diner." Last night's pay be damned.

"Look—"

"No, you look. Baldwin's in there doing one of those campaign breakfasts, right? Meet everyday folks, listen to the little guy. That's why the cameras are there."

"Yeah, I suppose so."

"So he's not going to have a conversation with me while that's going on."

"I never said you had to talk to him on camera. Just talk to him afterward."

"Okay, fine. I'll talk to him after. In here."

"But I gotta go in there. Baldwin's expecting me." He checked his watch. "I'm already late, damn it."

"So go in. I'm not stopping you."

"I said I'd have you with me."

I crossed my arms like a stubborn two-year-old. "I'm not getting out this limo, Frank."

"Two rides in my limo and she acts like she owns the damn thing." Lucado closed his eyes and pinched the bridge of his nose. "Headstrong broads give me a headache." He leaned forward and rapped on the partition again. It slid open. "Ain't that right, Gordon?"

"What, sir?"

"That headstrong broads give me a headache."

"Yes, sir."

Lucado made a face at me, as if to say, *See?* Then he opened the door and climbed out before I had a chance to tell him I wasn't a "broad." He pushed through the crowd on the sidewalk, half of them craning for a glimpse into the diner and the other half trying to peer into the limo. Then he disappeared inside the diner.

I leaned forward. "Hey, Gordon."

"Yes, madam?"

The head didn't turn; the eyes didn't flick to the rearview mirror. I spoke to the back of the chauffeur's cap. "Didn't anyone ever tell Frank not to call women broads?"

"Apparently not, madam."

"Well, somebody should."

"Yes, madam."

I could see that Gordon and I were not likely to have much in the way of a scintillating conversation, so I sat and stared out the window. Commuters hurried by on their way to work, some pausing to see what was going on in the diner, others rushing past without breaking their stride. Kane must be on his way to the office now, too. I wondered how he'd reacted when he found out his kidnapping scheme didn't work. He must've been mad as hell at those norms for bungling it. I'd bet his next move would be to call me up, pretending to play nice, like nothing had happened. He'd be in for a surprise.

A tall blonde emerged from the crowd in front of the diner. I couldn't tell whether she'd been inside or was one of the gawkers. But I knew who she was—Sheila Gravett, the biogeneticist. I ducked down in my seat, then realized she couldn't see me through the tinted glass. I watched her pull out her cell phone and talk for a minute, one hand to her ear to block the noise. It was likely she'd been in there, chumming around with Baldwin. She must love the guy, with his promise to take away PAs' limited rights. He'd make it open season on monsters like me.

Gravett snapped her phone shut and briskly walked away, toward the Common. I sighed, wondering what Gwen had decided about Maria. I'd try to talk some sense into her tomorrow, when we met for lunch.

I looked back at the diner. Why did Baldwin want to talk to me? Probably he needed me to take care of some Harpies for him. After all, that's how I'd met his buddy Lucado. Maybe Frank had given me a reference. Or maybe Daniel had briefed him that Difethwr was on the loose inside Boston. But there was no reason to do that, since Baldwin wasn't governor. Yet, anyway. So why would Daniel—?

Oh, no. Daniel. My heart sank. I was supposed to meet him yesterday to talk to the witches. I'd missed the meeting because of the kidnap attempt, but I'd forgotten all about Daniel. I felt like such a jerk. I remembered the warmth in his voice when we spoke on the phone, the way he'd squeezed my hand at Creature Comforts. This was terrible. I needed to let him know why I stood him up.

I leaned forward again. "Gordon, you got a cell phone?"

"No, madam."

Shit. "Then can you drive me to a pay phone? It'll take two minutes, I swear. Frank will never know we were gone."

Gordon was silent. I took this to mean he was considering my request.

"We'll tell him the cops moved us along, and you had to circle the block. Please, Gordon. It's urgent."

More silence.

"I'll give you twenty dollars. Twenty bucks, Gordon, for two minutes' work."

Gordon seemed to have lost the power of speech.

"Okay, fifty. It's all I've got on me—if you'll leave me fifty cents to make the call."

Still nothing. That chauffeur's cap didn't move an inch.

Then the engine started up, and we cut off a taxi as we pulled into traffic. Over the blare of the taxi's horn, I could hear, "Very good, madam."

20

I STOOD AT A PAY PHONE IN FRONT OF A DRUGSTORE, listening to Daniel's home phone ring. Butterflies galore, but this time there were lots of different kinds—the usual ones, definitely, but also anxiety that I'd stood him up and worry that he'd needed me at that meeting. I felt awful. It'd be reassuring just to hear his voice.

The line clicked as he picked up, and I felt my heartbeat go into overdrive.

"Hello?" said a woman's voice, thick with sleep.

I nearly dropped the phone. "Oh, um, I think I must have dialed the wrong number. I'm looking for Daniel Costello."

"No, Danny's here." *Danny?* "Hang on." There was a *thunk* as she put the phone down. Her voice called out dimly, "Danny? Phone's for you."

My heart was beating harder than ever, but now it was beating somewhere down in the region of my toes.

Daniel came on the line with a voice like sandpaper. "Costello."

"Did I wake you up?" Or maybe I'd interrupted some bedroom activity besides sleeping. The thought gave me a moment of grim satisfaction.

"It's okay. I'd have been up in a minute, anyway." He paused, and I pictured him running a hand through his blond curls. I wondered what he was wearing: Pajamas? A bathrobe? Boxer shorts? Nothing at all? "Um, who is this?"

"Oh, sorry. It's Victory Vaughn."

"Vicky! Thank God. I was worried about you." Relief colored his voice, but I couldn't help thinking *yeah, right, so worried that you just spent the night with some bimbo.* I almost said it, too, but I bit my tongue, hard enough to taste blood.

Be businesslike, I thought. I still wanted to know what he'd found out from the witches. "I'm sorry I missed our meeting yesterday. I ran into some trouble and couldn't get to a phone. But I—"

"Trouble? What kind of trouble?"

"Nothing serious. Just unavoidable."

"So you're okay."

"Yes, I'm fine. I just wanted to know—"

"It is so great to hear your voice. I even called around the hospitals. Sounds like something my mother would do." I could hear the smile in his voice, which brought up an image of the way his blue eyes twinkled. "But I was worried."

I didn't reply, because I was trying to figure out the best way to end this phone call both gracefully and fast.

"Listen, though," he said, "I've got a few questions for you. Plus, I want to brief you on what the witches said, see if I'm missing anything. If you've got time, I'd love to see you. Can you meet me around ten, ten thirty?"

I wasn't so sure I'd love to see *him* right now. But I might as well get it over with. "Can we make it earlier? I'm working dusk to dawn, so I need to get some sleep during the day."

"Sure. What time is it now? Seven thirty. How about we meet at the precinct at quarter past eight?"

"Okay." Hanging up, I felt a kind of sour pleasure in the thought that now he wouldn't have time to go back to bed. Whatever he'd been doing there.

I WAS BACK AT THE DINER BEFORE BALDWIN FINISHED HIS meet-and-greet. Gordon stared straight ahead, the back of his chauffeur's cap positively beaming with satisfaction.

Which wasn't exactly the emotion I was feeling. Daniel had sounded genuinely glad to hear from me; he'd kept that sexy warmth in his voice throughout the call. But he didn't live alone. No way that husky, sleepy voice that had answered the phone belonged to a housekeeper. Or his mom. I had to face facts. Daniel was married—so how come he didn't wear a ring, damn it?—or else he lived with someone. Now that I thought about it, his wife or girlfriend or whoever she was couldn't have been too pleased to overhear the conversation. It wasn't anything he said so much as the way he said it: *I'd love to see you*, all warm and glowing and promising myriad pleasures. He probably got away with sounding like that because she was in the shower. Or in the kitchen, making his goddamn breakfast. What a jerk.

"You know something, Gordon?"

"What, madam?"

"That phone call wasn't worth fifty bucks."

"Few are, madam."

Before Gordon and I could continue our philosophical discussion, the diner door opened. Cameras flashed like strobe lights as Lucado and Baldwin made their way through the crowd. Lucado barreled right through and got into the limo, collapsing on the leather seat like he'd just run a marathon. Baldwin, on the other hand, took his time, stopping to shake hands and give hearty thumps on the back. I didn't see any babies in the crowd, but if there were any, I'm sure he kissed them.

Baldwin looked different in person than he had on TV. For one thing, he was shorter than I'd imagined him, but then he'd been sitting down during the interview. Funny how sitting down can make short people look tall. Also, as he ducked his head to get inside the limo, I could see that he dyed his hair—gray roots peeked out at the part. Once seated in the limo, Baldwin opened the window and waved to the crowd. Gordon steered the limo into traffic. And we were off.

Baldwin shut the window, then leaned back and closed his eyes. His skin was doughy and yellowish—another difference from his TV persona. Eyes still closed, he pulled out a handkerchief and wiped his face. The effect was like a magician waving a magic wand. He sat up, eyes bright and attentive, looking almost as good as he had in the studio. He turned to me, smiling a big white shiny politician's smile.

"So you're Victory Vaughn," he said.

No need to contradict him on that one. I waited to see what else he had to say.

"I wish you had come inside and joined us. It would have been something for voters to see me having breakfast with the woman who saved that poor man from the monsters."

For one wild moment, I thought he was being sarcastic, talking about that thug I'd mauled in panther form. Then I realized he meant the director who'd gotten himself attacked in Creature Comforts, the norm who'd made me famous— temporarily, I hoped. I went for a nonchalant eyebrow raise, hoping my momentary panic hadn't shown in my face.

"I'm not here to help your campaign, Mr. Baldwin."

"No, I suppose not. You're involved with that werewolf lawyer, aren't you?"

Involved. What a word, especially since I had no idea what kind of involvement I had with Kane at the moment. So I dodged the question—not that Baldwin deserved an answer, anyway. "His name is Alexander Kane."

Lucado piped up at that. "Kane? That's the name you said before, ain't it? The guy you said couldn't talk you into doing an interview."

"Is that so?" Baldwin's finger tapped on the armrest.

"Shut up, Frank," I said.

Lucado opened his mouth, but he didn't say anything. He closed his eyes and pinched the bridge of his nose again, reminding me of his opinion of headstrong broads. Well, he'd just have to learn to put up with me. He'd have a hell of a lot more than a headache if the Destroyer visited and I wasn't around.

I ignored Frank and turned back to Baldwin. "Are we going anywhere special? I have to be at Government Center in half an hour, so you need to drop me off near there. If you've got something to say to me, Mr. Baldwin, you'd better say it soon."

"Direct. I like that." Coming from the man who was proving to be the king of beating around the bush, this was almost funny.

"I don't care whether you like me or not, Mr. Baldwin.

I'm just about out of patience here. Either get to it or drop me off."

"Frank tells me that you're working for him."

"I work for myself. But, yeah, I exterminated some Harpies, and now I'm his nighttime bodyguard."

"Against what, Miss Vaughn?"

"Didn't Frank tell you?" I certainly wasn't going to be the one to tell Baldwin that a Hellion was in town.

"He did. He said that you claim he's being stalked by a special kind of demon, bigger and nastier than people's personal demons. He said you called it the Destroyer."

"That's one of its names, yes."

"One of its names? It has others?"

"We don't speak those names, Mr. Baldwin. The Destroyer is not a Hellion you'd want to invoke by accident." I should know.

"It's a Hellion?"

"Yes."

Baldwin looked a little annoyed that he was the one doing all the talking. Sorry, but I didn't see any need to be a chatterbox around Kane's political nemesis.

"Frank also told me he doesn't know what it looks like."

"That's right," Lucado said. "I'm not even convinced the damn thing exists."

I shot him a glare to remind him that we'd already been down that road. "It exists, all right." But it wouldn't when I was through with it.

"I wonder," said Baldwin, "if you'd tell me a little about this demon—what it looks like, what its powers are."

I regarded him through narrowed eyes. Was this the point of our interview? Or was Baldwin trying to trip me up into giving away some other information? I didn't trust this norm. Even if he hadn't been a politician, which automatically gave him a dubious relationship to little things like honesty, his arrogance would make me wary. Still, I didn't see any harm in his question. I wouldn't tell him anything he couldn't look up in an Intro to Demonology textbook.

"It's big and blue and covered with slimy warts. Hideous.

Its mouth holds a couple hundred razor-sharp teeth, its claws are like daggers, and it can shoot flames from its eyes and mouth. Its purpose is to destroy."

"But a human can actually control this monster?"

"It's not a monster, it's a demon." I didn't like the way Baldwin defined anything that wasn't human as a monster. It reminded me of something Kane had said. "And yes," I continued, "a human can bind a Hellion and force it to do the human's bidding. But you'd have to be an extremely powerful sorcerer to try."

He laughed. "I have no ambition to try such a thing, Miss Vaughn. But tell me, what happens if the sorcerer isn't powerful enough?"

"The Hellion looks for every opportunity to break its master's hold. Then it kills the master. This particular Hellion will also try to destroy the master's soul."

"How does a Hellion kill?"

"It depends on the Hellion. It might tear a person limb from limb, peel off the victim's skin in half-inch strips, or rip out all the organs and leave them in a steaming pile on top of the victim's dying body." I glanced into Baldwin's eyes, but I didn't see any shock there. Only a kind of amused curiosity. Baldwin probably considered himself a cool head, but what I saw in those eyes was downright cold. "But since we're talking about the Destroyer, that demon's favorite method is to incinerate its victims—slowly, from the inside out. It's incredibly painful." The scar on my arm burned with the memory of the demon's touch. I rubbed the spot. "And if the victim's body isn't cut open to release the demon's essence, it also burns up the soul. Even after the body's dead, the soul suffers excruciating pain for days—weeks even—until it's completely destroyed."

Across from me, Lucado shifted in his seat and whispered, "Jesus."

Baldwin's voice, however, was clear and steady. "And that's how this Hellion killed your father?"

I looked up sharply. "Who told you that?"

Baldwin's eyebrows lifted in mild surprise. "Why, Frank did."

"I never told Frank."

"You did, when you first warned him about the Hellion. Didn't she, Frank?"

Something flicked across Lucado's face, then he nodded. "Yeah. Yeah, she did. And I told you."

My mind raced. Only a few people knew what had happened to my father. Gwen knew, of course. Kane knew, and Juliet. I'd felt it necessary to tell Daniel and Detective Hagopian in Kane's office. But I didn't let most people close enough to hear that story. Had I told Frank? I couldn't remember.

Baldwin's voice poured like syrup. "You told him the next morning, after you'd seen the Hellion in his condo. Frank didn't take you seriously, and you had to convince him that he needed protection." He glanced over at Frank. "Isn't that right?"

"Yeah," Frank agreed.

I was almost positive that I hadn't told Lucado. But seeing Difethwr had shaken me up, and the Creature Comforts fiasco had left my head spinning. And how else would Baldwin have found out? Daniel? I couldn't believe he'd tell. But then, I couldn't believe some woman would answer his phone, either.

Baldwin's lips curved in a half-smile, like he was enjoying my reaction to his question. Damned arrogant bastard. I stared straight into his brown eyes, my own eyes shooting sparks. "I will not talk to you about my father."

Baldwin's smile grew, as though I'd answered his question in spite of myself. "It really is a pity," he said, "that you won't help out with my campaign. Once I'm elected, I could find a position on my staff for someone like you."

I almost laughed in his face. "You're forgetting something: I'm one of the monsters."

"You're a demi-human. Inactive demi-humans will be allowed to stay in the state."

"Yeah, well, I'm an active demi-human. And that's just the name you blood bags give me. I'm Cerddorion."

He didn't flinch at my name-calling. "Like your father before you, eh? Only he couldn't change his shape, am I right?"

"I told you, my father is off-limits." I leaned forward and knocked on the partition, then slid it open.

"Gordon, I think I'll walk from here. Would you mind pulling over?"

"Sir?" he asked.

"We're not quite finished," said Baldwin. "One more time around the Common, please."

"Very good, sir."

"Gee, Gordon, I thought we were friends." Silence. Not even a *no, madam* in reply. Gordon had just lost his spot on my Christmas card list.

Baldwin looked out the window at Boston Common. So did I. The park looked lifeless; skeletal trees reached bare branches toward an empty sky. Benches sat vacant. A few people hurried through, their collars pulled up, rushing toward some warmer, more hospitable place. Like spooked-out norms passing through a cemetery at midnight.

As we turned the corner onto Park Street, Baldwin spoke. "If I'm understanding you correctly, a Hellion has somehow entered Boston. It would seem important to locate the sorcerer who summoned it, yes?" He waited for me to answer, but I didn't reply. "You said a Hellion will look for ways to escape its master's control. How does it do that?"

I kept looking out the window. As far as I was concerned, the interview was over. Baldwin had crossed the line by asking about my father, and we could circle the Common the whole goddamn day before I'd say another word. So I'd miss another meeting with Daniel. Given the way I was feeling about him at the moment, I didn't really care. Anyway, I knew that Baldwin had plenty of demands on his time. At some point, he'd have to be somewhere else: a Rotary Club lunch or a TV interview or his campaign headquarters.

Baldwin tried coaxing. He tried appealing to my expertise. He got Frank to threaten to fire me again. I didn't respond, not even to remind them both that Frank couldn't fire me. I just watched the damp gray Common go by. We circled three more times. Finally, with a curse, Baldwin told Gordon to pull over. We were on Beacon Street, so I'd have to jog across the Common and down Tremont to make my appointment, but at least I'd be out of that car. I got out, slamming the door. I'd rather be crossing the gloomy Common, adding a little life to the place, than cooped up in a limo with those two humans.

21

BY THE TIME I REACHED THE PRECINCT, I WAS BREATHLESS but only a couple of minutes late. I was signing in with the receptionist when a passing detective overheard us. "You're meeting with Costello?" she said. "Come on, I'll walk you back."

We went through double doors, up some stairs, and down a hallway to a door labeled Homicide. She opened the door and walked in. I followed her into a room crowded with desks. The detectives, all men except for the one who'd brought me here, were already in their shirtsleeves, pecking at computers or talking on the phone.

"There he is." She pointed. "Over there."

He sat with his back to me, but I recognized his curly blond hair. Half sitting on his desk, facing my way, was a woman. Her raven black hair flowed past her shoulders, and she wore a tight black skirt with knee-high boots and a clingy red sweater that showed off her curves. She laughed, white teeth gleaming against red lips, then leaned over to say something to Daniel. Well, how nice and cozy. This had to be the woman who'd answered the phone this morning. Today must be Bring Your Bimbo to Work Day.

I strode over to Daniel's desk. "Hello, Detective. Sorry I'm late."

He looked up at me and beamed, his smile like the sun rising over a dark hill. He stood and said, "Perfect timing. Let me take your jacket."

"That's okay. Our meeting isn't going to take long, is it?" I said it half in the direction of Ms. Desk Ornament, emphasizing *our meeting*, hoping she'd take the hint and leave.

Daniel's smile dimmed a few watts. "No, not too long, I guess."

The woman wasn't leaving. In fact, she was looking at me with a smile that rivaled Daniel's in candlepower. There we were, one big, happy family, having a grinfest around Daniel's desk. In another minute, we'd burst into song.

Daniel spoke. "Vicky, I'd like you to meet"—*Here it comes,* I thought, wondering whether he'd say *wife* or *girlfriend*— "Roxana Jade. She's the leader of the Witches of the Shield."

I blinked. One of the witches. Not Daniel's wife. Or his girlfriend. More relief than I'd care to admit washed over me. But only for a second. After all, *somebody* had answered his phone this morning.

Roxana pushed away from the desk and leaned toward me, her hand extended. "Victory Vaughn. Wow, I can't believe it. I've always wanted to meet you."

I shook her hand. "Um, you have?"

"Are you kidding? Your demon-fighting skills are legendary in my coven. I mean, it's one thing to create a charm that repels demons, but you exterminate them." She shook her head, pursing her lips. "You actually *kill* the buggers."

I shrugged, feeling a little too *aw, shucks* and not knowing what to say. I'd been all prepared to hate this woman and here she was, my biggest fan.

Daniel rolled a chair over from another detective's desk. "Why don't you both sit down? Vicky, Roxana can bring you up to speed on what she told me yesterday."

As we sat, Roxana was still gushing. "I told Daniel to call me the minute you got in touch. Day or night, I didn't care. When he called this morning, I was *so* thrilled. I look a mess, I know, but I had to rush over here right away. I wouldn't miss meeting you for anything."

If Roxana was a mess now, with her straight, gleaming hair and perfect makeup, I hated to think what I must look like. I hadn't even glanced in a mirror since last night's shower. I touched my own hair, fluffing it, then made myself stop.

". . . and then, when I saw you on the news yesterday, I

was bowled over. You were *so* brave!" She finally paused for breath, gazing at me like I was a rock star.

"Just another night in the Zone," I said, and she laughed like I'd said something witty.

Daniel watched her laugh with the expression of someone witnessing a miracle. Maybe he was one of those guys who flirted with anything female, no matter who he had waiting at home. He caught me scowling at him, and we both looked away.

I turned to Roxana. "I don't know much about witchcraft. All I know is what I saw on PNN after the plague, that you put up a shield to keep Hellions out of the city."

"Yes, because large-scale destruction attracts Hellions in droves." She put a hand over her mouth, blushing. "But of course *you* know that."

"They'd say legions. Instead of droves, I mean. That's what Hellions call themselves when they group together in an army." She nodded, and I went on. "What I don't know about is the shield. When it was created, I assumed—everyone assumed—that Boston was protected, a Hellion-free zone. So what happened?"

"Well, the shield is just a charm. A big one, woven from the magic of the best witches in the city, but still a charm. And charms grow old and fade. They need to be renewed. So we chose representatives from each of the local covens to maintain the shield. That's us, the Witches of the Shield. We meet every year on October 30, the night *before* the spirits pass through the veil, to renew the charms that support the shield."

I thought about explaining to her that "spirits," meaning monsters and demons, don't give a rat's ass about Halloween, but she looked like one of those humans who'd be disappointed by the news. Besides, we needed to focus on what had happened to the shield.

"So you're saying that the shield was weak, and somebody was able to punch a hole in it."

"The shield is never weak; we don't let that happen. We fortify it with Blood of an Evil Man."

"With *what*?" This came from Daniel, who looked a little

wide-eyed, like he was wondering whether he'd have to open an investigation.

"Not actual blood. Well, not these days, not with modern spellcraft. Blood of an Evil Man is a type of spell, an intensifier that adds power to whatever magic you're working with."

"So you don't really use blood?"

"Well, you can. Some old-school witches and sorcerers probably still do. But we've got better methods now to achieve the same effect. Cleaner. And blood can be hard to get." Roxana laughed, showing her white teeth, and Daniel smiled back. "People are often reluctant to part with it."

"Especially evil men, I'd imagine."

Roxana laughed again. "True. And how many people do you know who walk around going, 'Oooh, I'm evil'? Makes it hard to advertise for blood donors."

Daniel looked right into her eyes as they laughed together. Pretty rotten of me to break up their party. Or not. "Could we get back to the shield, please?" They both turned to me with the faces of scolded children who didn't feel one bit guilty. It was annoying. "So, Roxana," I said, "what you're telling me is that there was nothing special about the timing. The shield could have been breached any day of the year."

"Not by a Hellion. Not that, ever. But we never expected a magical attack. So you're right in a sense. After the thirtieth huh, that's today, isn't it—the shield would have been much harder to damage." She flipped a strand of hair back over her shoulder. "It's back to full strength now, though. Daniel told you we repaired it, right?"

"You *what*?" A hot, sick feeling possessed me, like I was suffocating. "With the Destroyer running around Boston? Are you crazy? You've sealed it inside!"

Those stupid witches. They'd trapped Difethwr inside the very city it promised to destroy. Which meant it was only a matter of time until the Hellion razed Boston, killing hundreds or even thousands of people. It didn't need a legion. It could do that all by itself.

What if I couldn't stop it in time? Those witches had sentenced half of Boston to death.

The sick feeling was swept aside by an electric jolt. My fist clenched, and along my right forearm, the scar itched and burned. I made the mistake of looking at Daniel as the demon essence flared, and I wanted to pound his smiling face into his desk over and over and over, until not even his damn wife would recognize him.

Whoa. Not that. I closed my eyes and forced my clenched fingers to open. They fought me, and my arm spasmed. I pushed the image of Daniel out of my mind and focused instead on opening my hand. If I could do that, I'd be in control. Me, not the demon mark. *Come on, Vicky,* I thought, *focus on the real enemy. Face up to what you're really afraid of. Difethwr. Sealed inside the city. Your city.*

The thought was terrifying. And rage felt way better than fear, so I let it flow. The mark pulsed as I allowed the rage to flame around the edges of my mind. The demon mark's pulse was slow and steady, nothing like my crazy-fast racing heartbeat. Instead, some deep, ponderous rhythm of Hell was coming alive in my body. *No!* I turned my rage toward that, toward the Destroyer itself. The demon that had killed my father and marked me for life. It was in the city, and it was trying to use its essence to control me. I wouldn't let it. I'd just have to kill the thing. That had been the plan all along, hadn't it?

My fingers flew open.

I inhaled deeply, then exhaled. I opened my eyes. Roxana was gaping at me, looking nervous. "We had to repair the shield, Victory," she said. "We've sensed a spike in Hellion activity; the Destroyer is assembling a legion. If we don't keep them out, there will be hundreds of Hellions attacking Boston, not just one."

It made sense. I didn't like it, but it was the less terrible of two really bad choices. And it was true that if Difethwr couldn't get out of Boston, it couldn't escape me. Not that it had been running away from me so far.

"We need to find out who breached the shield in the first place," I said, surprised that my voice sounded normal. "Who knew it was due for renewal?"

Roxana frowned. "That's what bothers me. Only the Witches of the Shield knew. We're all sworn to secrecy, and we take that vow seriously. The only reason I'm able to tell you and Daniel all this is because we had an emergency meeting and voted to cooperate with the authorities."

"It doesn't matter, you know," I said, deciding to clue her in after all. "About the date, the timing. Those spirits are always around. Halloween is just the day humans decide to notice."

Roxana's face clouded, and then she smiled. "Of course," she said. "So we can renew the shield whenever we want." She was quick; I liked that.

"And you can keep the new date a secret, or even change the date each year."

"Excellent." She beamed at me. "You're already helping us stay one step ahead of the demons."

"Except for the one we're dealing with now. So let me see if I understand what you're saying. You think it was a witch who made the hole?"

Immediately, the clouds returned. Her violet eyes now holding inexpressible sadness, Roxana nodded. "It had to be. Who else would know the date? Who else would know the charms we used?"

"What if a witch told somebody else?"

"Like who?"

"Like a sorcerer. The Destroyer didn't just show up. Somebody called it, then bound it. It has a master. No offense, but I've never met a witch powerful enough to do that."

Roxana nodded thoughtfully. "I see what you mean. It might have been a witch and a sorcerer working together. Or maybe one of the witches let some information slip."

"Hang on," Daniel said, jumping in. We both looked at him. At least I didn't want to smash his face anymore. "There's a difference between a witch and a sorcerer? I thought they were just different words for the same thing."

I shook my head. "A witch does magic by working with the energy of the earth. A sorcerer conjures demons and forces them to obey his or her will."

"Witches," added Roxana, "are forbidden to use their magic to cause harm, to themselves or others. Sorcerers don't have any such scruples."

"No kidding," I said. "How can you 'do no harm' when all your magic is tied up with demons? Sorcerers may fool themselves into thinking they command demonic servants, but the truth is that no demon ever served a human without taking a bite out of that human's soul."

"Wow. Okay, thanks." Daniel slouched in his chair as if trying to fade into the background again.

Roxana turned back to me. "I was afraid it was one of us. So at our last meeting, I put everyone under a truth spell, including myself, and asked each witch if she'd damaged the shield. Everyone said no. Now, it's possible to create a counter-charm that lets you lie under a truth spell, if you prepare it in advance. But I'd called the meeting with only an hour's notice, and I didn't sense that kind of magic happening. I'll try again, but this time I'll ask if anyone gave an outsider any information about the shield. Even if it was by accident, even if they've forgotten, the truth spell will bring it out."

"Kind of like hypnosis, huh? That's a good idea," Daniel said. "Let me know what you find out."

Roxana nodded. "I'll call another meeting today. In fact, I'd better get started. But before I go, Victory, I've got something for you." She dug through her purse for a moment, then pulled out a clear stone attached to a leather cord. "This amulet will call the Witches of the Shield to your aid when you next encounter the Destroyer."

"Thanks," I started, "but I don't—"

"Not to help with the fighting. You're the expert there. But what we can do is open a tiny, momentary hole in the shield, if you need it, so you can push the Destroyer out."

That sounded like a good idea. "How does it work?"

She held the crystal in her hand. It was a clear, unpolished stone in a lopsided teardrop shape, about two inches long. Golden wires caged it and connected it to the leather loop. "You wear it around your neck. The amulet serves two purposes: it glows scarlet in the presence of a Hellion, and in that state it also becomes a communication device. It transmits what you're seeing and hearing to a scrying mirror that my coven monitors constantly. If you need the shield opened, just call out and tell us, and we'll crack it right away. You can force the Destroyer out before another Hellion has a chance to enter."

"So I say, 'Open the shield,' and you'll open it." She nodded. "How long does that take?"

"About ten seconds. And the crack will remain open for another ten."

"So timing is everything, huh?" I reached for the amulet.

As Roxana handed it to me, the stone brushed my right forearm, right across the demon mark. I felt a hot tingle, and the stone glowed a pale pink. Roxana's eyes widened, fixed on the stone. She deliberately moved the amulet to find the source of the color, holding it over my scar.

My arm was burning now, and an image flashed into my mind: Roxana's face, her violet eyes bulging, her teeth smeared with blood, as I squeezed and squeezed her scrawny neck until the bones cracked and her swollen purple tongue protruded from that red-lipsticked mouth—

Roxana jumped, jerking the amulet away. The violent image faded. "What *was* that?" she whispered.

"It turned pink," Daniel said. "Why did it do that?"

Roxana's eyes were glassy with fear. She looked at me, uncertain, holding back the amulet.

"It's all right," I said, reaching for the amulet with my left hand. "The Destroyer's in town. I've got some unfinished business with it. Personal business."

Keeping my eyes on hers, I took the amulet and put it around my neck. The cord was long enough that I could look down and see the stone, which rested over my heart. It stayed crystal clear. Seeing that, Roxana nodded, but tentatively, like she wanted to understand but no longer quite trusted me. "We've felt a strengthening of the Hellion's power," she said, her voice almost a whisper. From her expression, she was trying to assess whose side I was on.

"It's hard to fight something that's inside you," I said.

She tilted her head, then nodded, as if this time she really did understand. "But it can be done," she said.

I nodded. "It can be done. People fight their own demons every day. Even me."

DANIEL DIDN'T ASK AGAIN ABOUT THE AMULET. HE WATCHED Roxana leave to call her witches' meeting, then turned back to me and grinned. He sure was smiling a lot this morning. "Wow," he said, "that was fascinating. I knew listening to you talk to a witch would help." He stood, taking his suit jacket from the back of his chair and pulling it on. "You want to get out of here? There's a coffee shop around the corner, and I skipped breakfast this morning. I'm starving. Can I buy you a cup of coffee?"

"No, thanks."

At my refusal, Daniel stopped, one arm in his jacket, looking crestfallen. "Why not?"

"I told you, I've got to get some sleep."

"Oh, right, you did. Sorry." He put his other arm through the empty sleeve and shrugged the jacket into place. He smiled again. "So can I tempt you with a decaf instead?"

I was sick of this guy acting like he thought he was Prince Charming. I narrowed my eyes at him and said, "What's your relationship to Seth Baldwin?"

"Seth Bal—? You mean the guy who's running for governor? Why would I have any relationship to him?"

See that? I thought. Answering a question with a question. He was trying to avoid telling me the truth. And the only way to fight evasion is to keep straight on your own course.

"Somebody told him that the Destroyer murdered my father." I watched his face closely, wishing I had one of Roxana's truth spells. Something flitted across his expression— he blinked, the smile dropped away, and he ran a hand through his hair—but I didn't know how to read him.

"You don't think I did?" His voice sounded hurt. "Jeez, Vicky, I'd never— You couldn't—" He inspected his fingernails. "What makes you think it was me?"

"Only a few people know: my family, my roommate, Kane—and you. I trust the others. You, I don't even know." I thought about the woman's sleepy voice calling him to the phone. "I don't know you at all."

He sat down heavily in his chair and spoke with his head turned away. "I've never met Baldwin. Hell, I'm not even voting for the guy. And I'm sorry that you think I could betray you like that. I swear to you, I haven't told anyone. I left it out of my investigation notes. You know, I'd really hoped . . ." He raised his eyes to meet mine. But he didn't finish his sentence, just looked down at his hands again.

Well, Daniel Costello's hopes were none of my business. Those were the concern of his live-in lover, whoever she was. As far as I was concerned, he and I had nothing left to say to each other.

Nothing personal, anyway. "If Roxana finds out who leaked the info about the shield, you'll let me know, right?" I made my voice sound as professional as I knew how.

He nodded. "And you'll tell me if you run into that Hellion again."

"Sure." But something told me that I wouldn't be calling him again, for any reason whatsoever.

As I was closing the door behind me, I knew I was right in my resolve.

"Hey, Costello," called a detective, "your wife's on line two."

22

WHEN I GOT HOME, THE APARTMENT WAS SILENT. I CHECKED for phone messages; nothing from Kane. At least he didn't want to continue our fight—or end it, for that matter. Either way, it would have been kind of nice just to hear his voice.

As I peeled off my clothes and got ready for bed, I realized that if Kane hadn't called by now, I wouldn't be hearing from him for a while. Tomorrow night was the full moon. That meant Kane, like all werewolves, had to report to a state-sanctioned werewolf retreat area before sundown tonight. He'd head for the Princeton retreat straight from his office. He'd be gone for three days.

It would be so good to talk to him, to drop our arguments and snuggle in together. I wanted to tell him about Roxana and the witches. I wanted to tell him how scared I was that I might be losing control. I wanted to feel his strong arms around me, to breathe in his woodsy, masculine scent. I wanted to feel the way I felt when we were laughing together. Safe. Happy. And if not exactly loved, then something not too far off.

Kane had wanted me to go on this retreat with him, but I'd said no. Now I was wishing he'd asked one more time before he left. Not that I'd have gone, of course; I had too much to deal with here in town—maybe even more than I could handle. Still, it would have been nice to be asked, I thought, as I pulled up the covers and turned out the light.

SLEEP BROUGHT NO COMFORT. I WANTED TO SINK INTO oblivion; instead, I felt as though I lay in an echoing chamber full of whispering ghosts. And all the whispers repeated a single name: Difethwr.

Only one person knew what it was like to stand alone against a Hellion. I needed to talk to Aunt Mab.

I used the dream phone. Mab's colors, blue and silver, rose up like wisps of fog, growing and filling my vision. I walked through the swirling mist of colors until they faded, then cleared away, and I found myself in Aunt Mab's library. The room looked exactly the way I remembered it: the floor-to-ceiling bookshelves, the French windows out into the garden, the chintz-covered wing chairs. A fire burned in the fireplace, its flickering light dancing around the room. But the cozy impression was ruined when I looked at the spot where my father had died. The shape of his fallen body glowed red, like the amulet Roxana had given me, as if Difethwr's fire inside him had never stopped burning. Again, I felt the mark of the Destroyer burn in my arm.

Staring at the place where my father had fallen, feeling an echo of that night's pain, I began to cry. The tears hit me like a tidal wave. I dropped to my knees and sobbed into my hands. That's when I became aware of Aunt Mab, sitting in her chair in front of me.

"Don't cry, child. He's ten years gone."

Her words only made me cry harder, rocking back and forth. God, it hurt so much. So much. Aunt Mab sat silently, waiting. It felt like I'd never stop crying. My father. Dad. Daddy. Dying for me, because of my stupid pride. And I couldn't reach him now, not even in my dreams. Could he be gone—really gone—as the Hellion boasted? I wanted to keep crying and crying, as though my pain could somehow bring him to me. But it didn't. And, gradually, the tears subsided.

Hiccupping, I wiped my eyes on my sleeve. Mab handed me a handkerchief, and I blew my nose, noisily. When I could speak, I looked at her and said, "I don't know if I can do this."

She looked at me, lips pursed, waiting for me to continue. But I'd just told her why I'd called her, and I didn't know what else to say.

Finally she spoke in her familiar, stern tone. "If you're waiting for me to say, 'There, there, don't worry, everything will be all right,' you'll be sadly disappointed."

I bit my tongue to hold back the tears that threatened to start again. That was exactly what I *did* want her to say.

"The Destroyer is a formidable foe, child. It has been the enemy of our family for many, many generations. If you challenge the Hellion and fail, you won't be the first."

"It's gathering a legion, Mab. To keep the legion out, the witches of the city have repaired the shield. That means it's sealed inside Boston. It says it's going to destroy the whole city, and I can't stop it. It says it will destroy me, too." As it destroyed my father.

She *tsk*ed. "If you refuse to believe you can defeat it, you will certainly fail."

"So I'm supposed to believe in myself? Just like that? What, and whistle a happy tune while I'm at it? Mab, this isn't somebody's Eidolon or Harpy. It's a Hellion." My voice dropped to a whisper. "And it's inside me." The horror fully gripped me then, and I clawed at my arm, raking it with my nails. The whisper rose to a wail. "It's *inside* me! Get it out, Mab, get it out!"

"Hush, child." She reached out and laid her hand on my hair. "It touched you; that's all. The fact that you survived its touch should give you hope. Don't forget who you are. Don't forget the prophecy. You have Saint Michael's sword. You've practiced with it. With these very eyes, I watched you grow in skill. You're a demon slayer, Victory." Her fingers felt like cool water on my burning scalp. "You know what to do."

"But I didn't tell you. When I faced the Destroyer two nights ago—my arm . . . I couldn't raise my sword arm against it. It's like the Destroyer owns that part of me." In my thoughts I added, *It's like the Destroyer* is *that part of me.*

The dream phone broadcast the unspoken thought to Aunt Mab as clearly as if I'd said it out loud. "You are not the Destroyer. The Destroyer is not you. Do not think that way, child. Open your mind, and you will see. I spoke the truth before: you know what to do."

The feel of her hand grew lighter, then misty. The room cooled and dimmed, until all I could see was blue and silver. Through the mist, Aunt Mab's voice echoed: "You know what to do."

"I don't," I whispered. Then darkness washed over me, and I knew nothing else but dreamless sleep.

I WOKE UP AT FOUR IN THE AFTERNOON WITH A STRONG sense of determination. Aunt Mab had said I knew what to do. Well, fighting was what I knew how to do, and whatever it took, I was going to learn to fight left-handed. If I had to practice every waking moment until my left arm became as strong, fast, and flexible as the right, so be it.

What my left arm was now, mostly, was sore. I winced as I pulled on a sweatshirt, getting dressed for practice. Ow. I rolled the shoulder a few times and did some windmills, backward and forward, to loosen it up. In the bathroom, I pulled up my sleeve and rubbed some liniment into the muscles to soothe the ache. It helped some, but I really need to work on strength—aches or no aches.

The living room was empty, but I heard Juliet moving around in the kitchen. I started pushing the furniture around to clear a space in the middle of the room. Juliet came in, carrying a mug of coffee. She stopped and stared at me.

"What are you doing?"

"Ugh," I grunted, pushing the sofa against the wall. When it was in place, I stood and surveyed the room. It'd do. "Clearing some space for a little sword practice."

She nodded, like it was a normal answer, and sat down on the sofa with her coffee. Juliet loved coffee—with lots of cream and about six teaspoons of sugar. Perfect way to ruin good coffee, if you asked me.

She sipped from her mug, watching me as I went over to the cabinet where I kept my weapons and got out the sword of Saint Michael. It was a beautiful sword, a double-edged falchion with a golden handle and a twenty-seven-inch, razor-sharp blade. It was the sword I'd be carrying with me every night; my best chance for sending a Hellion back to hell. I slashed it in the air with my right hand, listening to the *swish swish* of the blade. Then I shifted the sword to my left and made the same move. Too slow. The blade made no sound as it cut through the air.

That was the point of practicing: to strengthen my left arm, to make it quick and agile. As I'd done the previous night in Lucado's hallway, I started the basic routine: cut, parry, thrust. I wanted to make these motions second nature to my new fighting arm. Cut, parry, thrust. As I got into the rhythm of the motions, I increased the speed.

Juliet watched from the sofa. "You remind me of Jock," she said.

I laughed but didn't pause in my motions. "No one's ever mistaken me for a jock before."

"No, not *a* jock. Giacomo di Grassi. A fencing master I knew in Modena. That must've been . . . oh, around 1580 or so."

Okay, that made me pause. In fact, I stopped and stared. "You knew di Grassi? The guy who wrote *His True Art of Defence*?"

"Is that what they call it in English? I like the Italian title better: *Ragione di adoprar sicuramente l'arme, si da offesa come da difesa.* Wordy, but mellifluous."

"Yeah, very catchy. Wow, I can't believe you actually knew di Grassi. Aunt Mab made me spend two whole summers on that book. That's one of his routines I was doing."

"I could tell. But Jock fought right-handed. It looks odd, using your left hand."

"It feels odd, too. Believe me, I'd fight right-handed if I could." I explained how the demon mark made my right arm useless in the presence of the Destroyer.

"Too bad the Hellion isn't on your side. Think of the power that mark could give you."

"Power?" The thought turned my stomach. "It's the power to destroy; nothing more. This demon is threatening to annihilate all of Boston, killing as many people as it can. I wouldn't want that kind of power."

Juliet shrugged. "Humans come and go. Cities rise and fall. After you've lived through a century or two, it's not that a big deal."

"Well, I'm not going to be around that long, so it is a big deal to me. I've got to protect the things I care about." I practiced an upward thrust. "I've got to avenge my father's death."

"Now you sound like Jock, too. He was big on honor, vengeance, noble causes—all that sort of thing." Her eyes went a little misty. "I was crazy about him for a while. I offered to turn him, but he said no."

"Really?"

"He didn't want to be undead. He said he'd lose his edge as a swordsman if he knew he couldn't be defeated."

"Unless his opponent used a silver blade and got him through the heart."

"No one ever got near Giacomo's heart." She sighed. "Not even me."

She watched me for a few minutes, then said, "That's not how Jock would have done it. Lead with the same foot you thrust with."

"You're right." I tried again, lunging forward with my left foot as I made a sharp thrust with the sword, then brought my right foot forward to make them even. "It's hard doing it left-handed. It's like trying to be my own mirror image." I went through the move several more times.

"That looks better," Juliet said. The phone rang. "I'll get it. Might be tonight's dinner. He said he'd call." She stretched across the sofa to pick up the receiver on the end table.

As Juliet talked on the phone, I continued the move—thrust/lunge, step—then did the sequence backward to return to my original position. The trick was to get the movement so encoded in my body that I wouldn't have to think about it. I tried again, screwing up the footwork. Damn. I felt like throwing the sword across the room. Who was I kidding? I'd be lucky if I didn't trip over my own feet when I met up with Difethwr.

Juliet had put the phone down and was sitting up again.

"Who was it?" I asked.

"The garage. Your car's ready. You can pick it up tomorrow, but they close at noon."

The phone rang again. "Ah, this must be for me," Juliet said, reaching over to answer it. But she spoke only for a moment, saying nothing more than *hello* and *okay* before she hung up.

"That was Clyde," she said. "You've got a visitor on the way up."

Before I could ask who it was, there was a knock at the door. I lay my sword on the coffee table and went over to answer. I'd barely turned the knob when the door flew open and a furious Tina flounced into the room.

"Where were you?" she demanded.

"Huh?"

She pushed past me and went over to a chair, where she dropped the armload of extra clothing she'd been wearing to protect her skin from the late afternoon sun: baseball hat, hooded sweatshirt, scarf, gloves, sunglasses, even an umbrella. That left her with a pink T-shirt emblazoned with the word FLIRTATIOUS in sparkly letters and a baby-blue pair of low-slung jeans, along with sneakers that looked like astronaut shoes.

She put her hands on her hips and glared at me. "Where were you *yesterday*? When we were supposed to go over my *lesson*?"

"Lesson?" asked Juliet.

Tina answered Juliet but kept looking at me. "Yeah, Vicky promised I could be her apprentice. She promised to teach me about demon slaying. But obviously, she lied."

Oh, no. I'd forgotten all about quizzing Tina on the first twenty-five pages of *Russom's*.

"I'm sorry, Tina."

"So what were you doing?"

"Well, let's see—fighting off a kidnapping attempt and shapeshifting into a panther, for starters. I didn't even come out of the shift until after ten. And then I was late for a job, so I had to rush over to the North End."

Tina's bloodred eyes went wide for a moment. Then she rolled them. "Oh, please. You expect me to believe a lame story like that?"

"You're as bad as my client. How come nobody ever believes me? Ask Juliet."

Tina turned to Juliet, who smiled and held out her hands, palms up. "That's what she told me. Unless she was lying to me, too."

"Thanks a lot." I put my hand on Tina's shoulder, but she shrugged it off. "Did you even read the first chapter?" I asked. "When I saw you the night before, you didn't sound too interested."

"I read *fifty* pages. Go ahead; quiz me. Ask me anything."

"Okay. What kind of demons was I fighting in Mr. Funderburk's dream?"

Another eye roll. "That's so easy. *Inimicus somniorum*, popularly known as Drudes, or dream-demons. Here's their classification: kingdom, *spiritus*; phylum, *malus*; class, *demonia*; order, *terrificus*; family, *conjuratus*; genus, *Inimicus*; species, *somniorum*." She ticked off the categories on her fingers. "Drudes feed off fear, taking the form of whatever scares the victim most, causing nightmares. They're usually generated by the victim's own psyche, although they can be conjured. Occasionally, other kinds of demons can enter the victim's dreamscape by taking the form of a Drude."

"Wow," Juliet said.

I was impressed, too.

"What do you want to hear about next: Eidolons or Harpies?"

"No, no, that's okay, Tina. I believe you studied. And I'm sorry I didn't show up for the lesson."

"So let's do it now."

"I can't. I've got a lot going on at the moment."

"I knew you didn't mean it." Her eyes were accusing. "I knew you wouldn't really teach me."

"I will. Especially now that I know you'll study. But I can't start today."

"Why not?" She looked around the room as though she'd just noticed it. "And how come all your furniture is pushed over there?"

"Vicky's practicing fighting left-handed," Juliet said.

"Cool!" Suddenly Tina was all smiles. "Can I watch?"

I was going to say no. I probably should have said no, and sent Tina on her way. She needed to study demons for a full year before we moved on to fighting techniques—I'd studied books and books and more books for all those summers before Mab let me even look at a sword. But I felt bad about letting Tina down. Or maybe I'm just a pushover for teenage zombies with accusing eyes.

"Okay. But stay out of the way."

I picked up the sword and hefted it. My left arm was less sore and, I thought, getting stronger. Because of our flexible forms, shapeshifters' muscles are more responsive than those of humans. Results that would take a human six months of hitting the gym, I could get in a week. With each thrust and parry, I was getting a little stronger. And I was starting to feel it.

I went through the routine again, slowly, explaining each move to Tina. Juliet offered some pointers, too, tips that "Jock"—the great Giacomo di Grassi (I still couldn't get over that)—had told her more than four hundred years ago. Talking it through helped. My movements began to make more sense to me, and soon they were flowing almost naturally.

"That's a cool sword," Tina said.

"It's called the sword of Saint Michael," I explained. "My aunt gave it to me when I completed my training. Sort of a graduation present. It's got a bronze blade—"

"Because bronze is lethal to most demons." Tina smiled, proud of herself. "I read that in the book you gave me."

"That's right. And a golden hilt to represent purity of purpose. Before a battle, I prepare the blade with sacramental wine and bless it. When a demon appears, the sword bursts into flame."

"Awesome. Make it do that."

I shook my head. "Not here. It'd set off the sprinkler system. Anyway, it's not dark outside yet. No demons around to light it up."

Tina seemed disappointed, then she brightened. "Hey, I've got an idea. Why don't you pretend to fight me? I mean, you're doing really great and all, but in real life, demons don't just stand around and watch your moves, right? They, like, come right at you."

"Tina, it's too early to—"

"She has a point," said Juliet. "Jock said more or less the same thing: Even the most elegant swordsman must be able to stand against an opponent, or he's nothing."

I considered. It actually wasn't a bad idea. When Difethwr's master let it loose, that Hellion was going to put everything it had into destroying me. It wasn't about to give me a handicap because I had to fight left-handed. I glanced at Tina, who was watching me hopefully. She couldn't shoot fire out of her eyes (thank the gods), but maybe she could help me see and react to unpredictable attacks, blows coming at me from any direction. But Tina had zero fencing experience. And it really was too early to start her on swordplay.

I turned to Juliet. "I don't suppose you'd . . ."

She shook her head. "Not me," she said. "I might break a nail."

Yeah, let's focus on the important stuff. I sighed. "Okay, Tina. We'll give it a try."

The young zombie bounced up and down with excitement as I opened the weapons cabinet. "Wow," she breathed as she examined the array of swords, knives, crossbows, and guns. "Where did you get all this stuff?"

"Some of it's been passed down through my family. Some of it I had custom-made in Wales. A few pieces"—I picked up an automatic pistol—"I got locally. The modern stuff, mostly. There's a shop in Allston where you can buy all kinds of occult weapons. It's mostly for witches, but the owner also keeps an eye out for gear I can use. He sold me the dream portal and the InDetect I use to find Drudes."

"You mean that clicking thing you point around?"

"That's the one."

Tina's face lost its eager expression as I got out two wooden swords. I smiled, remembering I'd reacted the same way when Mab first taught me swordplay. "These are for practice," I said. "They can't do much more damage than a splinter."

"But I wanted to use that one." Tina pointed at a huge claymore taller than she was.

"Uh-uh. I don't want either of us to get hurt."

"I *can't* get hurt. I'm already dead."

"Yes, but if I slice your arm off, will you grow a new one?"

"No." She sulked for a minute, then brightened. "Okay, we can use the kiddie swords, I guess. It'll still be fun."

And it was. Tina was a little stiff, as zombies tend to be, but she was a fast learner and put her heart into it. After half an hour, I was panting for breath.

"Nice work," I said. "You have a talent for fencing."

She beamed. "You sit down. Rest. I'll put the swords away."

I gave her mine and flopped onto the sofa. The phone rang. "Ah, *that* must be dinner," said Juliet. "I'll get it in the kitchen."

Tina looked hopeful. "Did she order takeout?" I shook my head. "What, then?"

"Don't ask," I said.

Not only did Tina put away the practice swords, neatly closing the cabinet doors, she single-handedly moved all the furniture back into place—including the sofa, with me on it. Zombie strength could come in handy sometimes.

Juliet came back in the living room. "Dinner at eight," she said cheerfully. When she saw that the furniture was back where it belonged, she turned on the TV. I got up, and she settled back into her regular spot on the sofa to watch the local news.

"I've got to go to work," I said. "And you"—I pointed at Tina—"need to get ready for school."

"Yeah, yeah. So when do I get another lesson?"

"I can't make any promises right now. I'm on a long-term assignment, and there's a very nasty Hellion around that wants to kill me. Once I get those little matters sorted out, I'll let you know. And," I added, "It'll be a book lesson. No more fighting for a long time."

"What's a Hellion?"

"Look it up in *Russom's*. Chapter twenty-four."

"Okay. I'll tell you all about it next time. Whenever that is. I hope it's soon!" Tina's face glowed, as much as a zombie's complexion can. It was good to see her so happy. "Have you got any chips or cookies or anything? I'm starving."

I went into the kitchen and found some chips. Back in the living room, I tossed her the whole bag. She polished it off in about ten seconds—no wonder they don't let zombies enter hot-dog-eating competitions—then started bundling up to go outside. It was nearly sunset, but zombies couldn't be too careful when it came to sunlight.

"Hey, look," she said, pointing to the TV. "It's about the parade."

On the screen, norm anchorman Tom Cody sat in front of a picture from last year's parade—people in cheesy vampire and devil costumes or rubber masks of famous politicians mugging it up for the camera—as he began the story: "Ghosts and ghouls galore will march in Boston's annual Halloween parade tomorrow night, but you won't see any zombies."

The picture behind him changed to show a group of real-life zombies with a big red *no* symbol slapped across it. "The court has turned down an appeal to issue Deadtown's previously deceased humans a group permit that would have allowed them to enter a float in the parade. According to the mayor's office, no permits will be issued for the previously deceased to leave Designated Area One at any time on October 31. The Council of Three has sent a formal letter of protest."

"Big whoop," said Tina. "A letter of protest. The mayor's being *so* not fair. I think we should crash the stupid blood-bag parade."

"Tina, don't talk like that," I said. "You don't want to risk being picked up by the Removal Squad."

"What could they do? If few hundred of us showed up, they wouldn't be able to handle it."

I shook my head. "Not a good idea. Not this close to the election." God, I thought, I sound like Kane.

She shrugged. "You're probably right. Well, I'll see you when I see you." She walked stiffly to the door—a little stiffer than usual. I hoped she hadn't overdone it in our swordplay. With her hand on the knob, she turned back. "Were you telling the truth before—when you said somebody tried to kidnap you?"

I nodded.

"So you really turned into a panther and all?"

I nodded again.

"Good, I'll have to tell Jenna. She said she saw you last night walking down Winter Street, and you were wearing a garbage bag. She thought you'd gone all insane or something."

From the sofa, Juliet laughed, sounding more like a squealing teenager than a seductive vampiress.

"Well, now you know the truth," I said, pushing Tina out the door.

Ten minutes later, when I opened the weapons cupboard to load up my duffel bag, I realized something was wrong. The sword of Saint Michael was missing. Tina had stolen it.

23

CALLS TO TINA'S SCHOOL AND THE GROUP HOME WHERE
she lived produced nothing. She hadn't shown up at school,
and her house mother hadn't seen her since four in the afternoon, when she left to come over to my place.

I didn't have time to hunt her down. I had to get to Lucado's condo—and I couldn't be late. Not after what had
happened last night. But without the sword of Saint Michael,
was there any reason for me to be there?

Stop it, Vicky. I couldn't afford to think that way. When
the time came, I'd have to face Difethwr, regardless of how I
was armed. I just hoped, now, that the showdown wouldn't
come tonight. Tomorrow I'd find Tina and get my sword back.
Not to mention give her a good chewing out. If she ever did
anything like this again—*ever*—she could forget about studying with me. I wasn't sure I'd even give her that much of a
second chance.

If I had to fight Difethwr without Saint Michael's sword,
there might be no second chance at all—for Tina or for me.

From the weapons cabinet, I chose two swords: another
falchion and a cutlass, which had a slightly shorter blade. I
needed to try each of them out to see which felt better, but I'd
have to do it at Lucado's place. No time now. I packed them
in my bag, then grabbed a taxi and told the driver to floor it
to Commodore Wharf.

He did, and we got there at two minutes to seven. I ran
into the lobby, expecting to tangle with Rosie the doorman
again, but tonight a different guy was on duty, one who actually looked like a doorman instead of a hitman. He checked

the list, nodded, and called Lucado to let him know I was on my way up.

Lucado was waiting for me at his door, in a bad mood. "Well, good God—you actually decided to come to work," he said.

"Nice to see you, too, Frank."

"I'm busy tonight. So don't bother me." Judging by the smell of his breath and the way he slurred his words, he was busy getting drunk. None of my business. I didn't want to sit around chatting, anyway. "I'll be in my study," he said. "Long as you leave me alone, you've got the run of the place."

"Okay," I said, heading for the living room. "Have fun."

Falchion in hand—my left hand—I made a quick sweep of the condo: living room, hallway, kitchen, up the stairs to Frank's bedroom and the guest room, and all two and a half bathrooms. Roxana's amulet stayed clear and colorless. Back downstairs, I stood outside Frank's study, shifted the sword to my right hand and, left-handed, pressed the amulet against the door. Nothing. As I returned the sword to my left hand, my right arm passed a little too close to stone, making it a pink so pale it was almost white. I hoped that tinge of color wasn't enough to affect the scrying mirror. No point in putting the coven on the alert when it was just little old me.

"Um, hi, witches. Everything's okay," I said, just in case.

Back in the living room, I tried the falchion, then the cutlass, then the falchion again in my left hand, making cutting and thrusting motions through the air. The falchion felt better balanced to me, more like the sword of Saint Michael. It was the same kind of sword, after all, except that its hilt was steel, not gold, and its blade a half-inch shorter. The biggest difference, of course, was that unlike the archangel's sword, it wouldn't burn with holy flame in the presence of a demon. And I didn't know whether anointing its blade with sacramental wine would be enough to kill Difethwr. A lesser demon, yes. But a Hellion? I hoped I'd get Saint Michael's sword back before I had to find out.

I used Lucado's kitchen phone to call around about Tina again. It looked like she'd skipped school completely tonight, and she hadn't gone home. As much as I was furious with her for taking my sword, I also hoped she was okay. There are a lot of real nasties roaming around Deadtown—and Tina, really, was just a kid.

The clock on the microwave read 8:02. It was shaping up to be a long night. I wandered back into the living room, feeling restless because I was so frustrated. It seemed like the walls were pressing in on me, imprisoning me in this condo. There was so much I had to do: find Tina, get my sword back, make up with Kane—or break up, if he really had tried to have me kidnapped. Most of all, I wanted to send Difethwr back to Hell. But I couldn't make any of that happen right now. I was stuck here, waiting. Damn it all, I wanted to act.

I wandered back to the living room, where I paced back and forth across Frank's expensive Persian rug, burning off some of that nervous energy. If I kept that up, I'd wear a track into the rug. I looked around. Okay, if I couldn't spring into action, there was always TV. The room held leather club chairs, a fireplace, a bar, a round dining table in the ell—my God, there was even a bookcase. So Frank did know how to read. But there was no television. It seemed un-American somehow.

Then I spotted a remote on a table next to one of the club chairs. I went over and picked it up. It was a television remote, but where was the TV? I pressed the power button and heard a whirring noise behind me. I spun around, jumpy. The mirror over the fireplace was lifting to reveal a forty-two-inch plasma screen behind it. A clever disguise—I wouldn't mind something like that to hide Juliet's monstrosity at home. I pressed some more buttons. The screen moved out from the wall, and I could turn it to the perfect angle for viewing. Cool. I flopped into a leather chair and dangled my legs over the arm.

It was set to a sports channel that, right now, had one of those superfake pro-wrestling shows on. I watched it for a few minutes. They threw each other into the ropes, did somersaults together; one flipped the other out of the ring. Did anyone really believe this stuff? It was so choreographed it was more like dancing than fighting. I flipped through the channels. Shopping. Click. An infomercial about time-shares. Click. Some cheesy science fiction movie from the 1950s. Click. Cartoons, cop shows, political commentary. Click, click, click.

Two guys fighting on the screen. I sat up straighter to watch. Even though it was a movie—a seventies kung fu movie, from the look of it—the fighting looked real. More real than the pro wrestling, anyway. The combatants were fast, skilled, and graceful. And their eyes—each guy looked like he really wanted to kill the other.

The plot was a simple one. A warlord had terrorized a village, and the hero was out for revenge, making a steady advance on the warlord's heavily guarded palace. Nothing the warlord tried could stop him. The warlord sent his best warrior; the hero killed him. The warlord sent a troop of archers; the hero dodged their arrows and mowed them down. The warlord sent a seductive female assassin; the hero killed her, too. Increasingly panicked, the warlord gathered the best fighters in the kingdom. In a long fight scene, they attacked the hero hand to hand, with nunchakus, with swords. Nothing could slow the hero down. In the end, he killed the warlord.

Nothing about the story was any different from a hundred other king fu movies. But it moved me. The hero knew he couldn't set things right. He couldn't bring back the villagers that had been killed or take away the survivors' pain. But he could restore the balance of power. That was the problem: the warlord had all the power; the villagers had none. And it shouldn't be that way. Power not held in balance would always lead to tragedy, to exploitation and abuse. Juliet was wrong in thinking that tapping into Difethwr's power would be a rush. The Hellion's power was excessive. It wasn't in balance. It could never create or build up, only destroy.

With the Destroyer in Boston, it was up to me to restore the balance of power. Not because I was the best or even all that good. But because I was willing. And because, win or lose, I was the only one who could.

The movie's big battle scene had some interesting sword techniques I wanted to try. I turned off the TV and moved a couple of chairs to make room. I rolled up the Persian rug, then picked up my falchion. The sword felt good in my hand. My arm felt good, too—stronger, not sore. Concentrating, I played back the sword-fighting scene in my mind, then slowly started to follow the hero's moves.

"What the hell are you doing?" Lucado's voice came from the doorway.

"Practicing." I didn't even glance at him. That was good; left-handed fighting was going to require absolute focus. "Don't worry, Frank. I'll put the furniture back when I'm done."

"Well, watch what you're doing, will ya? I've got some priceless antiques and shit in there." He watched me for a second. I could sense him, feel what he was doing on the periphery, but I kept my focus on my moves. "Jesus," he said. "I'm going to bed."

"Nighty-night, Frank."

He grunted.

After I'd had a good workout, I put the sword away. Then, having second thoughts, I took it out again. Better to keep it close by. I was warm from practicing, so I opened the door and stepped out onto the balcony to cool off in the night air. I leaned the sword against the wall and looked out into the night. It was eleven o'clock on a Friday—the night before Halloween—and Bostonians were out and about for the weekend. An almost-full moon shone over the harbor, silvering the water. Sounds of laughter, music, and cars drifted up from the streets. When I looked to the right, I could see the North End's waterfront, down to Christopher Columbus Park. Couples strolled, hand in hand, on their way home from romantic dinners at cozy Italian restaurants. I sighed. With Kane mad at me and Daniel out of the picture, I didn't see any romantic dinners in my future any time soon.

Watching the norms, I felt the strangest sensation that someone was watching *me*. It started with goose bumps on my arms, then built to a creepy, prickly feeling along the back of my neck. Gradually, like a movie scene fading in, I realized that I was staring into somebody's eyes. Somebody who was standing on thin air, nine stories above the ground.

I leaped backward, groping for my sword, and the figure came into focus. Putting my hand on my crazy-beating heart, I let out a sigh of relief. It was only a vampire. Had to be an old one, because they didn't gain the ability to float or fly until they'd been dead a few centuries. Another minute, and I recognized him.

"Good evening, Councilor Hadrian."

"You know me." His dark eyes showed vanity, but not a jot of surprise.

I'd never met Hadrian, but I did know him. Everyone in Deadtown did; he was leader of the Council of Three and top dog among Boston's vampires. His photo was always on the front page of *News of the Dead*.

"What are you doing here?" I asked.

"Awaiting your invitation." As everyone knows, vampires can't cross your threshold unless you invite them in. It's one of the legends about vampires that's actually true.

"Gee, I don't know, Hadrian. This isn't my condo. Tell you what. I'll invite you onto the balcony, but not inside."

"Hardly hospitable. But for now, it will do." The vampire rose high enough to clear the railing, then slowly, gracefully, alighted in front of me. "Shall we have a seat?" he asked, gesturing toward the patio chairs arranged at the other end of the balcony.

Hadrian believed he was the epitome of civilization. You could see it in the graceful way he sat, smoothing invisible creases from his four-thousand-dollar suit. You could hear in his accent—proper Bostonian tinged with something European—and in the soft modulations of his voice. You could almost taste it, because looking at Hadrian made you think of full-bodied vintage Bordeaux and foods like truffles and escargot, foods you'd always heard about but never tried. Everything about him screamed—no, make that *murmured*— culture.

Only one thing was wrong with this picture. Hadrian ate people.

Well, not anymore; not officially. Now he'd take his legally allowed pint and say thank you and goodnight. But as a three-hundred-year-old vampire, he'd sucked his share of human bodies dry. And I had a feeling that whatever Hadrian wanted, Hadrian took.

He steepled his fingers and smiled that closed-lipped smile vampires favored. His brown eyes seemed to vibrate slightly. They made you want to lean in, look closer, and as you did, something in those eyes reached inside you, all the way down to your toes, and started to tease you out of yourself, slowly drawing you into those liquid depths.

I coughed and sat back, making him blink with surprise. "I'm a demi-human," I said. "Vampire tricks don't work on me."

He smiled again, this time showing a little fang.

"Forgive me—force of habit. After a few centuries of seducing attractive females . . ." He shrugged.

I'd bet his track record was pretty damn good. Hadrian was a little old for me—he looked like he must've gone vamp when he was about fifty, fifty-five—but he definitely had that sexy older man thing happening. A touch of gray colored his temples and shot through his neatly trimmed beard. He moved with casual elegance, and he had the kind of long, slim fingers that were made for bringing up goose bumps on naked flesh—

Whoa. Maybe those vampire tricks *half* worked on demi-humans.

I coughed again. "So what's up?"

"Juliet happened to mention that you were in the employ of my enemy. I wanted to see for myself."

"Enemy, huh? Good thing I didn't invite you inside, then, isn't it?

"That depends on how one defines a 'good thing.'" He smiled again. "I suspect that our definitions regarding the current situation might not mesh."

"Well, as you can see, yes, I'm working for Lucado. Believe me, I don't like the jerk any better than you do. But a Hellion came after him, and I'm not letting it get away." Aunt

Mab's voice echoed in my mind: *You know what to do.* I shivered, then glanced at Hadrian, hoping he hadn't noticed. If he had, he didn't let on.

"You know that Lucado has contributed a significant amount of money to Baldwin's campaign?"

"Yeah, and Kane's not too thrilled about that."

"No. I wouldn't imagine he would be." He leaned closer. "What I'd like to know is what kind of return our Mr. Lucado is expecting on that investment."

I shrugged. "Maybe he just doesn't like PAs. Or maybe it's you. If you get kicked out of the state, that's less competition for him."

Like Lucado, Hadrian was a real estate developer. After the plague, the state had taken control of both the quarantine zone—now Deadtown—and the buffer zone around it. Hadrian was the developer for Deadtown; he'd made a fortune using cheap zombie labor to reconstruct the area, then leasing residences to PAs for high rents. It was a captive market, since PAs weren't allowed to live anywhere else.

Frank Lucado didn't employ zombie workers—there was too much paperwork for norms who tried—so he had to pay union wages and carry workers' comp and unemployment insurance, expenses that would make it hard for him to be competitive if Hadrian was allowed to start bidding on projects outside of Deadtown. And to save money, Governor Sugden had proposed opening up state-financed construction projects to PA-owned companies.

"Yes," Hadrian agreed, "Lucado would undoubtedly prefer that I not compete with him. He'd lose. Presumably, he's also expecting to get preferential treatment from Baldwin for government jobs. Has he mentioned anything else?"

Hadrian was smiling, lips closed, as though he were just making pleasant conversation. Vampires rarely made pleasant conversation. He wanted something. "What's your angle, Hadrian?"

"My angle?" He shrugged, and there was something French about the gesture. "Know thine enemy, I suppose. I want a better understanding of the relationship between Lucado and

Baldwin. Something there doesn't feel right to me. Have you met Baldwin, by any chance?"

I considered lying but didn't see any reason to. "Briefly."

"What was your impression?"

"Let's just say I'm not inviting him over for dinner anytime soon."

He half smiled. "And what was your impression of the relationship between Baldwin and Lucado?"

"They seemed friendly enough. Lucado joined Baldwin at a campaign event this morning."

"Yes, I saw that on television. The Liberty Diner, wasn't it?"

I nodded. Hadrian sat back, stroking his chin as though thinking.

"That's the thing, isn't it?" he said after a few minutes.

"What is?"

"Don't you find it odd that Baldwin has cultivated a friendship with your boss?"

"He's not my boss. And why wouldn't Baldwin want to pal around with him? Lucado's contributing enough to his campaign."

"That's what surprises me, though. Lucado has a . . . shall we say 'shady' reputation. Baldwin has no qualms about being seen with him. Doesn't that strike you as strange in an election as close as this one?"

"Lucado has never been convicted of anything."

"A moot point. He has the appearance of corruption. He wears it on his face. Yet Baldwin doesn't seem to care. He seems, rather, to go out of his way to spend time with Lucado."

I thought about suggesting that maybe Baldwin just liked the guy, then I remembered we were talking about Frank. "Maybe he's after the Blood of an Evil Man," I said, attempting a joke.

But Hadrian sat up a little straighter. "Are you saying Baldwin has visited sorcerers? Do you know this for a fact?"

"You're kidding, right? Baldwin? He hates everything supernatural."

"Not if he thinks it will help him win. That man is all about power." Hadrian shook his head, looking almost admiring. "There have been rumors—"

But I never heard the rest of the sentence, because a man's scream tore through the night air. It was a horrible sound, ragged and drawn out, the kind of agonized shriek that must have rung through ancient torture chambers. I jumped up and ran to the balcony door, yanking it open. Another scream erupted—it was coming from inside the condo. From upstairs.

I grabbed my sword and dashed inside, taking the stairs two at a time to Lucado's bedroom. The screaming was constant now, like the cries of the damned echoing off the walls of Hell. I put my hand on the doorknob and checked the amulet. It was colorless, transparent, without a hint of light. With my heart beating so hard I could see the amulet jump, I opened the door.

Lucado twisted in his bed, screaming. There was nothing, no one else in the room. The amulet remained clear and cold. Lucado's eyes were closed; he was asleep. He must have been having one hell of a nightmare. I turned on the bedside lamp and balanced my sword against the wall. Then I went over to Lucado's bed and shook his shoulder gently.

"Frank," I said. "Shh . . . it's all right."

He grabbed my hand and sat up in midscream, his eyes flying open and rolling wildly. "Kill it, damn you!" he shouted. "Why don't you kill it?"

"Calm down, Frank. You were dreaming. Understand? It wasn't real."

He blinked, and understanding passed over his face like a sweeping searchlight. He let go of my hand and wiped his forehead. Rivulets of sweat poured down his temples. "Jesus. What a dream."

"You all right now?"

"Yeah, I guess so." His eyes remained a little dazed. I started to leave, but he reached out again and put a hand on my arm. "Wait. I . . . I gotta talk about it. Just for a minute. Just to make sure I'm really awake."

"Okay." I pulled a chair beside the bed and sat down.

Frank ruffled his hair, making it stick straight out on one side. His scar stood out vividly against his pale face. The guy looked shell-shocked.

"It was . . ." He paused and ruffled his hair again, like he was searching for the right words. "It was worse than those damned Harpies."

"You dreamed about a demon?"

"Some kind of monster. All blue, and huge. Slimy. At first its head disappeared into the sky, like there was no end to it at all. But then it came closer and . . . and . . ."

"And what?"

"It sounds stupid now, but the damn thing smiled at me. Its mouth was horrible, with hundreds of teeth—hundreds— and every one of 'em was bigger than that little sword of yours."

His description made my mouth go dry. Difethwr—the Destroyer had invaded Frank's dream. But how was that possible? The thing was a Hellion, not a Drude. And Frank only half believed in Hellions, so it couldn't be one of his greatest fears materialized. It didn't make sense.

Then it hit me. I remembered something Tina had said in her report on Drudes this afternoon. Sometimes other demons could take the form of a Drude. That's what Difethwr had done; it had created an avatar, an image of itself, and sent it into Frank's dreamscape as a Drude. I hadn't expected that. But what would be the point if I had? Even if I'd entered Frank's dreams to guard them, I couldn't have killed Difethwr in there. I'd only have destroyed the avatar.

Frank blinked; gave a little jolt. "Hey, wait." He scowled and grabbed my arm again; his fingers dug in, hard. "That thing you told Baldwin about in the car. That demon. This one was just like what you said. And when it smiled, it was like these flames shot out of its eyes and started burning me. I looked down, thinking, 'My God, I'm on fire,' but every- thing looked just like normal. I was burning on the inside." He gave me a strange look. "Just like you described."

"What you saw in your dream wasn't really the

Destroyer—" I started to explain, but Frank cut me off with a yell.

"You! You made that thing show up in my dream!"

"No, I—"

He interrupted again, his voice hysterical. "What the hell did you do that for? You want more money, is that it? You want more money out of me?"

"Calm down, Frank." I pried his fingers from my arm, laid his hand on the bed. "I didn't send that Hellion into your dream. It wasn't really there. It was an avatar."

"I don't care what the hell it was. I should've fired you, like I said yesterday. I'm not—"

"Shut up and listen, okay? If you think the dream was bad, you definitely do *not* want to meet the real thing." Frank shut his mouth. He looked at me, then closed his eyes and pressed trembling fingers against them. He looked ill, but maybe that would keep him quiet long enough so I could explain. "It was an avatar. That's like a representative, an image. It can't hurt you; not for real. But it can scare the hell out of you. You get all the fun of a Hellion attack with none of the actual damage."

"Lucky me."

Difethwr was taunting us. I had a feeling there was more to its appearance than playing the bogeyman. "Tell me more about the dream, Frank."

"That's it. The damn thing just burned me like I was a big pile of firewood. Then it laughed."

"That's all? It didn't speak?"

He frowned. "No, it did. It said something while it was laughing. Like a bunch of voices cutting through the laughter."

"What did it say? Do you remember?"

His lips were white as he whispered the words. "It said, 'Feel the obliteration of thy body and thy soul, human.'" As Frank spoke, other voices seemed to join his—a dozen or more. They rose in pitch and volume as he continued. "'This is how we shall destroy thee. Thou and all of Boston shall burn. Tomorrow there shall be no victory for thee.'" It was the voice of the Destroyer itself. Laughter rolled through the room.

I grabbed the amulet with my left hand and held it up. The stone glowed scarlet, but only for a second. Then it extinguished like a blown-out candle, all color gone. I watched it for a full minute; it stayed clear.

I sat with Frank, holding his hand like he was a frightened child, until he'd calmed down enough to go back to sleep. When he started snoring, I turned off the light and quietly shut the door.

Downstairs, I stepped out onto the balcony again. Hadrian was gone, but I hadn't expected him to hang around for the hour it had taken me to deal with Frank's nightmare. Laying a hand on the metal railing, I filled my lungs with the cool night air. Frank's dream had been a warning—a warning from a demon that believed it couldn't lose. *Tomorrow there shall be no victory for thee.* Victory. It was another play on my name. The Hellion was boasting to Frank—and me—that when it made its move, I wouldn't be able to stop it.

24

TOMORROW, THE DREAM-AVATAR HAD SAID. DIFETHWR— or its master—was planning the attack for Halloween. Of all the days of the year to heighten the terror of a supernatural attack, Halloween was number one. Humans associated Halloween with monsters and the paranormal. Even an intelligent witch like Roxana had made that mistake.

So Kane must have been right about one thing. The attack was intended to confuse the humans, to turn them against the "monsters"—Hellions, demons, PAs; it didn't matter. The creepy things that come out after dark would be blamed for whatever Difethwr and its master were planning. Whatever it was, I'd bet my best sword that it would happen during the Halloween parade. First the Destroyer would confront me here—*there shall be no victory*—and then it would attack the parade. If I could do my job right, it'd never get that far.

I was back in the living room, once again wearing a track in Lucado's rug. Too bad. I had to think, and pacing helped.

So the plan was to cause terror and blame the monsters. But it was personal, too; there was no doubt in my mind. Above and beyond Difethwr's servitude to its master, the Destroyer had a personal vendetta against me. How could it be otherwise? My family had been at war with it for hundreds of years, and here I was, the result of a prophecy, vowing to kill it. Surely the Destroyer believed that if it killed me, the last of my line, it would achieve the final triumph over the Cerddorion.

If I was the last of my line. We still didn't know about Maria.

I halted, my heart suddenly pounding in my throat. Gwen and the kids were coming into Boston tomorrow to meet me for lunch. That couldn't happen. I didn't want them anywhere near this city, daylight or no daylight. Not on Halloween. Not with Difethwr sealed inside, determined to end its centuries-old feud with my family.

I had to call Gwen and tell her to stay away. Stay in her nice, safe, charm-protected house in the suburbs. I hurried into the kitchen and picked up the phone, then noticed microwave clock—it read 1:46. Gwen and her family would be fast asleep. I didn't want to alarm the whole Santini household with a phone call in the middle of the night. I didn't want to alarm Gwen at all; she'd freak out if I told her I was preparing for a battle-to-the-death with a Hellion. I just wanted to cancel lunch. I'd tell her Boston was too crazy with all the tourists and Halloween festivities; we'd get together another day.

Calling her on the dream phone would be a better option. I'd have to guard my thoughts so she wouldn't hear anything in the background about Hellions. But I thought I could do that. The bigger question was, would she answer? Gwen had rejected all things Cerddorion, and for all I knew that included talking to family members through her dreams. It had been years since I'd tried to contact her that way.

I went back into the living room and settled into a chair. I needed to be relaxed, but not too much. Even though I didn't think Difethwr would be back tonight—it had delivered its message, its challenge—I didn't intend to fall into deep slumber. Only a light doze, just under the surface, more like self-hypnosis than sleeping. I made sure my sword was within reach of my left hand, then closed my eyes. Focusing on my breathing—in for four counts, out for four counts—I let my mind relax. In . . . out . . . in . . . out . . . Thoughts arose, but I gently blew them away on the out breaths. Starting at my toes, I imagined all tension flowing out of me, draining into the earth. Toes . . . ankles . . . calves . . . knees . . . Very gradually, gently, I nudged the relaxation upward . . . stomach . . . back . . . shoulders . . . dissolving all tension from my body. I wasn't sleeping. I knew where I was and stayed connected with my surroundings. But I was ready to place the call.

Gwen's colors are pink and gold. I focused on those, thinking of peaches, sunrises, the rose quartz necklace Gwen used to wear. Wisps of her colors appeared, but they thinned and faded. They didn't swirl up into the heavy pink-and-gold mist I needed to pass through to enter Gwen's dream. After a while, I gave up. Gwen wasn't answering. I'd have to try to contact her through human means in the morning.

SOMETHING KICKED MY ANKLE. IN A SECOND, I WAS ON MY feet, sword in hand.

"Whoa! Back off, Vaughn. Put that thing down." A scowling, scarred face came into focus. It was Lucado, standing three feet away in his striped bathrobe. I lowered the sword and rubbed my eyes. Sun streamed into the room. Despite myself, I'd fallen asleep.

"What time is it?" I asked, groggy.

"Time for you to go. Jesus, you've got to be the world's worst bodyguard. First you fall asleep on the job, then you practically stab me to death when I wake you up."

"That's an exaggeration. You weren't in any danger."

"Yeah, well, neither were the demons. You're fired." He headed toward the hallway, then turned back. "And this time I won't change my mind."

"Frank, you can't fire me—"

"You keep saying that. But I can. I just did. Get out."

"No, you don't understand. You can't fire me *now*. Just one more night, and it'll be over. I'll be out of your hair forever. That Hellion you dreamed about—"

"Was just a dream. And dreams don't mean nuthin' in the morning." He spun on his heel and left the room. I followed him into the kitchen. The room was warm with the smell of coffee, but this didn't seem like a good time to ask for some.

Frank sat at the table, a mug in front of him, writing something. He signed it with a flourish, and held it out to me. A check.

"There ya go," he said. "Two nights' pay. You can't say Frankie didn't keep up *his* end of the deal."

"Frank—"

"That's all you're getting out of me. Now leave."

He wasn't going to listen. I almost didn't blame him, having come downstairs to find me fast asleep in a chair. I took the check, folded it half, and stuck it in my pocket. The clock read 7:34.

"Can I at least use the phone before I go?"

"No."

"I need to call my sister."

He pounded the table with his fist, sloshing coffee out of his mug. "Then call her on your own damn phone. You got no reason to be here anymore."

When I see a battle I can't win, I know it. I shrugged and, without another word, left the kitchen.

In the living room, I packed up my gear and zipped the duffel bag. I wished I could brush my teeth, but I hadn't packed a toothbrush, and anyway, Lucado would probably call the cops if I tried to use his powder room. Carrying my bag, I went through the hall and opened the front door. Then I paused. I dropped my bag and went back to the kitchen, slamming the swinging door open with the heel of my hand.

Lucado still sat at the kitchen table. He was reading the paper. When I banged the door open, he slapped the paper down, looking seriously angry.

"Frank," I said, before he could speak, "listen to me for one minute. That Hellion doesn't make empty threats. If you don't want my protection, fine. But get out of Boston. Just for tonight. The Destroyer is trapped inside the city. If you're not here, it can't harm you."

With a grunt, Lucado raised the paper like a barrier, rattled it into shape, and ignored me.

THE FIRST THING I DID WHEN I GOT HOME WAS GRAB THE living room phone to call Gwen. There was a stutter tone indicating a voice mail, but I ignored it, punching in her number. I'd check for messages later.

The phone rang a couple of times before her husband answered.

"Nick, hi. It's Vicky. Can I talk to my sister?"

"Sorry, Vicky, she's on her way into town. I just walked in the door from dropping her and the kids off at the train station."

Damn. If that jerk Lucado had let me use his phone, I would've caught her.

"Okay. Thanks, anyway."

"Hey, maybe I'll see you this afternoon. I've got a squash date with a client at the Racquet Club. Give him a good game, then let him win." He chuckled. "But I'm meeting Gwen at Quincy Market afterward; should be there around one fifteen. So hang around a bit and say hi—if the kids don't drive you crazy first."

"But then you're going home, right? No trips to the aquarium? No parade?"

His tone indicated he thought it was a strange question. "We've got to catch the 3:10 train out of South Station. Gwen and I are going out for dinner—business stuff—and the kids have a Halloween party. Why do you ask?"

"Oh, it's just—you know how crazy Boston gets on Halloween nowadays. Swarming with tourists and partiers. Nutso. It's no fun when it's that crowded."

We exchanged a few more pleasantries, then hung up. I slumped back on the sofa. Gwen and the kids were on their way into Boston, and there was nothing I could do about it. Maybe it would be okay. I reminded myself that Difethwr couldn't make a move during daylight. But I had a bad feeling I couldn't shake. It worried me to have the whole family together, the entire Cerddorion population of Massachusetts, on the day the Destroyer was promising an end to Victory.

Still, it was daytime now. We had hours and hours before we had to worry about Difethwr. So I'd meet Gwen for lunch, act all happy and normal—and then personally escort the whole family to South Station and make sure they got on that train.

ON VOICE MAIL THERE WERE THREE MESSAGES FOR JULIET, including last night's dinner offering a second helping. His voice had the slow, dreamy tone of an over-the-moon vampire high.

The fourth message was from Daniel. Hearing his voice gave me a gut-level jolt, hot and cold at the same time. I couldn't help seeing those smiling blue eyes, and I couldn't help hearing that cop saying "your wife." Daniel had news from Roxana. When she'd called another meeting of the Witches of the Shield, one person hadn't shown up. The missing witch, Clarinda Fowler, was a paralegal who worked in Government Center. She hadn't come back from lunch yesterday, and no one knew where she was.

"We don't know for sure that she's the one who leaked the information about the shield," he said, "but right now it looks that way."

His message was short and businesslike, and I felt somehow shortchanged when he hung up. But businesslike was what I wanted, right? If I had to interact with Daniel Costello at all, let us both be brisk and professional. There was no other way.

I sighed, then listened to the next message.

"Um, hi, Vicky. It's Tina."

Tina! That thieving zombie. I sat up straight and gripped the phone.

"I, uh, know you're probably kinda mad at me right now . . ."

Kinda. That girl would be lucky if I simmered down to kinda.

"But I didn't steal your sword. Honest. I wasn't gonna keep it. I just wanted to show it to Jenna. It's, like, the coolest thing ever. I wanted to show her my moves."

See, that was the problem with starting weapons training too early. Tina didn't *have* any moves. But because I'd let her spar with me, she thought she did. What is it they say about a little learning—it's a dangerous thing?

Tina went on: "I was gonna bring it back tonight, but then me and Jenna had this really cool idea for our Halloween costumes—I mean, like, really cool—and I need it for mine. So, uh, I'll bring it back tomorrow night. I promise." She blew out a loud breath, then spoke really fast: "I hope you're not mad at me. Bye."

End of message.

I couldn't believe it. Using Saint Michael's sword for her Halloween costume. Sacrilege—that's what it was. Not to mention the end of the entire city of Boston if I didn't get the sword back before sunset.

I jumped up from the sofa. It was eight thirty. Tina would be tucked into her bed now, like all good little zombies. I was going to go over to her group home, and I was going to take back my sword. And while I was there, I'd confiscate *Russom's*, too. If Tina couldn't figure out the difference between the archangel's sword and a toy, there was no way she'd ever become a demon fighter. No way.

"NO, DEAR. TINA'S NOT HERE. SHE NEVER CAME HOME AT all this morning. I'm quite worried."

Tina's house mother sat behind a reception desk, looking like the zombie version of Mrs. Butterworth: plump face, gray hair pulled back in a bun, little half-moon glasses that she peered over when she spoke. Her looks made a weird combination with her spongy, pitted zombie complexion and bloodred eyes. She fluttered with anxiety about her missing charge.

"She's okay," I said. "She called me just before eight this morning." Tricky timing—she must've figured that Juliet would be asleep and I wouldn't be back from my job yet. Her best chance for getting voice mail instead of speaking to someone.

"Oh, I'm so glad! Such a relief. Where is she?"

"She didn't say."

Mrs. Butterworth shook her head, smiling. "That Tina certainly is a pistol, isn't she?"

"She's something, all right."

I thought of asking if I could search Tina's room, but I doubted Mrs. Butterworth would let me. Besides, there was no point. Tina hadn't been back here since she left yesterday afternoon. The sword would be wherever she was.

Maybe the house mother would have a clue about that. "Do you know where Tina likes to hang out?"

"Oh, I don't know. The usual teen places, I suppose. I just supervise the house."

Teen hangouts—in Deadtown? There was no such thing. Only a handful of teenagers and children had been caught in the plague zone. Like Tina and her friend. I had no idea where they went, besides school.

Maybe her friend could help. "Can I talk to Jenna?"

Mrs. Butterworth smiled. "That Jenna. She and Tina are like this." She held up two twined fingers. "It's so nice for the young ones when they have a friend. But Jenna's not here, dear. She didn't come home, either. Wherever one of those girls is, you'll find the other as well."

I TRUDGED AROUND DEADTOWN FOR A WHILE, TRYING TO think where Tina could be. I was alone on the empty streets. The werewolves were on retreat. Vampires couldn't come out into the daylight, and most zombies didn't dare. Stores were closed, everything was shuttered and silent. Deadtown was shut down for the day and, true to its name, wouldn't come back to life until after sunset.

Craning my neck, I scanned the tall buildings that housed Boston's paranormal population. Blackout shades blocked every window. Tina could be behind any one of them, but I'd never find her. Trying to locate a zombie here would be like groping, blindfolded, to find one particular grain of sand on a mile-long beach.

Hopeless, I wandered the streets until it was time to go meet Gwen.

QUINCY MARKET, NEAR BOSTON'S WATERFRONT, HAS BEEN a marketplace for nearly two hundred years. The Colonnade is the food hall, a central building made of granite, two stories tall and more than five hundred feet long. Visitors walk up a few steps and past massive granite columns to get inside, where they can stroll down the long central aisle and buy food ranging from sushi to cannoli to New England clam chowder, from kebabs to enchiladas to ice cream. On either side of the Colonnade are two other long, rectangular buildings, less grand, called North Market and South Market. These hold restaurants, clothing shops, jewelry and housewares stores, and carts where tourists can buy all kinds of souvenirs.

It was a beautiful, crisp, clear October day, and the market was packed. Tourists and locals jostled each other as they milled around, wandering through the pedestrian areas and in and out of buildings. I was glad I'd gotten there early; I'd had to wait more than half an hour to snag a table for five.

I was sitting in a pizzeria in North Market, with a good view of the open brick plaza in front of the Colonnade, a favorite spot for street performers. Right now, a one-man band played there, while "living statues"—Samuel Adams in bronze makeup, the Statue of Liberty in copper green—posed stiffly as passersby stopped to see if they'd blink. Occasionally, one or the other would move suddenly, making half the audience jump. I spotted Gwen and the kids when Zachary ran up and poked the Statue of Liberty. Gwen dragged him away, and thirty seconds later they stood in the doorway. I waved them over.

Act like everything's normal, I reminded myself as the older kids ran over, followed by a frazzled-looking Gwen, who carried Justin on her hip. In just a few hours, they'd be safely back in Needham. I smiled, hoping it didn't look like a grimace, and gave Maria a hug and a kiss on the top of her head. Zack shook my hand, all grown up at five.

I'd already asked for a high chair for Justin, and as Gwen got him settled, Maria and Zack argued about what kind of pizza to get. Maria didn't like anything spicy; Zack didn't like anything that remotely resembled a vegetable. We settled on a large plain cheese pizza for the kids and a small one with artichoke hearts and black olives for Gwen and me.

Sodas all around—no caffeine for the kids, though. "They've had enough stimulation for one day," Gwen said.

She produced three small boxes of crayons, and the kids got busy drawing pictures on the backs of their paper placemats. She watched them for a moment, then smiled at me. "I should've been a Boy Scout," she said. "With kids, my motto has become 'Be prepared.'"

She sat back in her chair, blew out her cheeks, and smiled at me. "Hey, I like your necklace." She motioned at the amulet. "You never wear jewelry."

"Thanks. It was a gift from a friend."

We chatted about normal stuff, Gwen doing most of the talking: how the kids were doing in school, Maria's soccer games—this was her first year in the Youth Soccer League—neighborhood gossip, Nick's hopes for a promotion at work. When the pizzas came, she chose a skinny slice from the plain and cut it into small pieces for Justin, who immediately started smearing tomato sauce all over his face. Zack wouldn't let his mom cut up his pizza for him; after one slice, his face wasn't much cleaner than his baby brother's.

"So what have you guys been doing all morning?" I asked. "You left awfully early—I tried to call around eight, but you were already gone."

Gwen's eyes slid away from mine. "Oh, we . . ."

"We went to the hospital an' saw a doctor!" Zack shouted. "We got stuck with needles this big"—he held his hands about ten inches apart—"an' it hurt!"

"Zachary." Gwen's voice held a warning tone.

Maria whacked her brother under the table. "Shut up, dummy! Mom said we're not supposed to tell," she said in a stage whisper loud enough to be heard two tables over.

Gwen smiled in a tight-lipped way that said she didn't want to talk about it. Fine with me. I was more than happy to avoid the details of the kids' medical charts.

Then it dawned on me. Oh, no. "Gwen, you didn't."

"I don't want to discuss this now, Vicky. Not in front of the kids."

"Sheila Gravett is not interested in helping you. I don't

care what lies she told you." My voice was rising, but I couldn't help it. "The woman has no ethics. You know how those were-wolf experiments turned out. What's next—a Cerddorion clone?"

"What does that mean?" asked Maria, eyes wide.

I took a deep breath, then let it out slowly. Okay, Gwen was right. I shouldn't be scaring the kids with tales of medical abuse. But talking about it was one thing—actually taking them to Gravett, letting her poke and prod them, was another. I glared at Gwen.

"It doesn't mean anything, honey," I said, smoothing a strand of Maria's blonde hair behind her ear. "I just got carried away. I don't like doctors." I wrinkled my nose to show my distaste.

"Me either!" proclaimed Zack. "'Specially not the kind with needles."

"She just drew some blood samples, Vicky. That's all she needed. I doubt we'll ever hear from her again."

I wasn't so sure. Gravett was greedy and ambitious. She didn't care if her research caused harm. And she'd lied to a mother about her intentions regarding her kids. If Gravett would stoop that low, she was capable of anything. Gwen had cooperated this far, and I'd bet she'd have trouble getting rid of Gravett in the future. We'd have to talk about it, but not now.

Searching for a topic that would get the kids' minds on something else, I asked about their Halloween plans.

"Mom won't let us watch the parade!" Zack's brow furrowed with the injustice of it all.

"Don't you want to go home so you can go trick-or-treating? You'll get better loot that way."

"Trick-or-treat was last night. Tonight's some stupid Halloween party at church. It'll prob'ly be like Sunday school with costumes."

"Don't say 'stupid,'" Gwen admonished.

"They'll have a haunted house," Maria said.

"So what? Bobby told me the Boston parade is gonna have *real* zombies."

"Not this year, Zack," I said. "Zombies aren't allowed in the parade. They have to stay in their own part of town. Anyway, zombies aren't all that scary—they're a lot like regular people."

"Yeah, except their skin is rotting and their noses are falling off and they got blood in their eyeballs!"

Not much I could say to that. It was a pretty accurate description.

Maria pointed outside at the plaza. "Look!" she said.

Zack turned so fast he must've given himself whiplash. "What? You mean that guy selling Halloween balloons?"

"No, I saw—"

"Look, look!" Zack shouted. "Somebody's doin' juggling! Can we go watch, Mom? Pleeeeeease?"

"Shh. Indoor voice, Zack." She turned to look outside. "If he's still there after we've finished eating, we can go."

"No, now. I want to go *now*."

Justin, bouncing up and down in his seat, echoed, "Now! Now!"

No indoor voices from either kid. They'd been good all through the meal. Let them have some fun. "We're pretty much done anyway, Gwen. You take the kids over there. I'll get the bill and come join you."

"Thanks," she said, standing. "Bathroom first, kids. We've got sticky faces to wash." With all three of them in tow, she disappeared in the back of the restaurant.

THE STREET PERFORMER WAS GOOD. BY THE TIME I GOT there, he was balancing on stilts, juggling half a dozen balls, and keeping up a patter that made the audience laugh. I didn't see Gwen and the kids at first, so I wandered around until I spotted my sister, who held Justin up on her shoulders. Zack had pushed his way to the front of the crowd. When the juggler asked for a volunteer, he ran out into the performance area, and the juggler laughed and told him he needed someone a little bigger. Zack puffed out his chest and yelled in his loudest voice, "I'm big!" The juggler pointed to a burly six-foot man, who stepped forward. Zack smacked himself in the forehead and yelled, "But not that big!" He was getting more laughs than the juggler. So the juggler told him to wait and he'd have a job for him. After the trick—which involved climbing up on the big guy's shoulders, juggling some dangerous-looking flaming torches, then doing a backflip to the ground—he gave Zack a hat and told him to make sure everyone put something green in it. Zack swaggered around the edges of the crowd yelling, "Put something green in. That means money! No frogs and no spinach. I want dollar bills—lots of dollar bills!"

I edged over to Gwen. "That young man has a future in sales."

She smiled, keeping an eye on him while she swung Justin down from her shoulders and perched him on her hip.

"Where's Maria?" I asked.

"She's right over there." She tilted her head to the right, then yelled, "Zachary Evan Santini, you give the man his money!"

I looked to the right but didn't see Maria. Zack came running over, a dollar grasped in his fist. "Look what the man gave me for helpin' him! He said I collected more money than he got all day!" His eyes shone. "Mom, where can I learn how to juggle?"

"We'll talk about it when we get home. Where's your sister?"

"How am I supposed to know? I was in the act!" He turned to me, waving his dollar and beaming. "Aunt Vicky, did you see me?"

"Maria!" Gwen called. There was no answer. She twisted one way, then the other, looking for her daughter. The crowd had dispersed, and there was no sign of a thin, blonde, ten-year-old girl.

"Oh, God, where is she?" Gwen grabbed Zack's hand and dragged him as she ran toward the performer, who was packing up. "Did you see my daughter?" she asked. "She's blonde, about this tall . . ."

"Sorry, ma'am. There are a lot of kids around."

"Maria!" Justin piped up, pointing.

I followed the chubby finger. A hundred feet away, a tall blonde woman was leading a girl toward Commercial Street. The girl was about Maria's height, but with so many people between us it was hard to tell from the back whether it was her. The woman leaned down and said something to the girl, then tugged her arm so hard it nearly made her fall. The girl looked back at us and waved, her mouth moving, but the woman grabbed other her arm and lifted the child off her feet. When I saw her face, even from a hundred feet away, there was no doubt. It was Maria, and she looked terrified.

I was after them like a shot.

"Maria!" Gwen screamed, and started running. She still held Justin and had Zack's hand. Zack couldn't keep up with her, and he fell, shrieking. Gwen stopped, but I ran harder. They were at Commercial Street now. Good. Traffic was against them. I'd catch them before they could cross. I put all my strength into it, pumping my arms, yelling at people to get out of my way.

But they didn't cross the street. Waiting at the curb was a dented black van. The side door opened. Arms reached out, grabbed Maria, and pulled her inside. The woman leaped in behind her. The door slammed shut. I was almost there. I was reaching for the door handle. But the van screeched out into the traffic, sideswiping a Jeep, and my fingers closed on empty air.

25

"WHAT DO YOU MEAN, YOU CAN'T DO ANYTHING?" Gwen's voice edged upward to a hysterical pitch. "We know who took her—Sheila Gravett. She forced my daughter into that van; I saw her. And Vicky got the license plate number. Why the hell haven't you put out an Amber Alert? Every second that passes— Oh God, I want my baby." She broke down in tears, but she didn't look away. She stared at the officer, her face contorted with suffering, demanding an answer.

"Mrs. Santini, I understand you're upset, but we can't help you unless you remain calm."

"You're not helping me! You're letting that bitch abduct my child!"

"We can't take action until we've determined whether in fact a crime has taken place." What the cop meant was that they weren't sure whether Maria was classified as a human or a PA. For a human child, they'd be broadcasting an Amber Alert, calling in the FBI, alerting Massachusetts and New Hampshire state troopers—the whole deal. But if Maria was classified as a PA, they didn't have to lift a finger. You can't kidnap something that's not human.

Gwen howled and launched herself at the cop. Three others closed in on her. Thirty seconds later, she sat restrained in the back of a police car. When they shut the car door, Zack started to cry. Then Justin joined him. The both wailed for their mother while a female cop bent over, shushing them. I tried to go to the kids, but a cop barred my way.

"Those are my nephews—"

"For God's sake, Morelli, let her go to the kids," said a voice behind me. The cop glanced past my shoulder, then nodded and stepped aside.

I turned to see Daniel, looking grim, his mouth set in a thin line. He wore jeans and a leather jacket, so he must be off-duty. I didn't know what he was doing there, and I didn't care. I just wanted to get to the boys. "Thanks," I said, and rushed over to them. Justin climbed up my legs and into my arms like a monkey, while Zack sobbed into my hip. "Why are the police hurting Mommy?" Zack said between hiccups. "Did she do something bad? Why did that lady take Maria?"

"Shh, Zack, it's okay," I said, smoothing his hair with my hand.

"Your mom didn't do anything wrong," Daniel said. "I'll get her for you."

Zack raised his head to watch Daniel walk to the police car and speak with an officer. Justin buried his face in my shoulder.

"Here she comes!" Zack's voice was an excited scream. "Mommy!" He took off running to Gwen, who caught him up in her arms and pressed her face into his hair. I handed Justin over to her, and while she hugged her boys I went over to talk to Daniel.

"Maria hasn't been classified yet," I told him. "We won't know whether she's human or demi-human until she reaches puberty. That means she should be treated as a human." I wished Kane were here. He'd nail these idiots on the legalities.

"I agree. But I'm not in charge on this—I'm not even supposed to be here." He pushed both hands through his blond curls, looking frustrated. "Chief Hampson is a Baldwin supporter. He's dragging his feet because he doesn't want to waste resources on a PA."

"What if she's fully human?"

"He's betting she's not." He paused, like he was wondering whether he should stop there, then decided not to hold back. "New Hampshire troopers stopped the van."

Gwen had come up behind me. She broke in, her voice excited. "The cops have Maria? When are they bringing her home?"

Daniel shook his head. "I'm sorry, but they let the van go. They said Sheila Gravett showed them a paper, signed by you, stating that Maria is paranormal and giving Gravett Biotech legal custody of her."

"That's a lie!" Gwen's face was gray, with bright red splotches on her cheeks.

"You didn't sign anything like that, Mrs. Santini?"

"Of course not. I only— Oh, my God." She caught her breath, and her eyes widened with horror. "It was just a formality. That's what that bitch said. She said she needed my permission to draw a blood sample. I . . . I didn't read the paper, but I signed it." Gwen grabbed Daniel's arm. "That can't be legal, can it? She tricked me!"

Daniel opened his mouth, but before he could answer, Nick appeared, looking worried and confused. Gwen collapsed against him, and both his sons started crying again. "What the hell's going on?" he demanded.

I explained the situation while Daniel went over to talk to another cop. After a few minutes, he returned with some new information. "We have an address, Mr. and Mrs. Santini. It's near Seabrook, not far over the state line. Two officers checked on her there, and she's all right. She's a little scared and wants to come home, but Gravett wouldn't dare do anything to mistreat her."

Not yet, I thought. Not until her legal status was resolved. But I couldn't say that in front of Gwen.

"You know where she is?" Nick said. "So go get her and bring her home."

"New Hampshire doesn't recognize PA rights, Mr. Santini. We can't just go in and take her; we have to determine her classification."

"Why?" Gwen wailed. "You're acting like my daughter is . . . is that woman's property."

"In New Hampshire, I'm afraid that's what the law considers her to be."

Gwen screamed. Her knees sagged, and her face was dead white.

"Daniel, don't," I said. "We don't know yet how the law will play out. Kane will be all over this when he gets back." But that wouldn't be until Monday—and I had no intention of waiting that long. God, what a time for a full moon.

"I'll get my lawyer on it right now," Nick began, then Gwen collapsed at his feet. He crouched down and held her, speaking softly.

"Take Gwen home first, Nick. And the boys." He looked up like he was going to argue with me, but he must have seen something in my expression, because he nodded.

When Nick had loaded his family into a taxi and left, I turned to Daniel. "Where is she? I want the address." I was already calculating how long it'd take to get to the garage and pick up the Jag before I could drive north. But—damn it all. The garage closed at noon on Saturdays. Well, that didn't matter. I'd break in if I had to.

"Vicky, you can't go charging off to New Hampshire. It's too dangerous." He put his hand on my arm. "They're not doing anything to her right now."

I shook him off. "You expect me to sit around while my ten-year-old niece is being held captive by that madwoman?"

"Slow down a minute. You drive a distinctive car. The New Hampshire cops know what's going on—they'll be watching for you. You won't make it a mile past the border."

He was right. Okay, so the Jag was out. I'd break into the garage and steal somebody else's car. Nothing was going to stop me from getting to Maria.

"Think about a young girl," I said, "locked in a strange room, crying for her mother. Think about a state that won't help her because they define her as property. She's a *little girl*, Daniel. And she's not going to stay with those bastards any longer than it takes for me to get her the hell out of there."

"I can't let you run off to a state where you have fewer rights than an animal."

"Listen—"

"But I can drive you there." He flashed a quick smile and jerked his head sideways. "Let's go."

THE ROADS WERE PACKED, AND WE WERE GETTING NO-where. Under good conditions, it takes nearly an hour to drive from Boston up into southern New Hampshire, but conditions were lousy. It felt like it took us an hour just to get across the Tobin Bridge into Chelsea. I checked my watch. Not an hour, but a very long twenty minutes.

When Daniel saw me check the time, he rolled down his window and reached under his seat. He pulled out a rotator light and stuck it on the roof of the car, then plugged it into the cigarette lighter. Splashes of blue light washed across the hood. He glanced over at me and shrugged. "I'm not supposed to do this, but . . ." He flipped a switch and a siren blared.

Cars began to pull over, and we got moving. Daniel weaved in and out of the lanes, picking up speed, coming up close behind the cars that wouldn't get out of the way and leaning on the horn to make them move. He was a good driver, tightly focused on the road. I let him drive. I looked out the window and watched the triple-deckers and convenience stores give way to strip malls, Cineplexes, and car dealers. When those thinned out, replaced by trees, traffic grew lighter. He turned off the siren and unplugged the light.

We drove the next several miles in silence. Then Daniel scratched his head and looked at me. "I don't understand why your sister let that crazy doctor examine her kids in the first place."

"Gravett led Gwen to believe that she could do some tests to determine whether Maria is fully human or demi-human. She was lying. If Maria *is* Cerddorion, her DNA will actually change when she reaches puberty and gains the ability to shift. Until then, there's no way to know."

"So why did Gwen believe her?"

I sighed. "Gwen is ashamed of her heritage. More than anything she wants Maria to be a human girl. She wants her daughter to grow up normal, giggling about boys and hanging out at the mall, not trying to control her moods so she won't shift into a warthog or a monkey." Of course, getting kidnapped by a mad scientist wasn't exactly part of a normal human childhood, either. "Gwen hoped Gravett could find a cure. That's what she called it: a 'cure.' That wishful thinking must be killing my sister right now."

Daniel steered into the left lane to pass an eighteen-wheeler. When we were past it, he said, "If there's no difference between human and Cerddorion DNA at her age, then the courts will have to rule that she's human."

"Maybe. There's no precedent for a case like this." Again, I wished Kane were here. He'd be filing motions left and right. "Anyway, I'm not waiting around for the courts to settle anything. I'm taking her home."

He nodded. We passed the exit for Byfield. Only about ten miles to the state border.

"You do realize," Daniel said, "that Gravett might be setting a trap for you, using your niece as bait."

"That doesn't matter." I had been thinking about it, though. There was a high likelihood that she'd try. As soon as I crossed the state line into New Hampshire, I'd lose the few rights I had in Massachusetts. Gravett could grab me and then, even if the courts made her return Maria, she'd have me as her own personal guinea pig. "She's already tried to snatch me once."

Daniel glanced sideways at me. "When?"

"Two days ago. Thursday. I got a distress call from a fake client at a bogus address. When I showed up there, three guys in ski masks jumped out of a van and tried to kidnap me. It was black van, the same one as today." I felt a twinge of guilt for thinking Kane had set that up.

"Jesus, I'm glad you weren't hurt. How did you get away?"

"I shifted into a panther and mauled one of them."

He turned and stared at me, mouth open. I met his gaze.

A horn blared as we drifted into the other lane. Daniel whipped his head around and jerked the wheel. After that, he kept his eyes on the road. We moved smoothly forward, but his knuckles were white on the steering wheel.

"It's what I am, Daniel."

He nodded but didn't reply. I watched the bare trees go by.

When Daniel spoke again, his voice was thoughtful. "So that's why you missed our appointment on Thursday. I thought I'd done something wrong." He ducked his head. "Or that you just plain didn't like me."

"I like you, Daniel, but . . ."

"But what?"

But you're married and you didn't bother to mention it. "Nothing. This isn't something to talk about now."

"You're right."

There didn't seem to be anything to talk about right now. The white lines flashed toward us, disappeared, flashed and disappeared, marking off the miles that would bring us to Maria. But Daniel pulled off at the Amesbury exit, still in Massachusetts.

"Why are we getting off here?"

"There's a checkpoint at the state line. You don't have a human ID, do you?"

I shook my head. My driver's license had PARANORMAL written across it in big red letters. I hadn't even thought about identification.

"They won't let you through without one."

"You know another way in?"

He turned on to a side street. "We'll have to hike through the woods for about a mile. A buddy of mine left his car for us on the other side."

"You were pretty sure I'd let you come with me."

For a second, his tense expression switched to one of those dazzling Daniel smiles. "If you didn't, I was coming anyway."

WE BUMPED ALONG A POTHOLED ROAD WITH WOODS ON both sides. Daniel parked in a pull-off. Two trucks and a car were already there.

"Popular spot," I commented.

"This is an easy place for PAs to cross the state line." He looked at a green pickup and frowned. "I hope that's who's in the woods."

"What do you mean?"

"There's a self-appointed civilian border patrol that watches this stretch of woods. If they catch us on the wrong side of the line . . ." He frowned at the pickup again.

I followed his gaze. The truck's empty gun rack suddenly looked ominous. "If they catch *me* on the wrong side, you mean. You'll be okay."

He took my hand. "I'm with you, Vicky. No matter what happens."

I started to pull away, but he tightened his grip, his eyes intent on mine. Okay, I could use his help. For the moment, I'd let him be on my side. Then he could go back to his wife.

We moved through the woods quickly, if not exactly silently. Both of us were city dwellers who didn't have the faintest idea how to move quietly through the woods. Autumn had left a thick carpet of leaves, and every single one of them crackled and crunched under our feet. It sounded like we were stomping our way across a giant field of cellophane.

"Shh!" Daniel squeezed my hand and stopped, gesturing with his other hand. I glanced around for a big tree to hide behind, but all the trees were slimmer than I was. So I dropped to a crouch, pulling Daniel down with me.

He dropped my hand, reached inside his jacket, and took out his gun, a 9mm Glock. He nudged my arm, then gestured with the gun. Fifty yards away, a potbellied norm in a fluorescent orange hunter's hat stepped through the brush, holding a rifle in both hands. He was looking away from us, so as quietly as possible, we stretched out flat on the ground. My nostrils filled with the dusty, loamy smell of dead leaves, and I pinched my nose to keep from sneezing. My heart pounded so loudly I couldn't tell whether the hunter was moving closer or farther away.

After what felt like an hour, Daniel tapped my arm. "He's

gone," he whispered. "But he went the way we were heading. We'll have to go around the long way."

I thought of Maria, locked away somewhere north of us, and every way seemed like the long way. We half ran, trying to be quiet, stopping every few yards to listen. Daniel kept the Glock out, but we didn't see the hunter—whatever he was hunting—again. Twenty minutes later, we emerged from the woods onto another road. Daniel paused, looking left, then right. "I think it's this way," he said, turning right.

We kept inside the woods, following the road. Twice we heard a car coming, and twice we dove for the ground. Finally, we rounded a curve, and there sat a blue Toyota with New Hampshire plates.

"Okay," Daniel said, holstering his pistol, "according to my buddy, the key's under a trio of rocks next to a birch tree."

"There's a birch tree," I said.

Daniel jogged over to it. "And here's the key," he said, coming back a minute later. He opened the passenger door with a flourish. "Welcome to New Hampshire!"

So far, so good. We'd made it in. Now all we had to do was find Maria, avoid whatever traps Gravett had set, and make it out alive.

26

GRAVETT BIOTECH WAS A FORTRESS, A COMPOUND IN THE middle of the woods surrounded by eight-foot walls topped with razor wire.

"How are we going to get in?" I said, looking at the high wall.

"You're a shapeshifter. Can't you turn into a bird or something and fly over?"

"I could. But then I'd be stuck in bird form for several hours, which wouldn't help get you in—or Maria out." Besides, I didn't want to shift on the day of the full moon, not after what had happened during the panther shift. No eating people today—not if I could avoid it. We'd have to find a norm way inside.

We ran alongside the wall, keeping low. Getting in would be the easy part. Gravett must be all in favor of welcoming me inside. It was getting out again that was going to be tough.

"Look!" I pointed to a place up ahead, where the trees stood close to the wall; the branches of one huge pine tree reached right across it. "I can climb up there, then drop to the other side."

Daniel shook his head. "Won't work," he said. "The branches are too thin when they get close enough to the wall. They won't hold your weight."

"I'm going to try." I ran to the base of the tree and put my arms around the trunk. It was sticky and smelled like pitch. I tried to shinny up it, but I couldn't get a foothold. And when I gripped the trunk with my knees, I couldn't figure out how to move upward.

Daniel caught up to me, panting. "Give me a boost," I said.

"Vicky. It's. Not—" he said between pants. But when he saw my expression he laced his fingers into a kind of step. I put my foot in his hands, and he boosted me up so that I could grab hold of one of the lower branches. From there, I pulled myself up until I was sitting on the branch where it met the trunk.

I was only about ten feet off the ground, but it felt higher. I could see far into the Gravett Biotech complex. Six brick buildings stood around a central courtyard. At the far side of the courtyard, almost directly across from my perch, was a barred gate. There was a gatehouse next to it, but from here I couldn't see whether it was occupied by a guard. We had to assume it was. Everything was still—no patrols, no guard dogs, nothing. No people in lab coats bustling around with clipboards. The stillness worried me. It was like the place was holding its breath, waiting for me to make my move.

Surprised at how unsteady my legs felt, I grasped the trunk, inching upward along it, until I stood at my full height on the branch. The tree seemed to shake with my own trembling. At chest level, another branch grew parallel to the one I stood on. I clutched the branch with both hands and took one step, sideways, toward the wall. So far, so good. Another couple of steps, and my confidence grew. But the branch began to thin, and the farther I moved from the trunk, the more it bent. This branch would snap or dump me before I got past the wall. From where I stood, I could just about jump onto the wall—to be sliced up by razor wire.

Then I had an idea. Clutching the higher branch with one hand, I shrugged off my leather jacket and dropped it to Daniel on the ground. "Toss that up so it covers the wire on top of the wall." He lined himself up with the branch and flung the jacket upward, hanging on to one sleeve. The first try, he missed, and the jacket slid down the wall.

On the second try, he got it. The jacket landed on a length of razor wire, flattening it. I'd have to jump carefully to make sure I hit the narrow strip protected by the jacket. I inched outward on the branch.

"Wait a minute," Daniel called. He took off his own jacket and threw it onto the wall next to mine. "Okay," he said, "I think you can do it."

I wanted to close my eyes, but I didn't. I kept them on my target, a four-foot-wide safety zone of leather. I took a deep breath, thought about Maria—and jumped.

FIVE MINUTES LATER, DANIEL HAD JOINED ME INSIDE THE wall. "She's in Building Four," he said. "That's what the report we got from New Hampshire said."

"Which one's Building Four?"

"Let's find out."

As I'd seen from the tree, the complex held half a dozen buildings. We dashed from the shelter of the wall to the nearest one. The place was still deserted. It was Saturday, but it seemed like there'd be more activity, more excitement, after they'd stolen a possible Cerddorion child. The wide-open stillness of the place made me nervous. It couldn't have felt more like a trap if they'd plunked down a big open cage in the middle of the lawn with a sign that read ENTER HERE.

Still, if there were no obstacles to getting in and finding Maria, at least they were making half of our job easy for us.

We edged along the side of the building until we got to the corner. Turning that corner would bring us into the courtyard, where we'd be in view of the other buildings. Daniel held up his hand, indicating I should wait. He pulled his pistol and held it pointing upward. Then he disappeared around the corner.

I squinched my eyes tight shut, waiting for the pop of gunshots. All was quiet—that eternal, unrelenting silence. In a moment, Daniel reappeared. "This is Building Three," he whispered. "Four is the next one over."

I nodded, and we backtracked until we stood behind Building Four. Again, Daniel went around the corner to check out the front of the building. I waited for him to motion me to join him, but when he returned, he took my arm and pulled me back. "This one's guarded," he said.

"How many?"

"Just one that I saw. A guy in a lab coat. I can't tell if he's armed."

Someone was in the building—good. I'd make the bastard take us to Maria. And we could use him as a hostage if we had to.

"Let's get him," I said.

We went for speed, bursting around the corner and through the front door. Daniel pointed his gun, but I'd jumped the guy and had him pinned to the floor before Daniel could yell *freeze*.

"Nice tackle."

"Thanks." I twisted Mr. Lab Coat's arm behind his back. "Where's Maria Santini?" I asked, twisting it harder.

"I don't— Ouch! There's no need for violence. No one named Santini works here."

"You know who I mean, damn you. Where's the little girl?"

"Oh, you mean—" He grunted. "There's no little girl here."

I grabbed a fistful of brown hair, yanked his head back, and slammed his face into the floor. "Are you sure?"

He groaned and tried to turn his head to look at me. Blood streamed from his broken nose. His glasses were crooked, and one lens had cracked, making it look like he had two eyes in one socket. "There's no little girl here," he repeated. "This is a research facility."

He was stalling—not good. It probably meant reinforcements were on the way. I smashed his face against the floor again, then climbed off his back. He half rolled onto his side and squinted up at me in surprise.

"Okay, Daniel," I said. "Shoot him."

It was impossible to say who looked more shocked—Daniel or the guy on the floor. I knew that Daniel would never shoot anyone in cold blood, but it took him a second to realize that I *did* know that. The guy in the lab coat, though, suddenly looked uncertain.

Daniel took two steps so his feet were planted in front of the guy's face. Mr. Lab Coat, wheezing in fear, curled into a fetal position and covered his head with his arms. His cracked lens glinted between them. Daniel aimed the gun and clicked off the safety. The sound of that click echoed off the walls.

"No, don't!" Lab Coat's voice came out in a high-pitched, half-strangled whine. "Don't! I'll take you to her."

I pulled the norm up onto his feet. He shook so hard his knees buckled, and I caught him before he hit the ground a second time. "Which way?" I asked. I'd twisted his arm behind his back again.

Daniel pressed the pistol against the guy's head, behind his right ear. He'd put the safety back on, but Lab Coat didn't know that.

He motioned with his chin toward the elevator. "Third floor."

"We'll take the stairs." I dragged him to the stairwell.

Daniel went ahead of us. "It's clear," he called down.

By the time I'd hauled Lab Coat up two flights of stairs, he'd recovered somewhat. When we emerged on the third floor, he led us quickly down a long corridor—or as quickly as he could, given the grip I had on him. The walls were gleaming white; so was the tile floor. The place smelled like a cross between a hospital and a zoo, strong antiseptic over musky animal odors. Every few feet there was a door with a small, square window about five feet above the ground. Wires crisscrossed the reinforced glass. I glanced inside one; the narrow room held a cot but was otherwise empty. In the next one, a wolf, mangy and thin, huddled in a corner, its back toward the door.

Next to each door were a magnetic card reader and a metal frame that held a printed card. SUBJECT 1375B, read one card. SUBJECT 1722A, read another.

We stopped in front of a door about midway down the corridor. The card here read SUBJECT 3564C. I looked through the tiny window and saw Maria, sitting on the cot and hugging herself tightly. She looked so small, so terrified and alone. I grabbed Dr. Lab Coat and pressed his face against the window until the glass cracked. I put my lips to his ear. "That, you asshole, is a little girl."

I picked him up with both hands and threw him, as hard as I could, down the hall. He grunted when he hit the wall and again when he hit the floor.

Maria had looked up at the movement at the window. When she saw me, her eyes went wide, and she jumped off the cot. I smiled at her, reaching for the doorknob. It was locked. And Lab Coat was crumpled in a heap against the far wall, out cold.

I pointed to the card reader by the door, turning to Daniel. "See if that jerk has an ID card. Something with a magnetic strip." I put my fingers against the glass and said, "We're coming, sweetheart. We'll get you out of here."

Daniel searched the guy's pockets, shaking his head. He pulled open the lab coat and said, "Bingo!" Handing me a plastic card with a photo on one side and a strip on the other, he said, "It was clipped to his shirt pocket."

I swiped the card, holding my breath. The lock made a telltale click, the knob turned, and the door flew open. Maria rocketed out and flung her arms around me. She didn't say a word, just pressed her face against me. I held her tight and showered her hair with kisses.

"Come on, kiddo," I said. "We're taking you home."

"We?" Maria looked around. Daniel smiled and said hi; she stared at him, her eyes wary, like he was a stranger who'd offered her candy.

"This is Daniel," I said. "He's a police officer."

Maria tensed. "A police officer already came. She said I had to stay here."

"Not Daniel." I gave him a half-smile. "He's okay."

The heap in the lab coat groaned. "Sounds like our cue to leave," I said. Holding Maria's hand, I started back down the hallway. Gray, furry faces with wide, rolling eyes peered out of some of the windows as we passed all those locked doors. As we neared the stairwell, shouts and hard-stomping footsteps erupted ahead of us. They were coming up the stairs.

We turned and ran the other way down the hall, toward a green-lit exit sign at the far end. A howl came from one of the cells we passed, giving me an idea. I stopped and swiped the ID card that had opened Maria's door. The lock clicked, and I pushed the door open. I did that at every door we passed. Growls and yelps filled the air behind us. A moment later, a voice yelled, "Stop!" then "Holy shit!"

As we neared the exit door, I glanced back. Wolves, half-men, and a few unidentifiable creatures looking like something out of a nightmare, charged the other end of the hall. A rifle went off, taking a chunk out of the ceiling. A human screamed. I pushed Maria into the stairwell, ducking in behind her.

BEFORE WE MADE IT TO THE BOTTOM OF THE STAIRS, AN alarm went off with a skull-splitting clamor. Strobe lights flashed at each landing. Maria covered her ears as we ran down the last few steps. At the bottom were two doors: one leading to the first-floor hallway and the other, marked EXIT, opening to the outside. At the exit door, Daniel put a hand up, telling us to wait. As he eased the door open a crack, I hugged Maria to me. I could feel the bumps of her spine under my hand as I stroked her back. She seemed so small and vulnerable; I didn't want to let go of her. The alarm kept up its racket.

Daniel opened the door a bit wider, then closed it and turned to us. The alarm was too loud for speech, so he signaled what we should do: out the door and immediately to the right. I nodded. I gave Maria a reassuring squeeze, then took her hand. Daniel opened the door, and the three of us slipped out.

To the right of the door were some overgrown yew bushes. We plunged into these for cover. The bushes grew close to the side of the building, but there was a little room to get through. We pushed our way through cobwebs and dusty branches. Maria sneezed, then sneezed again. *Bless you*, I thought, meaning it in so many ways.

When we made it to the corner of the building, we paused again. The next building, marked Five, was ten yards away. It was a rectangular brick building, three stories high, identical to the one we'd just left. But it was closer to the wall that surrounded the compound; the wall was only about five feet from the back of the building. If we could get inside, we could find something—a conference table or a ladder or a lab bench; something like that—to form a makeshift bridge between a second-story window and the wall.

The building wall that faced us, one of the short ends of the rectangle, had a metal door like the exit we'd just used. Next to it was a card reader. I still had Lab Coat's ID card; that would get us in.

The alarm still blared, maybe a couple of decibels quieter out here, but still deafening. I put my mouth right up against Daniel's ear; his curls brushed my lips as I spoke in a low voice, laying out my plan. He nodded. "I'll go first and open the door," I said. "You cover me." He nodded again.

Maria still clutched my hand. I bent down, brushed her hair behind her ear, and said, "I'm going to run over to that building and open the door. From there, we'll climb out of a window to get over the wall, okay?" She shook her head, looking panicked, and squeezed my hand.

"Don't go," she mouthed.

"Sweetie, you want to get out of here, right?" She bit her lip, then nodded. "This is how we have to do it. So I'll open that door. Then, when Daniel says go, run as fast as you can, straight to the door." A teardrop splashed on my hand. Another squeeze, and then she let go.

27

I STOOD AT THE EDGE OF THE BUSHES' COVER, TENSING TO run, when the alarm suddenly cut off. For about two seconds, the silence rang louder than the alarm. Daniel and I looked at each other, and I could tell we were thinking the same thing: Why hadn't anyone come running at the sound of the alarm? And who'd turned it off?

I didn't like it. But the situation wasn't waiting around for my approval. We couldn't get out the way we'd come in. We'd never make it out the front gate. Building Five, ten yards away, offered our only chance for escape. I leaned forward enough to get a view of the courtyard. No one there. The coast was as clear as it was going to get. I still didn't like it, but I ran.

I was halfway across the open space when Building Five's door burst open and four big guys wearing camouflage piled out, carrying automatic rifles. I veered to the right. But behind me I heard yelling, then a scream. Maria was screaming. I spun around. Four more soldiers—they must have come from behind the building—were dragging Daniel and Maria from the bushes. Daniel had his hands up. One of the men had his arm around Maria's waist, lifting her into the air. She kicked and flailed her arms, screaming my name over and over.

I started toward her, but both my arms were grabbed from behind. I started to yank away—it would take more than a couple of 250-pound norms to hold me back—then thought better of it. There were too many of them. If I didn't reveal my full strength now, I might be able to surprise them with it later. Outnumbered eight to two, with a little girl to protect, we didn't exactly have a lot going for us at the moment. Any advantage, no matter how small, was worth hanging on to.

A man stepped in front of me, acting like he was the one in charge. He had military-short hair, bug eyes, and a twisted, sneering mouth. He held a hypodermic needle in front of my face.

"Dr. Gravett wants to talk to you," he said. "But if you give us any trouble at all, I'll knock you out. Like I should've done the other day."

"Were you the one I clawed up? Too bad I didn't finish the job."

His grip tightened on the needle, then he shifted it to his other hand and backhanded me across the face. Everything went black for a second, and I heard scuffling and Daniel yelling. As my vision cleared, I tasted blood.

I shook it off and checked the others. Ten feet away, Maria hung limp and hopeless from the thug's arm, staring at the ground. Daniel stood tense, both hands on his head, while another thug pressed his own Glock into the base of Daniel's skull. The norm who'd hit me, the leader, spoke into a walkie-talkie: "Tell Dr. Gravett the situation is secure."

They herded us into the central courtyard. The leader went first, then me, flanked by two guards, with Daniel and Maria behind us. No one said anything. The crunch of boots on concrete and Maria's quiet sobbing were the only sounds. They lined us up in the middle of the courtyard, Daniel to my right and Maria to my left. The thug had put her down, and she stood, tiny and trembling, surrounded by two huge guards. I tried to catch her eye, but she wouldn't look up.

Sheila Gravett came out of the building nearest the gate and ran across the courtyard, her heels clicking on the walkway, her white coat flying out behind her. She was beaming. She stopped in front of our little group and clapped her hands together, clutching them under her chin. "Oh, well done," she said.

To my right, Daniel spoke. His steady voice rang out across the quiet courtyard. "Dr. Gravett, I'm a detective with the Boston police department. I came here to investigate a report of a kidnapping." One of the thugs punched him in the stomach. He gasped in pain and started to double over, but the one who had the gun on him grabbed his hair and held him upright.

Daniel was struggling for breath, but he kept talking. "Assaulting . . . a police officer"—he could barely get the words out—"is a serious . . . charge . . . I suggest—"

His captor pistol-whipped Daniel with the Glock. There was a sickening crack as the gun made contact with Daniel's skull. His eyes rolled back and he went down. Blood trickled down his neck.

Maria collapsed, too, curling into the fetal position with her hands over her face.

Gravett smiled.

That's when I lost it. Drawing on all my strength, I yanked my arms away from the two guys who held me, then grabbed them, one in each hand, and smashed them into each other like cymbals. They dropped. The one with the needle rushed me. I dodged, circled behind him, and got him around the waist. I lifted him over my head and threw him, hard, into the two guards who stood over Maria. All three hit the ground. That made five down.

I was turning to find the next one when I was hit from behind in a low tackle. I twisted as I fell, and we rolled in the grass, struggling. Hands closed around my neck.

"For God's sake," Gravett shouted, "don't damage the adult female!"

That distracted the guy, and I broke his grip. I heaved him off me and jumped on him, my hands on his throat now, squeezing. He clawed at my hands. I squeezed harder. The demon mark was on fire; I felt strength like I'd never known. I could squeeze this asshole's head right off.

"Hey, freak!" called a man's voice. *I'll kill this one now,* I thought, *and then I'll pulverize his friend.* "Hey! Your boyfriend's in trouble." Boyfriend? Did he mean—? Keeping the pressure on the fallen guard's neck, I looked up.

Daniel lay on his back, still unconscious. A guard stood

over him, pressing a rifle barrel into his throat. "Give up now, or I'll kill him."

Gravett stepped between us. "He could do it," she said. "That man entered the premises illegally, and armed. You attacked my private security force. Everyone would swear it was self-defense."

Everyone who counted, I thought. As a PA, I couldn't testify in New Hampshire.

The guy with the rifle kept his gaze locked on mine, his slitted eyes daring me to defy him. Waves of hatred swept over me, hot as the burning demon mark. I could kill the guy, easy—snap him in two in a second. Then I looked at Daniel, vulnerable and deathly still.

I removed my hands from the fallen guard's throat. He convulsed under me, gulping in air. The other guard lifted his rifle.

"Good," Gravett said briskly. "Take the juvenile back to her cell. And I think the adult needs to be tranquilized until we've secured her."

The guard I'd nearly strangled pushed me off him. I fell on the ground and just sat there.

I'd lost.

I'd never leave this place; I'd be tortured and imprisoned for the rest of my life. Worse—far, far worse—I'd failed to rescue Maria from whatever horrors they planned for her. That bright, happy girl, reduced to less than an animal. To some kind of lab specimen.

Gravett approached me, holding a hypodermic needle upright and flicking its tip. I looked at the woman and felt a hatred deeper than anything I'd ever known. Daniel lay unconscious and bleeding on the ground. Maria was rolled up in a ball, howling with fear. And Gravett was coming to knock me out until I woke up in a locked cell.

I wanted that bitch to suffer. I wanted her to hurt as badly as all those creatures she'd locked up and experimented on, as badly as she'd hurt my family. Something stirred in me, some deep, savage hunger. I wanted to feast on her screams, to drink her tears as she pleaded for a mercy she'd never get.

The hatred twisted my limbs. A bubbling—fast, frantic, boiling—started under my skin. My spine contracted and kinked, and the longing to tear Gravett's eyes out made my toenails become thicker, sharp, steely. At the same time, my legs withered, grew thin and tough.

"My God," Gravett whispered. "Who has a video camera?" she called out. "Quick, someone get a camera—we have to record this!"

I feasted on my hatred, pushing the emotion through my veins, filling my lungs with it. Revenge. Revenge! A shock of pain went through my body. My arms stretched, feeling like they were being pulled out of their sockets, and kept stretching. Widening, the hairs thickening, becoming feathers. Another jolt of pain as my torso compressed, crushing and reshaping each rib. My lips pursed as if expecting a kiss, then my nose melted into them, the skin hardening into a new form. A tingling shot through my scalp, and I heard a soft hissing that seemed to come from all directions.

Maria screamed, and I turned to comfort her. Then I realized she was screaming at me.

I wanted to say something to her, but my voice came out as a squawk. Then the world's colors bled away. I closed my eyes, then opened them again. Everything had changed. Colors were dimmer, overlaid with gray like a layer of ash. But shapes were sharper. I picked out an ant crawling up a tree trunk fifty yards away. I turned my head, looking. I didn't know this place; what I *did* know was that I had a mission here. My hunger—deep and gnawing and demanding satisfaction—told me so.

Prey. There was prey nearby. Where? I tossed my head, flinging my lovely, living tresses of snakes that hissed and wriggled with the movement. Harpies are proud creatures, vain, and rightly so. I tossed my head again. With the movement, I noticed a small human lying on the ground, hopped toward her. There was fear there, lovely, but the hunger didn't flare. Not this one.

A large female stood a short distance away, rooted to the spot, her mouth hanging open stupidly. She wore a white garment, and her hair was the color of brass. The sight of her sent a sharp knife of hunger into my bowels. Hunger spiced with hatred, with cruelty and revenge. Demanding satisfaction, demanding gorging until I could feed no more. And I knew: *This* was the one; *this* was my prey.

I shouted with triumph and delight. The idiotic humans covered their ears. I hopped, flapping my wings to get airborne. The snakes hissed their excitement as I climbed into the air. Higher I flew, and higher. So high that the humans looked no bigger than field mice. I circled once. I marked my target and dove.

Shouting, shouting my glorious cry of battle. The pleasure of watching the prey's face as it came into focus, surprise tensing into terror. I slammed into her chest, gripping it with my talons, and took her to the ground. She writhed and screamed under me, writhed like the dancing snakes. I dug my talons deeper into her chest. I joined her screams with a song of my own, using my talons to cut and tear, to make her sing new notes. Then, I prepared to feed.

"No!" A sweet young voice—the child's?—made me pause. "Aunt Vicky, look out!"

The child. There was some kind of danger here. And I was supposed to . . . help her? I? I looked for her, confused. I dimly felt something, some impulse that was foreign to me. Something to do with the child.

Ridiculous. I was hungry; I was here to feed. That was my mission. I struck my beak into the soft, doughy flesh of my prey, searching for tasty entrails. She screamed. What a delicious sauce.

A blast thundered, and something struck my wing. I looked up, a morsel dangling from my beak. The snakes snapped and spat. A human, a male, pointed a weapon at me. The man had dared to fire! I rose into the air, screeching my rage.

Of course the wing was unhurt. I laughed. The human did not know enough to use the death metal. Humans are such fools.

But so delicious.

I rose higher in the air, and saw one of the men pulling at

the child's arm. She was crying. I cocked my head. Something about this one . . . Most humans made me frantic with rage. But the girl, somehow, calmed me. I wanted to sit beside her, let her stroke my feathers, gently pluck morsels of food from her small fingers.

A strange desire, but a pleasant one.

A movement from one of the buildings caught my eye. A door opened and out rushed a group of creatures—wolves and odd-looking furred men. They bounded toward the humans, toward my prey, sending up a howling that made my snake-hair hiss in response. I added my own voice, my wondrous, piercing cry. I soared in wide circles above the battlefield as together, the creatures and I proclaimed our war on the humans.

My pulse quickened, my hunger grew sharper. I trumpeted my excitement. War is something I understand.

The creatures bounded across the lawn with breathtaking speed. The humans panicked, breaking ranks and running. Waves of fear shimmered in the air. Guns fired; pack members fell. But still the pack advanced.

On the ground lay a human, a male with yellow curls and closed eyes. From the air, I could see blood in his curls, on his neck. My stomach rumbled. This one's flesh would be firm and ripe. But the hunger soured. Something about him made me think, *No, not this one*, and I blinked, trying to remember. It was the brass-haired female, the one who made the child cry. She was the prey.

A wolf paused by the fallen man and sniffed at him, then, with a pink tongue, tasted his blood. The sight filled me with fury—why, I didn't know. But I dove. Landing beside the man, I spread my wings and screeched at the wolf. *Stay away!* I warned. The wolf growled, lowering its head and showing its teeth. Its ears lay back; its hackles raised. I lowered my own head and shook it, as the snakes strained to strike the wolf anywhere they could reach, in its muzzle or eye. One of my beauties struck home, because the creature yelped and jumped backward, yanking my head and then pulling away. It turned and ran across the lawn, its tail between its legs.

I flapped my wings and screamed. *Anyone else?* I challenged the pack. No creature approached. None dared. Hunger stirred again, and I looked for my prey. At the spot where I'd downed her, one human foot stuck out from a pile of creatures. The screams that pushed themselves from beneath those furred bodies were sweet, sweet sounds. But they belonged to me; that brass-haired woman was mine. Mine! Shrieking, I hopped toward the group, ready to fight those others for the prey.

Then I heard a small sound, like an injured chick. I stopped, cocked my head. The sound came from a clump of bushes. I hopped over to see what was making it.

It was the child. Again, the sight of her flooded me with calm. I wanted to be alone with her somewhere, away from humans and creatures alike. I wanted to soothe and protect this one as I would my own chick. I thrust my head into the bushes. The snakes might frighten the child, so I cooed to her, clucking reassuringly. She screamed and buried her face in her hands. But then she peeked out from between her fingers. "Aunt Vicky, is that really you?" she whispered.

Vicky—a familiar name, although I couldn't place it. But the child's eyes held hope when she said it. How strange. Hope was an emotion I'd never seen in a human's face. On this one, it was lovely. I bobbed my head up and down. I backed up a few paces, keeping up the soft cooing, then looked back. *Follow me.* I did it again. *Follow me, little chick.* The child hesitated, but then she crawled out of the bushes.

I spread my wings, then looked at her. I repeated the gesture. She wrinkled her forehead, then nodded. She understood. She spread out her arms, as I'd asked. I jumped into the sky and alighted on her shoulders, gently closing my talons around her outstretched arms. No tearing, just holding. It was an odd way to deal with a human.

Then, flapping my mighty, powerful wings, I lifted us both into the air.

In a moment, we'd cleared the treetops. Below us, the ground flowed with the movement of creatures. I could see no more humans, save for the yellow-haired man I'd chased the wolf away from. He lay still and alone. For a moment, I felt I should do something for him, lift him away from that place in the same way I carried this child. I shook my head; my tresses hissed softly. The strange feeling faded, and then the yellow-haired man was out of sight.

Below me, the child sobbed quietly, but she didn't struggle. Trying to soothe her, I sang to her, but she cried, "No, no!" so I fell silent. I flew without direction, content simply to be with the child. Holding her small arms felt so good, and I felt we could fly this way forever.

Then I heard a sound, one that was unfamiliar yet beautiful. I listened with a sense I didn't know I had. It was a call. Someone was calling this child. Not with words, but with the heart.

Hearing the strong, constant heart-call, I had no choice but to heed it. We flew south, the setting sun to our right, shadows stretching across the land below us.

28

HARPIES, OF COURSE, ARE SUPERIOR TO OTHER WINGED creatures. We're larger, we're fiercer, we're more beautiful. And we fly faster, because we have access to portals that flesh-and-blood birds do not. Within minutes, I'd locked on to the heart-call that beckoned the child I carried. Following that call, we came to a landscape cluttered with human dwellings, laid out in rows. A good hunting ground for another day. For now, that pure, clarion heart-call guided me like a beacon. It came, clear and bell-like, from a square white dwelling surrounded by grass.

"There!" the child shouted, squirming. "That's my house!"

We alighted gently, so as not to hurt her. The house's door flew open, and a woman rushed down the steps. "Mommy!" The child ran to the woman and wrapped herself in her arms. A picture came to mind of a chick enfolded in its mother's wings.

The picture lasted only briefly. I stood on the grass, tensed and ready to flee. This dwelling was not a place for my kind. The woman, who'd lifted the child from the ground and pressed her face against her, raised her eyes to search the lawn. When she saw me, she gasped. She put down the child and stepped in front of her, protective, then approached me, making shooing motions with her arms. "Get out of here, you damned Harpy! I will not have a revenge demon invade my home!"

I screeched in anger, but I hopped back.

"Mom, no—" The child stepped in front of the woman and grasped her wrists in her small hands. "It's Aunt Vicky. She brought me home."

"Vicky? Oh, my God. How did—? You can't—? A *Harpy*? That's impossible."

"It's her, Mom. I saw her change. Look, it's wearing Aunt Vicky's necklace."

"Vicky?" the woman said, tentatively putting out her hand.

The name meant nothing to me. I tossed my head, setting the snakes to hissing. I was to be feared, not petted. The female snatched back her hand and held it to her chest. Good.

We stared at each other. But no waves of fear rose from either woman or child. Their eyes held something, some emotion that I didn't understand. Confusion filled me. The snakes hissed impatiently. There was no prey here—why was I wasting my time? The woman, her eyes bright, said, "Thank you." I cocked my head. I'd never heard such words before; I did not understand their meaning.

Then, like a jolt through my marrow, I felt something that I did understand, something I knew well. It was a call. Not the heart-call that had compelled me to carry the child to this woman, but the trumpet sound of a call for revenge. Revenge! I stretched my wings; my beauties sang their hissing songs.

This was a call from one of my own kind—not a Harpy's voice, but a demon's. It spoke a language I understood. The voice carried power, great power. It called to me, and my heart sped in excitement. Bloodlust, eagerness, a hunger for vengeance, those delicious feelings, all swelled within me. I called out my answer: *Yes, yes, I'm coming!* Shrieking my excitement, I rose into the air.

"Vicky, where are you going?" yelled the grown female. But I had no thought for these humans or their strange ways. A call had gone out, a call to all demonkind. I must obey. I flapped my powerful wings. With all the speed I could muster, I flew east, into the gathering darkness, toward the city.

THE CALL THUNDERED THROUGH THE NIGHT SKY. ALL around me, other demons flew, clamoring their replies. We were an army, a mighty force of vengeance. I trembled with anticipation, eager to find my target. My prey. I had not fed sufficiently before, and hunger seared my innards. To war!

The city sparkled with lights. Nighttime. Feeding time. Just outside of it, huge, hulking shapes stood—a whole legion of them—shaking their fists and pounding against thin air. Hellions, they were, held back from the city by some kind of magical boundary. They roared their anger, nearly drowning out the call that brought us all here.

Around them, even under their feet, humans walked blindly, oblivious. Out here, cut off from the leader that summoned them, the Hellions were powerless to materialize. The humans saw nothing of the mighty demons that stalked their city. Fools.

Whatever barrier stopped the Hellions, it was nothing to me. A slight tingle as I passed through, a current of cold air raising chill-bumps beneath my feathers. Past the barrier, the Hellions' noise subsided, and the call came stronger. I laughed and followed it, moving deeper into the heart of the city.

Some kind of procession moved slowly below. Humans marched down a long street, dressed in colorful outfits, some seated on slow-moving platforms. Among them, here and there, were some living corpses. More humans lined the street, cheering and waving. The sights and smells, all that blood coursing just beneath the flesh, all that sweat and a whole buffet of emotions, sharpened my hunger.

But the call. The demon sending it was strong. There was power in that call—power and promise. I followed its summons, as did my sisters all around me. Shouting and singing, we followed it to a street in front of a crumbling building in a deserted part of town, not far from the marchers. More living corpses here, but those bloodless creatures were of no interest. The sky was thick with unmaterialized Harpies. Too many. Surely there wouldn't be enough prey for us all. I shrieked my hunger, greedy, and targeted a Harpy below me. I grabbed her with my talons and flung her aside. She howled with anger. Good. Let her fight me for this feast. I'd fight them all. Nothing would keep me from prey tonight.

The call boomed out, and I could see its source—a shadowy Hellion invisible to weak human eyes. An impressive Hellion, this one. Powerful. In its full glory, it stood taller than some of the buildings, its skin the bright, eye-hurting shade of daytime skies. I admired its sharp, pointed teeth, so good for tearing. The Hellion spread its arms in welcome, gesturing to all of us: *Come, come.* We came. Hundreds of Harpies alighted before it. I joined them, ready to do the bidding of this demon that had called us.

We milled around the Hellion's feet, hundreds of us, like a flock of hungry pigeons pecking for scattered crumbs. I was hungry, ravenous. I didn't want to share with these others. Too many sisters, too crowded. It was hard to get enough air. A body's length away, a Harpy stared at me, not at my face but at a spot in the middle of my chest. I squawked at her—*go away!*—then turned. In a flash, the Harpy lunged at me. I felt a tug, then something snapped, was pulled away from me. The Harpy ran off at a fast waddle, holding something in her beak, but I lifted myself into the air and landed in front of her, blocking her way. I lowered my head, snakes hissing, and spread my wings menacingly. She froze.

From her beak dangled a string with a stone at the end. The stone gave off its own light, like a small sun, but the light wasn't clear like sunlight; it was the color of the setting sun. And it was mine. I wanted it back. I screamed at the thief and lunged for her feathered breast. She screamed back and dodged, dropping my stone. I grasped it with my talons and flew to the top of a nearby building, away from the flock. Mine.

The roof was spacious, quiet. The air filled my lungs better here. I hopped to the edge and peered at the crowd of Harpies. They strutted about on the ground, cackling, arguing, lunging at each other. The hissing of their snake-hair filled the air like the sound of rustling leaves. A human approached—in a street crowded with demons, he remained blind to our presence. But he stopped suddenly, as if he sensed something, and shivered. He turned up the collar of his coat, moved his head left and right, then chose a different path.

Another blind fool. He'd see us clearly enough once we ripped into his flesh to dig out his juicy liver.

But the thought of feeding dulled my hunger. Why? Hunger grows sharper and sharper until a Harpy must feed. That is the way of things. Yet at this moment, in me, the hunger was fading. *Not* hungry. I barely knew myself without the feeling. Why did the thought of dining upon that human cause me to feel odd, almost ill? He was a paltry human, nothing more than food to satisfy a Harpy's raging hunger.

A light caught my eye. It was the strange stone. I hopped back to where I'd dropped it and pecked at the thing. Mine. I wanted it. I must have it. I would kill any Harpy that tried to steal it. But I didn't know *why* I wanted the thing. I couldn't eat it. It was too small to use as a weapon. It was merely a shining stone. But it was mine. Mine. For some reason, it was important that I keep it.

Below, the Hellion spoke, claiming my attention. Its many voices rang through the night. "Harpies!" it bellowed. "Into this building. Now! Follow us!" It turned and lurched into a tall building with boards on the windows. Was the prey there? The site of so many eager Harpies piqued my hunger once again. They swarmed in behind the Hellion. I pushed my stone into a hole in the wall, hiding it. Then I followed my sisters.

The building was old, long abandoned by humans. Debris covered the floor. Along one wall, a few remaining windows, some shattered, let in a little light from the street. Torches flamed at one end of the huge room. My sisters gathered near the torch-lit end. Even from the rear of the crowd, I could smell human.

I pushed forward, straining to see. Was this was our prey? It would not be enough. More, we needed more! In the center of the room stood a brown-haired human male, wearing gray. Hungry. But something slapped back my hunger from this one. This was no mere human; this was a master. Power glowed from him like the light from my stone. A small female, puny, cringed beside the master. That one was nothing; I had no interest in her. They stood before a table covered in black cloth; something bulged beneath the covering. At the ends of the table, torches blazed.

The Hellion halted in front of the master—the room was silent, even our snake-tresses quieted their hissing as we awaited the signal to attack. But the Hellion, in stiff, resisting movements, bowed before the master, then fell to its knees. "Master," it said, "we are yours to command." The Hellion's words begged to serve, but their tone oozed with hatred, with a strong desire for revenge. A murmur rippled through the Harpies.

The master nodded, and something in the gesture stirred my memory. I knew this human. His female servant picked up a robe and slid it over the master's clothes. The robe was black, covered with symbols that shimmered and glowed with light. His power surged. My sisters drew back, again murmuring. Even the Hellion cringed, bowing lower.

I'd never seen a master such as this one. Why did I feel I knew him? The female servant handed him something. He lifted it: a knife that sparkled with gems. Turning in a slow circle, he displayed it to all present. The shining weapon brought my stone to mind. I wanted it. Now. I wanted it more than ever.

"Tonight," the master said, "we will reduce this city to ashes and rubble. We will crush all humans within it. Difethwr, my servant—" The Hellion growled, and the master smiled. It was a smile I knew well, a smile of pleasure in another's pain. "My servant Difethwr shall direct you. You Harpies, now gathered here, are the foot soldiers of my attack. In addition, Difethwr, in obedience to my will, has assembled a legion of Hellions. Even now, this legion waits outside the shield that protects this city." He smiled his cruel smile again. "But the shield will fall, and we will prevail."

With a flourish, he pulled the black cloth from the table. On it lay a naked human, bound at the wrists and ankles. His eyes were closed, and he didn't move—only the slight rise and fall of his chest showed that he lived. I climbed into the air to see better. It was not an impressive human, neither large nor fleshy. And the face was marred: a long, thick scar ran from his eyebrow to his mouth.

That scar. Something nudged at my mind. I felt I knew this human, as well. A strange word whispered through my mind: *Lucado*. I didn't know its meaning. Confused, I dropped back to the ground.

"With the blood of this man and the fire of the Destroyer, we shall pierce the shield!" the master shouted. Excited Harpies cheered and shouted. But I didn't join their battle cries. The *Lucado* word wouldn't leave me, buzzing at the edges of my thought. Again, hunger faded, replaced by an unpleasant, queasy feeling. I wanted my shining stone.

The master covered the victim with the black cloth. "Clarinda," he called. The female servant came forward and took the knife. "I must prepare my spell." He smiled and puffed his chest. This was an arrogant master. "The spell that will open the shield and subject a legion of Hellions to my command! Where's my servant? Where's Difethwr?"

The Hellion still kneeled in its spot before the master. Rage flamed behind its eyes. "Here . . . Master."

"Send forth these Harpies. Start the attack!"

"We obey." Flames roared and shot forth from the Hellion's eyes but stopped short of the master. The Hellion stood and raised its arms. "Harpies, attack! We charge you to avenge this master on all humans within the bounds of this city. We charge you to sow confusion and terror! Go! Now! Attack their parade!"

Screeching with excitement and bloodlust, the Harpies rose in a dark cloud. The cloud hovered, then exploded into a hundred different directions as my sisters went forth to seek their prey. I rose into the air also, but I felt no hunger for human flesh. I felt no hunger at all. The Hellion's vengeance command was not for me. All I wanted was to retrieve my shining stone.

Lucado, Lucado, the night whispered as I flew back to the top of the building. As I landed, another word—*Vicky*—arose. That word was one I'd heard today. The child. The woman.

Vicky, both had said, as though that word was my name. Vicky. My name.

Vicky was my name. I shook my head, snakes hissing. No. Like all Harpies, my name was Vengeance.

I hopped to the hole where I'd hidden the stone and plucked it out. Its light was dim now, not the glowing bloodred I'd seen before. Red—the stone must be red. It was important. And I had to do something when the redness returned.

I picked up the stone by its string and launched into the air. I'd take the stone back to my nest, and . . . Where was my nest? I didn't know. How could that be? All Harpies have nests. But the thought of *nest* was a blank spot in my mind.

In confusion, I landed in the square. All the Harpies had gone. In the distance, I heard their battle cries and the screams of humans. I dropped the stone on the ground. Did it shine brighter here, redder? I bent to pick up the stone but knocked it with my beak. It skittered away, toward the building where my sisters had gathered. The stone glowed redder. Yes, its color had both deepened and brightened. I pushed it again, on purpose this time. The color brightened more. Carrying the stone in my beak by its string, I waddled into the building.

Inside, the shining of the stone was stronger, its color deeper. Beautiful. I felt happy, but still confused. I was supposed to do something now, but what? I flew up into the rafters to puzzle it out.

Below me, the female servant and the master placed items on a second table. The bound man—*Lucado,* something whispered—remained motionless, covered with the black cloth. The Hellion stood close by, tense with coiled fury, watching the master, its face a mask of hatred. I drew back on my perch. The Hellion's expression was repulsive, hideous. Had I admired this demon? Now, hatred answered hatred. A chaos of feelings roiled in me. Anger. Hunger. Fury. Revenge. Prickling, burning sensations bubbled through me. I saw the Hellion, and I hated it. I wanted to fly into its loathsome face, pluck out its eyes, rake its skin with my talons.

The thought came from nowhere: *My father. This Hellion killed my father.* I didn't understand, but I knew it was true.

Screaming, I dropped the stone and dove at the Hellion, crying vengeance. Vengeance! The demon turned, surprise and rage twisting its features. Vengeance! I aimed for the eyes. Vengeance! But just as my talons were about to strike, I fell. One wing, seared with fiery pain, collapsed and hung limp. I veered to the side and fell, hard.

When my body slammed into the floor, it broke into a dozen pieces—that's how it felt as the pain exploded through me. Agony in my head—like my skull had split, my brain mushroomed. I couldn't hear the hiss of my beautiful tresses. My legs swelled up into large, soft, sausagelike things, while my wings were losing their feathers, growing small and stick-like. As every part of me wracked with pain, I writhed on the ground.

"What's that Harpy doing here? And what's wrong with it?" A man's voice pushed through the wall of pain.

"It's not a Harpy, Master. It's the shapeshifter."

I hurt, hurt, hurt—as though I were being burned in a furnace, stabbed with spears, and pulled apart all at once. Twisting and struggling, my body gave up its Harpy form. As I found my way through the haze of pain, I knew who I was.

And I knew I was in trouble—naked, weak, unarmed, in-the-presence-of-my-worst-enemy trouble.

When the last spasms of the shift had shuddered through my body, I opened my eyes. Difethwr loomed above me, flames licking from its eyes as if hungry for my skin. It showed its teeth in a horrible laugh. "Hast thou forgotten, daughter of Ceridwen? Our mark is upon thee."

The pain had drained from my body—all but my arm. The demon mark was on fire with searing, burning pain. That was why I'd fallen. My arm, still demon-marked while in the form of a Harpy's wing, had failed when I tried to attack Difethwr.

The sorcerer appeared, standing over me. The symbols on his black robe seemed to glow and move. "Good evening, Miss Vaughn," said Seth Baldwin. "Your timing is wonderful."

"Go to hell, Baldwin."

"No, that's where I'm about to send you." He smirked, running his gaze down, then up, my naked body. "A pity, perhaps." Then his voice went hard. "Clarinda! Prepare a second altar." He turned and disappeared from my field of vision.

Clarinda—I'd heard that name before. The witch who'd disappeared. Clarinda Fowler was the witch who'd leaked the information about the shield. All at once I remembered Roxana's amulet, the shiny stone that had so fascinated me in Harpy form. I'd dropped it when I tried to attack Difethwr. Was it working now? Could the witches see—or at least hear—what was happening here?

I tried to sit up, but the shift had left me weak and my right arm was useless. I rolled onto my side and looked for the amulet. There it was, glowing with its soft light, about twenty feet away. So far, no one had noticed it. I flopped onto my stomach and crawled on my belly across the cold concrete floor. It was slow going; I couldn't use my right arm at all.

Difethwr growled. Flames hit the floor two inches in front of my face, blocking my way.

"Let her be," said Baldwin. "Come over here and assist me. She won't get far."

He was right; I didn't get far. Just far enough to reach the fallen pendant. Checking over my shoulder to make sure the others weren't paying attention, I reached out and grabbed it with my left hand, the hand that was still mine. The right, marked arm lay heavy and useless like a dead tree trunk.

"Where do you think you're going?" Baldwin sounded amused. Hands grasped my ankles and dragged me backward. The floor's grit scraped my naked skin. I clutched the glowing stone in my hand, trying to keep it hidden, hoping the witches could hear us. Maybe they'd send help. But what kind of help could stand against the Destroyer? That was supposed to be my job.

Baldwin dumped me near the second altar.

"Give it up, Baldwin," I said. "There's no way you can blast a hole in the shield from an abandoned building in the New Combat Zone." *Can you hear me, Roxana?* "Where are we, Washington Street? It'll never work."

"Stupid. Location makes no difference. But your blood will. Shapeshifter blood, mixed with the Blood of an Evil Man, will shatter that damn shield beyond repair." He laughed and turned back to his preparations.

Clarinda stepped over me to place lighted candles on the altar.

"Clarinda," I said. "Why are you doing this? You're a witch. You took a vow to do no harm."

She stepped over me again and didn't answer. But she glanced at me with pain-filled eyes.

"My servant Clarinda is not permitted to speak," Baldwin said. "She renounced her vow and bent her will to mine after she'd seen a small demonstration of what a Hellion can do. Her uncle, it was. I believe he was a client of yours."

I stared at him. "Are you talking about George Funder-burk?"

"Funderburk. Yes, that was the name. She'd created a charm to protect him, but obviously it did no good. When I explained that her child would be next if she refused to serve me, she gladly agreed. You see, I could create a spell to neutralize a single charm, but the shield was too powerful. I needed assistance. Clarinda's has proved adequate."

"So you sent the Destroyer after Frank, too. It wasn't coming after me."

"Not then, no. But it was delighted to find you there. As was I. I hoped I could deepen my knowledge of demonology through you, but you had nothing to teach me. I was already far advanced beyond your primitive skills." He made a dismissive gesture and turned away.

I had to keep him talking. Even if the witches couldn't help me, at least people would know what had happened here.

"What changed you, Baldwin? You wanted to be governor of Massachusetts—and now you're bent on destroying Boston."

"You're right. At first I did want to be governor. I made ridding the state of monsters my issue. That weakling Sugden, with his zombie daughter, would never get tough on paranormals. So to win I had to increase people's fear of the monsters. I summoned Difethwr, bound the Hellion to my will. My plan was to send an army of Harpies to disrupt the Halloween parade. With that kind of terror three days before the election, how could I lose?"

Exactly what has happening out there right now. "But that wasn't enough for you, was it?"

"Governor." His lip curled with disdain. "Who cares about being governor? That's not power. Real power, as my servant Difethwr helped me to see, has nothing to do with humans and their puny institutions. Real power is irresistible. Real power crushes whatever opposes it, whatever it wishes to destroy. Binding Difethwr has given me a taste of *that* kind of power. It's intoxicating, like nothing you could imagine. And tonight, as I bring an entire legion of Hellions under my command, my power will be limitless."

He scooped me up as though I were a child and dumped me onto the makeshift altar. The amulet fell from my hand. Baldwin saw it and laughed. He held me flat on the altar. I struggled and kicked, but I hadn't recovered my full strength. I did land one good kick in Baldwin's stomach. He gasped and doubled over. I slammed him in the forehead with another kick.

He staggered back, but my bare foot hadn't done any real damage. Where were my stiletto-heeled boots when I needed them? I jumped off the table and ran for the door.

"Difethwr, you fool, stop her," Baldwin wheezed. I'd winded him, but the Hellion still heard the command. It appeared in front of me, its teeth bared, its eyes simmering with flame. Slime dripped from its warty blue skin. It reached for me, and I backed up, my right arm throbbing with fiery pain. Difethwr advanced, laughing, its eye-flames inches from my skin. It forced me back, until I bumped into the altar table behind me.

"Bind her," Baldwin said. "She's wasted too much time already."

Difethwr reached for me. Flames sparked from its fingertips, sheets of fire shimmered along its skin. I felt the heat approach, smelled sulfur and charred flesh. "No!" I screamed. I couldn't let it touch me. I couldn't. Still it came closer, reaching. I leaned back over the table until I was half lying on it again. I was trapped. Difethwr reached out to touch my right arm, which lay unmoving, obedient, awaiting the Hellion's will.

Our mark is upon thee, it had said.

It's inside me, I'd told Aunt Mab. *I can't get it out.*

The Hellion touched me. It touched my defenseless arm, and the mark exploded with new pain. The demon essence, in contact with its source, burned through my arm in an enormous surge of power, like a never-ending lightning strike. I screamed and screamed.

Difethwr bellowed, its own voice rising into a howl of pain. It tried to pull back its hand, but it couldn't. It was locked onto my flesh, onto the demon mark, as though welded there.

Baldwin appeared, furious. "Difethwr, what in hell are you—?"

Words poured forth from me in a torrent. I didn't know where they came from; I barely recognized my own voice: "This Hellion is mine! I have the greater claim; our marks are upon each other. I repudiate your mastery, human, and bind Difethwr to me." A sound like a thunderclap shook the building, as furnace-fierce heat blasted through the room. Difethwr reeled backward, its hand free, and for a moment everything froze.

There was no sound, not even a whisper of wind through the broken windows.

The first thing to penetrate the silence was Difethwr's laugh, a low rumble that rose in pitch and strength until it sounded like a roomful of damned souls howling. Baldwin's mouth dropped open. Fear glittered in his eyes. Difethwr moved toward him, each footstep shaking the ground. Blue and yellow flames shot from its eyes, its mouth. Its entire body blazed with fire.

"No! Stop! I command you!" screamed Baldwin. He commanded nothing now. The Hellion advanced. Baldwin turned and tried to run, but he tripped on his long black robe and fell hard, facedown. The flames of the Destroyer singed the hem of the garment. Baldwin whimpered in terror.

"Stop, Hellion!" I called. *"Arhosa!"*

Difethwr jerked, then stood still, as though some hand had yanked an invisible leash. It turned, slowly, and glared at me with bottomless hatred. It gnashed its teeth and made slashing motions with its claws. Its eye-flames shot toward me, but extinguished before they came near.

I climbed down from the altar and stood as tall as I could. I pointed at the demon; it cringed and wailed and howled. The Hellion's flames flared out in all directions. Except mine.

"Difethwr," I said, the words ringing clearly, "I banish thee back to the Hell whence thou came."

The Hellion shuddered. It contorted its body, bending its spine and twisting its limbs, and moaned in pain. "We cannot go," it whimpered. "The shield holds us in."

I picked up the amulet from the floor and held it to my mouth like a microphone. "Now!" I shouted. "Open the shield!"

Nothing happened. Ten seconds, Roxana had said, but I couldn't count. There was no time in this moment—how can you pick ten seconds out of eternity? Difethwr moaned and writhed, and its moaning and writhing were eternal, the fate of the damned.

Then a whirling light appeared, and time began again. Faint at first, the light quickly intensified, spinning faster and faster into a funnel shape directly above the Hellion's head. Faster and brighter it whirled, until Difethwr began to grow misty and whirl with it, sucked into the vortex, inch by inch. The demon bellowed and roared, but the sounds grew faint, like an animal's cry half-heard across a foggy marsh. The vortex of light sucked Difethwr into the air. In another moment, the Hellion was through the vortex and gone, except for the fading echo of an angry, tormented howl.

29

THE MOMENT THE SHIELD SNAPPED SHUT, I COLLAPSED LIKE a marionette whose strings had been cut, landing in a heap on the cold floor. The light of the vortex still dazzled me; I couldn't see past the colored spots that swarmed across my vision. Every inch of my body shook. My teeth chattered. Nausea suffused my stomach. But in the cold, trembling, aching lump of flesh my body had become, one feeling predominated.

And that feeling was nothing. I felt nothing whatsoever in my demon-marked arm.

The nothingness wrapped around me like a cocoon. Far off, I could hear scuffling and muted shouting. I tried to rouse myself and go after Baldwin—I couldn't let that son of a bitch get away—but I was shaking too hard to stand. I raised my right hand, amazed that it obeyed me, and flexed my fingers. They were shaky, but they worked. No twinges. No tingling or burning below the skin. My arm was my own.

"Are you all right?" A woman's voice pushed through the cocoon. A face materialized in front of me and came into focus, the eyes squinting with concern. Clarinda, the missing witch.

"Where's Baldwin?" I asked, trying to jump to my feet but losing balance and falling back again.

"It's all right," she said, putting a hand on my shoulder to keep me from getting up again. "He's not going anywhere. I immobilized him with a binding spell."

"But how—" I began, and then I realized. Baldwin's power came from Difethwr. When I severed their bond, all his power crumbled, all his spells failed. He was helpless against Clarinda's magic.

She nodded, as though she'd read my thoughts. "Here," she said, holding out a bundle of cloth. "You're shivering."

I reached out a shaking arm and took the bundle. It unfurled from my hand—a black robe with mystical symbols painted on it. Baldwin's magician's costume. Nothing glowed or shimmered now, but the robe was wool and looked warm. I pulled it over my head. It was like wrapping a blanket around myself, and I felt better immediately. The shaking diminished, then stopped. And still the demon mark was quiet. Almost as if it had never been there at all.

I flexed and straightened my fingers, fascinated, twisting my wrist this way and that.

"I've been in touch with the coven," Clarinda said. "The police are on their way."

Given Baldwin's attack on the Halloween parade, I suspected it might be a while before the cops got here. I opened my senses to the demonic plane to see what was happening out there. Nothing but blessed silence. No shrieks, no screams, no maniacal laughter. Like the spell that bound Clarinda, the call to the Harpies had fallen apart when Baldwin lost power over his Hellion. For tonight, maybe for a few nights, Boston was a demon-free zone. That was good. I could use a vacation.

Behind me, a growl started low and rough, and then swelled to a roar. Not on the demonic plane—this was a human sound. "What the hell is going on?" yelled Frank Lucado.

Clarinda jumped. "I didn't cut him loose yet," she said, her eyes wide. She turned to the altar, then back toward me. "Is he really an evil man?" she whispered.

"Evil? Frank? Not really. Annoying's more like it." Clarinda ventured a thin smile at that. I didn't know much about sorcery, but I suspected Blood of an Annoying Man wouldn't add much firepower to a spell. Even if it was sometimes tempting to shed a bit of it, I thought, as Lucado's cursing grew louder.

I climbed to my feet, feeling steady now. "Don't worry," I told Clarinda. "I'll take care of Frank."

Lucado was thrashing around as much as he could, yelling and swearing, doing his best to break free. But he was tied down tightly, and so far all he'd managed to do was lose the cloth that had covered him.

"Hang on, Frank," I said. "You're going to injure yourself."

Lucado went rigid. His head whipped around to face me, the scar as red as his rage. Then he sighed. "Jesus," he said. "I should've known."

"Don't look at me like that. I'm here to save you. Hold still and I'll cut you loose." I picked up Baldwin's would-be sacrificial dagger.

"Hurry up, for God's sake. And throw that sheet back over me. I ain't decent."

"Just what I've always said about you, Frank." I moved to cut the ropes that held his wrists to the altar, then paused. "Wait a minute. Didn't you fire me again?"

"Whaddaya mean, fire you? You're always yammering about how nobody can fire you. Anyhow, I'll hire you back. I'll give you two weeks' pay. Just quit screwing around and get me off this goddamned table."

Two weeks' pay. Nice. I wouldn't hold him to it, but it was good to be appreciated. With a single slice, I cut through the ropes that immobilized his wrists. Another swipe, and his ankles were free. As Frank sat up, rubbing his wrists, I picked up the altar cloth from the floor and dropped it in his lap. He wrapped it around himself like a shawl and glared at me.

"Why is it," he asked, "that any place there's trouble, there's you?"

"You're just lucky I like you so much, Frank. Your buddy Baldwin was going to use your blood in a spell to destroy the city. Then he was going to give you to the Hellion to play with."

Frank's eyes went wide. "That blue monster? That thing's

around here?" He turned his head frantically, clutching at the altar cloth.

"Relax. It's gone."

"Really? You ain't gonna show up at my house tomorrow and tell me it's out to get me?"

"Baldwin's the one who sent it after you. He thought he was some big powerful sorcerer. But I took his demon away from him and sent it back to Hell." I was just hoping Difethwr would stay there.

"Seth? A sorcerer? Are you kidding me? He hates that spooky shit." Lucado's brow furrowed, and he cocked his head. "Wait a minute. I remember. He gave me a Scotch that tasted funny. I felt wasted after two sips. And I remember—" He jumped from the altar and stormed over to where Baldwin sat on the floor. "You son of a bitch!" Lucado stepped back and kicked Baldwin hard in the ribs. Baldwin didn't move. He didn't even make a noise—Clarinda must have laid a silencing spell on him, too. But his eyes brimmed with fury and pain.

Lucado pulled back his leg for another kick. I ran up behind him, got both arms around his chest, and lifted him off the ground. He struggled and cursed, but I was stronger. I backed him away from Baldwin and held him until he stopped struggling. When he went limp, I put him down.

"Don't beat him up, Frank. Let the cops handle it."

Lucado stood, breathing hard, staring at Baldwin. "All right," he said, moving toward his former friend, "but I'm not going to stand around freezing in a goddamn sheet while that asshole wears a nice warm suit."

A couple of minutes later, Baldwin sat naked on the floor, a little blue with cold but bound too firmly by Clarinda's spell even to shiver. Frank wore Baldwin's gray suit. It was too tight, and the sleeves and pant legs were too short, but he looked better than I'd ever seen him. Alive looked good on old Frank.

That's when the cops burst in. Guys in uniforms fanned out across the room, guns drawn, and everyone put their

hands up. Everyone but Baldwin, that is. When the cop nearest me—a kid with acne on his chin—saw Baldwin, his eyes
went wide with recognition, and he swung the gun in my
direction. I couldn't blame him. Baldwin looked pathetic
sitting there on the dirty floor, all paunchy and goose bumpy
and pasty-fleshed, and I was the one wearing the funky wiz-
ard's costume. It was Halloween of course, but this kid was
probably already spooked out by the Harpy attack on the
parade. Now, his eyes rolled, and the gun he pointed at me
shook.

"Take it easy," I said. "I'm not a threat. I can explain—"

"Watch that one, Collins," said a voice behind me. "That's
one damn slippery freak."

I didn't have to turn around to know whose voice it was.
A second later, Norden appeared in front of me, sneering,
followed by his zombie partner, Sykes. It figured the Goon
Squad would be in charge—we were in the New Combat
Zone. But why did it have to be these two? Norden lived to
give PAs like me a hard time. Well, tonight I wasn't putting
up with his crap. Guns or no guns, I dropped my hands and
put myself right in his ugly, pitted face.

"I'm not the bad guy here, Norden," I said. "Seth Baldwin
tried to destroy the city. He was practicing unlawful sorcery,
using the black arts to cause harm, and probably half a dozen
other violations."

Norden glanced over at Baldwin. A cop was trying to help
him stand, but Clarinda's binding spell meant that he kept
flopping back into the same position on the floor.

"Yeah," Norden scoffed. "The guy looks real dangerous.
Why should I believe you?"

"Listen, blood bag, you'd have been Hellion food by now
if I hadn't—"

"Victory! Thank the Goddess you're all right." Roxana
Jade pushed past the Goons and stood in front of me, beaming. "Magnificent job! You were wonderful. Just wonderful!"

Norden snorted, like "wonderful" was the last word he'd
associate with me. But he stepped aside. In another second I
saw why. Roxana was with Tony Bergonzi, head of the Goon

Squad. Captain Bergonzi was a norm, but he was respected in Deadtown.

Roxana looked gorgeous, as usual, but tonight she looked more like a practicing witch than when I'd last seen her. She wore a long, midnight blue gown, and a silver circlet of stars glittered on her raven hair. I was suddenly aware of how filthy I must be. Well, fighting demons was dirty work. Almost as dirty as being one. I sniffed to check for any lingering eau de Harpy, then thought the hell with it. We were at a crime scene, not a charity ball.

Roxana introduced me to Bergonzi, who impressed me by shaking my grimy hand. I could see why the monsters didn't mind him having some authority on our turf. Bergonzi turned to Norden, who'd pulled out a magic meter, which was used to detect the quantity and kind of magic present in a place, and was trying to turn it on. The thing hummed half to life, then sputtered. Norden swore under his breath and banged the instrument against the palm of his hand.

"Don't worry about that now, Norden," Bergonzi said. "You and Sykes go interview Mr. Lucado." He jerked his head toward Lucado, and I got the feeling that Norden and his partner were being dismissed.

Norden must have felt that way, too, because he scowled at me. On second thought, that was probably his natural expression. He thumped the magic meter again and muttered, "Damn piece of junk," shot me another scowl, and then said, "C'mon, Sykes." The partners went over to Lucado, who leaned against the altar where he'd been held captive.

"I don't think Frank will remember much," I said. "He was passed out for most of the fun."

Bergonzi nodded, a far-off look in his eyes as though he was thinking about something else.

I was ready to get the hell out of there and go home, so I said, "I guess you'll want me to make a statement."

Bergonzi's eyes focused on me again. "Yes," he replied. "But we already know what happened here."

"You do?"

"We got the whole thing," Roxana said.

I raised my eyebrows.

"We plugged the scrying mirror into the coven's computer and captured the transmission in digital. I burned it to a DVD and gave it to Captain Bergonzi."

Wow. Ancient earth magic meets high tech. Who knew?

"I'm the only one who's seen it," Bergonzi said. He cleared his throat, and a calculating look crossed his face. I wondered what was coming. "And that brings me to what I wanted to say. We'd prefer to keep it quiet that a Hellion was inside Boston. So I'll take your statement myself. Next week at headquarters would be fine."

Keep it quiet? Was this bozo planning to protect Baldwin? Maybe I'd judged him too kindly. "I don't care what you'd 'prefer,' Captain. There's no way in hell I'm going to let Baldwin walk."

"No, no. I didn't mean that. He'll be charged with conjuring demons to cause public mayhem, for sending those Harpies against the parade. Believe me, Baldwin's not walking away from this. He's going to prison for a long, long time." He gestured at Baldwin, who was being handcuffed as Clarinda prepared to remove her binding spell. "But there's no need, is there, to publicize the fact an amateur, unregistered sorcerer was able to breach the shield? That the city was nearly destroyed by a legion of Hellions? We don't want any other would-be sorcerers getting ideas."

I considered. I certainly didn't want another run-in with a Hellion anytime soon. And maybe—just maybe—keeping this quiet would keep my face off TV for the next news cycle.

"Okay," I said. Bergonzi gave me a politician's smile and clapped me on the shoulder, then walked past Norden, who was fiddling with the magic meter again, to talk to Clarinda.

I watched him approach the witch, who cringed, looking as though she'd like nothing better than to disappear. If witches really could pull tricks like that, I'm sure she would have.

I turned to Roxana. "What will the coven do to Clarinda?"

Roxana pursed her lips. "She broke the first rule of witchcraft: harm none. There's no more serious offense in the Craft."

"Go easy on her. There were extenuating circumstances—Baldwin used the Destroyer to kill her uncle, then threatened to do the same to her child."

"I know. We heard Baldwin through the scrying mirror."

"And what does 'harm none' mean in a dilemma like that? Resist Baldwin and let him kill your child in the most horrible way possible? Isn't *that* doing harm?"

She kept her lips pursed and didn't answer.

"Besides, your scrying mirror didn't show what happened after the Hellion was gone. Sending that thing back to Hell knocked me flat. Baldwin could've got away. But Clarinda stopped him. She didn't harm him"—I'd have killed the guy if I'd been her—"she immobilized him. And then called you."

"I see your point. We'll take what you've said into consideration." Then she smiled at me in a girlfriend-to-girlfriend way, clearly wanting to change the subject. "But let's talk about what *you* did, Victory. That was brilliant, the way you yanked the Destroyer away from Baldwin's control. I didn't even know such a thing was possible."

Neither had I. And I wasn't ready to think about the consequences yet. "Let's find your amulet," I said. I could change the subject, too. "I must have dropped it when the shield opened. That was a pretty intense moment."

"I'll say. Look how far down I chewed my nails." She splayed a hand, the nails short and ragged, dried blood along the index finger's nail bed. Good to know there was one thing about Roxana that wasn't perfect.

I led the way to where I'd been standing when Difethwr had been sucked through the vortex, and we kicked through the debris on the floor. "Here it is," Roxana said. She picked it up, tied the leather loop ends together, and hung it around her neck. She crossed to my right side—and the amulet lit up. Not a pale pink this time, but a shining, bloodred crimson, bright as the lights on a fire truck.

I stared at it. The damn stone was as bright as it had been in the presence of Difethwr. Had the Hellion come back?

Or—good God—was it *me* making the amulet light up? I still felt nothing from the demon mark.

Norden came sprinting over like an alarm had gone off, holding his magic meter out in front of him. "What is it? What's happening over here?" He swept the magic meter back and forth.

Roxana glanced at me as she strolled casually toward him, placing herself on my left side. The stone faded back to clear. "Residual energy," she said. "Victory was showing me the spot where Baldwin stood when he launched the Harpy attack. There were thousands of those demons here. It takes a while for that kind of energy to fade."

Norden pointed his meter at me, and the damned thing clicked like a Geiger counter in a uranium mine. My heart was beating almost as fast. He motioned me away, and I realized he was pointing at the spot where I stood, not at me. I took a couple of steps back. He frowned as the clicking slowed down and pointed the meter at me again. It revved right up, and I stepped back again, this time involuntarily. He moved toward me, still frowning. Then the meter sputtered to a complete stop.

He swore under his breath, shook it, and swore again, audibly this time. "I knew this was a piece of junk."

"For some kinds of energy," Roxana said, "the old ways work better. Look—" She dangled the amulet in front of him. I made sure to stay well back and keep my left side toward the amulet. "See? The amulet is crystal clear. The demonic energy is gone now. Might as well put that thing away."

Norden squinted at the amulet. Then he shook the meter one more time, frowning, and stuck it in his pocket. "I'm done here anyway," he said. "Captain," he called to Bergonzi across the room, "I'm heading back to headquarters to write up my report. C'mon, Sykes." The zombie shambled over to him, and the two of them left together.

When Norden was gone, Roxana winked at me. "Jamming spell," she said.

"Thanks."

"Captain Bergonzi would've reined him in, but there's

no point in creating an awkward situation with the Goon Squad."

Especially not with that particular Goon.

Roxana put the amulet in her purse. "What does it mean," she asked, tilting her head, "to have that Hellion bound to you?"

"I don't know." I'd thought that the demon's mark had given Difethwr power over me, but apparently it went both ways. Hellion power corrupts, as Baldwin had proved, but could my own power affect the demon? I rubbed the demon mark and flexed the fingers of my right hand. Still nothing. "I don't know," I repeated. "But I'll do my damnedest to make sure it stays in Hell where it belongs."

I WAS HOME BEFORE TEN. JULIET WAS OUT, BUT THAT WAS no surprise. Halloween was a major feast night for her. I took a long shower to wash away the grime and any last traces of Harpy. Then I threw Baldwin's sorcerer's robe in the trash and put on some normal clothes: tan leather jeans and a thick brown ribbed turtleneck. Feeling a little more like myself, I picked up the phone and called Gwen.

"Vicky! Thank God. Are you all right?"

"I'm fine. How's Maria?"

"She'll be fine." Gwen's voice held a strained note, suggesting that "fine" might be a long-term goal.

"Can I talk to her?"

A long pause answered my question.

"She doesn't want to talk to me," I said at last.

"She's just a little girl," Gwen said. "She needs some time."

"Yes, sure. Of course. So how about I come out next weekend and treat the kids to a movie?"

Another pause. "Let me call you, Vic. When I'm sure the time is right."

All of a sudden, my eyes were stinging. I wiped them on my sleeve. "I understand. Well, keep in touch, okay?"

"You know I will. And I'm really glad you're okay. We all are."

I wondered if that meant Maria. Two days ago, I'd been her hero. After what had happened today, how could she see me as anything but a monster—a real one? I said good-bye to my sister and started to hang up.

"Wait!" she said.

I waited. Gwen took a deep breath. "I just wanted to say thanks. For going up there and bringing my baby home."

"Oh, Gwen. How could I have done anything else?"

As I hung up, I wiped my eyes again. The phone was still in my hand, and I needed to make a decision. I had to find out about Daniel. I'd asked Bergonzi if there was any news from New Hampshire. He either didn't know or wouldn't tell me, acting like he had no clue what I was talking about. I'd have to call Daniel's apartment, talk to his wife. But I'd do it in the morning. By norm hours, it was too late to call now.

You're chickening out, I told myself.

Yeah, you're right, I told myself back. But I'd face it— whatever "it" was—tomorrow.

There'd be a lot, in fact, to face tomorrow. Maybe too much. What had happened to Daniel. Whether I'd be able to rebuild my relationship with my sister's family. Where I stood with Kane. And most of all, how I was going to handle my new, deeper bond with the biggest, baddest Hellion out there. I could drive myself crazy trying not to think about all that now. Or I could go out and get Axel to pour me a shot or two of tequila. Just enough to chase away my own demons, just for tonight.

I pulled on a jacket and headed for Creature Comforts.

The New Combat Zone was surprisingly busy for ten thirty. I'd never seen so many zombies on the streets here. Norms, either, for that matter. They traveled in groups, zombies and humans walking together, talking and laughing. It was like a big party.

Creature Comforts was packed. I could barely get in the door. Just like on the streets, the crowd was all zombies and norms. Humans did hang out at Creature Comforts—vampire junkies and thrill-seekers—but never this many, and hardly ever any zombies. What was going on? Poor Axel ran up and down the bar, pouring and serving drinks as fast as his long legs could carry him.

Before I could figure out what was going on, a cheer resounded and the crowd started singing: "For she's a jolly good zombie . . ." At the back of the room, some guys hoisted a zombie into the air and set her on a table. My God, it was Tina. And she was holding my sword.

With energy I didn't know I had left to summon, I pushed my way through the crowd. Tina waved the heavy sword around like a conductor's baton, in time with the music. She was smiling and laughing. When she saw me, she waved. "Hi, Vicky!"

"We need to talk," I shouted over the noise.

She nodded, then went back to conducting the song. When it was finished, the room burst into applause. Tina bowed to all sides, then climbed down from the table. "I've got a booth over there," she said, pointing. I followed. She plopped herself onto a red vinyl seat, next to her friend Jenna.

"I want my sword back," I said, sitting across from them. "Now. You had no right to take it."

Jenna popped her gum. Tina opened her mouth like she was going to argue, but then she handed me the sword of Saint Michael across the table, hilt first.

"This has been the best night *ever*," she said. No apology. No promise to leave my stuff alone. "Did you hear what happened? We saved the parade!"

I was so flabbergasted that the lecture I'd been preparing flew right out of my head. "You saved—? What happened?"

"Well, like I told you in my phone message, me and Jenna had this amazing idea for our Halloween costumes. Do you like them?"

Both girls were dressed in head-to-toe black leather. "What are you supposed to be?"

Tina rolled her eyes. "We're demon slayers. Duh."

I thought of Maria in her Aunt Vicky costume and had to blink a couple of times. "Yeah," I said, "it's all the rage."

"It is? Well, anyway, now you know why I needed the sword. And Jenna needed a weapon, too. So we snuck out of

Deadtown today and went that that store in Allston, the one you told me about."

"You snuck out of Deadtown? Without a permit? You are so lucky you didn't get snatched by the Removal Squad."

Tina shook her head. "Uh-uh. We were safe. We went as zombies." This sent her and Jenna both into peals of laughter so severe that Jenna almost swallowed her gum. "This year, all the blood bags—I mean humans—wanted to be zombies. It's the most popular costume. So we got two rubber zombie masks and wore them when we went out. Brilliant, huh? They protected us from the sunlight, and everyone thought we were norms goofing around in costumes."

"You risked an awful lot." But I had to admit it was a clever plan.

"So, like, we took the T out to Allston and found the place. Oh my God, it was so cool. We got guns and bronze bullets and swords and daggers—"

"You walked in there wearing rubber masks and they sold you all that?"

Tina shut her mouth. Jenna said, "'Course not. We boosted it." *Pop* went the gum.

I shot them both a stern look. "I'll take it all back for you next week."

Jenna looked ready to argue, but Tina hit her under the table.

"So then what happened?" I asked.

Tina bounced up and down in her seat. "We came back to Deadtown. A bunch of zombies were planning to crash the parade, so we, like, put on our costumes and joined them."

I vaguely recalled noticing some undead in the parade when I'd flown over it in Harpy form.

"Except," Tina continued, "instead of zombie masks we wore movie star masks. 'Cause, you know, you're, like, kinda glamorous and all."

"How flattering."

She beamed, missing the sarcasm. "We marched in the parade, along with everyone else. All these blood bags were around, and nobody *knew*. Nobody screamed or ran away or gave you that look like you belong in the toilet or something. It was fun." Her red eyes widened. "But then, out of no-where, all these Harpies just appeared. I knew they were Harpies from that book you gave me. There were hundreds of 'em—thousands—and they swooped in and started attacking. Norms were screaming, running around. It was, like, really bad. I didn't even think about what I was doing. I just jumped up and started killing demons."

Tina had led the zombies in fighting off the Harpies. From what she said, the zombies fought hard, attacking Harpies with their bare hands, tearing them limb from limb. Harpies don't eat zombies, but they'll fight anything that threatens them. Some of the zombies had been badly injured. And zombies don't heal. A zombie gets its face slashed open, it stays that way. They'd been brave.

For humans, Harpy wounds disappear at sunrise. I hoped the same would be true for zombies.

"You know what was weird?" Jenna said. "All that human blood, and I didn't even get hungry."

"I know why," Tina replied. "It's 'cause the blood was only real in the demonic plane. Right, Vicky?"

I nodded. "In normal reality, it's an illusion."

"Yeah," Tina said, "so we couldn't smell it."

"I don't get it." Jenna shrugged and chomped industri-ously on her gum.

"It's all in that book," Tina said. "You should read it. It's really good."

I got up to go. "Well, Tina, it sounds like you're a hero."

"Yeah," she said happily. "I'm gonna be on TV tomorrow, too. Maybe even on *Oprah*."

Kane would love it. Without knowing it yet, he'd found the face of PA propaganda. A face with green skin, bloody eyes, too much mascara, and pink lip gloss.

Later, I'd give Tina the lecture on why it takes years of training to become a demon fighter. She needed to under-stand that the expulsion of Difethwr had scattered the Har-pies. Tonight, though, I'd let her bask. The kid had done good.

30

I SPENT SUNDAY AND MONDAY MAKING UP FOR SOME SE-
rious sleep deprivation and hanging around the apartment. I
tried Daniel's number four times but never got an answer. On
the last try, his answering machine was full. There was nothing about him or Sheila Gravett on the news. I was due to
give Bergonzi my statement at Goon Squad headquarters on
Wednesday—and the good captain was going to come up with
some answers about Daniel, or I'd go public about Baldwin
and Difethwr. I still had the phone numbers of half a dozen
reporters who'd love to put me back on TV.

In between attempts to call Daniel, I stared at the phone
and wondered whether to call Kane. He'd returned from his
werewolf retreat on Monday afternoon. On the one hand, I
was still kind of mad at him. On the other hand, I just plain
missed him. Just when the desire to hear his voice started to
win out over my stubbornness, he called me.

"How was your retreat?" I asked.

"Lonely."

I didn't want to get into that discussion again, so I went
for a lame joke. "Well, you *are* a lone wolf."

"True. But I missed you."

"That's funny. I was just thinking the same thing about
you."

"So how about we get together? I've got tons of work to
catch up on today"—*same old, same old,* I thought—"but I'd
love to come over tomorrow night. We can watch the election
results together."

"Ah, so it wasn't me you missed. It was Juliet's TV."

He chuckled, a feral sound low in his throat. "Believe me,

Vicky. It was you." I caught my breath at the sexy promise in his voice. He chuckled again, but when he spoke, his voice had grown serious. "There's something we need to talk about. Not now. Tomorrow, when I see you."

That got my stomach flip-flopping all day on Tuesday. Even though the apartment didn't need it, I cleaned the place just to distract myself. I was sure that Kane was going to lay down an ultimatum about next month's retreat. And if he did, he wasn't going to like what I had to say.

I was all fluttery with nerves—and I'm not a flutterer, damn it. I knew what the problem was: there was too much I wasn't facing. But you can only face one thing at a time. And sometimes you needed to get your feet back under you before you could face anything at all.

By the time Clyde called to announce that Kane was on his way up, the apartment was spotless, the TV was on, and I even had little snacky things—cheese and crackers, peanuts— laid out on the coffee table. Still feeling fluttery, I opened the door. And there he was. God, he looked good, dressed in jeans and a black sweater that made his hair seem even more silvery. Kane, the cooler-than-a-cucumber trial lawyer, was never one to be nervous, I thought. But then he kissed me—a mere peck on the lips— and I wondered. What did Kane have to be nervous about?

"Man," he said, looking over my shoulder, "look at those numbers." He walked around me to sit on the sofa, his eyes on the TV.

I wondered what was so fascinating. Governor Sugden was winning reelection by a landslide. No surprise there, though, seeing as how his challenger was in prison awaiting trial on charges of practicing sorcery without a license and aggravated assault by black magic. What was surprising was how many norms turned out to vote. You'd think they wouldn't bother, for a one-man contest. But voters had gone to the polls in record numbers. A few cranks voted for the disqualified Baldwin—making a statement, I guess—but 98 percent of the votes went to Sugden.

"It's a whole new era for human-PA relations," Kane exulted. I sat on the sofa, leaning against him, his arm slung loosely across my shoulders. His body was solid, both strong and relaxed, and I could almost feel the energy buzzing through him. He was always like that, revitalized, when he returned from a werewolf retreat. It felt so good just to be close to him.

Then Kane clicked off the TV and turned to me. His gray eyes searched mine. "Vicky, about the retreat—"

"Please don't ask me to go to the next one. I can't." I took a deep breath and held his gaze. "This isn't easy for me to say, but I have to say it. I'm not a werewolf. And I can't straitjacket myself into pretending to be one. Not for you, not for anyone. I've got to be what I am."

He nodded. "I know. I was wrong to try to make you into something you're not." His hand brushed my cheek. "You're pretty terrific the way you are."

I closed my eyes and leaned forward for a kiss. But it didn't come. Kane straightened and pulled back his arm. I opened my eyes again and blinked at him. He jumped off the sofa and started pacing.

"I've got to say something difficult, too. Hard as hell. But—" He stopped and nailed me with those piercing gray eyes. "I'm going away. To Washington."

Color me stunned. The way I gasped and gaped, I'm surprised I didn't shift into a fish out of water. After a minute, I found my voice. "When?"

"Tonight. I have to leave for the airport in about twenty minutes." He sat again and took both my hands in his. "It won't be forever. I've got a six-month PA visa. But it's happened, Vicky. I'm preparing a civil rights case for the Supreme Court."

He glowed when he said it, like someone had flipped on a spotlight. This was Kane's dream—the chance to establish PA rights at the federal level. "That's great, Kane. It's what you've always wanted. I'm sure you'll win."

"It'll be a long, uphill battle." He grinned, a little wolfish. "But winning is exactly what I intend to do." He squeezed my hand. "I know you don't care about politics, but—"

"No, that's changed. After what happened to Maria . . ." I pictured that poor, sweet child huddled all alone in a cell. "Believe me; I'll be rooting for you. The norms are going to have to figure out how to live with the monsters."

"Don't say—" He stopped himself, smiling, and nodded. "There's one other thing I need to say. While I'm gone . . . I'll be working hundred-hour weeks. Work, sleep, work, sleep."

"The usual routine."

He smiled again. "But what I'm trying to say is . . . For me, this case will be everything. Everything. And I don't expect you to sit around waiting for me. You should see other guys. If you want."

"We were never exactly going steady to begin with."

"True. I knew I was crossing a line, asking you to come with me on the werewolf retreat. I'm sorry I pushed." He let go of my hands. "I kind of thought you and that human detective—"

I put my finger on his lips to shush him. And now the kiss came: long, warm, deep, and sexy.

When it was over, I snuggled against his chest. He sighed, stroking my hair. "But if there is anyone else, he'll have to fight me for you when I get back."

LESS THAN AN HOUR LATER, KANE WAS GONE. I COULDN'T believe it, but he was. And I wouldn't see him for six whole months. I sat at the bar in Creature Comforts, feeling glum and half listening to Juliet chat up a Harvard graduate student who was studying Renaissance drama. He wanted to interview her for his dissertation; she wanted to drink his blood. Same old story.

Creature Comforts was busy—not as crowded as the night of Tina's victory party, but doing good business. More norms had been coming in, as well as zombies, who were now allowed to roam the New Combat Zone without a permit, expanding their range beyond Deadtown by several blocks. Zombies couldn't get drunk, but they sure as hell got hungry.

Axel had had to quadruple the number of bar snacks he carried. "How's business?" I asked him as he lumbered past, pushing that seven-foot body as fast as it would go. He grinned, showing his big square teeth, and gave me a thumbs-up.

"Hi," said a voice to my left.

I turned on my stool to see Daniel standing there, smiling. Daniel. Alive and in one piece. His hair was a little shorter, and his blue eyes sparkled.

We took the same booth we'd sat in before. "You're okay," I said. I couldn't help smiling back at him.

"Good as new."

"I tried to call you. No answer at home, and at the precinct they said you were on leave. I had to hope that meant you were all right."

"I had a concussion. No big deal. But they kept me out of sight for a few days while they figured out how they were going to spin this thing. You wouldn't believe who got into the act: Massachusetts cops, New Hampshire cops, the Goon Squad, politicians, FBI, even Homeland Security."

"I haven't seen a word about it on the news."

"They're going to make an announcement tomorrow. Sheila Gravett was attacked and killed by one of her werewolf experiments when a keeper inadvertently left a door unlocked." Well, that much was true. Sort of. "There'll be nothing in the news about me. Nothing about you or Maria."

That was good. I didn't want Maria being dragged through the publicity machine. I felt a pang, hoping she was okay. I hadn't heard anything from Gwen.

Daniel was silent for a while, picking at the label on his beer bottle. When he looked up, the sparkle was gone from his eyes. "I wasn't much help to you up there."

"You're kidding, right? I never even would have made it across the state border without you."

"Yeah, and then I got knocked out with my own gun." He paused, looking down. "I saw what happened, Vicky. Security tapes, and Gravett had a video camera going. I watched everything. You saved my life."

So he'd watched the shift, seen me in Harpy form. The knowledge of that squeezed at my heart. It hurt. I didn't know what to say.

"What did you . . . ? What *was* that thing?" he asked, his voice low.

"I shifted into a Harpy. I didn't even know it was possible for me to change into a demon." I suspected it had to do with the Hellion mark, but that was a question I'd have to ask Aunt Mab. And I was still in avoidance mode—part of me didn't want to know.

"I didn't save you, Daniel. That Harpy wasn't me. Well, it was, but not the real me. I wasn't in control." How could I explain this to him? "I don't know why I chased that wolf-creature away from you. Maybe I wanted to eat you myself." I reached across the table and touched his hand. Just lightly, just for a moment. "I'm not human. You've got to understand that."

"I do." Now he looked at me, something fierce in his eyes. "I also understand that it *was* you, whatever you say. The spark that's Victory Vaughn didn't go out just because you changed form. So you wanted to kill Gravett. I'd have killed her myself, given the chance. But you weren't just some demon bent on revenge. You protected me. You saved Maria. Hell, from what Roxana told me, you saved the whole city of Boston. All of that was *you*, Vicky. All of that was brave and loyal and . . ." His hand captured mine and held it. "And beautiful."

I blinked, because I'm not the kind of person who gets teary-eyed. "Thank you for saying that."

"I should be thanking you." His smile lit up the dim bar. "And I was hoping to do it with dinner this weekend."

I drew back my hand. "I can't."

The light faded from his smile. Why did it hurt to see that?

"Is it because I'm human?" he asked.

"No, Daniel. It's because you're married. I'm not going to get between you and your wife."

A little wrinkle appeared between his eyebrows. "But I'm not married."

"Please, don't. I appreciate that you came here to say thank you. And what you said just now, it means a lot to me. Don't spoil everything with a lie."

"I'm not lying. I'm *not* married."

This was too much. "Who answered your phone that morning?"

He frowned. "What morning?"

"The day after I missed our appointment. The day I met you at the precinct."

A light dawned. "That was my wife, but—"

"See? Give up on lying, Daniel. You're lousy at it." I pushed myself out of the booth.

He got up, too, and blocked my way. "My *ex*-wife. Her name's Elise. We only got divorced two months ago. I haven't gotten used to calling her my ex yet."

"Your ex." Yeah, right. "So what was she doing answering your phone at seven o'clock in the morning?"

"Staying in the guest room. She sold her condo because she's moving to Chicago. The timing worked out that she needed a place to crash for a few days." He ran a hand through his curls. "Sit down again. Please. I'll explain."

He looked so eager and sincere that I slid back into the booth. For a minute, anyway. "Okay," I said. "Explain."

He opened his mouth, then stopped, like he didn't know where to begin. He bit his lips. Finally he spoke. "Elise and I got married right out of high school—way too young. It was a mistake, but not a terrible one. We grew apart. No big fights or anything, we just kind of drifted down different paths. I'm a cop; she's an architect. We didn't have any kids. After a while, there was nothing to connect us anymore." He paused, glanced at me. "She moved out two years ago. We stayed friends, but we were both happier living apart. When Elise started thinking about taking a job in Chicago, we decided we might as well go ahead and get the piece of paper that says 'divorce.' But our marriage ended a long time ago."

I tried to digest what he was saying. "Is this true?"

"It is, I swear. Call Elisc. She'll tell you. In fact, I think you two would like each other."

"Whoa, let's take this one step at a time." I wasn't exactly ready to become pals with the ex-wife yet.

We set up a dinner date for Saturday night in the North End. And then we talked for hours. He was warm and funny and full of stories, his blue eyes flashing as he told them. And my stories didn't freak him out. Since he'd seen me shift into a Harpy, he'd already seen me at my worst.

Or maybe it wasn't my worst. Maybe there was a little bit of me in there, like he'd said. A spark, he'd called it. Maybe that spark was the real me.

BEFORE I FELL ASLEEP THAT NIGHT, I THOUGHT ABOUT MY father. I remembered when he was teaching me to drive: showing me how to work the Jag's clutch, staying patient even when I kept stalling out in traffic with half a dozen cars honking behind us. I saw him dancing Mom around the kitchen as he belted out Welsh songs, Mom laughing and trying to pull away before the potatoes boiled over. I remembered sitting close to him on the sofa, Gwen on one side and me on the other, as he read to us from a book of Welsh fairy tales. And I saw him teasing Aunt Mab, his eyes twinkling, as my stern aunt blushed like a schoolgirl. He was the only person I knew who could get Mab flustered.

He was gone, and I'd never get him back.

But I had set things as right as I knew how. I'd restored the balance of power, sending my father's murderer back to Hell, where it belonged. At what cost, though? I wondered, my guard down as sleep approached. To conquer Difethwr, I'd had to bind it to me. And a bound Hellion is a treacherous thing.

You know what to do, Aunt Mab had said. But binding Difethwr had never been my plan. I didn't know where that binding spell had come from; the words had simply arisen and poured forth, erupting from me like a geyser. Had those words come from me, from my spark, from some deep-buried ancestral knowing? Or had they come from the Destroyer in me, a demon's trick to escape Baldwin's bondage and strengthen its mark in me?

I didn't know. But the thing was done. Difethwr and its legion were in Hell, and I was free of the mark's torments. There still had been no burning, no weakness, no surges of uncontrollable anger. All seemed well. For now, anyway.

As I slipped into sleep, I heard a noise. It sounded like a laugh, a deep rumble that rose up through the floor and grew, many voices joining together in a crescendo before sinking back into silence. I'd heard that laugh somewhere before, hadn't I?

Or maybe it was just a dream.